PUNK AND ZEN

Visit us at www.boldstrokesbooks.com

What Reviewers Say About BOLD STROKES Authors

KIM BALDWIN

"Force of Nature is filled with nonstop, fast paced action. Tornadoes, raging fire blazes, heroic and daring rescues…Baldwin does a fine job of describing the fast-paced scenes and inspiring the reader to keep on turning the pages." – L-word.comLiterature

ROSE BEECHAM

"…her characters seem fully capable of walking away from the particulars of whodunit and engaging the reader in other aspects of their lives." – *Lambda Book Report*

GEORGIA BEERS

"Beers weaves a tale of yearning, love, lust, and conflict resolution. She has constructed a believable plot, with strong characters in a charming setting." – *JustAboutWrite*

RONICA BLACK

"Wild Abandon tells how these two women come to realize that 'life was too precious to be ruled by…fears, by…demons.' While these two women struggle with their issues, there is some very, very hot sex. If you enjoy complex characters and passionate sex scenes, you'll love *Wild Abandon."* – *MegaScene*

GUN BROOKE

"Course of Action is a romance…populated with a host of captivating and amiable characters. The glimpses into the lifestyles of the rich and beautiful people are rather like guilty pleasures…a most satisfying and entertaining reading experience." – *Midwest Book Review*

CATE CULPEPPER

"…an exceptional storyteller who has taken on a very difficult subject …and turned it into a spellbinding novel. As an author, she understands well that fiction can teach us our own history." – *JustAboutWrite*

JANE FLETCHER

"The Exile and the Sorcerer is a mesmerizing read, a tour-de-force packed with adventure, ordeals, complex twists and turns, and the internal introspection of appealing characters." – *Midwest Book Review*

JD Glass

"*Punk Like Me*...is different. It is engaging. It is life-affirming. Frankly, it is genius. This is a rare book in that it has a soul; one that is laid bare for all to see." – *JustAboutWrite*

Grace Lennox

"*Chance* is refreshing...Every nuance is powerful and succinct. *Chance* is not a novel about the music industry; it is about a woman discovering herself as she muddles through all the trappings of fame." – *Midwest Book Review*

Lee Lynch

"Lynch, with a dozen novels to her credit dating back to the early days of Naiad Press, has earned her stripes as a writerly elder. She was contributing stories to the lesbian magazine *The Ladder* four decades ago. But this latest is sublimely in tune with the times." – *Q-Syndicate*

JLee Meyer

"*Forever Found*...neatly combines hot sex scenes, humor, engaging characters, and an exciting story." – *MegaScene*

Radclyffe

"...well-plotted...lovely romance...I couldn't turn the pages fast enough!" – Ann Bannon, author of *The Beebo Brinker Chronicles*

Susan Smith

"This disparate duo's lush rush of a romance - which incorporates reincarnation, a grounded transman and his peppy daughter, and the dark moods of a troubled witch - pays wonderful homage to Leslie Feinberg's classic gender-bending novel, *Stone Butch Blues*." – *Q-Syndicate*

Ali Vali

"Rich in character portrayal, *The Devil Inside* by Ali Vali is an unusual, unpredictable, and thought-provoking love story that will have the reader questioning the definition of right and wrong long after she finishes the book." – *JustAboutWrite*

PUNK AND ZEN

by

JD Glass

2007

CREDITS
EDITORS: SHELLEY THRASHER AND STACIA SEAMAN
PRODUCTION DESIGN: STACIA SEAMAN
COVER PHOTOS: SHANE SALEK
GUITAR PHOTO COURTESY STAN JAY, MANDOLIN BROTHERS
COVER DESIGN BY SHERI (GRAPHICARTIST2020@HOTMAIL.COM)

By the Author

Punk Like Me

Acknowledgments

You already know that CBGB was a real place. So was the Red Spot, and the former owner loves hearing it talked about.

Adam's Rib was a real band, but Adam's Rib America bears absolutely no resemblance or relation to Adam's Rib Canada (they pinched the name!). That's one of the major distinctions.

The owner of Mandolin Brothers is also happy to be mentioned in this work—and the place really is one of the best globally for fine fretted instruments. If you play, or love someone who does, you should go there. Make sure you say hi to Stan and tell him JD sent you.

Thanks to Jennifer Harmon, Nell Stark, and Ruth Sternglantz for patiently going through the creation process with me, and Shelley Thrasher for everything. Shelley, you are a graceful Job(ette) and I am grateful. A debt of gratitude always to Radclyffe, for vision, for faith, and for the continued vote of confidence—thank you.

And Shane? Nothing would happen without you. *Te adoro.*

Dedication

For the feelers and the thinkers, the fighters and the bleeders; to those of heart, both heavy and hollow, for the red, the white, the black and the blue, and every shade in between:

We are legion; you are not alone.—Nina, Punk Army

We are the music-makers, and we are the dreamers of dreams—Arthur O'Shaughnessy

I know that it's easier fought than won
Everything that's good? Already done
Nothing ever seems to work out right
Close your eyes and dream tonight

When everything just falls away
You learn that nothing gold can stay
Love Calls Again

When the world comes crashing in
And the good guy never wins
Love Calls Again

I know what it's like to push too far
Perception makes it all seem so hard
Just don't stop—don't throw yourself away
You can make it to another day

When everything just falls away
You learn that nothing gold can stay
Love Calls Again

When the world comes crashing in
And the good guy never wins
Love Calls Again

from "Love Calls" by Life Underwater

LOVE BITES

My face is green now it's turning blue
I think I got it from fucking you
Make it go away

"Make It Go Away"—Adam's Rib

Let no one fool you. Love? Sux, period end. There, I've said it, and I'll say it again. Love sux. Luv sucks. Luuuuuvvvvv sssssuhhhhhhkkks. I think I've gotten my point across.

Now, that's not to say anything bad (well, not really) about sex. Sex, at its worst, is always better than a day at work, and more so if it's twice on Sunday.

Here's the deal about love, such as it is.

First, there they are, the boy/girl/alien of your dreams, and they are bee-yoo-tee-fool, with an emphasis on fool. And, of course, they have a tragic story—what else could make them so alluring, if they weren't just so strong and vulnerable, so needing to be rescued and loved? And, of course, you and me, the idiots with the good hearts, do just that—rescue and love—hoping, because we're so darn noble, and worthy, and deserving, and, darn it, just so *nice*, that when the pain is over, the boy/girl/alien will see that love was here with them all along, inhabiting our bodies.

Second, of course, there are challenges, obstacles along the way. You have to prove your love, prove that the object of your affections is worthy of love because, of course, being so damaged, they're not very trusting, and we'll just have to understand that, be patient. It's not us, it's them, and after all, they knew they were never very lovable to begin with—they just somehow seem to push everyone who loves them away.

We, of course, swallow this hook, line, and sinker, and vow to ourselves that *we*, *you*, *I* will be the one, *the very one*, because of our goodness and purity of love, to prove to the damaged basket case of a boy/girl/alien once and for all that yes, love is real, life is good, and sex, well, okay, it would be nice (oh so very, very nice), but not necessary, because, after all, this is true love. And there are no conditions on true love, especially for those (read: *us*, the suckers) who are noble of heart. Besides, that's not what we're all about, since we're so noble and good and all, and we don't want the poor wounded boy/girl/alien to think we're just in this to get laid—really.

Third, and it never fails, comes the come-here-no-go-away sequence. Conversations tend to run along these lines: "This is never going to work; it's not you, it's me—get out," followed by tears and groveling, vehement statements as to why we, the hero of this epic, aren't really good enough; the tragic departure scene; and then, a call on the car phone (if you can afford one) halfway home on a five-hour drive: "Baby, I'm sorry, I miss you, I need you, come back." Whereupon, the knight turns the steel horse around (or gets on the bus or the plane, pulls out a bicycle, or walks) back to the scene of the original bloodletting, all forgiveness and understanding because, after all, they're hurting, they've had a damaging past, and we're here to heal that—*all* of that.

At about this point, casual friends and distant cousins have started to make comments, like, "Hmm, why don't you hang out with *us* tonight? We have a few friends coming over, remember [insert name of puppy-love crush]? Yeah, we just ran into each other, and wouldn't it be great? If we all hung out?" or other such things like, "Geez, are you okay? Wanna talk about it?" And our most intimate friends and family are just telling us directly, "Lose the crazy boy/girl/alien—you're getting, no, wait, you *are* brain damaged. C'mon, we'll get you drunk, and laid, and you'll feel much better."

The sad thing is, how did they know we weren't getting laid? All this suffering, and no loving to make up for it. Oh, yeah, maybe, a couple of times, maybe a lot—the first few weeks—but then, all that baggage shows up (damage, remember?) and, well, it just ain't happening anymore.

After a long time of this (and we, the noble rescuers, put up with this for a while, sometimes years, because the boy/girl/alien never really breaks it clean, so we have hope), we finally realize that we've been had, taken for a ride, to the cleaners and back, tire tracks on our backs, nobility wasted, heart sore and certainly not nearly as trusting or as nice as before. Sometimes the rescuer becomes the boy/girl/alien to some other undeserving good sort, and the cycle continues: hallelujah and pass the ammunition.

This is one type of love, and I'm sad to say, I've not only witnessed this happen to beloved family members and friends, but I myself have followed this sad, sad pattern.

STUDIO B

I've been dreaming again and something tells me
I'm standing on the wall—if I don't jump, I'll fall
I've been feeling again and I remember
There's nothing left to gain drinking from the pain
I say good-bye for the moment—I say good-bye and I'm
frozen
I say good-bye for the moment—I say good-bye and I'm
golden
...
Don't cry for me

"I Say Good-bye"—Life Underwater

I sat alone outside the control room because, with the exception of the bassist who was doing some backup vocal takes, everyone else had found somewhere else in the building to be for the moment, grabbing food or cigarettes or some other such stuff. No such luck for me, though. I was sucking down a cup of tea that was probably too cold to do any good, as well as missing milk and sugar—which is the way I like it, but unfortunately milk was out if I wanted to sing—and trying to collect myself.

Through the soundproof glass doors I could see the hands of Mr. Jeremy J. "Bear" Jenns, the engineer, flying over the hundred thousand points of light, buttons, sliders, and whatchamacallits, eyes closed and grooving to the sound that wasn't merely enough for him to have flowing through his headset, but also had to be pumped through the studio monitors.

As for myself, I couldn't tell if my teeth were rattling and hands bouncing because I was nervous or because I could hear the tracks for myself, and they were making circular waves in my cup. So much for soundproof, I thought wryly and grimaced, then downed the rest of the tepid brown water.

I crumpled the cup in my hands, tossed it in the can, then picked my ass up and off the sofa I'd parked myself on to hustle back into the studio. It sounded like the backup vocal had been nailed, and that meant it would soon be my turn to do a final lead vocal take.

"All right, then, baby. Let's give it a listen," Bear said into the microphone on his board.

An alto female voice floated back into the room through the monitors. "I'd like to try that again."

"Well, it sounded pretty damn good," Bear commented mildly, "not pitchy or anything. Come on, take a break, hear it for yourself, and then see what you think," he persuaded, waving "come here" through the window into the studio. "We'll roll it under Nina's take."

Now a word about Bear. He was, well, big. His chair was custom made, large enough to hold three people comfortably, and still it bent under him. And though his military-style beard was neatly trimmed, his hair was wild—curly and long, sticking out at crazy angles. He used that mane as a holder for this foot-long, inch-wide pencil he used to manipulate the knobs and faders he couldn't reach by himself across that tremendous sound board/mixing console/mother ship communication center.

In a word, he was huge, larger than life itself, and more real than stereo color. Of course, my mind may have overreacted to the situation by painting things in hyper-realism, but then again, I'd never been in my own recording studio before, or worked with my own hand-picked engineer. Five years. It had taken five years to get to this point, and only by sweating every detail.

I heard the pop of electric disconnect, the headset being put down, then Bear slid his chair along the huge board to open the door to the right of it.

The foam-padded door opened, revealing dark long hair pulled back into a ponytail parked over a pair of usually clear, but now stony blue eyes, and lips that weren't smiling. A shirt that had been pulled off due to the threat of heat exhaustion hung from the waistband, leaving only a black tank top over black jeans, and a bass guitar slung over a strong bare shoulder to complete the picture. Words floated in with the body.

"Dude, I think there's one section—a measure toward the end of the break—that I'm going to need to redo," she said, voice slightly hoarse from effort.

"Ya know, baby, you're just a perfectionist." I smiled, walking toward her. "Because from what I heard, I think you nailed it."

Samantha's eyes lit up when she heard my voice.

"Hey, you're back!" she answered with delighted surprise. A smile that's just for me graced her lips, and she reached out as I neared her. Caught up in the pull I always feel between us, in less than a moment I was where I wanted to be, and her lips were where I needed them, on mine.

No kidding, no shit, and I'm sure to some, no surprise, either, I live, and I mean live, for those kisses, soft and sensual, filled with tenderness and love, or hard, demanding, and speaking in the most direct way of good ol'-fashioned primal lust.

All of them inflamed desire, but this wasn't the time or place. We had a job to do, and we were paying by the hour. A greedy moment or two, okay, well, maybe it was more, of that sweet fullness, a line of fire running from the tip of her tongue through me, and we broke off, breathless, my face flushed and warm, just in time to hear Bear speak under his breath.

"Okay, if I balance the highs here and pan through the mids—"

"I'm ready to give it a shot, Bear," I interrupted, and he faced us, pushing that mutant pencil back into his tangled curls.

"This is one hell of a hot track." He grinned. "You sure you inspired her enough there?" He nodded his chin at Samantha. "I mean, don't let me interrupt. Do what you need to do to get her, uh," he flushed into his beard, "get it down, er, done."

I glanced over. Either Samantha was blushing or she was feeling the aftereffects of our friendly little greeting; her face was as red as mine. I squeezed her hip and let go.

"Time to get this show on the road," I murmured in apology and eased toward the sound room door, but Samantha tightened her grip and reeled me back.

Her lips brushed against my ear. "We'll finish this later," she told me quietly, sending warm chills along my neck.

"Definitely," I promised in just as heated a tone and twisted my head for a quick kiss, but a flash exploded in my face, blinding me momentarily.

I heard a familiar laugh.

"Oh, that was perfect, love. Just keep going," the laughing voice said. "Don't let me stop you."

I blinked away the white and green clouds in my eyes. "I'm blind. Candace must be here," I said loudly. The light clouds faded and shifted from green to purple, and a slight figure approached and resolved itself.

"Hey, you know I couldn't miss this," she said in that slight Brit accent of hers, giving us each a hug. "You didn't do your takes yet, did you?"

How to describe Candace? A few inches taller than me, currently she'd been coloring her wavy hair black and keeping it short so that it never came past her chin. She had incredibly beautiful green eyes, deep and dark forest green, and Candace made up in sheer energy for at least two people. Her presence was so vibrant, you had to stop to count how many people were in the room—and usually most of them were her, her and her whatchamacallit, her aura. Well, that and her camera, too.

Outside of being one of the most dynamic people I'd ever met, Candace was a class-A, number-one photographer, who just happened to specialize in rock'n'roll. I for one was glad she'd gotten sick of doing "A&R" ("Artists and Repertoire") work for the label we'd all worked for and took up the flash.

Her photography was so fantastic, I actually liked the way she made me look in photos, and that's saying something. I generally hate my pictures. Besides her wonderful eye for composition, Candace was a friend, and when it came to the band's link to the public, I trusted her either to take our pictures or guide us in the right direction professionally. She knew her shit, she knew it cold, and she knew she knew it, too.

The light flare finally faded from my eyes, and I could see clearly again. "I'm just about to go in," I informed her. "Glad you could make it."

"Hey, just wanted you to have that 'live' feel." Candace smiled and flashed her camera at me again. "And I wouldn't miss this, anyway."

I kissed Samantha's cheek, still light-blind from the second flare. "Let's do this thing," I told her, nerves shaky in my throat, and I turned again for the door.

"Sit and listen with me," Samantha invited Candace as I pushed through the foam baffling to the doorknob, twisting it firmly. I could see the overflash through the room as Candace took some shots of Bear and the sound board.

"You know, love, when these girls get down, they rock it all night," I heard her tell Bear, and I smiled as I closed the door behind me and made my way to the microphone that had been suspended from the ceiling for me. A mounted one would have picked up sound from my feet as I danced and grooved. A set of headphones hung from an otherwise empty mike stand, and I slipped them on.

I glanced around at the drum set behind me, which sat on a riser filled with sand to dampen vibration, then looked at the various amps and guitars next to them in stands. I'd been in a vocal booth in the corner of this room before doing "scratch" vocals—a guide track for the band so that the recording would feel "live"—but that had been with the whole band, together. Now I was standing in the center of the studio, alone. I reached up to the microphone and made minute adjustments for my height and comfort.

"Okay, Nina baby, you hear me?" Bear asked in my ears, his voice almost too loud in its stereo clarity.

"Yeah, you're fine," I answered into my own microphone.

Through the glass I could see one or two people moving past the glass window in the sound booth so they could sit behind Bear. Probably the rest of the band, I thought.

Samantha's voice cut into the silence of my headphones. "Kitt's here, love."

"Hey, Kitt," I greeted through the mike and waved to the glass. One of those shadows might have waved back.

Suddenly I felt strange; a huge lump formed in my throat. This was completely different from either the rehearsal studio or a stage performance, and it was so very weird, singing in front of the band, having them watch instead of play with me. An idea struck me.

"Do me a favor, Bear?" I asked. "Lower the lights out there, and give me a dim spot, okay?"

"You want the smoky night club effect?" he asked, his voice perfectly stereo-balanced in the center of my head.

"No, I want the it's-so-dark-in-here-we-can-barely-see-our-instruments-never-mind-the-audience effect," I explained, "where the light is so weird it makes the space very intimate, and everyone's hanging on to the sound and just feeling everything going on—like a low-burning fire."

"Uh-huh, uh-huh." Bear nodded and the lights dimmed. I could barely make out Bear's figure behind the board, and Samantha, Candace, and whoever else was there dissolved into vaguely humanoid shadows. The sound stage blackened around me for a moment, then a small, warm light resolved above my head, directly in front and over the microphone. The overall effect was similar to candlelight, but without the fitfulness that wax and air display.

"That good?" I heard Bear ask, his voice almost hushed in the environment we'd created.

I forced the air in and out of my lungs slowly. Focus, determination, I thought to myself, and drew up in my mind the song and its structure.

"That's perfect," I answered in a steady voice, letting my breath out gradually.

I breathed again, still slow, still focused on muscle and air. I tried to ignore the sounds through my headphones of Bear readying the console and chairs scraping behind him.

Chairs? I asked myself. *Who's watching this now?* But I shoved that thought away. It had no place here, in this now.

"In a moment, Nina." Bear's voice came again—strong, sure, and confident in the semidarkness. This was what he did, and did best— capture musicians, music, and emotion blended and expressed, phrase followed by phrase, note replaced by note, building and shaping the ephemeral for all time.

No pressure, no, none at all, I thought. *This is just going down on permanent record.*

I swallowed and nodded, drawing all the emotions that I needed to do the music justice into my gut and the events that had created them into my mind, because before this studio, before the music for this recording ever existed, this was my life—before all of it, even before Samantha and I finally got together. Suddenly, it all clicked. I was there, in the moment. I was ready.

My headphones came to life again when drumsticks clicked the opening time into my ears, cuing my entrance.

"One, two, three, four..."

GIRLS JUST WANNA HAVE FUN/DOMINION

I remember innocence around me
I remember looking at the sky
I remember heaven used to ground me
I remember knowing how to cry

"I Fall"—Life Underwater

I was at the in place, the hot spot, the place to see, be seen, and be cool. Welcome to the Red Spot, located on ever-so-friendly Bay Street on Staten Island, New York, home of antiques and "junque" by day, and *the*, I mean the coolest, place in the counterculture by night.

My second year of college was over for the summer, my apartment was only a few blocks away, and I didn't have to be anywhere but school in September and work on Friday. But since it was only July, and this Thursday, I didn't have any obligations for at least another day yet, and that wasn't until ten at night, baby.

"*Más tequila!*" Van roared, slamming his shot glass down on the bar in front of him, hair falling over his chin. He stared through the strands at his glass, as if fluid would magically appear in it.

"What are you talking about, 'more tequila'?" Trace teased from behind him, and, shoving his shot glass to the side, she slid into his lap, beer in hand. She held her green bottle to his lips, and he gulped at it desperately.

"That's your fourth Flaming Sambuca, and the third time you've almost set yourself on fire," she reminded him in her honeyed-whiskey voice, and, withdrawing the bottle from him, she replaced it with her lips. Her wavy, long black hair fell down in a curtain over them both.

Well, that was more than enough of a show for me, and turning my eyes from what had evolved from a makeout into a mauling, I decided to check out the scene.

The bar was built on top of an old long-ass, bright red Cadillac convertible with the chrome sticking out just far enough to make a comfortable footrest, and in the long, narrow corridor the front bar created (because there was a back room, too), a couple of TVs hung from the walls, showing cartoons and underground videos. Sound bins hung alternately from the ceiling throughout the room, pumping up the music from the jukebox, and the light was just enough to make out faces, sit in a corner and write pretentious poetry, or read your beer label, but not enough to show the tiredness, sorrow, or the effects of too much partying—which was probably a good thing.

I put my own drink down on the bar, just an orange juice mixed with cranberry. I'd already done a pitcher (or was it two?) of Red Death shots with Trace, so I was slowing down a bit. Oh, and by the way, Red Death is an Alabama Slammer mixed with Kamikazes—that's the best I can explain it.

I had all night to play and I didn't want to get too messed up, you know, so I made my decision. I was going to the back room to dance. The scene up here in the front was lame, and no way was I going to play appreciative audience for Trace, who just loved to perform for whoever was available, or just watch the damn TV. I could do that back at my apartment.

As I wove through the press of bodies to the back corridor, then took the sharp right to the couple of steps into the dance room, I nodded hellos to people who greeted me. I loved those steps; they were painted to look like a giant, triple-level piano keyboard.

The guitar riff from the Cult's "She Sells Sanctuary" gave way to the opening harmonics of the New York Choral Society and the start of "This Corrosion," by the Sisters of Mercy. At ten minutes long, this song was incredible lyrically as well as awesome to dance to, and my feet were already moving toward the center of the dance floor.

I waved to Darrel up in the DJ booth, his blue Mohawk proud and high on his head and bobbing in time to the rhythm. He returned my greeting and continued mixing. I lost myself in the throb of the music.

Spinning and twisting to the beat, dancers mixed and mingled as people admired each other's style, either of dancing, clothes, or body, and I ended up dancing with a girl I didn't really know but had seen there before. Darrel and I referred to her as "Blue," because that's the color she always wore.

Tonight was no exception. Her latest variation was a body-hugging electric blue minidress with a skirt that ended a scant two, maybe three inches below her definition, leaving several inches of bare leg above her spiderweb-patterned thigh-high stockings and dark hair teased up into a tousled bunch. It was too dark to tell what color her hair really was, but I'd definitely seen her in that dress before. We didn't say a word, just smiled and played moves off each other. For the record, she danced very well.

"Thanks for the dance," I said, and smiled at her as the song changed into the next.

"No, thank you," she responded with a smile of her own, and we said nothing for a moment or two. Awkwardness crept into the silence.

"Well, I'll see you around the dance floor." I grinned to end the silent discomfort, neatly ending this interchange. My line was polite and just a touch charming, and always my preferred ticket out of an awkward situation.

"Hey, yeah, see you 'round," she returned.

Grin still in place, I waved and made my way to the bathroom. Might as well check my hair, I figured.

I nudged my way through the body press again, up three little stairs that took me out of the back room, and slipped into a narrow corridor toward the female-designated plumbing facilities.

Odd, I thought, when that place was empty, it was as cold as a meat locker, but add people, then music, and you could barely tell the place was air-conditioned it was so steamy, unless you were in the small corridor, or in the bathroom, like me.

I waited patiently for a spot to open in front of the mirror-wall opposite the toilet stalls, and, once there, I gave myself the once-over starting with my hair, the most important part. Amazingly, it still looked good.

Shaved to the skin right to the top of my ear, buzzed to fuzz another half inch, and an inch-long layer to the temple level with my brow, the rest of it flowed straight and long across my head and down to the center of my back in a modified Mohawk that spread to the width of my temples, as opposed to a simple narrow stripe down the middle of my head. I'd brushed it over to the right, and it arched across perfectly, leaving a curtain I could hide behind if I wanted, or push back if I didn't. Right now? I didn't.

My main mission accomplished, I checked the rest out. No need to worry about makeup. I rarely wore it, with the exception of a little eyeliner and mascara every now and then—hey, that stuff will ruin your skin, ya know. And I inspected my clothes, making sure everything was where it was supposed to be.

Skintight black cotton and Lycra covered my body from throat to not quite midthigh, with sleeves that came to my wrists. I twisted to see my back—yup, everything was in place, or not, depending on your point of view. I was covered in the front, but the back was open to my waist, and the sleeve tops were cut out in such a way that my shoulders, shaped from years of swimming and a few other sports, were bare to the top of the tricep. Sheer black stockings, calf-high black riding boots, and a simple silver ankh on a black velvet choker around my neck completed the outfit.

I like the look, it's working for me, I thought. It was definitely a female look, no mistaking that, but not, you know, girly. Strong, yes, maybe even a little dangerous. I liked it. Woman with an edge, I thought to myself, and nodded slightly with satisfaction.

It was my night off, I was buzzed just enough to feel good but not out of it and filled with restless energy that dancing with a pretty girl only stoked hotter and higher, making my skin tingle. I was definitely ready for anything, and I wasn't going to merely wait for it to come my way.

A face reflected next to mine in the mirror. "Hey, fancy meeting you here." It smiled at me.

"Small world." I smiled in return at the reflection of my dance partner and skimmed my fingers through my hair, just to make sure nothing was out of place. I faced her head-on, leaning against the little ledge that ran the length of the mirror, and crossed one booted leg over the other. Of course I had "cool" attitude. Bathroom or no, this was my place to work, to hang out—my world, my territory.

I watched with an amused grin as she checked her makeup and decided it was okay, then inspected her hair, which in the well-lit room was light brown with a few blond streaks. Whether they were from the sun or chemistry was up to the eye and mind of the beholder.

However it got that way didn't matter, though. In my beholding eye, she was definitely, no doubt about it, very pretty, and she had great legs, too.

"I don't mean to sound trite," she started, "but have we met, before, I mean? You seem so very familiar." Her voice had a musical lilt, her words a very slight accent, as she spoke with a little half smile. The quirk of her lips told me she wanted to play that old game.

Ah, but I was feeling just too good, and I don't like to play some games, especially old ones. If she wanted to play, we'd do it my way. I merely arched an eyebrow at her and recrossed my legs.

"Funny you should say that," I answered, glancing casually down at my nails before looking back up at her, "because I know exactly where I've seen you before." I straightened and put my hand out. "I'm—"

"Nina!" Trace came calling into the bathroom. "Richie asked if you could take over for Darrel. He's sick or something." She barely glanced as she walked right past Blue and slid next to me by the mirror. "He said he'll pay you double your shift. Just remind him at the end of the night."

Trace stopped herself a moment and studied me, as if she hadn't just seen me ten minutes before. I returned her perusal with a bland look; her inspection bothered me. "Very good look for you, by the way." She smiled and lifted slender fingers to tweak the forelock that fell over my cheek. "God, you're so fucking cute," she added, cupping my chin. Her steel gray eyes locked with mine a moment, and the longer the moment held, the more my discomfort grew. She was just a little too close for comfort.

Her intensity pulled at me, began to cut through my shell, and as I felt the muscles grow tight in my neck, I tried to talk myself down, away, and just somehow out from the feeling that swelled within me.

She always does this, she doesn't mean anything by it, I reminded myself, fixing the image of her draped over Van's lap firmly in my head. She'd approach that edge of flirting, though she'd never outright proposition me, then pull something like, well, making out with Van, and it always made me feel pretty darn rotten, like if I'd just done this, that, or the other thing, she'd be with me instead of whoever. Tonight, though, instead of making me feel bad, it was just pissing me off.

"Thanks," I answered shortly, and twisted my head away from her hand. I scowled at the mirror, checking my hair. I hated my hair being messed up, I hated my head being messed with, and I hated being called cute. Teddy bears were cute. Puppies and ducklings? They were cute.

My mother thought I was cute. Then again, my mother also wanted me to be straight. We were working on that—my mom understanding, not my being straight, I mean—fuck that, and fuck cute. I didn't want to be cute, I wanted to be hot. Woman with an edge, dammit, not Lil' Bo fuckin' Peep. Besides, she was making me lose points in front of this girl. Cute, damn.

You know, points are all about the respect of your peers and your chances of getting laid. That's it. Period. On the imaginary scoreboard, "cute" was dismissible, not desirable. Cute and horny did not, do not, and will never go together. Hot, though. That's something else altogether. Hot gets some; cute gets a pat on the head. Did I mention that I hate that? I felt like Trace was trying to say, or rather imply, that I was a teddy bear with teeth, and how ridiculous is that?

But I didn't let any of that show. My boss needed an answer, and Trace was waiting to deliver it. What the hell, I thought. I could lose myself in the music, which was always a good thing as far as I was concerned, and I could earn a few extra bucks toward a guitar I wanted.

Work was work, I decided, and besides, I was only a little buzzed—just enough to feel the edge. So as long as I didn't drink anything fermented for the rest of the night, I'd be fine. It's not like I was operating heavy machinery or driving. "Tell Richie I said yeah, and see if he can have Darrel cue up the next one. I'll be there in half a minute." I decided to not to theorize out loud exactly why Darrel was suddenly so ill he couldn't spin tunes anymore, but I suspected one too many jello shots mixed with some pharmacology up in the booth.

"I just want to—" I indicated my hair to Trace.

"Ohmygod, you're Nina, the DJ!" Blue interrupted excitedly from behind Trace's shoulder. "I'm here every Friday and Saturday you spin the Elemental Experience, and for your Experience-the-Experiment Wednesdays." Her eyes were wide with recognition (or admiration or something I didn't recognize at that time), and those eyes staring over Trace's shoulder were green, like a pine forest at dusk, and I've always been a sucker for dark green eyes.

But sure, right, like she didn't know who I was before, I thought a little cynically with an inward smile. I remembered what nights Darrel and I had both seen her—and debated which of us she'd rather date. I told Darrel I didn't fucking care one way or another, but I also didn't tell him I'd have put the money on me. Outwardly, I grinned at her anyway over Trace's shoulder, and Trace spun so quickly to face her, I'm surprised she didn't hurt the floor.

"Oh, I'm sorry," she apologized, "didn't mean to interrupt." Trace didn't look the least bit repentant as I watched her check the girl out for herself. "Okay, well," she addressed me, her inspection complete, "I'm gonna drop off your message and grab everyone. See you in a few," and she strode off to the door.

"Oh, one last thing?" She poked her head back in. "Don't do anything I wouldn't do." She smiled evilly at me and nodded her chin toward Blue.

I cocked an eyebrow at her. "That leaves me with a lot of options, you know." I shook my head in mock confusion. Trace just kept smiling her wise-ass smile and disappeared.

I took a step in that direction, then stopped and looked over my shoulder at Blue and that incendiary dress. I didn't want to just leave her hanging. She seemed nice enough, and the lines she used could have just been a casual, sincere attempt at conversation. Besides, that would have been rude. Right?

"Hey, I'm sorry, but I've gotta go," I excused myself with a smile. "Work calls. It was very nice meeting you. See you out on the dance floor." I returned through the corridor to the back room.

Darrel had left a slow ambient track flowing through the sound system and the dance floor lit by a dim orange-red glow. The last tune had filled the room with a dark and throbbing energy, a low and restless feeling, not so much sexual as sensual, but lacking joy. Darrel had brought these people down. Where was I going to bring them, I asked myself as I made my way to the booth in the very back corner of the room. I opened the door and leaped up three steps to my little world.

This little square in the sky, the "skybox" as we sometimes called the DJ booth, was surrounded by walls on three sides, and the front that faced the dance floor had a sturdy bench that held the sound board, microphone and headset, two turntables, a disc player going from the middle to the right, all the way to the wall, and a space for discs, drinks, or sometimes, dates, all the way to the left. A Plexiglas wall separated the DJ from the crowd so that whoever was spinning could observe and be observed, but still have that illusion of separateness. Except for the empty space all the way to the left—there was no Plexi there, because that's where people could call up requests or attempt to talk with the DJ, and the waitress could drop off water or whatever other substance had been requested.

The back wall was filled with bins of records and discs, as was the space under the turntables. I flipped through the discs Darrel had set aside. No, no, no, I thought as I quickly discarded each selection, not where I was going. What the hell had he been thinking? Sure, the music he'd picked was decent, but he'd provided no direction, no theme, not even a unifying mood, except for the bleakness his ambient tune was setting.

I had a few more minutes to pull out the next set of tunes that would create the mood I wanted, but no way could I just abruptly alter the environment Darrel had created, even if it was confused. That would have been terribly uncomfortable for the people out there and would leave them feeling disoriented.

No, I was going to evolve it—bring them down, all the way down, then raise them to where I wanted them to be, the fall and the redemption, all in one night; and I'd provide the soundtrack that would guide them all the way through.

I ran my fingers lightly through the racks, pulling this disc out, discarding the next, setting my program up and in order: the songs, the occasional patter, the lighting. I was set.

I took my selections and, instead of placing them on the prep area, put them on the stool before the turntable so I could make faster changes. Besides, since I just had to move my hands, I wouldn't have to break my groove. It's always a good sign if the DJ's dancing too. But this arrangement had another benefit: it made me less accessible to the crowd, since I almost never had to step directly in front of that open space.

Under the counter was a small shelf (and under that was a wastebasket) crammed with paper towels, electrical odds and ends, and baby wipes—you know, premoistened and soaped towelettes, but without the lotion—and I grabbed one of those, quickly wiping my hands free of any detritus they might have picked up. Hey, have to keep those discs clean. My hands now lemony fresh, I hung the headset around my neck so that I could slide the phones up to my ears without messing up my hair and set up the first disc, listening for the groove I wanted to slide myself into. Oh yeah, that low dark throb I was going to take down, all the way low down through, then twist it up. *Take that musical moment and dance, baby*, I thought as I brought the faders up for the first piece I'd selected.

I raised my eyes from the board to scan the room and feel the vibe, and watched as Trace and Van ambled into the dance area and settled about fifteen feet away from the booth. Trace waved to me, then pointed. I followed the line of sight she drew out for me and saw Blue dancing her way over to the booth. I shrugged. "So what?" I mouthed to Trace.

Trace just smiled back at me, and, maintaining eye contact, she slowly and deliberately snaked out her tongue to lick Van's neck. Why did I keep looking as his eyes fluttered shut? Though I couldn't hear it, I could feel the groan that I knew was making its way from his lips. Still watching me watch her, Trace proceeded to trail up into his ear. At that point, he pulled her into his arms and they were mauling each other again.

I shook my head and broke eye contact. I didn't have time for this shit; I had work to do. I slid my headset over my ears, careful not to mess my hair, then smoothly set my mix, letting the heavy opening cadence of that first tune fill my head and the room.

I took a breath and let it out slowly. It was time. Reaching for the microphone, I keyed it open. "Darrel and the Daze have left the building for the night," I intoned solemnly. "You are now…" I let the first riff swell through and watched with a small smile of satisfaction as the music started to take effect, "in…" I let the chords build through and conquer the older tune as it faded out of hearing, "Dominion," I breathed, letting the song of the same name sweep through the room. This was another Sisters of Mercy tune, and by the by, the Sisters of Mercy is a very cool band, sort of. Well, dark and sensual and danceable all at the same time, the *Floodland* album is phenomenal. But still, what a tune to pick for first choice, I reflected. Boy, I was in some mood.

I set the lights to give off a bit of a flicker, since there's nothing like the "dungeon-disco" effect, and checking my mix for the next tune, I closed my eyes and sank into the groove, at peace and at home in my little musical world, feeling fine, just fine, thank you. Of course that moment of peace couldn't last. What is it they say, "When you least expect it, expect it?"

I felt a gentle touch on the bare skin of my back, and as I opened my eyes, I saw a hand holding a plastic cup of water. That was nice.

Wow, sometimes Trace could really set me off, and sometimes she could be just so damn sweet, so considerate, it drove me fuckin' crazy.

It was like she'd been raised in my home—nobody ever said they were sorry. Okay, well, my parents would force us to say it if we got caught doing something, but otherwise, nobody ever said those words; they "did" it instead.

For example, if Nico and I had an argument and it was his fault? Later on, he'd say something like, "Hey, um, wanna go play some video games? My treat." Or if it was me, I'd catch up with him and hand him a cup of hot chocolate or something. Our parents did it too. I mean, if they were "wrong" (which, of course, never happened), they'd pick up a book one of us wanted or take that person out for a Saturday afternoon—something along those lines. We "did" it; we didn't just say it. Well, okay, I was known to say it on occasion, but I always backed it up with an action because "actions speak louder than words."

Trace "did" it, too, although she might every now and then say it, but usually not.

I took the cup and gratefully tossed back and swallowed more than half of it before I realized it was a tequila pop (tequila and 7-Up) and not water. As the combination of sourness and soda fizzled against the back of my throat, my eyes opened wider, and I gulped down what was left in my mouth before handing back the cup.

"Hey, thanks, Trace, but I'm not drink—" It wasn't Trace. It was Blue.

I was momentarily speechless as I pushed my headset from my ears. No one ever, and I mean *ever*, had entered that booth before that either I didn't know or didn't personally invite. This was unheard of. This was—

"Your friend let me in," she told me, neatly plucking the cup from my fingers with a smile. "She figured you wouldn't mind."

A setup. That's what this was. I looked back out into the room and didn't have to scan far. Trace was right by the "request" window, smirking at me, and I leveled my eyes on hers as I leaned over to catch her ear.

"Trace, what the fuck?" I asked her in a loud whisper. Invading my domain and all—sheesh, you know?

Trace tweaked my hair again. "You're so fucking cute when you're mad." She laughed, then reached up and kissed me. Her lips were soft and full but pressed hard against mine, and when she finally let go, she bit my lip. I tasted blood.

"If you did some of the things I would"—she stroked my cheek—"you'd have more fun." Trace drew a finger across my lip, taking the red stain she'd left with it, and I watched, angry, stirred, and mesmerized, as she slid it between her lips. What was wrong with me, that I let her get to me like that? I couldn't stop her if I wanted to, and I wasn't sure I did.

Trace smiled as she brought her hand down. "Mmm, delicious," she commented, then smirked at me. "Now go have fun. I fuckin' dare you." Her smile turned wicked, a flash of teeth, eyes sparking her challenge. She held my eyes a moment, then gave me her back, dismissing me.

My mind swirled as I straightened up and faced my "guest." The carbonation burned through my stomach, the tequila sent a flush through my body, warming my skin and thrumming in my chest.

Blue simply observed me, cup in hand and eyes narrowed in consideration. "I told your friend I wanted to speak with you, and she said she'd help me out, since she'd interrupted," she paused a moment and set the cup on the ledge behind her, "our earlier conversation." She stepped closer to narrow the short distance between us.

Okay, so this game was a little different than I thought it would be. I wasn't expecting this more, well, forward sort of behavior. Okay, though, maybe that was my fault. I'd been the one to start changing the rules, anyway. She reached out, and I stepped back a little nervously, smacking against my sound board.

Oh yeah, the sound board. I was working—or supposed to be, anyway.

"Okay, yeah, sure," I agreed and smiled. "We can talk. I, um, I've got to set my tunes," and I gave my attention to the board. We were so close my hip brushed against hers. Did I mention this wasn't a very big space?

I slipped my headphones back on and checked the play status on the disc. Everything was going smoothly and exactly where I wanted it to. I ran nimble fingers across the dials, then grabbed the next two discs, setting them up in succession; they would fade beautifully into one another. I closed my eyes as I tested the mix, listening, sinking into the music's mood, my fingertips resting lightly on the knobs as I adjusted the program, tweaking a bit here and there to get it perfect. Oh yeah, there it was. This was going to be nice, very nice. I swayed along with the beat and set a few automatic times, tweaking the sound and moments until they were perfect too.

A soft fingertip slid slowly down my bare back, and I forced myself to control the light shiver it caused. Hands strayed to my hips, and Blue danced with me. I could feel the heat of her body on my back as I locked the mix on the board, and as we swayed in time together, I realized she was slightly taller than me.

She was subtle as she pressed up against me, and I felt the light touch of her lips on my neck as I caught the rhythm with her and swayed to the beat. She nibbled her way up to my ear. God, I love that. Well, if I hadn't been stirred before, which I was, this situation had just jumped me up a little higher, but it was time, more than time, to take it in hand. Maintaining body contact, I twisted around, and, glancing up at her eyes for a moment, grasped her hips, bringing us closer. We moved together for a few moments, then I brushed my lips up along the line of her neck, then to her ear. She inhaled sharply, and I smiled. I love it when things work the way they should.

"I have to check the board," I whispered, lightly kissing the skin right below.

"How are you going to do that if I don't let you go?" she murmured into my hair, readjusting the grip she had and holding me firmly.

I brushed my lower lip against her earlobe, then looked up into her eyes. "Just like this." I grinned and, neatly sliding my leg between hers, pulled her closer and pivoted, using our combined weight for leverage. I controlled her descent by holding her hips, and her back landed neatly and with the slightest heaviness to the left of the board. Now I could face the room, if I wanted, and the controls.

But God damn that system had good shocks; the sound never skipped.

"This work for you?" I asked her with a smile, releasing her hips so I could ease up my headphones. As I leaned over and across her to reach for the console and the microphone so I could introduce the next song, my lower body pressed into hers.

She hooked a leg around my hip and reached up, pressing her breasts against me and burrowing her lips into my neck. "This works just fine for me."

"Good," I whispered, enjoying the pattern she was weaving on my throat. What can I say? I'm a sensualist at heart. "Shh," I cautioned, indicating the microphone as I brought it up. She stopped and nodded. Headphones in place, I keyed the mike.

"Brothers and sisters, boyz and grrlz, lovers and leavers, this is the Dominion," I informed the dancers as I scanned the now-crowded floor. Wow. A lot of people had come into the back room since I'd started, hopefully drawn by the music. Hey, all was cool; it meant they liked it and that I was doing my job well.

Blue slipped her leg up between mine and pressed it firmly where it meant business, and I had no doubt in my mind what kind of business she meant.

The throb that flew through my body mingled with the music and the buzz I already had, and a low and throaty "mmph" escaped my lips into the room as I set the sound flying and returned the pressure Blue was sending my way.

We spent a few more moments like that, moving with one another to a beat that was sensual to begin with and heated further by our contact, so when she sat on the small available space on the board and arched her neck back, quicker than it takes to tell, she dropped the leg that was pressed against me and I was between hers. Still dancing, just a slight movement of hips and shoulders, I dipped my head to the line that ran the length of her throat and trailed it very softly with my lips until I reached hers. I gently nipped at her lower lip, requesting access, and received it.

Her lips tasted like cherry-flavored balm, and her tongue had that sweet beer taste. For a moment, I was caught up in a memory—the smell of the ocean and lips so soft and tender that to kiss them was to worry for a moment about bruising them before losing myself entirely. But the mouth I was kissing was certainly not like that, and that event, that possibility, was too far away to be brought back, I thought fleetingly.

But Blue was a good enough kisser that I was able to shove the memory aside and focus on the mouth under mine. As I smoothed along her ribs, a hand ran up and down my back and sides, and one snaked into the space where our bodies met.

Tempting, very tempting, but not where I wanted to go, not in this place, not on these terms. She wanted to play and—this was now my game. Carefully, I took her hand away from me and my lips from hers.

"No, baby," I gazed into her eyes and whispered, bringing her hand to my shoulder and holding it there, "this is all about you." And reaching for her mouth with mine, I rounded her hips, massaging her firm ass.

She moaned into my mouth and gripped my ribs with her knees. Almost lazily, I encircled her waist and drew a soft line along her thigh with my free hand until it was under what was left of her skirt. She'd already pushed it up and mostly out of the way. Skirts are great sometimes, ya know? I like 'em, lots. I grazed the spot where the thigh meets the body, stopped kissing her for a moment, and stilled my hands to consider—what, exactly, I'm not sure—but this was going a bit further than I'd originally intended.

Raising my head, I scanned the room once again. Everyone was grooving; the mood was working, both in the room and definitely in the skybox. A hand waved in the air and caught my eye—Trace, trying to get my attention. I nodded and gave her a small smile.

"I dare you!" she mouthed at me.

I shook my head. "Fuck you!" I mouthed with a grin and rolled my eyes.

"I'm not the one you're fucking!" Trace yelled back, laughing. She spun Van around until they were both out from my line of sight.

Blue merely waited for me, stroking my ribs as I removed my hands, and I took advantage of the moment to make some final adjustments to the board. I had a ten-minute song followed by an eleven-and-a-half-minute one. The music would be good to go for a decent length of time without my direct attention. Blue's legs relaxed a bit and rested on my hips.

I'd reached for the last set of knobs that would lock my current settings when, suddenly, Trace was at the request window. I stared at her. "What?" I asked silently.

"You're such a baby, just so really fucking adorable. You know that?" she yelled up at me with an evil smile, then danced away.

God damn, how did she manage to always fuckin' do that to me? I reached blindly for my cup of water and drank, forgetting—again—that it wasn't water, but what was left of the tequila pop. The drink was like acid in the back of my throat and burned all the way down.

Fuck it, I thought as I finished it and tossed the cup into the pail under the board. I stood there a moment staring at nothing, letting everything run through me, burning like the tequila—the frustration with Trace, the arousal from Blue, and the normal restlessness that rides everyone's blood on a summer night. Okay, maybe that's just hormones, but you know what I mean.

Maybe the moon was full, or I'd had more to drink than I thought. Could be I was still a little annoyed, maybe even a little raw about the "cute" comment. I don't know why I had such a need to have Trace see me differently (okay, maybe I do know, but let's just move on), but I was scanning the dance floor, finding Trace's cold gray eyes and holding them with my own. Blue twined her arms around my neck, and I tangled my hands into her hair, drawing her head back. My lips were almost on her throat, just a breath away, before I broke that eye contact with Trace, and this time, definitely on my terms.

Cute this, I thought as I brought my teeth to bear along the column of Blue's throat, and my hands were in the mix, too. I had both of them by the twin junctions of her thighs and was alternately scraping along their length with my nails (yes, I keep them short, but not bitten) and massaging the firm muscle. She was busy, too. Gratifyingly responsive to my kisses and caresses, she hungrily licked and sucked on my neck, her hands tracing the contours of my face, her knees now firm against my ribs.

I lifted my head away from the assault, then dipped it, questing for her mouth. My hands rested lightly on her parted thighs, and as I slid my tongue between her welcoming lips, I softly brushed my thumbs along the narrow strip of material that held her secrets. She gasped into my mouth, and her body surged forward. I pressed my thumbs harder against her and could feel the valley she wanted to welcome me into under the damp material.

"Are you sure?" I whispered into her ear, interrupting the meeting of the mouths, and she bit my neck in response. I glanced up a moment, toward the dance floor, and found Trace's eyes upon me, an unreadable expression on her face. Burying my lips into Blue's neck, I lifted the flimsy material away with my right hand and stroked over the fine damp hairs that lined her cleft with my left. Her clit was hard and wanted my attention, and I complied, sliding my thumbs around its base, stroking it.

She was soft and slick, swollen with want and wide open to me. Shifting my left hand palm up, I poised my index and middle fingers right at her wet and welcoming entrance.

She moaned softly and eased back on her elbows, her head hanging between her shoulders.

I leaned forward over her and slid my free arm around her waist. When she raised her head to mine, I kissed her. "Are you sure?" I murmured into her lips. "We can stop if you want."

She grabbed my wrist. "Please, Nina," she asked, and kissed me deeply. "Fuck me," she whispered into my ear, and as she leaned back again, she pulled me with her, but still I stayed my hand, at her entrance, but not in it, "just fuck me."

Hey, you never deny a lady a direct request, right?

I kissed her again, slowly and sensually, and explored the lovely rich wetness between her lips. With small and steady movements, relishing the feel of her, I entered by slow degrees, getting to know her, making sure she was more than ready. When the very tips of my fingers were inside her, I felt more than heard her anticipating groan. That, and the complete opening of body—you know what I mean, that sudden, total, there's-just-no-barriers-here-I'm-wide-open-to-you welcome that tells you "Now, right now!"—were the cue I wanted, had been waiting for. It's all about timing. I pulled her closer and in one swift, almost savage movement, slid my tongue all the way into her mouth, pressed my thumb hard against her clit and my fingers almost as far as they could go into her pussy.

She gasped and shuddered, gripping the edge of the bench with both hands, and, bringing one knee straight back, she stretched the length of her leg over my shoulder. I slid even deeper inside that slick, tight space, and the rhythm I set was fast and furious, the time for formality and shyness way over.

I felt her pussy tighten around my fingers, and, instead of sliding in and out, I stayed deep within her, moving easily through her wetness, fucking her with short thrusts as her hips pushed back against me.

"That's it, baby," I whispered, "that's it."

Encouraged, she groaned, grabbing the edge of the board with one hand, a leg now pinning my arm, a heel dug into my ass, and she groped around for something else to hold on to. She grabbed the microphone.

"Oh, yeah, baby, fuck me like that, just like that," she groaned, chest heaving, her body a glorious wave. Using my hips, I pressed farther into her, the weight of my body against hers adding intensity to the pressure on her clit and the fingers inside.

Her pussy tightened again, a hot suck on my fingers as she undulated against me. My clit, already throbbing, jumped with intensity. I love, I mean, really love, the feeling of a woman getting ready to come.

"You're so tight," I whispered throatily. "Go ahead, squeeze me, baby, hold me in you." She was gonna come, and I was making sure she would, but good. Fucking hard, and fucking good. I increased the pace.

Blue let out a small, high-pitched gasp and gritted her teeth a moment. I painted stripes along her neck with my tongue, then found a spot to focus on. Nibbling and sucking, I stayed there and realized she was speaking, chanting something, over and over.

"So good, so fuckin' good," she ground out repeatedly through her teeth. The sound of her fuck-heavy voice seemed to surround me, and for whatever reason, I looked up a moment.

Suddenly I realized where I was, stretched across this girl, buried deep in her cunt, the knee on my shoulder pressed almost all the way back to hers, her head and shoulders thrown back against the Plexi, and the microphone keyed in her clenched hand.

Her pussy kept rocking, sucking my fingers, then started to spasm, squeezing and releasing. "Oh yeah, yeah," she gasped out, and as her voice floated over the rhythm that played in the room, I thrust in her hard, fast, and steady.

I found Trace's eyes upon me as she stood still upon the dance floor, the only one not dancing, really, and Van had seemingly departed to parts unknown. He'd probably gone for another drink or to the bathroom. Trace folded her arms over her chest, definite anger on her face as she watched me. Fuck her. This moment wasn't about her.

Blue cried out, a sensual, breathy sound that floated over and around the dancers, mixing perfectly with the beat in the room, and with a final surge of motion, her body rose, sealing her chest against mine, her legs coming down tightly around my waist. She released her grip on the bench and tossed the mike to parts unknown, then put both hands on my face, bringing our mouths together. She sent that primal cry down my throat as I felt the waves go through her. I wrapped my free arm around her, supporting her, holding her close and my fingers still while her pussy softened and relaxed, and Blue buried her lips into my neck, whimpering softly.

"Shh…" I soothed, and I rocked her gently against me for a few moments, murmuring nonsense into her hair, hearing her breathing ease. She wrapped her arms loosely around my shoulders, and I very carefully withdrew my fingers.

"Boy!" she exclaimed airily as we came apart.

I cocked my head. "Not hardly." I grinned. She caught the grin and smiled back, and in a moment we both laughed.

"For which I'm thankful," she responded, laughing some more. She hopped off the bench and straightened her skirt. The scent of sex, her sex, hung in the box as I dug under the bench for the baby wipes. Now I knew why Darrel always made sure we had plenty.

I grabbed a few out. "Here," I reached up and gently wiped off the light sheen that glowed on the skin of her face and neck, "how's that?"

Blue took my hand and kissed the palm. "Very nice, thank you." She smiled.

"It certainly was." I smiled in return because I didn't just mean the wipes. "Thank *you*." I took my hand back, and in moments both of them were lemony fresh again. I gave the board a quick glance to make sure all was good in the world, and Blue began to ease toward the door.

"Hey, where you going?" I asked her, slightly confused. Hadn't she originally said she wanted to talk?

"I guess…I should, um, let you work, right?" Despite the smiles all around, hers didn't seem all the way right, and her eyes questioned me.

Oh no, this was going to become drama very soon if I wasn't careful. "Hang out a sec?" I requested. "It's okay," I reassured her. I decided to scan the room—I wanted to catch the waitress's eye—and when I finally did, I waved her over. She deftly picked her way through the crowd to the request window.

"Hey, Andra," I greeted, "I need a plain cran and orange juice and"—I looked over my shoulder—"what are you drinking?" I asked Blue. She had to at least be thirsty, right? Besides, she was a guest in my booth.

"Corona." She smiled at me, and this time her smile looked genuine or, at the very least, relieved.

"A Corona," and I glanced back over my shoulder with a grin, "with lime," I finished.

"I'll be right back with that." Andra smiled up and batted her heavily lashed eyes at me. "Anything else? Are you sure you're, um," she raised her eyebrows, "satisfied?"

Huh, what do you know. I'd always suspected Andra might have been flirting with me, and now I knew for sure. Cool.

"Hey, I'm just getting started," I grinned back with a quirk of my lips, "but thanks—I'm totally fine."

"So we hear," she shot back, now smiling widely. She turned to go, then stopped. "I like your mix tonight. You've really got the, um, mood," I watched her mouth as she ran her tongue along her teeth, "going." She favored me with a smoky look, then slid back into the writhing throng.

"Thanks," I called to her retreating form.

I glanced at my meters and returned to Blue, who had made herself comfortable along the back bench.

"Listen, I've got about forty-five seconds to set my next mix. Just hang back here a minute, go through the discs, see if there's some tunes you'd like to hear, and I'll see if I can fit them in, okay?" I asked her with a smile. I didn't want her to think that I'd fucked her and wanted to forget her, but I really did have to pay some attention to my job. I was supposed to be working, after all.

I focused on the board and replaced my headphones. Andra was right, I mused, swaying to the beat; it was a good groove. I checked the next tune and adjusted my fades and timers for the next insert. I hadn't spoken to the room for a bit, so it was time to be a little more interactive—with the whole room, I mean.

I reached for the microphone. Fuck. Where was my mike? Finally I saw the wire trailing across the board, where it had been tossed over the dividing screen. I grinned to myself. Well, hell, if it had gotten wrecked, at least it had been for a good cause, I figured.

Slowly reeling it back, I placed it carefully down where I needed it, checked my volumes again, and listened for my entrance. Okay, there it was. I eased the fade in, the end of one song flowing into the beginning of the next. I'd already brought the mood down as far as I wanted it to go. The one that was about to end had started the climb back up, and this next one would cement that move.

I reached for the microphone and keyed it. "Fellow freaks and frenzied followers," I brought the mix up slightly and the volume down a bit, "you are in the Dominion with Nina," I reminded them.

Whoops, hollers, and applause broke out across the room, and I stared out at the crowd as the dancers all paused to cheer me in the skybox. Usually, when I announced songs or just uttered some encouraging enthusiastic phrase, I got some enthusiastic hollers, but this, this was a standing ovation. I was momentarily stunned.

"Do it, Nina!" someone yelled over the music.

I was shocked out of my daze, and my ears burned with embarrassment because I was pretty sure that was not a reference to my DJing, although it could have been. Most people looked at the floor and each other when they danced, and they couldn't really see anything behind the partition except for heads. Anything they heard they probably thought was just part of the mix, add-ins by the DJ to enhance the music and the mood. It seemed to have worked, intentionally or not.

"Experience Dominion!" another person yelled, and the crowd picked up the cry until it became a chant that reoccurred over the closing strains of music and beat that flowed through the room.

"Dominion! Dominion!" The sound from the eager dancers seemed to swell and grow.

I placed my hands on the board and studied the crowd a moment longer, their attention firmly on the skybox and not on the music, apparently. Hoo boy. I'd started something I'd had no intention of even beginning, and I wasn't sure of how to go on or what they were asking for.

Scratch that. I knew. Fuck it, though. This wasn't something I'd normally play with, but I was feeling reckless anyway, and the burning in my ears was nothing compared to the burning in my skin or the rising flood threatening to overwhelm me that being with Blue had done nothing to stem.

I set my headphones firmly, placed a hand on a fader, and keyed the mike. I brought the level up as I spoke. "Is that what you want?" I asked the room in a low and throaty voice. Cheers broke out. "Are you sure?" I pressed in the same low voice, bringing the fader up a bit more. The mix was still in the background, but now discernable through the other song. More cheers and applause.

I checked my timing and went with the rhythm. "Fine, then," I purred. *Careful now, timing, that's what it's all about,* I reminded myself, listening for the entrance, "have it."

I brought the faders up on full, and the mix was complete. The room was off and grooving, and I grooved along with them to the music.

I pulled out the next few selections and positioned the tune that would follow on the board, checking my levels for time and volume.

Andra had come back with our drinks and set them in the request window. Done with my board for the moment, I picked them up—a cup of cran and orange for me, a bottle of Corona for Blue, and, wait. There was a third? Yes, another cup of what looked like cran and orange.

"Thanks," I told Andra, who had waited to make sure I saw the drinks, "who's this for?" I asked, pointing to the second cup I had left on the ledge.

"For you," Andra grinned, "in case you're too busy, um, grooving, to remember to get another."

"That was very cool of you, thanks." I smiled back. It was true, that was both cool and nice of her to do.

"You're very welcome," she answered, "oh, and by the way?" She stuffed a piece of paper into the hand that held the cran and orange cup. "You can start with me, anytime." She gave me an appraisingly smoky look, then walked away.

Stunned, I blushed, then managed to collect myself. "I'll keep that in mind," I grinned and called to her back. Andra heard that and gave me a saucy smile, then wove her way through the dancers back to the main bar.

I shook my head. Yep, definitely flirting, I thought, bemused. Drinks in hand, I found Blue still sitting on the back bench, and she favored me with a smile as I handed her the beer.

"Thanks for your patience." I grinned at her, holding my cup up in toast.

"No worries," she answered, seeming amused. "You'll want to keep that." She pointed with her beer.

"Keep what?" I asked, confused.

"That..." She reached over and plucked the paper I'd forgotten out from between my hand and my drink. She folded it neatly and tucked it into my sleeve, stroking my wrist as she did so. "You'll want to keep it." She grinned at me. "She's very pretty."

I wasn't sure of what exactly to say, so I thought it wise to say nothing and merely gave her a little smile of my own. Sometimes, it's the only thing you can do.

Blue merely smiled wider, then clinked the top of her bottle against my cup. I gratefully lifted the cup to my mouth and drank, the juice nice and cool, soothing even, as it slid down my throat. I was thirstier than I thought and drank rather quickly, and it was only somewhere between the second and third swallows that I realized there was more than juice in my cup. Ah, well, there went stopping for the rest of the night.

I finally settled back along the ledge next to Blue so we could chat. While the mix I had on wasn't terribly long, at least not as long as the ones I'd had on before, it was long enough that I could take a break if I wanted.

"So, do I detect a bit of an accent?" I asked, remarking on the slight lilt in her voice. I'd noticed it much earlier, but this was the first chance I'd had to ask about it. We had been rather, um, distracted.

"Um, yes." She glanced down. "Most don't hear it," she said finally, looking at me with what I suspected were pink cheeks and a faint grin.

"Ah, well, most don't spend all their time listening for inflections in sound." I smiled at her. "I tend to hear things others don't. It's charming, by the way," I added with honest admiration. "It adds this lovely little roll to your voice. It's really quite musical."

This time she was definitely blushing. "No one's ever told me that before. What a nice thing to say," she finally said, and she studied me seriously.

I let her inspect me for a moment, not sure why she was so somber. And it was true, about her voice, I mean. The lilt underneath her words made everything she said lyrical, so why shouldn't I mention it? It was lovely, even a bit sexy.

The silence grew longer. "Something wrong?" I asked lightly. The mood was getting way too serious, and I wasn't comfortable. I also wouldn't let it continue if I could help it.

Blue seemed to give an inward shake and collected herself. She shook her head.

"No, nothing." She nodded, then took a sip of beer. "It's just, you're not just trying to charm me, are you?" she stated more than asked.

I focused my gaze on her with greater intent because that confused me. Charm? For what? I didn't get it—what the fuck was that all about? All I'd said was that her voice was lovely. Oh, she meant... Well, wouldn't I have done that before we, um, I, uh, well, you know, before I let someone use my microphone for distance tossing? and I said as much.

Blue sighed, almost grinning in relief. "You've a point there, don't you?" she commented, and rubbed my thigh.

I felt the strength of her fingers as they ran up and down the muscle, then lightly took her hand in mine and twisted a bit on the bench to face her. The flood that had risen through me before was starting to ebb, and I was finally starting to feel a little normal again—whatever that was.

I took a small sip of my drink and considered, then took another. Nope, it really wasn't just juice. Funny how you couldn't tell right away.

Finally, I put the drink down on the bench behind me, then faced Blue again. "So," I began with a smile and her hand delicate and warm in mine, "you still haven't told me where you're from."

Blue laughed, a sensual and somehow sophisticated sound. "I'm from the UK." The curve of her lip was undeniably attractive as she spoke. "I'm spending the summer holiday here on the advice of a friend, well, an ex, um, sort of." She grinned, but seemed slightly embarrassed. I can't tell you why, but I found that attractive, too. "You know how these things can be."

I nodded in polite agreement. In reality, I didn't—know, that is. I dated, I occasionally fooled around, but my first girlfriend I hadn't spoken to in quite a while, though I'd seen her at the club from time to time, and besides, I never dated anyone long enough to become anything other than friends, and didn't want to, either. People, once you trusted them? Fucked you over, and I'd been fucked enough, thanks.

"She's an American, from here, I mean. New York, actually," Blue added.

"Don't ask me if I know her." I laughed. "New York's a very big place." That was something everyone from everywhere did, and as far as I can tell, still does, you know, the "hey, I'm from X," followed by "oh, yeah? I know Y in X—do you know him/her/it?" I think it's funny and sort of cute, even heartwarming in its own way, how we all want to reach for these connections, bridge the gaps of time and space/place.

"How big is Staten Island?" she asked me with a small twist of her lips and appraisal in her eyes. "Because that's where she's from."

"Not nearly as big." I answered, amused. "Sooner or later, you find that everyone's someone's cousin or sibling or something like that."

"Well, that explains it, then." Blue smiled. "You must be a cousin." She put her bottle down beside her.

That was weird. "What do you mean?" I asked. As far as I knew, all the cousins I had in this state, and there were only two of them, were in grammar school, and in fact, they lived with their mom in my parents' house.

"You look so very much like her, and there could hardly be two of you, could there? I mean, she never mentioned a twin of any sort, especially not with the same name."

My head started to tingle, and I could feel the skin on the back of my neck tighten. This was more than the alcohol, this was a sign, a part of my brain said. Have another drink and don't be a moron, the other part told me. Since that was the part that I thought made sense, I listened to it and took yet another sip of my this-is-*not*-juice juice. But still…

"What's your friend's name?" I asked, more than curiosity piqued. It could be possible. I mean, maybe I did have a cousin I hadn't known of before. Lord knows, history, hell, the world is full of stories like that. Some of them even true. *Okay, that's the alcohol thinking for you*, said the part of my brain that had just told me to have some more.

"Oh, no, not my Ann, but a girl she knew a few years back," Blue corrected. "She has pictures, from secondary—I'm sorry—high-school yearbooks, and you look very much like her friend. But," and as she paused, the expression in her eyes softened, "sadly enough, Annie's friend passed away quite some time ago and you, " she ran a finger along my cheek, "you're quite alive." Blue smiled sensually and showed me her teeth as she gently stroked my chin with her thumb. Her eyes lingered appreciatively on my lips.

My cheeks grew hot, but still I considered what she'd said. It was possible she was talking about my high school and yearbook. I mean, I'd been in pictures all over it for each of the four years I attended, but I didn't remember anyone named Ann, at least not that I'd hung out with, and I couldn't remember anyone who'd died, at least not recently.

I mean, there had been one girl who'd been a freshman when I was in my sophomore year, a lovely girl named Susan who'd been born with an incomplete heart wall—a blue baby. Sadly enough, for whatever reason, that poor heart finally stopped one day, and the entire student body mourned the loss of the beautiful soul that she was and the person she could have become.

But still, even with the sad death of Susan, I couldn't think of who it could be. Besides, she and I had looked nothing alike, unless you subscribe to the general sentiment that all *Homo sapiens* look alike. She'd been a light ash blond to my auburn-infused brunette, and due to her condition, Susan had been very slightly built. On the other hand, while I wasn't terribly tall, I had definitely been more robust. Well, I had to be. I'd been on the swim team, after all.

It must have been simply that the DJ booth was dark, and, clearly, Blue and I had both been drinking. Ergo, she must have made a mistake. Just because I didn't know or remember an Ann at school with me didn't mean there wasn't one in some other school. After all, there were at least two other all-girl ones, not to mention the almost dozen other coed and public ones, on Staten Island.

"No." I slowly shook my head. "I've never gone to school with an Ann," I told Blue. "Do you know what school she went to?" I asked, thinking that if I didn't know her, there was a good chance that I knew someone who did.

"Oh no, Annie, Ann," she smiled broadly and reached out to touch my shoulder, "that's her nickname. Her name is really—" but she never got to finish the sentence.

The door to the booth slammed open, and as Trace flounced up the three little steps, the force of her shove allowed the door to bounce back shut again. She looked upset.

I jumped off from my seat in alarm, and Blue followed suit. I stepped toward Trace. "What's wrong?" I asked with concern as Trace's eyes burned. Correction. Definitely upset, very upset, and possibly angry.

"What the fuck do you think you're playing at?" she spat out venomously. "Just what the fuck do you think you're doing?"

My concern vanished; I knew what was going to happen. Trace was just about to pull one of her famous jealousy scenes. I'd witnessed a few in the past, all of them unleashed on her current boy toy. But this time, for whatever her reasons, she'd decided to focus on me.

I quickly checked over my shoulder, ensuring Blue was safely behind me—there was absolutely no need for her to be in the line of fire, after all—and stepped closer to Trace.

"My job," I answered Trace coolly, "and *nothing* that you wouldn't do," I ripped back at her, and pointedly studied her a bit. Who the fuck was she to question me, anyway? She'd set me up in the box with Blue in the first place. Fuck her if I called her bluff, and fuck her and her jealousy. She had no right to it.

"Don't be a fuckin' smartass, Nina," Trace warned. "I mean"—she gestured at Blue, but continued to glare at me—"her."

"I was just showing…" I paused a moment. Fuck. My fingers still knew what it felt like to be inside her, and I didn't even know her name. Christ. In my head, she was Blue, but I was sure she had a name other people used, like the one she'd been born with, perhaps? I glanced at her, and, luckily for me, she picked up on my thoughts.

"Candace," she whispered to me.

"Thanks," I stage-whispered with a quick and what I hope was a reassuring smile before I faced down Trace again. "I was showing Candace the booth, and letting her pick out a few tracks. She's keeping me company," I added blandly. Well, what else was I supposed to say?

Blue, I mean Candace, slipped beside me and slid next to Trace by the steps.

"I can see you and your girlfriend have some things to discuss," she said a bit hurriedly, "so I'll just say good-bye now," she said.

"She's not my girlfriend," I affirmed to Candace, while Trace spoke at the same time.

"I'm not her girlfriend," she ground out from the corner of her mouth.

I watched as Candace studied Trace, and I realized for the first time that she was more than a bit older than me, maybe mid to late twenties. Not that I cared, that's not a big deal or anything. It's just that I hadn't noticed before.

"No, you're not that," she said with a thoughtful expression as she made her own discovery of Trace, "and not quite a friend either, I see." Blue, um, Candace took a step back toward me while Trace mulled that over. I tucked the statement into the back of my head to think about later, because at this moment I agreed with Candace. I suspected she might have spoken truer than she knew.

Candace leaned toward me. "Watch out, love," she whispered into my ear. "That one has fangs." She kissed my cheek briefly but warmly, and I returned the kiss as we gave each other a quick embrace. I admired the lines of her legs as she climbed down the steps to the door.

"Lovely meeting you," she told Trace politely, her hand on the latch. "Nina?" her voice lifted and she smiled at me.

"Yes?" I couldn't help but smile back at her in inquiry. I really liked the sound of her voice.

"You're simply lovely. I'll see you soon," and with that, she was out the door, closing it behind her.

❖

I downed what little remained of the "not juice" I'd already started, then tossed the empty cup into the waste pail. Grabbing the one Andra had fortuitously left for me, I sipped it as I ignored Trace, who simply stood there glaring at me with her arms folded, and went back to my board. I'd lost all feeling for the night. No flood, no rush, no buzz—just an emptiness that was heavier under my skin than the restlessness from before. But it didn't matter if I'd lost the feeling; I still had a job to do. Plenty of people were still out there counting on me to provide their good time, and I was going to do that.

Donning my headphones, I checked the meter and set my fades, timing for the next cue, sliding it into the mix. Scratch what I said before. I wasn't numb, I was drained. I could never figure her out— Trace, I mean. She was ready to fuckin' chew me a new asshole, and I didn't even really know why. She'd sent Candace to the booth in the first place; what in the world was she so mad about? I finished my drink and looked back up and over the dance floor. I spotted Andra, and, when she finally saw me, I signaled for another round. She nodded and disappeared.

Funny, I mused as I pushed the headset off my ears and around my neck, then sorted blindly through the discs I'd pulled earlier to lay them out in their upcoming order, once you passed the second or third sip, you really didn't taste the alcohol anymore.

A gentle hand touched the bare skin of my back, and I stiffened slightly. "I'm sorry, Nina," Trace whispered into my hair, and kissed the soft skin behind my ear. I worked on in silence as she etched light patterns onto my skin. That was just typical Trace. In like a flash flood, out like a gentle spring rain. Okay, more like a hormonal spring flood. But me, well, she just left me confused at best.

If I was angry, I couldn't stay that way, and if I was happy, I couldn't stay that way. No matter what I did, it wasn't the right thing to do, and whatever I was, it apparently wasn't the right thing to be. And now she was sorry. What an ugly joke—I should have just kicked her out of the booth—but her apology softened my anger, and she began massaging my neck and shoulders, adding light, sensual kisses to the back of my neck between pressure points.

This proved one thing, I thought. I was a complete idiot. As I added the finishing touches to the mix, affection for Trace rose and blended with the frustration and the sensual stirring that Trace created wherever she went.

I let myself lean back into her a moment, then caught myself and stopped. Trace wrapped an arm across my shoulders and one around my waist, anchoring a hand on my hip.

"Come on, Nina, you know how I am," she cajoled softly, following up with little kisses.

"Yeah," I answered shortly. Andra had already come back and dropped off another beverage without a word. I grabbed the new one and downed it. Trace was driving me crazy, and she knew it. She was manipulating me, and I knew it. I didn't respect myself for responding, even if I didn't let on how effective she was. In fact, I was angry—with Trace for trying to play me, and with myself for being so damn easy to play. I found more knobs on the board to adjust. Trace pulled me tightly into her arms.

"Nina, you know how I feel about you," she persuaded in her honeyed-whiskey tones, and she let the very tip of her tongue play across that sensitive spot right behind and under my ear.

I set my mix and, with a shrug of the shoulder, we were face-to-face, and I caught her eyes with mine. What the hell was that supposed to mean? What the fuck was she trying to say? Why didn't anyone ever just come right out and say what they meant? Also, what had she done to Van? Was he sitting, brain melted and blood drained, in a corner somewhere? She done with him, too? My skin felt like it was on fire, and my throat burned. The constant sexual tension and half-toned seduction, the all-too-confusing words—I couldn't, I just couldn't anymore. My chest felt like it would explode with pressure.

"No, Trace, I don't," the words tore from my lips, harsh and jagged, "you've never told me." I stared into her eyes as they flashed silver even in this dim light. "You," I started softly as I reached for her face, "play games." Before I fully realized what I was about to do, I kissed her, hard and full, on those baby-soft lips that answered mine with a surprisingly slick sensuality. A moment, then another. Putting my hands on her shoulders I pushed her away, breaking the contact. Trace stared at me, her expression indefinable.

"You kiss me, you pet me, then you go fuck whoever, and when they lie, when they hurt you, I'm the one." I placed my hand over my chest, heat running so high within me I could feel my ears burn. "Me, I'm the one to heal you and hold you through it, until you feel better, until it's time for the next one."

Trace waved a hand in confusion and reached for my shoulder. "Nina, I—"

"No, Trace." I brushed her hand away in impatient frustration. "You tell me we're friends, that what we are together is beautiful." I raised my fingertips to her cheek and touched it lightly, brushed my thumb gently against her lips. "Oh, Trace," I sighed as she kissed my thumb softly. "I'd fuckin' die for you if it would make you happy, but I think you'd just laugh." I watched her face for a reaction, any reaction, as I tried to control the short, hard bursts that forced themselves through my throat and passed for breath.

A part of my mind—probably the part that had called me a moron—marveled inwardly. I'd never spoken to anyone, especially not Trace, like this before. I was always the understanding friend, the supportive, comforting presence. In the past, I'd been hurt, I'd been confused, but never before had I been furious and let it show. I might not have understood it, but I was definitely just going with it. Well, hell, I'd already been doing that all night.

With surprising speed, Trace grabbed my wrists and held them to my side, then, using the height she had on me to her advantage, she backed me into the board, pinning me with her hips. My back thudded against the ledge, though I barely felt the pain. This time the sound did skip. My headphones slid off my neck and back behind me onto the board.

"Nina, that's not true, you know how I feel"—she leaned her forehead against mine—"about you." I swore I could hear the beginning of a laugh bubbling in the back of her voice.

Alarmed, I tried to free myself from her grip to at least rescue my headphones, but I could barely move my arms. Man, what the hell was wrong with me? I couldn't move and, believe me, I tried. My muscles just wouldn't obey the commands my brain was sending.

God, I was drunker than I thought, and I was scared, scared because I couldn't move, and really scared for the first time of Trace—

the intensity of her words and the raw power of her body against mine. I'd forgotten, or maybe just ignored, how for all her delicate looks, Trace was also incredibly strong. And it had never occurred to me, for even a moment, that things would go in this kind of physical direction.

"What do you want from me?" she hissed into my ear, then scraped it with her teeth. With a quick twist of her hips, Trace pressed between my thighs, and, with a strong sweep, she spread my legs so wide I would have fallen over if she hadn't had me pinned to the board. How the hell did she do that? Her arms pressed mine even more firmly than before, locked down by my hips, and yet she was still able to reach all the way around and grab my ass, the very tips of her fingers on my inner thighs, up against the sides of my pussy.

Whatever this was, wherever this was going, I didn't like it, and I wanted it to end. "Trace, stop!" I ordered with as much strength as I could muster. I didn't want this between us.

Heartbreakingly beautiful, Trace was a striking combination of slender lines and strength, a vulnerable fortress. How many nights since I'd moved into the building that we shared had we spent together, in her apartment or mine, my arms around her while she cried because of old wounds that still ached, new ones that still bled, or just because there were things in the world that simply touched her that deeply? How many mornings had she woken me with kisses and caresses, made me breakfast, and made sure I took my vitamins? And then there was time we spent together, just cuddled up, talking of nothing, everything, listening to music, just wrapped up against each other, listening to one another breathe.

But in all that time and all that closeness, even with all the flirting and sleeping skin to skin, we had never, and I mean never, gone to that next step. Slept together, yes, but it was sleep, and not sex. Hell, this was the first time we'd ever really kissed—I mean, without an audience, that is. I'd never wanted to push for anything. I'd just wanted to let things between us go the way they naturally would, whatever that was.

But maybe Trace was tired of waiting, because she ignored my request. "You want me to tell you how I love you, that I want you." Her lips slid along the sensitive column of my neck. Teeth replaced her lips with such strength that I knew she'd drawn blood. But then, when didn't she, one way or another?

"You want me to tell you that when you hold me I feel peaceful, and my dreams are filled with you, holding me, loving you," and she slid a fingertip along the slight depression that marked my lips, "that if I let you, your love makes me feel whole." She pressed harder, massaging me with her fingertips through my stockings.

"Trace, you don't want to do this," I said as steadily as I could. My heart pounded, my head swam, and though I couldn't explain then how I felt, I can say it now. I loved her. I pitied her. I wanted her. She scared the shit out of me.

I was caught between horror and desire. Yes, I wanted her, but I wanted something between us to be real, not real scary. This just felt so wrong, so very wrong. *Man, I hope I wake up soon. Real soon.*

"But I do," she answered, ripping at my lower lip with her teeth. I could feel her fumbling for the seam, and I felt her fingers gain purchase and pull, her hands hard against me. "You want me to…" she whispered into my ear. Jesus Christ, she wasn't going to stop.

Her mouth continued working on my neck, weaving exquisite patterns on my throat while her fingertips continued to trace my outlines. I could feel the groan that she uttered as her lips nipped a particularly sensitive spot, and as I arched my neck and offered her my throat, I began to think, okay, maybe this was what she needed to be able to let go and just be, be real. If I surrendered completely maybe, possibly, so could she.

The part of my mind that wasn't drunk surged forward. What was I, fucking crazy? More likely, she'd suck my soul dry.

Summoning strength from I don't know where, maybe it was just that Trace's grip slipped, or that my brain and spine had decided to communicate with each other again, all together my brain, spine, and I remembered an old move from the judo I had been forced to study in high school. My legs set as they were, I couldn't move up, so I managed to bend my knees a bit and slid down. Rotating my arms outward and applying pressure from my elbows to hers, I was able to break her hold and bring my arms up, while removing Trace's hands from my body. Emphasis on *my.*

Don't get me wrong, I'd been aroused earlier, and this situation wasn't doing anything to lessen that, but it was my body that responded, not my mind, not my heart. I didn't want this, not this way, and I discovered something: there was a limit to just how much I could give. Nightmare over. I was wide awake now.

"God damn it, Trace," I spat out as I wiggled free, "fuckin' enough.

Just stop." I pushed up against her chest, and she fell back a step. But still, her words were spinning through my head, confusing me, twisting me. I managed to bring my legs together and stand somewhat upright. My chest felt like it had two jackhammers playing off-rhythm to one another, and my head was starting to feel like someone had sped the merry-go-round up a bit too fast, but still, through the hammering and the dizziness, all I could think was that maybe she was right. Maybe that was what I wanted. Everything.

My eyes burned as I went back to my board. Where were my fucking headphones? Oh, there. I grabbed them and set them firmly around my neck. I ignored Trace completely as I reoriented myself to the board and my world, and a drop of water fell onto the soundboard. What the fuck? Oh, it was me. I hate tears, especially mine. What the fuck was I crying for, anyway? The leak stopped.

I could feel Trace as she approached my back. Her hand was gentle again as she touched my shoulder. I reached for the microphone.

"Nina, I'm sorry," she began softly, her mouth inches from my ear, but I held up a hand to forestall her. I needed quiet at the moment. I was, after all, still on the job. I watched my fingers tremble, betraying how my body and mind felt as I took a deep, shaky breath, and keyed the microphone.

"Boyz and grrlz, the freaks are out tonight." My voice came out steadily and with the right tone as the audience clapped and howled in agreement. I waited a few beats for my next statement. "Tonight the moon is on the rise—better watch out, 'cuz no one knows in who a monster hides," I finished, bringing the mix back up on full.

I shut the mike, then squared my shoulders and set my face. A burning cold hardness that I had felt only once before, once when I'd had to defend myself from the people who were supposed to love me, filled me, and I turned around to look at Trace directly. There must have really been something in my face, because as her eyes met mine, she stepped back.

We watched each other a moment, her eyes confused, evaluating mine hard. She reached out for my face. "Nina, truly, I didn't mean—"

I'd had it for the night, maybe forever; who knew. But either way, my expression stopped her cold, midword and midmotion. I stared at her hand, suspended between us, until she dropped it.

I crossed my arms over my chest and settled back against the board, languidly stretching one leg over the other. My guts shook, my head hurt, and the spot I was leaning on ached in the way only an incipient bruise can, but I'd be damned, twice damned, if I let her see any of that. I was back in some semblance of control, and, real or no, mask or no, I was going to hold on to it for dear life if I had to.

I took a slow, deep breath and let it out silently. Focus. That's what I needed, and that's what I was after. "Trace?" I inquired quietly, arching an eyebrow at her. An eerie, hyper-real calmness filled me, and I was as steady and strong as a rock.

"Yeah?" she answered softly, and her eyes were wide, shocked, as she studied me.

"If you want something, you have to ask," I stated quietly, and let those words hang in the air. I observed her face and took in the quirk of her lips and sharp jawline, the hint of pain and confusion in her now-darkened eyes as they studied me in return.

Trace took a step closer. "I'm sorry, I don't know what—"

"Stop," I interrupted, my voice low and hard. "Trace?" I asked again softly. "Get out."

Unused to these tones from me, Trace held her hands slightly away from her body, as if she didn't know what to do with them, and she stared at me, more in shock, I suspect, than anything else. No one, as far as I knew, ever told Trace what to do—ever.

"Now," I said, unfolding an arm and pointing toward the door, and it became a contest of wills as we stared each other down. My gaze was steady and unflinching, and my hand never moved from the direction it pointed in.

Trace's expression changed from shock to sadness as she dropped her eyes from mine, and her heels scuffed along the carpet as she walked to the steps, gazing floorward. I recrossed my arms, just watching her. As she reached for the door, she looked back up at me.

She seemed both sad and frightened. "We need to," she began. "I mean, I want…" She trailed off, gazing at me with an uncharacteristic uncertainty.

By now, though, I had no patience left. This had to end before I softened again, gave in and let her kidnap my soul. "We'll talk," I promised, knowing what she wanted. At the moment, all I wanted to be was alone. I was angry with Trace, yes, but much more than that, I was furious, disgusted, with myself, with what she'd made me see.

Trace searched my face a moment, then finally nodded and stepped out, closing the door behind her. I stared at it, almost expecting yet another person to burst in. Finally, I stood up straight and stretched my back. It hurt. Ah, well, I thought cynically. Another day, another bruise. Besides, I would have plenty of time for self-loathing and analyzing later. I still had to get through the night.

I took my headphones off and forced myself to go slowly, to think of nothing, to catch and direct my breath as I measured my steps to the door.

This time I locked it.

SHE SELLS SANCTUARY

One day I was introduced to power
She hardly spoke—she never said her name
I was preying in my darkest hour
And she whispered to me, "Blood cannot be tamed."

"I Fall"—Life Underwater

That night, after I collected my pay, I was so tired I practically crawled home and made straight for the shower, since no one else was around. Trace, I knew, wasn't there yet, or if she was, she hadn't come upstairs, and my roommates were still out and about—working, drinking, doing whatever it was they did.

Once in the bathroom, I started the water running in the shower, kicked off my boots, and stripped quickly. Balling the dress up, I tossed it in the hamper, then inspected the stockings. Yep, ruined. Absolutely wrecked. There were several holes along the seam. For a moment, I could feel the bruising strength of Trace's hands pressing against me, but I shook that feeling off and tossed the nylons into the garbage pail.

I checked my back in the mirror briefly. The promised bruise had materialized and would be tender for a few days, and a few scrapes along my neck stung when I touched them. Ah, well, what was life without a few bruises? Probably nice and painless, I thought wryly.

I wondered if my buddy, you know, my pal, my girl, my best friend, my favorite body part, would end up with a couple of bruises. Trace had been pretty rough, especially when she was ripping through the nylons.

What a fucking event that had been, I mused as I stepped into the shower. I got soaked as quickly as possible and went through the routine of bathing. Finally, when I'd rinsed off the soap, I stood under the shower itself and simply let the water pour over me.

Trace's words pounded through my head, so hard that my head ached. It was time to get out so I shut the taps and reached for a towel.

My hair wrapped, I grabbed one of my robes from behind the closed door (I have three of them: tiger stripes, leopard spots, and black), wrapped myself in the black one, and began to rub my aching head with the terry cloth. Suddenly, it occurred to me that perhaps my head hurt because I was a little hung over, and my follow-up thought was maybe, just maybe, Trace had been a little drunk as well, because I could think of nothing else to explain her behavior.

But that made things more confusing, because didn't alcohol lower your inhibitions? Supposedly, it just lowers your guard; your brain is definitely not functioning well enough to come up with new and novel ideas, thanks to the effects of oxygen deprivation. So what did that mean? Yeah, I'd wanted more between Trace and me, but I didn't "go" for it, and Trace had pretty much literally attacked me, which was still just unbelievable.

And I'd frozen. What the fuck was up with that? I'd been fine, or at least I'd thought I was, just a little while before she appeared. Was it really the tequila pop? Or was it something else? For a moment there, I'd honestly considered just letting things happen—if I'd just, well, given over, it would have been what Trace needed, it would help her to be whole.

Why fight it or her anyway? I mean, it's not like I didn't know that it didn't matter who Trace was with; she always wanted to be with me in the end. Except perhaps now, after this, this thing, she wouldn't. I admit that something inside me was afraid, and I wasn't sure what I was more afraid of—that we'd continue the way we'd been, or that maybe, just maybe, it was finally over and I was free.

Free. That was a strange thought, and I shied away from it. Free from what, really?

But something in my mind insisted that I'd done the right thing, that this whole issue wasn't just about whether or not we ever fucked. I mean, look at me and Blue, um, Candace. What happened between us was pretty damn intimate, can't really get much closer, physically. But

I felt no tie, no connection to her, other than a warm friendliness and an honest lust. The only game between us had really boiled down to this: she was interested, was I? And there was no deceit about it. Yes, I was. Okay, maybe it had gone a little further faster than I normally would've let it and, for chrissake, in the skybox of all places, but really no harm, no foul. She wanted, I wanted; it was very happily mutual.

Too much, it was too much to think about—the words, the feelings, and this strange sense of shame all floating together. That was weird, the shame, I mean. I didn't feel any about Candace, but from what had happened with Trace. I felt like my whole body was as raw as my neck, as if I'd lived out that nightmare everyone has sooner or later—you know, the one when you go to school and suddenly realize you're naked.

I brushed my teeth (I'm a Crest baby), and somewhere during the rinse and spit cycle, I realized that my hands were shaking.

Maybe my blood sugar was too low. It had been quite some time since I'd had anything solid to eat, I rationalized. Besides, that made sense, in a purely biological sort of way.

Wrapped in my robe and stepping out of the bathroom finally, I walked into the kitchen and drank some orange juice. That would take care of the sugar. I left the light on over the stove, since it would shine nice and dimly in the living room, then went to the bedroom that I shared with my roommate, Jackie.

Oh, yeah, roommates. I had two. Captain, otherwise known as Cap, who was a police officer and had a room of his own, and Jackie, a good friend who'd invited me to move in when life became unlivable at my parents', since they'd given me the boot because I couldn't fit in with their master plans for my life. But that's another story.

Fuck it. Since the room, located right off the living room, was really small, Jackie and I shared a bed, which wasn't quite the hardship that it would seem, given that I spent half my time downstairs in Trace's. But when Jackie came home, and she would soon, since she worked at another local bar and was probably doing the after-hours hangout, she'd want to talk, at the very least, and I was in no mood to chat or to sleep next to anyone, at all.

I took a pillow from the bed and a blanket from the closet and made myself a nest on the sofa. Why is it that a pullout sofa feels terrible when you pull it out, but leave it closed, and it's great for sleeping? I was glad I'd left that light on by the stove because I hated sleeping in the pitch-black dark, and Jackie always shut off the small lamp I'd leave lit on the dresser in our room.

Satisfied with my bed engineering, I lay down on my side. Definite mistake. The moment my knees touched, my favorite body part twinged. My poor buddy, all pain and no gain. I didn't have another pillow, and since I hate to let my head droop to the side and I didn't feel like sleeping on my back, I scrunched up the blankets between my knees. That was better—not much, but better.

I don't know when I fell asleep, but I thought I was dreaming when I heard Jackie come in, talking with Trace. I guess they must have gone to the after-hours together. That wasn't too surprising. Jackie and Trace had been best friends since high school (in fact, I'd met Trace through Jackie) and were twenty-three and twenty-four, respectively, to my twenty. They were definitely a lot more used to partying than I was, on every level.

"Hey, she's sleeping." Jackie's voice was pitched low.

"Yeah, well, it's been a full night," Trace whispered back. "She hooked up with this girl and…" The rest trailed off into a quieter whisper that I couldn't make out, and I didn't care. I snuggled tighter under the blanket, forcing myself back to deeper sleep.

In that mostly unconscious state, I thought I heard Trace say that she needed to talk with me, and I heard Jackie say good night and go to bed.

I drifted further into darkness, everything silent, and I was warm, toasty warm. A body pressed against my back, and arms wrapped around and held me firmly, but with love.

I dreamt of the beach, and ocean-colored eyes, and for the first time in ages, held warmly in that embrace, I dreamt of an old friend, maybe the best friend I'd ever had, Samantha, standing before me by the surf as the sun went down, the light catching on the pendant I'd just given her as a birthday present.

She smiled at me in the setting sun. "If you're ever lonely, come to me. I know what it's like to be lonely. If people hurt you, because you're not like them, come to me. I know what it's like to be different. When you hurt, when you ache, let me take that from you. I ache, too," I heard as a whisper in my ear. A soft hand caressed my cheek, and the sun, surf, and Samantha disappeared. I had truly been dreaming, after all.

I missed her so much my muscles cramped with the longing, a hard ache that ran through my bones the way it does when you've spent the night sleeping cold, and a chill chased after it as I realized it was Trace's voice I heard. But this time, I really couldn't move at all; I was just too damned tired. Trace had somehow wrapped herself behind me on the sofa. Her body pressed against mine, her arms held me, her words sank into my brain. Every single one of them broke my heart.

"Let me take care of you. You will never feel lonely, or hurt, or sad again," she insisted. "Just come to me. Give yourself over to me, make me your world, and I swear you will be mine." The arm beneath my shoulder pulled me closer, and the warmth, the feeling of genuine affection that poured from her was wonderful. "I will love you and protect you." She punctuated each promise with a soft kiss and a caress. "You will never, ever, need anything again. I promise you, Nina," she swore, and kissed my cheek gently.

The warmth, the words, the emotions were tempting, and I wanted to believe them, all of them. I wanted to believe her. I almost gave in because in that moment she felt so like her, so like Samantha. I was going to snuggle deeper into her, throw my arms around Trace and nuzzle against her neck as I'd never done before, but as I shifted my legs, the bruise at their apex throbbed, and instead of turning inward, toward her, I twisted further away, almost onto my stomach, the blanket clutched firmly around me. Samantha would have meant it, would have never hurt me first, would have said those things to me face-to-face, not waited until I was bruised and sleeping.

"No," I whispered, still only half awake, and safely tucked away, I fell back into a deep sleep.

Trace was gone when I finally woke up, on my stomach and half off the sofa. I blinked a few times and rolled onto my back. Ouch. Bad idea. I'd forgotten about that bruise there and the other one that nestled up in my crotch. Both reminded me of their reality, and I remembered how I'd gotten them.

Geez. What the fuck was I going to do? No way would I tell Jackie or Cap about it. I mean, Jackie and Cap were both friends with Trace first. I wasn't sure they'd believe me, and even if they did, somehow, I was sort of sure that it was my fault, anyway, which meant that I'd been dumb.

Besides, what was I going to say? It was no secret that I felt strongly for Trace; Cap would probably tell me I was an idiot for not going for it, and Jackie? She'd never, ever, believe it. She'd tell me I misunderstood, that I didn't understand Trace, that I was just too young, too immature.

I could just imagine Cap—his cocoa face, high and tight military-style buzz cut, and wide, bright grin. "Two, in one night? And one of them Trace? Not bad, kid, not bad," and he'd slap my shoulder and laugh.

And I could see Jackie's face as well, auburn hair and porcelain skin broken only by the firm line of her mouth. She probably wouldn't say a word. Hell, she probably wouldn't talk to me for a few days, then, at the end of that time, walk in one night after work and start yelling about the spoon in the sink or something. We'd have a big talk, or rather, she would talk, and I would listen, while she told me how and why exactly I was wrong.

I sat up and swung my legs off the sofa, the blanket half covering me, and bracing my hands on my knees, I stared at the floor. It was starting to occur to me that maybe, just maybe, I didn't have the best friends in the world—at least, not to live with.

I stood up and stretched, letting the blanket fall to the floor. Everything was a little sore, but that was no big deal. Glancing down, I realized I'd slept in my bathrobe and I had terry-cloth textured skin. I tied the ends of the belt together and crept to the shared bedroom.

Opening the door slowly, I stuck my head in. Jackie was out like a light, and I was surprised to see she had her arm thrown over Trace, who was asleep on top of the blankets in a T-shirt, facing the wall.

I didn't want to wake either of them, so I slipped very quietly to the closet where our clothes were and grabbed a T-shirt, a pair of shorts, some pants, socks, underwear—you know, the usual. It didn't matter what it looked like; most of it was black, anyway.

As I sneaked back to the door, Trace shifted.

"Nina," she called quietly. I froze in place. I certainly wasn't ready to talk with her. Trace moved again and resettled on her side. Good. She was just sleeping. A part of me hoped she had nightmares, then quickly felt guilty. I knew better than most that she did.

Back in the living room, I dumped my stuff on the sofa and neatly folded the blanket.

If you sat on the couch, the bedroom was behind you, TV in front, windows to the left, kitchen to the right, and the door to Cap's bedroom just a bit past. Since his door was firmly shut, which it hadn't been when I'd gotten in last night, he was home and sleeping too.

Good. I didn't want to deal with anyone, anyway.

I dressed and began a set of floor stretches. The thigh stretches were a little more painful than usual, but otherwise, everything was in good working order. Warmed up, I was ready to go for a run. I didn't exercise all the time, but today seemed like a good day. Running is similar to swimming in that your mind goes blank sort of, but not really. Somehow, while you're focusing on the very basic steps of breathing and moving simultaneously, your brain figures all sorts of things out. Besides, exercise, especially strenuous exercise, was and is good for breaking down all the stuff your body creates when it's stressed, and I was for sure feeling stressed.

The table was right by the door, and all of us roomies put our shoes under it when we came in, to avoid tracking crap across the floor, literally or figuratively, so I sat for a moment at that 1950s off-white Formica and glitter-topped table, focusing very clearly on tying those knots just right. I do "bunny ears." I know, it's supposed to be "rabbit in the hole," but hey, my laces never come loose. It's my thing.

Sneakers on, I grabbed my keys, tucked them into a shorts pocket, and was out the door. The sun was brilliant and still climbing; it was going to be a warm day. I stretched again, then started running—down the block to Bay Street, past the park, up the hill (yes, we have hills in Staten Island), and back down Broad Street, the street I lived on, past the projects and the firehouse, past my apartment, and did the circuit again.

I'd gotten into a nice rhythm by the second go-round, and in the third set, I was deep in the flow. Cars, trees, cement, burnt lots, and lost auto pieces, all part of the whole—step, breathe, step, breathe, the air was a continuous flow in and through my body, the sun shining and warming my skin. Bits of glass winked up at me from the asphalt as I glided past.

I didn't know what exactly I was going to do when I got back to the apartment, besides shower and dress, but I was certain on one score: I needed to find something new, maybe completely different.

My feet kept hitting the ground, flying past the scenery. I had enough money for the rent for at least another month tucked away, and if I watched my expenses, I could pick up that guitar today. I had my eye on a beautiful double-cut Ibanez Artist, and it had a sound so sweet,

I couldn't wait until it was mine, all mine, to have and to hold, to play until my fingers bled.

I was about two, maybe three blocks away from the apartment, and coming up to the firehouse, when it hit me—not only had I worked the night before, I'd supposedly gotten paid double-time for it. I hadn't even counted the money Rich had put into my hand, but I calculated that working from about midnight, which would be a little after Darrel had left, to four a.m., I should have a little over two hundred dollars.

Since I owed only another hundred on the guitar, I'd be able to pay it off, put half away, and maybe have a little fun with the other half. Hey, cool, I smiled to myself, in happy anticipation. I'd go get my guitar today and let the rest work itself out somewhere in the back of my mind. I frowned a little bit at that strategy. Hope it came up with something soon, though. As clueless as I could be sometimes, I had the nagging feeling that I might have been in more trouble than I knew.

❖

As I approached the firehouse, I managed a last burst of speed for my end sprint, and I was cooking by the time I flew past the steps that led up to the three-story brownstone I lived in. Someone was sitting on the top of the steps, and as I finished my sprint, I recognized my brother, Nicky, waiting for me. No, Nico, I mentally corrected. Everyone called him Nico now, I reminded myself with an inward grin.

I stopped before I crossed the street and took a few deep breaths, then jogged back to my door, waving to Nico.

With a genuine smile, he jumped down the steps as I approached. "Hey, Nina!" he greeted, and opened his arms for a hug.

With the same smile on my own face, because I love him so much and I was, then and now, always happy to see him, I moved into his arms with a hug of my own. "Nico!" I called, drawing out the "oh" sound in a way I knew he enjoyed hearing.

We gave each other a kiss on the cheek, but I didn't hug him as tightly as I normally would.

"Hey, I want a real hug," he protested, squeezing me.

"I don't want to get you wet," I explained, a little breathless still from the run.

"Wet, shmet, I don't care," Nico replied, increasing the pressure, and I hugged him tighter, resting my head on his shoulder. "It's just a little water and salt." He leaned back, picking my feet up off the floor, bouncing me a little.

Though he was my younger brother, he had finally beat me in the height department. Oh, we were still shorter than most people our ages; we had (and have) that slower metabolism thing going (which our baby sister, Nanny, didn't—she was bigger than both of us), so we'd both still grow over the next few years, but he had an inch or so on me. Since I'd been bigger for so many years, say approximately our whole lives up until then, he loved to tease me about my height. By picking me up and bouncing me.

I held on to him as if I'd fall off the planet if I didn't, and not just because of the bouncing. Despite the natural endorphin goodness of the run, I'd been feeling pretty darn alone, and now, I wasn't. I had Nico, and I'd be fine or, at least, better.

A few more moments of Nico's testing the strength of my rib cage, then he put me down, but I continued to hold on.

"Nina, are you crying?" he asked, and I could hear and feel his concern.

I guess, maybe, a little, I realized, raising my head and noting the little wet spot I'd left on his shoulder. "Naw, Nico." I grinned at him lightly, because I just didn't want to go there yet. "It's just a little water and salt."

His eyes, the same shade of blue-gray as mine, except that his had a thin butter gold ring in the center that you could only see when he was really mellow, searched my face.

"You'll tell me later?" he asked, brow furrowed and not put off or fooled by my joke.

I glanced up at the door to the building, then back at him. "Yeah," I promised quietly, "I'll tell you later." I meant it. I would talk with him, but for now, the sun was shining, the birds were singing, well, somewhere anyway, and it was a beautiful summer day.

"Come on up," I invited him with a bright smile, and started up the stairs. "Hang out while I shower, then let's blow this pop stand." I pulled my keys out and opened the door. "You eat breakfast yet?" I asked him, staring pointedly at his stomach. One thing for sure, neither of us ate often, but when we did, watch out, especially if we were together. Whole gallons of milk, entire loaves of bread, and full cartons of eggs were known to be transformed into French toast and disappear around us.

"Yeah, I grabbed something, but," he grinned at me, "I'm not fully fueled yet."

I was pretty hungry too. Usually, I made myself something, and if Nico and I were together, we'd cook together, splitting up prep work and cleanup, a tradition we'd started years ago when our parents would work overtime on Saturdays and we were home alone with Nanny, but I wasn't sure what was in the refrigerator upstairs, and I really didn't want to hang out in the apartment longer than I had to. For some reason, the thought made me queasy.

"I worked last night and got paid," I told him as we rounded the first landing. "You want to go to Jerry's? My treat." Jerry's Pancake House, on Bay Street, looks like a dive from the outside. Oh, hell, the whole neighborhood was divey, but Jerry—there really was a Jerry—made the best pancakes around, with all sorts of variations of fruit, chocolate, ice cream, whatever; and he served huge portions, enough to make even me and Nico happy, for a very reasonable price.

"Oh, cool, yeah," Nico enthused as we reached the top landing, "I'm getting strawberries and bananas, then." I smiled to myself. Nico ate so many bananas, he was living proof that humans are related to apes, and in fact, our dad used to call us monkeys (in a nice way) when we were small and being silly. Of course, we were monsters if we were bad, but that's another thing altogether.

Once inside, Nico dropped casually into a chair by the table, and I walked back to the sofa, to gather my real clothes for the day.

Cap's door popped open and he stood in the doorway, yawning and stretching.

"Hey, Nina," he greeted me through a yawn, scratching his chest, his eyes still half closed with sleep. I should probably mention he was stark naked.

"Morning." I nodded in Nico's direction. "Nico's here."

Cap's eyes popped open. "Oh, geez. Hey, Nico," and he took a step back into his room, shutting the door. It opened again a moment later, and he stepped out, wearing a pair of boxer shorts.

"Hey, man, sorry about that." He grinned at Nico and clapped him on the shoulder.

"No problem, man," Nico answered noncommittally. But I noticed the tips of his ears were a little pink as he bent over to fiddle with his shoelaces. Cap grabbed another seat at the table.

What is it with some guys? They don't care if you see them naked, but another guy, oh, then they're all modesty, unless it's a locker room. Then they're all smacking each other with towels and stuff. Or maybe it's just me. I mean, I'm not much interested in the package so it doesn't matter whether I see it or not, and not just because of the male-female thing. If it was a girl, I wouldn't have had a problem being completely neutral either. Well, that could have been from too many years in locker rooms myself. Okay, maybe there had been one exception, a long time ago, but let's not go there. That hurt so much to think about I couldn't breathe. Maybe it depended on the context, I mused to myself as I walked over to the kitchen sink to get a glass of water.

Cap yawned and stretched his arms over his head. "You hanging for the day?" he asked Nico midyawn. "You guys want to watch stuff with me?" He brought his arms down and looked from Nico to me. "I got a few new videos," he wheedled in his most tempting tone. "Lots of babes in action."

Nico and I looked at each other a moment. We knew what Cap meant, and it wasn't movies—at least not big-screen ones with ratings for the general public and leading ladies rescuing people, no dialogue, but enough explosions to keep the keenest pyro happy. No, it was more like things that could only be filmed in certain places (I hear tell a few spots in California "specialize," but that ain't necessarily true) so the cops wouldn't arrest the crew, half of which would be naked, and all the explosions would be of a more, um, limited, biological sort.

Not that Nico or I were particularly averse to pornography. I mean, we'd seen every video our dad had ever hidden in his workshop, and discovered that they were really funny if you played them in fast forward or reverse (and the faster you play them, the funnier they get). Besides, they were, in their own way, a valuable educational tool. I mean, when a person gets to that part of their learning, no one ever talks about technique, just anatomy and ducts. And, really, once you understood the mechanics of fertility, pregnancy, venereal disease, and AIDS, no one ever taught anything else—like how to enjoy it. I mean, really. Everyone wants to tell you how your genitals work and all the things you should be paranoid about for them (and for good reason, too), but not how to use them, so we'd gotten a lot out of those flicks.

Still, sitting and watching one with Cap didn't appeal. I was sure it wouldn't be a popcorn-throwing, smart-ass-commenting, technique-dissecting session. In fact, from the look in Nico's eye, the suggestion made him just as uncomfortable as it made me.

I finished my water. "Thanks, but we got stuff to do today," I answered, not missing the grateful grin Nico flicked my way. "We're going to pick up my guitar."

Both guys looked to me, eyes wide.

"Oh, wow, you're gonna get it today?" Nico asked, smiling. "That, Nina, is so cool."

"Hey, nice, very nice, congratulations." Cap nodded, looking impressed. "How'd you manage to pull that one off so soon?"

"I worked last night, so I got paid a bit extra." I smiled with real joy. "And now, I'm going to shower, so we can run out there."

"Well, hey, don't let me keep you," Cap said, "but if you get bored, you know where I'll be."

"Yeah, I do," I answered as I made my way to the bathroom. And I did know. He'd be on the sofa, eyes glued to the screen, with one hand on the remote, watching blow-job scenes and "money shots" over and over. The other hand, well, you know where it would be—and not motionless, either. Not that I cared. I mean, masturbating is a healthy thing; it was just, well, no thanks. Didn't want to see that.

I took a shower and did my hair in record time. Dressing was just as quick. Required undergarments, a black *Love and Rockets* T-shirt with Hopey (my favorite character) playing with her band on it, button-fly black jeans, and a pair of engineer's boots. Black, of course. Did I mention that I wore a lot of black?

One last check in the mirror, and I was good to go. Let's see. My hair was up, my clothes were on, and I was ready to rock and roll.

I stepped out of the bathroom and headed for the door, stopping only to grab an old army bag that held my wallet (complete with last night's pay), sunglasses, cigarettes, lighter—you know, stuff, all the stuff that you need during the day.

"Hey, Nina," a female voice creaked out at me as Nico stood to join me, and I looked for its source.

Jackie stood in an extra-long sleep shirt by the sofa back, a cup of tea cradled in her hands. Her hair was disheveled and her face still swollen with sleep. Add in her knee socks, and she looked all of twelve or thirteen years old, except her eyes. They were slitted and glaring at me over her mug as she sipped.

"Morning, Jackie," I returned with cheerful wariness. I couldn't tell if the glare was her usual morning grumpiness—because Jackie could be an absolute horror show before she finished her morning caffeine ritual—or something else. I was erring on the side of caution, either way.

She drank deeply, then lowered her mug to her chin, watching me over its rim. "We need to talk when you get back," she said finally. "I have a few questions for you."

Oh, great, just great. I inwardly rolled my eyes.

Over by the sink, Cap's shoulders shook with suppressed laughter. "Someone's in trouble," he singsonged to me with a smile.

I gave him my own sickly approximation of a smile, then gave Jackie my full attention.

"I'd prefer"—she sipped again—"to talk now, though." She finished her tea and stared longingly into her cup when she realized it was empty before she was ready for me. "Hello, Nicholas," she greeted my brother, without a smile, without so much as a glance. Her eyes were fixed on me, and her face was grave as Nico muttered a low greeting in response behind me.

"Well, I think I'll just scoot along," Cap interrupted, a mug and a bowl in his hands—coffee and Cheerios drowning in milk, from the looks of it. "If you'll excuse me." He bowed slightly toward me and Nico.

He faced Jackie, square on. "I hate to get in the way of these sensitive chats," he told the room in general, his voice as flat as his expression. Cap gave me a shrug. Well, he was right. What could you do?

"You didn't do anything, kid," he muttered to me from the corner of his mouth. "Bear with it, then ignore it. Later!" He grinned brightly and briefly to me and Nico, and with that, he walked the few steps to his room, opening the door with his foot. It closed behind him with a sharp slam, and Nico and I stood there for a moment as the air settled from the sound.

Apparently more than one conversation had gone on while I'd slept, I quickly concluded.

"I, um, I'll go bring the van around," Nico said into the awkwardness that had descended into the room, then nimbly slipped out the door.

Jackie stalked over to the sink and washed her mug in measured silence before she turned on me. "What the fuck do you think you're doing?" she launched at me. "What the hell did you do to Trace?" Her eyes blazed, and her voice ripped at me with anger. She folded her arms across her chest, waiting for an answer.

I stood there staring, mute, attempting to comprehend Jackie's anger. How was I supposed to answer that tirade? What did I do, anyway? Okay, maybe there was a reasonable way to respond. Jackie was, generally speaking, rational, and she'd been a good friend for a while. If I explained, she'd be able to help me find the middle road between responsibility and blame, and if there was blame to be laid upon me, bring it on. I wasn't, then and now, afraid to face myself or my faults.

But first things first.

"Where's Trace?" I asked. I don't know why I cared, but I did. If we were going to work something out and still be friends, I wanted to know if she was okay. Despite my bruises, the memory of her curled up on her side sleeping, the gentle vulnerability she revealed when we were alone, touched, softened me. I couldn't really be too angry—I loved her.

Of course, a little voice in the back of my head warned me, too. If Jackie and Trace ganged up on me, I was done for. I was trying to ignore that voice, but it was insistent, and it told me that I'd been calumniated, if not, at the very least, misrepresented. Shut up, voice, I thought; suspicion isn't very honorable. I'd hear this out before I came to any conclusions.

"She left before you came back," Jackie said softly, anger diminished for the moment. "She said she couldn't bear to talk with you yet." Jackie shifted and leaned back against the sink. "So, I'm asking you again, what did you do? I've already heard about your," her mouth tightened for a moment, "escapades. Did you drink too much? I can understand that," she told me quietly, "and I can understand that things may be coming to some sort of head between you two." Jackie paused and glanced down, studying the floor as she considered her next words.

Finally she looked up, the lines of her face hard and set. Well, she certainly didn't look sleepy anymore. "What I can't understand, though, is how, is why," she shook her head and held her hands up as if they'd help her ask and understand, "why you," and her eyes now held both anger and tears, "you of all people, would want to fuck with someone's head like that? Haven't we all been your friends? Didn't I take you in when you had no place to go?" Jackie's voice rose. "You're here because of me!" she yelled.

"She pays more rent and more often than you do," Cap called out from his room. I glanced at the door, then back at Jackie. *Thank you*, I thought silently. *At least I'm not completely alone in this.*

Jackie gathered herself again, folding her arms and still leaning back on the sink. She took a deep breath, visibly forcing herself to be calm. "Be that as it may," she stated, "you share my home, my bed, for Christ's sake. How could you do that? How could you go and fucking treat a friend, *my* friend," she emphasized, "like that?"

Told you so, the little voice in my head said, a bit smugly too, I might add. Well, okay, I'd heard her out. I could even understand how she felt. I mean, I'd feel the same way if someone I'd trusted had, or I thought had, hurt a friend of mine. But that's not what happened—at least, not as I saw it. I'd just have to explain my side of it or, at least, most of it.

I was going to leave some stuff out, like where and how I was bruised. I couldn't really bring myself to talk about it—not here, not now, especially not at this moment, although I knew the information might flip those tables so fast we'd all see double. But that didn't seem right to me. It seemed sort of, like, I don't know, hunting for butterflies with atom bombs or something. Besides, somehow, I can't really explain why, I felt like this was my fault.

"What exactly is it that you think I did?" I asked in an even tone. If I was going to attempt to be a rational adult, it wouldn't do me any good to attack in return. Right? Yeah, I thought so, too.

Jackie straightened up from her position and stepped toward me. "Don't," she hissed, "don't you dare use that prep-school cool on me." She waved a finger in my face. "Right now, you're fucking nowhere and no one, and I'll kick you out of here faster than you can...you can...you can just go fuck yourself if that's how you're going to be."

I stepped back. Not only do I have absolutely no love for anyone invading/encroaching on my personal space without an invitation, especially when they're angry and waving their hands (and God help the person who actually makes a move to my head or face), but that icy heat was starting to burn into my face. Right now I still had control of my mouth and my body, but if she got louder, if she fuckin' so much as touched me in anger, I couldn't guarantee that I could maintain my cool.

At that moment, Cap's door opened, and we both looked as he stepped out, T-shirt and jeans on this time.

"Okay, if anyone has anything to say about who lives here, it's me. And right now, all three of us live here," he said firmly as he approached us. Outside, I heard a car horn blow, and I could tell from the way they cocked their heads that Jackie and Cap heard it, too. Nico must have brought the van around and was waiting for me.

We stood in that little area in the kitchen, facing each other in a triangle. "Nina, go, have a good time with your brother. I've thought of a great space for you to put your guitar in," Cap told me very calmly, motioning me toward the door. "Jackie," he addressed her and continued, "lay off. Nina's one of your best friends. You don't know what really happened, and you know that Trace, well"—he hunted for the right words—"she's Trace."

What else was there to say about her, anyway? Liar was too strong, because I didn't know what she'd really said, and drama queen wasn't exactly right, either. Crazy wouldn't have been hard to prove. But this wouldn't have been the right time to find the right adjectives, anyway.

Jackie and I glared at each other a moment longer. Finally, I'd had it and strode rigidly to the door, then opened it. "I'll see you guys later," I tossed back as I slung my bag over my shoulder.

Running down the stairs, because I didn't want to keep Nico waiting, I reviewed the "discussion" in my head and thought about different ways I could have handled it. The French have a phrase for it: *esprit de l'escalier* or, roughly, "spirit of the stairway," which is what happens when you run down the stairs thinking of different ways you could have done or said something, now that you had a moment to think about it. That's what I had, stairway spirit, I thought as I passed the landing that held Trace's door.

Not that I could think of anything else to have said or done, really. I guess I could have just interrupted Jackie and, using sheer volume, explained my side of the story, but that just wasn't my style.

I could still hear Cap and Jackie upstairs. "You never stop to think, Jackie," Cap growled. "You forget, I know Trace better than you do." Jackie's reply faded as I got to the bottom.

Nico peered anxiously out the passenger side window of the hulking gray behemoth that was his pride and joy, a gunmetal gray conversion van converted from utility to mini rec room, complete with pullout sofalike thing in the back (and a box of assorted toys—footballs, Frisbees, baseball gloves, swim fins—stuff like that, as well as towels and T-shirts), a little porta-potty in its own privacy cupboard, and sink with assorted car-type parts and tools that might one day prove useful beneath it.

"You okay?" he asked as I strode over to the door and jumped in.

"Oh, yeah, I'm fine," I breathed out as I buckled myself in. I rooted around in my bag for my pack of cigarettes, found one, then lit it, the first for the day.

Nico nodded his head in understanding and pulled away from the curb as I blew smoke out the window. I let my thoughts drift with it as we drove in silence.

Nico respected my need for head space, and soon I was able to recapture my "good morning" mood. I would have time to let the back of my mind work toward solutions. Besides, my stomach rumbled, reminding me that I needed food, and, really, who can think if they're hungry?

"So," I asked conversationally, "we still going to Jerry's? Cause if we are, you're headed the wrong way," I informed him as we went in the opposite direction.

"Oh, yeah," Nico grinned at me, "we can still do that." He sighted down the street for a likely turning block and set a signal.

As we drove, sunlight flashing on the sidewalk through the trees, it occurred to me that it was July, after all, and though the summer felt endless, we didn't have all that many sunny and free days left. Soon enough I would have to wait in line for registration, buy books, and juggle classes and work schedules, and Nico would be off with his trunk packed with new undershorts and linens to his own schooling. Fuck it. I don't like to waste rare, beautiful days. We could go to Jerry's some other time, when it was raining. Now was now. Even if I didn't swim, I could still roll my jeans up, and Nico most likely had a couple of spare shorts in the back of the vehicle somewhere. And they were probably mine. Besides, I could pay off and pick up my guitar after the sun went down.

"You know, we could just grab some bagels and chocolate milk and go to the beach," I suggested. "Whatchya say?" I grinned at him.

"Shit, yeah, the beach," he responded, his eyes shining brightly at me for a moment before he had to return his attention to the road.

"Sun and sand, here we come," I sang out, visions of the surf crashing against the shore filling my head, and the taste of an egg bagel with a little mustard and Muenster cheese followed by a Nestle Quik chocolate milk to wash it down filling my mouth. I was there already.

SEXY EIFFEL TOWERS

Let me tell you something darling,
You're doing fine…
Now you've shown me all of yours I'll let you into mine
But me, I like a pretty boy, I love a hard-edged girl

"For The Love of Boyz'n Grrlz"—Life Underwater

Trace and I didn't speak for days, but it wasn't as if we had a chance. Between Cap's and Jackie's schedules, combined with mine as well as Trace's, it was a wonder any of us ever got to see each other. And I honestly wasn't trying too hard.

I did see Candace, though—the next week, in fact. Totally sober and with the door safely locked, headset tight over one ear and off the other so I could hear the sound in the room, I grooved in the skybox, eyes closed and feeling fine, swaying along with this phenom beat I'd discovered a few days ago. A voice with the loveliest hint of a British accent floated up to me.

"Hey, lovely DJ. Do you take requests?"

I slipped my headphones down around my neck and opened my eyes to see Candace's smiling face.

"Maybe," I played. "It depends on what you have in mind."

"I'm thinking…French," Candace replied, her even white teeth sparking up at me.

"Ah, too bad." I shook my head with mock regret, pretending I didn't know what she meant. "I can't read minds in French."

"Colonist!" Candace smirked back at me. "Can you even speak anything other than that fractured language you borrowed from us?"

"Hey, I take offense at that." I scowled good-naturedly. "My grandparents are from South America, and I happen to be fluent in Spanish," I told her, which happens to be true. "And don't forget, this is Staten Island. I can speak and read a little Italian as well," which was also true. And in that part of New York? Occasionally necessary.

"Well, that explains quite a bit, then," Candace said as she reappraised me.

"How about you—imperialist?" I asked her, half joking, half challenging. I mean, yes, as Americans, many of us have natural ties to Europe, with its grand culture and history. On the other hand, we invented the steam engine, the car, the Internet, and rock and roll, not to mention a few other things. Besides, other countries and continents had lent us their best people, too, and though I liked Candace, I wasn't going to deal with any my-country-is-better-than-your-country bullshit. Even if that might have been true at different times in history, past and future.

"I give, I give!" Candace held her hands up in mock surrender. "Now forgive me and let me take you to dinner, *ma cheri*." She smiled charmingly.

"Oh?" I asked, intrigued despite my attempt at distance—her pronunciation was excellent. What can I say? I have a thing for sound.

"It's a little place I've discovered in the East Village called Port Marseille. I'm so full sure you'll love it!"

I couldn't. I had to work, I had guitar practice, and I certainly didn't want to get involved past, further, or more than what had already happened—and I hadn't even really intended for that. Well, at least not in that way, anyhow. Friends. I wanted to be friends, and that meant no dates. What Candace suggested sounded more than vaguely like the latter as opposed to the former, but as I tried to form an answer that wouldn't sound offensive or hurtful, Candace's face wore an expression of such obvious sincere affection that I had difficulty thinking.

"My schedule's really tight," I replied instead. "When where you thinking of—"

Candace must have noticed some of my internal struggle. She interrupted me with a wave of the hand and reached through the request window. "No pressure, Nina." She patted my hand. "Whenever you'd like."

Cool. Okay then. "Okay," I answered slowly. "I'll let you know."

"Hmph," she answered and took her hand back, then smiled, a Mona Lisa smile that could have meant nothing, that could have meant anything, and somewhere in my head, it made me want to crawl, crawl behind it and discover more. "I'll see you later," and with that, she melted back into the crowd.

She wasn't wearing her usual blue, I noticed before she disappeared from view; the body-skimming one-piece Candace had on this night was black.

I returned to my board and slipped my headphones back up on my ears. Hmm...

Setting my faders for the next mix, I grabbed the microphone, waiting for my moment. "Oh, yeah," I encouraged the crowd. "It's time to set the night on fire!" I began to bring up the next tune into the current one, a heavier beat mixing well with the tail of the one still playing.

"Scorched-earth mix," I announced, and brought the song in fully as I faded the other out completely, sending the custom compilation flying through the room where the people cheered in anticipation. I set the lights to pattern reds through yellows, with occasional flashes of blue thrown in for dramatic relief.

After dancing along for a bit, I assessed my selections for the night. My set was in good order, and as long as there were no changes, the music would cycle through moods—from earthy hip to fiery house and on to airy techno, finally ending with liquid trance. Hmm...

I dug under the shelf for a pen and piece of paper, then leaned over by the small work light to scribble down the settings for the light shows per segment. Done, I reviewed my work. It was solid, a nice piece of musical experience, even if I did say so myself.

I reached for the microphone.

"Duh Darrel, come to the sky. Duh Duh Darrel, come to the sky," I singsonged to and through the beat, searching for Darrel's bobbing Mohawk among the dancers. Of course he'd be around. Don't ask me why, but for whatever reason, when you work in a club, you tend to hang out there on your time off. Of course, we used to say that the Red

Spot wasn't just a place, but a way of life. You know what? It really was.

"Duh Duh Darrel, come to the sky. Duh Duh Darrel, come to the sky," echoed the crowd, thinking it was part of the performance. Well, it was in a way.

I finally spotted him on the other side of the room, leaning against the wall chatting with one of the many pretty young women who frequented the place. Catching his attention, I waved him over.

"What's up?" he asked when he reached the request window.

"Come in," I said, then walked over and unlocked the door.

"Hey! What's up?" he repeated, this time a bit more seriously as he mounted the steps.

I got right to the point. "I need you to take over for me," I explained as I returned to the mixing board. I visually checked the faders and knobs, just ensuring everything was where it had to be, then grabbed my list and handed it to him. "Here, everything's already set and in order." I pointed to the stack of discs. "And here are all the lighting switches and their cues."

Darrel studied the paper a moment. "Nice, Nina. Nice music, nice setup." He pursed his lips and nodded with what I could swear might have been honest admiration. It was definitely approval, at the very least.

Fuck nice, it was good, really fucking good, and I knew it. And it was good to have someone else, someone that did the same work too, I mean, think so.

"So, why you leavin'? You all right?"

"I'm okay." I smiled widely because I knew why I was okay, and why I was leaving, and he didn't. "Just something I really gotta do."

I searched through the Plexi window among the throng. Where was she? Not this corner, not that one. My eyes continued to roam. Ah, there. She was harder to pick out among the crowd now that she wasn't wearing her trademark blue.

"Oh," Darrel drawled. "I got it. You mean *someone*."

"Huh?"

Darrel gave me a knowing smirk. "It's not some*thing* you have to do," he explained, "it's some*one*." He snorted.

"Shut the fuck up." I backhanded him none too gently on his well-defined ribs, though I grinned while I hit him. If I didn't mention it before, let me say it now: Darrel was quite the hottie. From his blue Mohawk and silver-blue eyes, to his sharply drawn cheeks and delicate mouth, down his wide shoulders and well-defined upper body—which no one could miss, since he usually wore either very loose or very tight tank tops—Darrel was beautiful. And he knew it.

"Abuse! Abuse! The DJ's trying to kill me!" Darrel joked, clutching his side as if he'd been dealt a mortal wound.

I rolled my eyes at his antics, but I couldn't help smiling. For Mr. Stud Muffin, he could be such a goof, and he reminded me in a good way of Nico.

"C'mon, man, will you do it?" I repeated, once his agonies had abated. He scoured the crowd, to see for himself again who it was.

"Nina," he asked slowly, "is that Blue?"

"Candace," I corrected without thinking.

"Candace? Candace? As in I-want-a-piece-of-candy Candace?" His voice rose as his eyebrows climbed higher—I thought they might disappear into his Mohawk. With surprising speed Darrel whirled and seized my shoulders. "Nina, you must go. For the honor of the order of hot DJs everywhere, of which we are but a humble two," and I snorted with self-derision as he gave me a little grin, "you must go."

"So, you'll cover for me?" I asked again, torn between impatience and amusement. I lightly knocked his hand off my shoulder, and he removed the other without assistance.

"She's fucking hot—ah!" He clapped his hands to his face.

"Great. Thanks." I grabbed my jacket from the bench. Black, of course, and leather, too. Highway-patrol style. It was late summer, after all, and as scorching as the days were, the nights were starting to cool a bit after midnight. I slid it over my shoulders as I jumped down the stairs, then grabbed for the doorknob.

"Thanks again, Darrel," I called back to him. "Thanks for covering for me—see you tomorrow."

I was on a mission, and I probably said hello to everyone in the club and on the dance floor before I finally found Candace in the ladies' room, checking her hair in the mirror.

"Hey there!" I greeted her reflection as I slid into the spot next to her and put an arm lightly around her waist. "Let's go."

She dropped her hands from her hair and faced me, and I kept my hand on her waist.

"Now?" she asked, while the shine of her eyes and the delicious curve that grew along her lips told me I'd made the right decision. "You mean, right now?"

Mmm. Her tones and accent were so alluring that as her hands fluttered up to play with my collar, I felt a desperate need to just forget about everything—dinner, whatever—and take her home, if we made it that far. Darrel was right—she was so fucking hot—but I didn't really need him to tell me that. I already knew it.

I didn't give in to that feeling, that pull on my blood, completely, though. Instead, I let it show in my voice as I leaned in close to whisper in her ear. "Well," I drawled, blowing softly behind her ear, "I do recall you were thinking in French." I nuzzled her neck, gently pulling at the skin with my lips.

"That's nice." Candace exhaled and arched her throat toward me. "I thought you couldn't read minds," she said as she twined her arms around my neck. I placed light kisses along that center column, until she shifted slightly to lay butterfly kisses in the hollow above my collarbone.

"Only in French," I reminded her as I closed my eyes and enjoyed the sensations. Just forget going home, my car was closer. "I can't read minds in French."

I twisted my head away and sought her mouth with mine, and tonight's kiss tasted like cherries and bubble gum. As that kiss deepened, Candace's fingertips moved from behind my neck to patter light touches from my neck to my chest. I brought my hands up to her face, brushing my lips right behind her jaw. We really had to leave.

The bathroom had started to get a bit crowded—either our little makeout session had drawn a crowd or it was merely that communal time. Whatever we were going to do, it couldn't continue here. Most of the women either acted bored or impatient as they waited, and as I caught the eye of one or two, they blushed and looked away. I didn't care, though, because unless this was their first visit to the club, I was definitely not the only woman who'd kissed another in that bathroom or any other place in the club. For some of the patrons, that was part of the attraction and definitely part of the club's reputation.

Fuck the occasional total straights that came in there. They either came for the show, or they left soon enough. I did mention earlier that this was one of the coolest places to see and be seen, and that meant a lot of try-sexual activity. There, in the corner by the sink, was proof.

Two girls I'd observed on the dance floor, with what I was pretty sure had been their boyfriends, were leaning together face-to-face, stroking each other's hair, occasionally kissing each other's cheek, trying to get up the courage to take it to that next step. I knew what that was like, I thought with a smile.

I glanced back at Candace, who'd noticed what I had. "Do you want to get going?" I grinned at her and indicated the girls in the corner with my chin.

She glanced their way, then back at me. "I thought we already had," she murmured and caught my hand. "Yeah, let's go," she agreed decisively.

I led the way through the press to the door, and as we passed the girls by the sink, a sudden inspiration made me pause.

"Hey there," I greeted each of them—first a very pretty girl with a deep tan and red and gold streaks in her dark hair, whose back was against the counter, then an equally stunning almond-eyed brunette, who looked slightly familiar to me from somewhere other than the club. Well, Staten Island really was a small place in many ways, after all. Maybe I'd seen her on the bus on the way to school or something over the years. "How you doing?"

To their credit, while they may have both blushed, they neither stopped holding hands nor changed positions. Why is that to their credit? Because it meant that they weren't ashamed or embarrassed. Good for them. Maybe I'd have to reevaluate my estimation of their male companions' status as boyfriends.

"Okay," answered the girl with the tan noncommittally, with a slight shrug. Her head bent closer to her companion's shoulder.

"Fine, thanks," answered the other. "You spin great tunes by the way, really love these Experience Nights." She beamed shyly.

"Thank you," I told her, honestly taken aback. I hadn't thought I'd be recognized. Perhaps that was foolish. I mean, it's not as if I was completely invisible up at the booth, and let's face it—neither my hair nor my attire was nondescript, especially when I was working. And quite frankly, as long as I was still in the club, I was still on the job, especially since this was supposed to be one of "my" nights.

"Oh, you're DJ Nina!" exclaimed the girl with the tan. I couldn't help but smile as I noticed her arm steal around her companion's waist. "You really play great music!"

"Thanks, thanks a lot, really." I blushed a bit myself. "It's very nice of you to say that." From the corner of my eye, I could see Candace pull her phone out of the bag slung from her shoulder.

The brunette stuck a hand out. "Oh, I'm Gina, by the way," she introduced, and I shook her hand, "and this is—"

"Mary," the tan girl interrupted, putting out her free hand. "I'm Mary."

"Nice to meet both of you," I answered sincerely. "And right now, it's just Nina, Nina Boyd," I said as I shook her hand as well, "and this is," and I turned to find her staring at me as she spoke into the phone, "Candace."

She shook her head a moment, and instantly her expression changed. "Hullo, girls." She waved, then directed her attention back to her phone. "Yes, on Bay Street, wonderful." She closed her phone with a snap.

"We'll have a car in ten minutes," she announced with satisfaction. "Let's go have a drink in the front while we wait?" She offered me her arm.

"Oh, okay." I slipped my arm through hers. "Nice meeting you guys," I said to Gina and Mary. "You have a great night."

"You too," and "Nice to meet you too, Nina," they answered severally as we left.

"Oh, by the way?" I turned back and asked.

They now had their arms around each other and glanced up in inquiry.

"Don't do anything I wouldn't do." I winked, and they laughed as Candace and I left.

"Barbarian!" she jokingly scolded, lightly slapping my bicep.

"That's 'colonist' to you." I licked my teeth as we squeezed through the corridor to the front bar. "You called a car?" I asked. "So we're going to, what was it, Port Mar See?" I exaggerated my bad pronunciation to see if I could get a rise out of her.

"Port Marseille," she corrected, amused. "You aren't going to let the 'colonist' thing go, are you?" she asked, rubbing the bicep she had just slapped as we walked through the hall arm in arm.

"Hmm…" I considered playfully. "You know what? 'Colonist' is such a novel thing to be called," I said, smiling to take any possible sting out of my remark. "I mean, I've been called many things, but still…"

Stopping as we reached the front of the Cadillac bar a few feet from the door, I freed my arm from hers, put my hands on my hips, and faced her. "I think it's going to take some time," I told her in mock seriousness.

"Well, then," she said coyly and brought her fingertips to the edge of my neckline while she played with my collar, "let me buy you a drink, and we can let the reparations begin."

With my fingertips, I drew gentle lines down her cheeks, and her skin was so very smooth. "Oh, so now you're trying to seduce me with your decadent European sophistication?" I asked. "Besides, you can't."

"Can't what?" she asked in a throaty whisper, kissing my ear. "Seduce you?"

I closed my eyes and let her continue. "You can't buy me a drink," I murmured as she licked the hollow in my throat. "I work here—it's one of the perks. So," I asked as her ministrations continued, "what would you like?"

"You…" she said, nipping lightly on my neck, "on silk." That sounded good to me too, and as her lips reached the hollow of my throat, a light growl escaped me. As I opened my eyes, I realized—the club, we were still in the club. We were supposed to be leaving, and I was supposed to be doing something. Oh, yeah! Drinks! I was getting those.

"I meant…what would you like to drink?" I finally sputtered. "Since you're getting dinner, let me get you a drink."

Candace trailed her fingertips up and down the column of my neck as she straightened. "You know," she said, "that's not a bad idea. Do you recommend anything specifically?"

"I do recommend you stay away from doing entire pitchers of Red Death," I told her, ruefully twisting my lips as I remembered my recent occasion of overindulgence. Oh, but I did have an idea. "Would you mind if I surprise you?"

"Hmm, surprise away, then," she said. "I'm sure you've got good taste, if your clothes and your musical choice are any indication." She waved at me.

"Great, I'll be right back," I said, and walked to the end of the bar.

"Hi, Dee Dee!" I called to the bartender, yet another stunning example of women the powers-that-be have placed on this earth. A statuesque "five foot twelve" as she called it, Dee Dee had skin the color of coffee with cream, very curly blond hair, and startlingly hazel eyes that shaded from golden amber to an incredible light green, depending on her mood. Honestly, I couldn't tell you what I found most attractive about her—her eyes, her personality, or her drop-dead gorgeous accent. She was sexy all around.

Born in Bonn, Germany, of a Japanese-American father who'd been stationed there while in the army and the wife he'd brought there from Port-Au-Prince, Dee Dee, the living example of how beautiful human beings would be if we all just got along, had come to the United States not quite a year ago to finish her education and currently went to a local private college where she was getting a master's degree in chemistry—which was probably why she was such a great bartender in the first place, sort of an extension of natural talent, I guess. Why she lived and worked on Staten Island was beyond me—she had the rest of the city to choose from, but I knew that I, for one, was glad she was there.

"Hallo, Nina!" Her eyes were on the cocktail she'd been mixing. "You're well tonight?" she asked, tossing a little flurry of ice flakes on the concoction she'd just finished and passing it to the waiting customer.

"I am...*wunderbar*!" I answered, using the only German word—wonderful—that I knew. Well, there were a few others, like *hamburger*, *achtung* and *mach schnell*, but I don't think any one of those would have been appropriate, especially since I'd learned them watching movies.

"*Wunderbar*, eh?" she asked, widening her eyes at me. "And is that the reason?" She pointed with her chin toward Candace, who was watching from a window for the awaited car.

I glanced down at the bar to hide the rising red in my cheeks. "Maybe." I paused. "Can't it just be a beautiful summer night?"

Dee Dee pursed her lips in what I recognized as amusement and picked up a glass. "Right. A beautiful night. Yet another for you, then?" she asked with a little smirk as she focused on polishing the glass.

"I don't know what you're talking about," I told her with as straight a face as I could muster. "Most summer nights are beautiful, don't you think?"

"Hmph," Dee Dee snorted, putting the glass down and wiping the bar. "What I think is that you are going to get lai—"

"Ladylike?" I interrupted before she could finish the word. "Lazy?

How about literal or, better yet, literary?" I smiled. "Shall we discuss our favorite authors?"

I don't know why I wouldn't let her say "laid." It's not like I didn't know what it meant. It's just, well, it didn't seem right or polite somehow, as if it would be disrespectful, both to me and to Candace. That's it—it would have been disrespectful, and I didn't want that.

"Hah!" Dee Dee laughed and threw the rag under the counter. "Good for you, Nina." Her cheeks dimpled slightly as she looked me up and down with unmistakable approval. "Good for you. So," she continued, "what do you want at my bar?" She spread both hands on the counter to lean on her elbows and talk with me.

"We're going out for a late dinner, French, so what do you recommend?" If anyone knew what went with what, it was the bartender, and Dee Dee was one of the best.

"Hmm." She pursed her lips and considered. "Start with a merlot? Or what about a white?" She shifted to another part of the counter and searched under the bar.

"Here," she presented me with two glasses, "start with white for now," and she filled the glasses about halfway, "for a fresh palate and," she searched a shelf and came back with a dark bottle, "finish with a good Bordeaux!" She set the bottle on the counter in front of me with a flourish.

I stared at the bottle. "You're not seriously giving this to me?" Even with drinks on the house, that was a pretty pricey gesture.

"Why not?" Dee Dee shrugged. "You never really get anything from the bar. Most of the time, that is." Her lip curled slyly. "Besides," she continued, "this way you will impress her and you can get, um, literary." That sly curve twitched when I raised an eyebrow at her.

Still, I was rather doubtful. I mean, I would have rather paid for the wine and said so.

"Nina, you make the club lots and lots of money. Think of it as bonus!" she insisted. "Now, go!" she ordered. "Go give her the glass, and I will put this in a bag for you." She waved her hands at me, shooing me along. "Well, what are you waiting for?" she demanded, a hand on her sharply arced hip when I didn't move fast enough.

"I'm going, I'm going." I raised my hands in mock alarm and jumped away from the bar, taking the wineglasses with me.

"Don't forget the Bordeaux!" Dee Dee called to my back.

"I won't!" I assured over my shoulder, and I carefully returned to Candace, trying not to spill anything. I didn't want Dee Dee's rag to make a sudden and snappy appearance near me or, even worse, on me.

I had a very visceral memory of the sponge. You know, the you've-got-some-dirt-on-your-face, come-here-and-let-me-clean-it-for-you stinky sponge that every household in creation has. Not that Dee Dee's rag was like that; she was a bleach fanatic. It's just, well, that's what it made me think of. I shuddered, remembering the nasty, wet smell of that sponge, but controlled my hands quickly—I didn't want to spill the wine.

"Try this." I offered a glass to Candace as I neared, relieved to not have to balance it anymore.

"Thank you," she said as she lifted the stem from my fingers. "White wine for a fresh palate?" She swirled the wine, then held up her glass. "To a beautiful summer night?"

I stared a moment, surprised to hear the words I'd said moments ago to Dee Dee, but I recovered quick enough. "To a beautiful summer night," I agreed. Candace lightly tapped her glass to mine, then took a sip. I did the same—not bad, not too dry, not too sweet. Knowing Dee Dee, it was probably a German Rhein.

"Very nice," Candace commented contemplatively. "Wonderful, in fact." She sipped again, finishing the glass.

I nodded agreement and did the same.

"So, ready to go?" she asked, regarding me over her glass. "Because I think," and she peered out the window, "yes, our car is here."

"Oh, yeah, would you just, um," I glanced over at the bar, "give me a moment?" I took her empty glass. I wasn't going to forget Dee Dee's gift since she was so politely insistent, and I figured it certainly wouldn't hurt my karma if I made the waitresses' job a bit easier and took the glasses back to the bar.

"Certainly." Candace shrugged good-naturedly and touched my shoulder. "I'll meet you in the car, then?"

"Great. I'll be right there." And back to the bar I went.

Dee Dee hurried over, package in hand, as I approached.

"Here," she announced, placing a medium-sized, baby blue gift bag on the counter as I set the glasses to one side. "If you don't get to discuss your books, it will not be the fault of the wine!"

She laughed as I peered into the bag. She had wrapped the bottle in black tissue paper and placed a little silver ribbon around the top. As I reached into the bag for it, Dee Dee stopped me.

"No, that is for later, after the books!" Dee Dee grinned with secret mirth. "Promise?"

"Fine, I promise," I agreed. Impulsively, I leaned over the counter and kissed her on the cheek. "Thank you. That was just so very nice of you."

Dee Dee stood up straight, put her hands on her hips, and nodded from side to side. "So, go!" she shooed finally, picking up her rag to wave at me. "What are you waiting for?"

"Have a great night, Dee Dee." I lifted the bag from the bar so I could go meet Candace.

"French—hah!" I heard her call to my back. "You let me know when you want *real* food, *liebchen*!"

I laughed as I walked out, visions of sausage and sauerkraut with large mugs of beer in my head, although maybe I was wrong. I'd have to investigate, I thought, just to make sure—and maybe take some Southern Champagne, otherwise known as Coca-Cola, with me, just in case it was truly, well, whatever. Coke would make it all better.

I was still thinking about Coke as I walked to the car, owned by one of the many local companies that exist on the Island. For whatever reason, there are no yellow cabs or gypsy cabs on Staten Island; the county doesn't allow them. If you want a car, you have to call and reserve one. That's just the way it is. Most of them seem exactly like regular cars and don't have any identifying marks except the phone number on the door. But I could tell which one I was going to because the door was still open for me.

"There you are!" Candace exclaimed as I slid in.

"Where we going again, ma'am?" the driver asked as I settled the bag by my feet. I didn't know, of course, so Candace gave him directions.

"By the way, earlier, did you say your surname is Boyd?" Candace asked with studied nonchalance as she settled into her seat. I could tell it was an act, though, because her eyes were way-wide, and she pursed her lips too tightly.

"Yes, why? What's yours?" I asked her with a grin, trying to set her at ease. You know, for a moment there, she'd looked as if she'd seen a ghost.

Candace blinked and recovered herself. "Oh, it's…I didn't hear you clearly, that's all. Mine is Neilds, by the way. Candace Lindsay Neilds, actually."

"Well, it's nice to officially meet you, by the by." I held out my hand. I was surprised that I hadn't told her my last name before. I usually always tell people because there was one thing that really, really bugged me, to the point where I'd promised myself I wasn't going to do it. What is it with lesbians and no last names? That just so pisses me off.

Candace stared at, then finally shook my hand. "The pleasure is all mine." She grinned back. "So then, what's in the bag?" She reached over me for it, but I caught her shoulders as she lunged across my lap.

"Hey, that's for later," I reminded her as I released her.

Candace twisted her body so that she faced me, and she reached across my legs to lean on her hand. "Confident, aren't you?" She reached her free hand around my head and pulled me toward her.

"Now, now," I admonished as my mouth closed in on hers and I wrapped my arms around her waist, "that's colonist to you," and I lightly flicked my tongue between her lips, then slid it in. Oh, but she could kiss, and when she sucked on my tongue, squeezing it with her mouth, the sensation sent a chill down my throat, through my chest, and shot through my stomach. I could feel my lower abs tingle with want, not to mention everything else. Great technique, I thought. I'd have to try it sometime.

We made out the whole way to Manhattan, and by the time we got to the restaurant, I was stretched out along the backseat with my back against the little side window and Candace on top of me. Somehow, the driver got paid, and we stumbled out of the car, bag in one hand and the rest of me busy with Candace. I don't know how we got through dinner, but I do remember that the maitre d' gave us a private table, and between feeding each other with our fingertips, sharing glasses of wine, and trading little kisses throughout, I don't even know what we ate, never mind how we left the place or came to the conclusion that we would go to hers. It made sense, though—it was definitely closer and positively more private than mine.

Finally, somehow, maybe the Bordeaux we'd opened as we walked had teleported us, we were in her apartment—somewhere on Sixth and Avenue A, I think—and in her bedroom, the Bordeaux half gone as I sat on the edge of the bed and poured out another couple of glasses on her night table.

Candace lay on her side propped on an elbow, watching me through hooded eyes and wearing nothing but her boots. "I love the way that looks on you," she purred, an appreciative light in her eyes.

I glanced at myself, then back at her. "Glad you like it, since you requested it." I smirked slyly.

It had been an unspoken yet understood thing between us tonight—despite the fact that I doubt either of us had questioned that this was exactly where we'd end up—we weren't rushing, perhaps to compensate for the last time. No matter what the reason might have been, we teased, we tortured, we tantalized each other to that promise of sex, and whereas we mauled each other on the way through her apartment to her bedroom, we slowed as we got through that door, and Candace fumbled for, then found, the light switch.

We blinked at each other for a moment in the half-light, then kissed each other languidly. She removed the bottle and the bag from my hands and led me to the bed. I slowly rolled her dress up and off her, and she rolled mine down. I have to say, that as sexy and revealing as Lycra combined with whatever other material can be, it's really not that easy to remove. It's for looking, not for touching, that's for sure, and we giggled a bit as we fumbled with the stretchy fabric.

We stopped kissing and caressing a moment when Candace grabbed my jacket from where it had landed.

"Would you wear this?" she asked me with a sensual twist to her mouth.

Wordlessly, I put it on and Candace slipped her arms beneath it, pressing her skin to mine. I had to have some wine before I just fucked her again and again.

"Drink," I muttered hoarsely, gasping for air. "I need a drink."

Which is how we ended up as we were at the moment, as I handed her a glass.

Candace accepted it with a smile and held her glass up to me in silent toast, and I matched the gesture. Candace sat up to twine her arm around mine and switch drinks so that I'd have hers and she'd have mine.

We each took a sip, and then it was time, and more than. I placed my glass on the nightstand and leaned into her, kissing her neck, gently pushing her back onto the pillows. Our mouths met again as I slowly lowered my body over hers, and as I shifted more fully onto the bed, she reached a leg over mine and urged me between her thighs.

"Are you okay?" I murmured softly in genuine concern, propping myself up on my hands so I could see her expression for myself and know for sure.

Candace gazed up at me, raised her arms over her head a moment, then placed them on my ass, running soft trails up and down my spine under the jacket. "Fabulous," she said into my eyes, then trailed her glance to my chest. "Magnificent, your breasts are magnificent," and she brought her hands away from my back to touch them, tracing their contours, filling her hands with them.

I arched my back, pressing my lower body into her and my nipples into her palms. My eyes closed when her thighs came up to embrace my hips, and she tilted hers in such a way that her lovely cunt met mine. I opened them again when her hand reached between us to spread those luscious lips—hers and mine—and I don't know which one of us sighed as my aching hard clit moved against hers, sliding and grinding in warm wetness.

I spread my thighs and pressed them against her, increasing the contact and the pressure, moving slowly, building the sensation.

"Oh, this is wonderful," Candace moaned, and I admired her expression, open-mouthed and head back, below me. When her eyes finally met mine she smiled, then reached for the wine. She took a sip, then passed it to me.

I took it from her, riding her pussy in a smooth, languid wave as I straightened my spine and tossed my head back to drink. "Mmph, it is," I agreed, handing her back the glass.

She set it on the table and reached to shut off the lamp.

"Don't," I requested rather breathily, and Candace's eyes questioned me.

"Don't shut off the light," I asked again. "I like to watch," I explained, smiling sensually as I rolled my hips and slid against her in such a way that she arched her neck.

"Kinky," she breathed out as she undulated under me, the muscles in her stomach rippling and her breasts heaving. "I like it."

"You're the one," I sighed, "who insisted I keep the jacket on," I reminded her.

I picked up the pace, my movements a little sharper, harder, just more deliberate, and Candace her spread her legs farther as her cunt licked mine. Occasionally my clit would slide right into her, and we'd both gasp.

"Oh, yeah," I breathed when her hands grabbed my ass, squeezing and massaging the muscles, pulling me closer. Her legs spread wide, and her ass moved with the rhythm I now set. I tossed off the jacket so I could feel free, then grabbed each of her ankles in turn, pulled her boots off—and tossed them wherever.

"Yes, yes," she hissed, her clit thumping solidly against mine as we drove for that final push, unable to tell whether she was moving me or I was moving her.

She scraped up my spine and down my shoulders to my ass, and I arched into the added sensation, tossing my head back and lifting my upper body, power building as I felt heat rush up from my happily moving cunt, a flush that rose steadily up my stomach.

"Oh God, you are beautiful," Candace gasped as we fucked in desperate earnestness, that hot slide a pussy-pounding glorious sensation. "Fucking magnificent," she breathed again, and her hands came off my ass to trail across my shoulders and my breasts, and when I felt a drop of sweat slide down my neck and opened my eyes so I could see Candace, really see her, she wiped it away with a finger, then just so sensuously slid that finger into her mouth.

"Ooh," I groaned as I watched her, the erotic thrill adding to the roll of my hips, "fuck, yes." I wanted so much to feel more, but the sensual haze I'd been caught in slipped away. She scratched a sharp trail down my rigid biceps, then squeezed my ribs before moving back down to my hips.

"Fuck, yes," Candace echoed, "fuck, yeah, oh, yeah, yeah!" she groaned, her hands clenching and unclenching my ass.

Her face revealed an almost unearthly beauty as her head tossed back and her cunt strained in mine. "Your pussy is so hot," I told her. "You are so fucking hot!"

When that crimson flush began to crawl up her body, painting her breasts with a rosy glow, she arched her back and pulled me into her as hard as she could. "Oh fuck," she groaned, and I could feel her clit throb against mine as her hips bucked, her thighs squeezing my waist.

"That's it, baby," I encouraged, firmly holding her hips so that no matter how she moved, the pressure would stay where she needed it most. For myself, honestly, I felt nothing. Nada. Zippo. I don't know why that happened, but it did. One moment, I'd be riding the wave and getting to the top, and another, well, I might as well be playing in the bathtub, for whatever that was worth. But if only one of us was going to come, I was glad it would be her. I would make sure of it.

"Oh, yeah, that's it, that's it!" Candace ground out from her clenched jaw, her body tensed under me, the tendons evident in her neck and shoulders as her hands dug into me, and I felt a pleasant rush shoot from my chest to my head.

"God, Nina," she purred as her legs relaxed and she rolled her head from side to side a bit as she lightly stroked my lower back. "What did you just do to me?"

I rested my head on her chest a moment and stroked her arms lightly as I caught my breath. I could hear the deep and steady pounding of her heart. "Hmm," I exhaled, "what felt right, I guess," I answered honestly. "Did you like that? I mean, did you..." I leaned up on an elbow to see her face.

Candace stretched under me, bringing her arms over her head. "Come?" she filled in for me, and her lips curved gracefully in the way I so liked. "Can't you tell?" she teased, and brought a hand to my shoulder and the other skimmed my nose, while I played with the tendrils of hair near her temple.

"But you didn't," she stated softly, the corners of her luminous eyes crinkling with observation.

I smiled gently. "It's okay," I reassured her, then nuzzled her neck. "I like making you come," I whispered as I slid my body down hers and painted circles on her breast with my tongue.

"Oh," she groaned softly as her nipple hardened between my lips, "but Nina..."

I switched my attention from one breast to the other and twirled the one wet from my mouth between my fingertips as hers dug lovely trails up my neck.

"Shh," I gentled her and kissed the center of her chest, "let me..." I licked a path to her navel, scratching lightly down her ribs.

Her hips jumped beneath me a moment, and I could feel the hair from her pussy rub against my sternum.

"Fine, then," she sighed as I fit my shoulders between her legs and lightly bit and licked at her thigh. "So," she breathed, "what do you think of French?" she asked in an attempt at conversation.

"Well..." I paused a moment, glancing up at her. Her eyes were closed and her head tilted back, exposing the long length of her throat and opening up her breasts to my view. *"Je comprends le Français un peu,"* I told her in mock seriousness, then sucked on the tendon that ran from her thigh to the light brown hair of her pussy. That brought me another rewarding, somewhat anticipatory groan, and Candace shifted her hips.

"Eh, *je parle un peu,"* I told her as I brought my hands up to her hips and my thumbs massaged along the edges of her lips. *"Mais, pas très bien,"* I finished, grinning at her.

Candace leaned up on her elbows to stare at me. "You understand a little French, and you speak a little?" she asked, shaking her head incredulously.

I blew softly on the curls before me before answering. *"Mais, pas très bien,"* I reminded her.

"But not very well," she translated, then smiled at me in appreciation of the joke. "Is there anything else about you I should know, you wicked, clever girl?"

I drew my lower lip up against the length of her lips before answering. "Yes," I breathed against her. "I'm an American, not an idiot. They're not synonymous, so no more assumptions," I requested as I lightly parted her lips with my thumbs. I glanced at her a moment, hoping she could tell from my eyes that I was playing. "And you were right," I whispered, "I am a colonist." I flicked the tip of my tongue against her clit, then drew it into my lips.

CHANGE YOUR PRETTY MIND

Send a perfect hero for one day
Ride right in—take all the pain away
The hero halo's broken—another lie is spoken
And I've a broken heart when the image falls apart

"Lead Me On"—Life Underwater

It's funny. After I had picked up my guitar, I locked myself in the only private place in the apartment—the bathroom—and played for three hours, enjoying its full and glorious voice. Well, as full as it could be without an amplifier. When I finally quit playing for the night, I eased it into its hard-shell case, and, for the first time, I really could see its beautiful amber-honey burst. The sound and feel of it had so entranced me since I'd first played it in the shop, I didn't even know what color it was until that moment. It wouldn't have mattered if it was avocado green with pink stripes; it played with delicious ease and sounded so incredibly fine. Okay, maybe avocado green and pink stripes might have mattered, but still, it wasn't an eyesore; it was both functionally and visually beautiful.

Cap had left me a note on the table that night, letting me know I could use the large empty closet in his room for my guitar, since it would be safe there and out of the way of general traffic. Funny thing. Despite the fact that Cap, Jackie, and Trace had all gone to high school together, I always got the feeling that, somehow, Cap was older, though he wasn't—not at all.

I'd mentally thanked him and added a note to the end of his:

You, dude, are awesome. Thank you. Nina.

I played every day (still do, in fact), getting used to the different feel of an electric guitar as opposed to an acoustic in my hands in those first few weeks of having it, and that night, like the first, I reluctantly slid the case into the walk-in closet in Cap's room and went to work. I was still actively avoiding my roommates—Cap was always working anyway, Jackie still had no kind words for me, and Trace, well, the whole thing just confused me. Since I didn't know what to do with my feelings, I decided I better get my head clear before we spoke again rather than be so off balance when I saw her. Given the mutual work-shift craziness and my penchant for traveling into Manhattan and staying over at Candace's on occasion (well, not staying exactly—I never really slept there—I went back to Staten Island—"the Rock"— around sunup), it was pretty easy not to see anyone.

I was coming home kinda late. I'd stopped at a local studio so I could finally plug in my guitar and play it at its full honey-throated throttle—I had a bona fide, honest-to-goodness possible new band audition/meeting the next day, and I wanted to be more than ready for it. After I'd played till my time was up, I'd stepped out to pay for it and ended up speaking with the owner, and then some guys came in, and the next thing you know, we were back in the studio just jamming out some tunes for fun.

Needless to say, I was in a really great mood, so when I rounded the landing on the second floor and ran right into Trace, it didn't throw me as far off track as it could have.

"Hey, Trace," I said with my usual smile. Ah, what the hell, right? I was feeling way too good, the rhythm and the melodies running through my head, and as I shifted my gig bag on my shoulder, my fingers twitched with playing memory.

"Hey yourself," she drawled back, the beginning of a smile edging her lips.

"Off to work?" I asked. It wouldn't be unusual for her to pick up a night shift.

She hesitated a moment before she answered. "No, just, you know, hanging out. You?"

I smiled widely, too happy to contain it. "Just getting back—from the studio," I told her. "I have an audition tomorrow."

Trace nodded and smiled, and when she did, her eyes grew wide and deep. "That's really cool, Nina, really cool. You're gonna do great," she said with the warmth she usually had for me in private.

"Yeah, well, we'll see how it goes, you know? I'm a little nervous," I admitted.

"Well, you know the cure for that, right?" she asked.

I kinda sorta thought I did—preparation and focus—but maybe she had a better idea. "What?"

"A good run. Gets the nerves right out."

I smiled despite myself. "I was kinda sorta gonna do that anyway."

"Ah," she grinned at me, "but it's always better with company. Want some?"

That startled me. It had been so long since we'd really spoken, and even longer since we'd run together, especially after what had happened between us—well…I thought about it. Oh, hell, why not, right? Maybe we'd be able to communicate; maybe we could work things out.

"Yeah, sure, that'd be really cool."

"Set then," Trace returned, clapping her hands together briskly. "Come get me in the morning?"

"Sure. Cool."

"Yeah, cool."

We said our good-byes, and I continued up the stairs to my apartment. I took loving care of my guitar, checking out the strings, wiping off the fingerprints, then giving it a good polish before I carefully put it away. I took a few moments to pick out what I'd wear the next day, hit the shower, then dropped into bed after I snapped my little light on, and I made sure I left enough room for Jackie when she got home.

So, early enough in the morning, I carefully wiggled out from the bed, holding my breath so I wouldn't wake Jackie, and I was dressed and ready in minutes. I hurried quietly down the stairs to Trace's apartment in the early morning silence and knocked, but no answer. Probably still asleep, I figured, so I let myself in like I'd done a thousand times before. I opened the closed door, expecting to find Trace in bed. I did.

She leaned over the mattress, forearms braced against it as Van pumped her furiously from behind. She must have heard me, because her expression changed from a curious, somewhat inward concentration, to concern.

"Nina, wait," she called out to me as she straightened up, trying to shake Van off her. He snaked an arm around her waist, and she slapped it.

The sound snapped me out of my shock, and I shook my head as I closed the door.

"Get the fuck off me," I heard her tell him as I walked to the exit, and I heard the sound of hurried feet as I jogged down the steps. I had to get my run in.

As I opened the front door, Trace called from the hallway above. "Nina!"

"Later, Trace!" I answered, waving behind me. I refused to even glance back once as I shut the door. I went for my run, hating my stupidity and the expression on Van's face when he finally opened his eyes and saw me. That fucking smirk—like Trace was a toy we were fighting over. Bastard. Like he even really cared about her.

I ran for miles—I don't know how far. Dumb, dumb, dumb. That word beat itself into my head with every other breath I took. In between, all I could think of was how everybody kept saying I was cute, how they treated me like some stupid kid with a cool haircut.

I couldn't talk to anyone. Nico wasn't around; he had his own stuff to do for school. Jackie would, at best, ignore me; at the next level, try to tell me how I'd misunderstood because I was so uninformed; or, at worst, tell me how I'd brought it on myself or it was my fault anyway.

I didn't know what Cap would say, but as much as I liked him, I wasn't as close to him as I had been to either Trace or Jackie, and I didn't think watching porno was the answer to all issues. Forget talking about anything with my parents. Now that I no longer lived within the range of tossed items, we were only first being civil to one another. Anything that reminded them that I was gay wouldn't be helpful. God, I missed them, though.

No. I needed my own space. The large walk-in closet in Cap's bedroom where I kept my guitar was about eight feet by five feet wide, and, by a design quirk, it not only had a door into his room (which locked from the inside), but also an egress in the back. If you walked to the end of the wall, you'd discover an opening about two feet wide;

go through it, and you were in the front closet by the entrance. And it had its own door.

Jackie could, as a "senior" roomie, close the door to "our" room whenever she wanted, especially if she had company. When that happened I'd have to wait or get comfortable on the sofa or at Trace's.

Hmm...maybe that's why I had previously spent so much time down at her place. But I didn't want to do that anymore—the sofa or Trace's. And I was tired of always having to go to someone else's place if I wanted to spend time with them. So what if I had to walk through the closet? At least I'd have my own door. Besides, the closet thing was funny if you thought about it, and I've never been one to ignore an inherent irony.

The way I saw it, I really did pay more rent than Jackie, and Cap wasn't using that closet for anything except my guitar. Besides, it also had its own window, with a southeastern exposure. I love the light in the morning, and Jackie insisted that the room we share be blacked out, all the time. I was tired of living in a small, dark, cramped space. I wanted to be able to read at night if I wanted, roll onto my back and smile back at the clouds in the morning, and not worry about jamming my elbows into anyone or being jammed in return.

And I wanted my privacy. Not that I had anything to hide or something like that, it's just that if I wanted to be alone with my thoughts or my guitar, I wanted to really be alone. And after what I'd seen this morning, I wanted, no, I *needed* to be alone.

❖

I approached Cap about it that day, after I'd come back, showered, and dressed from my morning run, and he'd finally come out of his room.

I sat at the kitchen table, which had been shoved up against the wall, two feet from the entrance. Well, it wasn't the world's biggest apartment. I had placed my chair so that I could rest my arm on the table, but I looked out onto the rest of the room, my back against the wall, drinking a cup of tea (Earl Grey, with milk and sugar, thanks), reading the hardcover graphic novel *Camelot 3000* for the who-knows-whatever time, and smoking a cigarette, my first of the day.

I figured I'd let my subconscious compose the words I'd need while I entertained the forefront of my brain with futuristic sci fi, King Arthur, his Round Table of knights, including a Tristan who had been reincarnated as a woman. Besides, it got me away from my thoughts, which were beyond confusing at the moment.

I was just getting to the part where Tristan runs into and remembers her true love, Isolde, when Cap stepped out of his bedroom door, dressed in the usual—the skin he was in.

"Coffee's made," I told him as he grunted a feeble hello and trudged to the counter.

"Thanks."

He seemed surprised, and I exhaled smoke calmly as I waited for him to join me at the table, cup in hand.

"No problem." I slid my cigarette pack and lighter across the table toward him, and with another grateful nod, he took one and lit it, inhaling deeply.

"How ya doin', kid?" he asked me finally.

"I'm all right." I closed my book with one last look at the four-color panels, sliding it over by the wall. "How about you?"

"I'm good." He nodded. "Just hunky-dory." He took a deep breath, then downed his coffee as I watched his face change from sleepy softness to a more alert tension. Not a negative thing, mind you. Cap was always pretty cheerful in the morning. It's just that I could see his brain was starting to engage.

I waited until he put his cup down with a small exhalation of satisfaction.

"That hit the spot." He smiled contentedly and dragged on his cigarette. We sat for a few moments in companionable silence, and I carefully gathered my words.

"Hey, Cap?" I started. "I'd like to ask you something."

Something in my tone must have worried him, because he instantly looked concerned.

"You can ask me anything, you know that. Everything okay?" he asked, favoring me with his I'm-a-policeman squint. "Is Trace giving you shit? Do you need to—"

"No, no, nothing like that," I raised a hand and interrupted. Besides, I wasn't ready to talk about it yet. "It's about the living arrangements. I'd like to propose a change." I launched into my request and explanation while Cap sat silently the whole time, his eyes focused on mine.

"So," I concluded, "what do you think? I'm pretty quiet anyway, you know that, and I've never been disrespectful of your things."

The silence dragged on, so long that I thought he'd say no, until I saw the tiniest bit of a grin tugging at the corner of his lips.

"Well, you know, I have to think about it," he started, but the effort not to smile was too much, and he burst out laughing.

"You bastard," I laughed as I wadded up a napkin and threw it at him, "you had me going for a minute there."

"I gotcha good!" he chortled, batting away the second and third missiles I sent his way.

"But..." and his face went somber, "there's one thing. I have to move something out of there, and I want you to know where it is. I also want you to know how to use it."

I stared a moment, puzzled as I tried to figure out what he meant. Oh, I got it! Of course, he had a large footlocker in there, and he was a cop. He could only mean one thing—his gun.

"Oh," I said. What else was there to say?

"In fact," Cap continued, "are you free this afternoon?" He watched me expectantly.

"Um, yeah, I don't even have to work tonight. I was just going to catch up on some stuff," I answered. "What do you have in mind?"

Twenty minutes later, I was in the passenger seat of Cap's jeep pulling into the lot of the local firing range, a huge one-story brick building with no windows. Well, I guess those just wouldn't be necessary, right?

I found myself in a little cubby staring down a lane at a tiny target that seemed to be at least a hundred yards away, with others separated by a distance of several feet on either side.

"Put these on"—he handed me some yellowish-tinged shooting glasses—"and these"—he handed me a pair of headphones—"but wait until after you fire your first shot."

I slipped the glasses on and curled the ends around my ears, then carefully placed the headphones on the rug-covered ledge in front of me that stood slightly higher than my waist.

"Okay, now," Cap began, and I faced him. He held a matte charcoal pistol in his hands, barrel pointed up, its profile facing me. It looked like something out of a movie, any movie with a bad guy. In fact, it looked like a bad-guy sort of weapon, not like the revolvers that officers seem to have either in their holsters on the street or even on screen. First off, it looked like it was metal, all metal. And second of all, there was no round chamber section—you know, like the ones you see cowboys twirl and—never mind.

"This is not my service revolver," Cap explained.

Well, yeah, I figured that. But I said nothing. All I could focus on was that real live gun in front of my eyes.

"This…" and he paused, "is a Glock 9 millimeter. This"—he clicked something and a cartridge fell out of the pistol grip into his other hand—"is your ammo." He slid a finger into the cavity and, finding nothing, eased the top forward and back. "In case there's a round in there, that'll pop it out. You never know," he cautioned me.

"Okay, you load it like this." He demonstrated, pointing the weapon toward the floor and popping the cartridge home. It audibly snicked. "Then set your safety." He twisted the gun so I could watch him thumb it. "You try it." He handed it to me.

I was very conscious of its cold weight as I somehow managed to slip the release, the clip gliding out easily into my free hand. I examined it. It seemed full to me; bullets practically bristled at the very top.

I faced the range so I wouldn't accidentally point the gun at someone. I admit it, I was afraid, and I didn't know if there just might somehow be a stray bullet in the chamber.

"This a full clip?" I asked in as casual a tone as I could muster as I sighted down the hopefully empty gun. I handed it to him.

"Yeah, it should be," he answered, examining it carefully. "But you're doing the right thing, pointing it away from yourself or others. Never look down the barrel. There could always be an unfired round in the chamber." He put a gentle hand on my shoulder; I guess he could tell I was scared.

"Here," he handed me the clip, "now before you put this in, make sure to see if anything's in there."

I checked as I had seen Cap do it, and slid a finger in. I felt nothing other than the contours inside.

"Okay, now clear it and double-check."

It took a moment to figure out, but I did it and safely inspected the chamber. Nothing fell out, so that had to be a good sign, right? Man, I hoped so.

I glanced over my shoulder. Now what?

Cap answered my unvoiced question. "Load it, Nina. Load it…
and shoot." He had put on his shooter's glasses.

I took the clip and pushed it in. When it didn't click, I let it slide
out about halfway. This time, I slapped it in with my palm and was
rewarded with a solid "snick." I set the safety.

Staring at the target, I carefully wrapped my right hand around the
handle, and my left cradled it for stability. Both thumbs were pointed
at the target.

"Nice, Nina," Cap said softly behind me, "that's the way. All right
now, release the safety."

I eased my thumb over the safety and carefully curled a forefinger
around the trigger.

"Whenever you're ready," Cap whispered behind me.

I swallowed and nodded nervously. Straightening a bit, I squared
my shoulders and sighted the target—a humanoid figure with a gun—as
best I could.

"You okay?"

"Yeah, I'm fine…just trying to aim," I responded through dry lips.
In truth? I was stalling. I didn't think I could do it—aim, shoot, hit the
target. I was caught between scared and incompetent, and neither of
those options felt very good.

"If you're too scared, you could just watch me," Cap offered,
voicing my feelings, and while his voice sounded friendly, I was sure I
heard something else—not mockery or derision exactly, but more like
a hint of disappointment, like he'd expected something different from
me.

Great, now I wasn't tough enough either; that was just the end.
Not old enough, not smart enough, not enough of whatever it was Trace
wanted—too cute, too intense, too stupid, too much me and just not
right.

"I'm fine," came curtly out of my mouth. I breathed out softly, and
in that same moment, I found my target line, then promised myself I
wouldn't blink. I pulled the trigger.

The blast was louder than I'd expected and seemed to echo in the
concrete chamber as I looked around the range. I could feel the kickback
from the shot in my hands, like catching a baseball barehanded, and my
palms stung lightly.

The skin of my knuckles stretched and whitened as I brought my hands down and rested the pistol on the ledge.

"Nice shooting!" Cap clapped my shoulder. "Let's take a look at it." He edged in next to me and pressed a button I hadn't noticed before. A chain creaked its way on a pulley, bringing the target back with it.

The paper fluttered and grew larger as it came closer, and I could see the results for myself—a neat hole with slight scorch marks around the edges went through what had been the drawn shirt pocket of the figure.

"Man, oh, man, straight for the heart—great shot! You're a natural, Nina. Let's try that again."

Cap pressed the button, and as the chain wound its way back, another target appeared at the end.

I could smell something in the air, I didn't know what, and my ears still rang. Oh, my God, I had a loaded gun in my hands and was afraid to let go, to drop it, to move in any direction and accidentally hurt someone.

That possibility kept repeating itself in my head. I could decide at any second to turn that gun on Cap, on myself, at anyone, and that would be that. I could kill someone, including myself, thanks to this thing in my hands. How could someone not be overwhelmed by that possibility? There was, there is, no other purpose for a gun. I couldn't use it to dig, or to plant, or to build. All it did was what it was made to do—make holes in things, and maim or even kill living ones.

I couldn't find anything redeeming in that fact, and I couldn't put it down because I couldn't think or see any place that would be safe.

"Put the earphones on this time," Cap reminded me.

I cocked the safety with my thumb and pointed the gun at the floor, then looked at him. "Um, which hand should I use?" I asked a touch more acidly than I'd meant to, "the one that steadies it or the one that pulls the trigger?"

"Give me that," he laughed, "and put those on." He indicated with his chin toward the ledge where my phones sat.

I let my left hand relax off the grip, but still careful to point it down, I handed him the gun and noticed as I did that he wore both a pair of green-tinted shooting glasses and bright orange earphones.

My rental ones were blue, and they felt heavy as I slid them on, not at all like my DJ headphones.

"I'm gonna take a shot, okay?" Cap asked, his voice muffled and distant through the protective ear gear as he squeezed beside me to aim down the range.

"Yeah, sure, go ahead," I answered as loudly as I could so he could hear me, and nodded as well, just in case he didn't. I backed out of his way as he leaned his elbows on the ledge and took aim.

"You so do not shoot like a girl," he chortled, thumbing the safety and taking position at the ledge. I watched over his shoulder as the sound of a distant firecracker went off and light flared for a moment from the end of the pistol.

I tapped him on the shoulder to get his attention. "What's that supposed to mean?" I asked him with real curiosity and a touch of annoyance.

"I'll show you." He grinned, then quickly set himself up to pop off another two rounds.

He pushed the recall button, and as the target swung its way back to us, I could see three holes: one in the same place mine had been, another in the belly, and the third dead center of the pants zipper.

"You see," he explained, pointing, "girls tend to go for the gut and the groin, even when they're not looking at the target."

He pressed another button that would set up a new target, then glanced at me with a slitted, sidewise look.

"Always remember that, Nina. Girls will always go for the gut or the groin."

"Hey!" I protested, "that's not fair. I'm a girl, and that's not what I—"

"You're a woman, Nina," he interrupted me, waving a hand, the other one holding the gun securely on the ledge and pointed toward the range, "a young one, but still a woman. And one with an edge, at that. Even more, you're an adult—something rare."

He looked at me very seriously, and I arched an eyebrow in return.

I didn't feel very adult or womanly—edgy, maybe, but I figured that was due to hormones. I mean, I didn't think I knew what I was doing or had some sort of internal sense of, I don't know, certainty maybe, or direction, something—something I assumed that adults had, but I didn't.

Cap must have understood the expression on my face. "Keep shooting straight for the heart, Nina, and you'll be fine."

We were silent, Cap letting his words sink in, and I quietly absorbing them. Then Cap grinned. "Come on, it's your turn. Let's work on your technique and make sure you know what you're doing."

We spent a whole lot more time getting me comfortable with a gun, and between that and the whole morning thing, I had a lot to think about on the drive back to the apartment.

I so wished I didn't feel like I was always trying to catch up to everything and everyone around me, I thought as I watched the streets fly by from the window.

"Trace," Cap said quietly as he drove, "she's not it for you, right?"

Great. Awesome. Straight to the one thing I didn't want to talk about. Forget shooting for the heart—this went straight for the gut.

Pain bubbled up in my chest, so big, so hard, it squeezed me airless, and even worse, it *hurt*, throbbing in time with my heartbeat, because deep down, I knew what, I knew who was it for me and it was never going to happen.

Cap swung the jeep over to the curb so quickly we almost tipped. He set the car in park and twisted in his seat toward me. "Nina, what happened?" he asked me, his voice full of concern. "Is it Trace? She get a little too, ah, nuts with you?"

I faced the window, took a breath and then another as I got swamped between waves of memory—this morning and Van's eyes and the very visceral memory of my Samantha, my Sammy Blade. I missed her so much my blood flayed me within as it flowed and all my brain was able to form was her image and Van's expression, and they were twisting together over and over and making me nauseous.

But it wasn't just that or them—thinking of Samantha made me think of all the other friends I'd had, friends I hadn't seen in years. Fran, Francesca, whom we'd called "Kitt" on the swim team and her perfect smile, a really good friend, someone I'd even liked and spent a lot of time with outside of school. Laura and her flaming red hair, so determined, so fierce. Even my first girlfriend, Kerry, who'd been my best friend for a time. You'd think she'd have shown up at the Red Spot every now and again; after all, she'd introduced me to it.

But I saw no one—except Nico when he was around and very occasionally our parents and little sister Nanny since I'd moved/been kicked out/run away—that perspective depended upon who you asked. But still, even with the buffering presence of my aunt and cousins, that was strained at best. Everyone else was new to me in one way or another, and I always felt like I was struggling to catch up or something, because I just wasn't where they were at.

God, it sucked. After some unknown time, I was finally able to breathe through it, the nausea, the weird coldness that sucked at my skin and left my chest hollow. I tore my gaze from the window to answer him.

"It's not Trace, I mean, not right now, anyway," I said finally as I faced him.

Yeah, that was lame, but that was all I had—I couldn't tell him about this morning, I mean, what the fuck, Trace went out and got laid, big deal, right? She had every right to, didn't she? I should've either just played it off or stopped down later. Dammit, though, why should it have bothered me? How did I explain that? How could I explain it? Silence settled between us like the heavy humid air.

"Why don't you tell me about whoever it is, then?" Cap asked, his words cutting through the silence. "I can see that someone still means a lot to you and...Trace will never be it, and she knows it, too."

Floored, I stared at him wordlessly. Trace made me hurt, in ways I didn't know I could, and I'd been through quite a bit already, but the ache Trace left in me was a ghost, a ghost of the yawning chasm Samantha's absence had left within me. He was right—it would never be Trace, but it would never be Samantha, either. It had been years since I'd seen her, and even had I wanted to, I had no way of even knowing where to start looking if I wanted to find her—or anyone else, for that matter.

Who knew? Cap had taken me out to teach me how to handle a gun, and he'd given me the key I needed to break free. That...was the past, not the present. And not the future either, my brain told me mournfully, but I told that part to stop. It was way past time to get over it.

I took a deep breath and considered before I answered. "Cap, Trace could've been it. We could've really had something, something really good, if she just didn't—"

"Attempt to seduce every living being in front of you?" he finished wryly. "You know she's just playing the I Dare You game, don't you?"

"Huh?" Did he know what had happened this morning? If he didn't, I wasn't going to tell him. I fished my cigarettes and lighter out of my back pocket. If this conversation was going to continue in the direction that I thought it was, I was going to need nicotine.

"Nina, come on. You show me yours, I'll show you mine, that game?" he hinted.

I thought he'd left his mind behind in the shooting range. Besides, it wasn't as if Trace and I hadn't seen each other naked. We'd taken showers together, for chrissake, and slept skin to skin half the time. Well, before now. That was never going to happen again.

"Um, Cap? I've seen Trace naked." I blushed as I said it, thinking of just how naked I'd seen her this morning. But otherwise, it wasn't as if he didn't know. Plenty of times he'd bounced into the bedroom and onto the bed, waking us both up and forcing one or both of us to cover ourselves or each other. Actually that kind of—no, wait. It did piss me off. But now wasn't the time to discuss it.

Cap snorted. "Yeah, I don't mean that. I'm talking about feelings—show yours first, then she'll show hers."

I exhaled slowly and let the smoke drift away. I'd been on the right track, then. It really was about mutual surrender, and one concession on mine would have meant one on hers. But I wasn't comfortable with that scenario. Why did it have to be this whole dramatic submission thing? I voiced that part to Cap.

He grabbed a cigarette of his own and lit it. "Why did you turn her down, kid?" He exhaled. "You had no problem with that chicky you'd just met—the one up in the DJ booth."

What was this about? Did he and Jackie and Trace get together to discuss my affairs, or had the story merely made the rounds? Or was I just currently their only topic of conversation? Either way, I wasn't happy about it.

"Hey, look," I began, defensively. I mean, none of this seemed fair, you know? "First off, Trace sent her in there. Second of all, it's nobody's fuckin' business, and you know what? She didn't play any fuckin' games with me. She was honest about what she wanted, and I was feeling loose enough to go with it!" I retorted. What the fuck was up with these people? What, everyone's allowed to screw around but me? Oh, hell, they probably all got together when I wasn't around to laugh about me.

Cap's eyes narrowed. "I'll bet you didn't let her touch you, though, did you?"

My cigarette burned unheeded as I stared at him in shock. "What the hell did you just say?" I finally blurted out.

Slowly and methodically, Cap ground out the end of his cigarette into the ashtray until the unburned tobacco fell out in shreds. "I said," he began very slowly and evenly, "you don't let anyone touch you."

I shook my head from side to side in disbelief. "I can't"—I waved my hands before me in negation—"this is just…" I didn't know what to say. I flicked that dead cigarette far out into the street, then ran my hands through my hair, making it stand up higher.

That was it. Enough was enough. I'd had it, and this conversation was over. I unsnapped my seat belt and hopped out of the jeep. "I'll meet you back at the apartment. Thanks for the lesson," I told Cap as I closed the door and started walking. Oh, hell, it was only about a mile back to the apartment. I ran more than that, so this wasn't really a big deal.

I stared blindly at the sidewalk as I mechanically moved my feet. God, how un-fucking-believable, though. What made him even think of saying that? True or not, that was beside the point. What gave him or anyone else the right to discuss whether or not I allowed anyone to touch me? My body. Period, end. There should be no discussion; at least, that's how I saw it.

Cap and his jeep pulled up alongside me. "Get in the jeep, Nina. This is a bad neighborhood. You don't want to walk through here."

"Yeah, well, I know how to handle a gun now. I'll be fine," I shot back at him with a glare. I stopped and quickly lit a cigarette, then kept going. Cap paced me with his jeep.

We traveled that way for a few moments, me walking, him trailing me with the jeep, until finally I stopped and faced him. Cap cut the motor.

"Why do you care?" I asked him across the space between us. "What does it matter, anyway? It's my body, and I decide, not you, not anyone else, what I want and don't want on it, in it, or around it."

I placed a hand on a hip and waited for his answer while Cap stared down into the passenger seat. No answer came.

"Exactly," I muttered. I waved my hand in disgust at the whole exchange, as if that could erase it. His comment and following silence left me angry and gave me added motivation as I stalked off back toward the apartment.

I heard the roar of the jeep as Cap started it up again, and seconds later, Cap caught up with me.

"Nina," he called, "come on. You have to trust somebody, sometime. Please, just get in."

I walked a few more steps and considered. Maybe he had a point, maybe I had to change something. I already knew that I needed something different; maybe this could be the start.

"Okay," I said finally, and went back toward the jeep. I put my hand on the latch. "But," I cautioned, "I won't discuss my sex life with you. It's nobody's business except mine, and it wasn't necessary for you to say that, either."

Cap listened, then nodded. "Fair enough. I should have put that differently, and I won't ask for details, except when I need some pointers."

I let go of the door and was about to step back, when Cap threw a hand up. "I'm just joking, just joking. Come on, let's go home."

I finally opened the door and climbed in. Once I settled in my seat and snapped on the seat belt, Cap pulled forward.

"Nina, I'm just trying to let you know that you're not the only one hurting. Trace hurts over it, too. I mean, she kind of put herself out there for you, and you turned her down. And it's not like you don't want her or anything."

I rolled my eyes and shook my head. "You know what, Cap? She didn't offer. She tried to—never mind, just fucking forget it." I sighed.

"Look," I tried again as the scenery rolled by, "do you really want to give your heart to someone who's fucking everyone in sight? Ever think for a second that's what everyone else does? Fuck her, then forget her?"

I paused, then continued. "Yeah, so she comes on to all of them—and of course they respond. Who wouldn't? I don't want to be one of those, I don't want to hurt her, and," I took a breath, "I'm not going to be another fuckin' notch for her, either."

We rounded the corner of our block, and Cap pulled into a space across the street. He unsnapped his safety belt and lit a new cigarette. "Take one," he offered.

"I've got, thanks." I took one of my own out, but didn't light it. It was just something to hold on to for the moment. Cap smoked quietly, and I sat there with him while we both considered what we'd been talking about.

I cut through the silence. "Don't you think if someone was really into you they wouldn't go after anyone else, especially in front of you, want you to watch, wouldn't play with you like that?"

"Nina, what about you? You did that girl. You didn't seem to have a problem with that. And if it's just sex, then why don't you just go for it?" Cap look genuinely puzzled as he spoke. "Besides, what the hell is it going to hurt? I mean, it's not like you have to worry about getting pregnant or anything." He smirked the last part at me.

"You just don't get it, do you?" I countered, exasperated. "It's not just about sex. Okay, yeah, with Candace at that time, it was sex, but for chrissake, I was fucking drunk. Give me a break. And it was honest, at least. I didn't have to lie to her or pretend shit or try to, to break her will or anything. Dammit, leave me alone already. If I pull out the phone book, you guys have fucked half of it."

I lit that cigarette and took a deep drag. "Just because I don't have to worry about getting fucking pregnant doesn't mean there aren't any fucking rules," I told him, "at least for me. Yeah, I fucked Candace, okay? I fucked her because she was there, and she wanted me to, and Trace dared me to, and you know what? I never do that, never just pick someone up. I actually go out on dates first. So what, I enjoyed it, enjoyed her, so sometimes if we get a chance we hang out and talk or something, because I like her. She was totally up front, she hasn't stopped being that way, and I *like* honesty. That's the way to get me, okay?"

"Whoa, girl." Cap held up his hands. "You're preaching to the choir about just enjoying it, and that's what I'm saying. You should just stop being so damned guarded all the time, let someone in, ya know?" He paused and took a drag on his butt. "Once you and Trace...you know..." and he exhaled, "things'll probably calm right down." His tone was reassuring, but his words proved he didn't understand me at all. Maybe I wasn't saying it right. I thought I was.

I blew out a frustrated breath. "No," I told him flatly. "It's never going to happen, don't you get it? I want it for real. I really, truly love, um, care about her, understand? As long as I'm not involved with anyone, I'm a free agent, but believe me—and it has nothing to do with my own past—if I had an honest-to-goodness real clue that she could even partially be what I need, I wouldn't ever, ever, fuck around, not with anyone."

I took a drag on my butt and blew it out. "Candace would never have happened," I continued, "but I'm not gonna fucking waste my time. Do you get me yet? Someone, someday, is going to be there for me, and I wish, I would love it to be Trace, but if it's not, well, why I should I pretend? Why should I let her pretend to me? Oh, hell." I threw my hands up in confusion and frustration, then undid my seat belt. "Just forget it, man. I'm going inside."

I didn't even know what I was trying to say anymore, and I was tired of trying to understand myself. "I've got to practice, I've got a rehearsal-audition today," I told him as I opened the door and slid out of the car.

Cap undid his belt and got out, double-checking to make sure the alarm was set. "Hey, you've got your own room now, have fun." He smiled at me as he strode to the steps.

We climbed up together in silence, and I tried to clear my mind. I really did have to get myself together. I was hooking up with some people I'd met at the bar a couple of nights before: Stephie and Jeremy. They liked my style, they liked the tunes I spun, and they liked me. We'd see what would happen, if we clicked musically. There was no drummer yet, but we'd work that out, if the first couple of rehearsals gelled in the way I thought they would.

"Nina, you really are a virgin, aren't you?" Cap broke into my thoughts as we approached our door.

I rolled my eyes. "Can we just leave that alone?" I asked, exasperated. I keyed the lock and let us both in, then went right to my closet to get my guitar.

"Yup, thought so," he said mostly to himself. "Not that there's anything wrong with that," he added hastily. "Just that it sorta makes sense of everything else."

I faced him, hands on my hips. "You know, just because I don't let just anyone who wants to fuck actually *fuck* me doesn't mean I don't know what sex is about or feels like," I informed him. I'd had it with this heavy conversation. It was time, more than time, to add a little levity somewhere. "Besides," I added with a grin, "have you ever had anyone do it better than you do it yourself?"

Cap stared at me for a second, then started laughing. "No, I've never experienced that."

"Well, there you go, then," I told him with a smile. "Maybe you're a virgin too."

He guffawed. "That'd be the best line, Nina. I think I'm gonna use it." He laughed again. "That's just too good."

His mood was infectious, and it was such a relief to not feel like I was on the defensive, I joined in.

"Feel free," I offered, still grinning. "I figure I'll probably marry the person who can make it feel that good." I clapped a friendly hand on his shoulder, then went back to my guitar.

"Nina." Cap's tone was serious, so I faced him again. Damn. I really needed to practice.

"I never thought of it like that before. You know, if you can trust someone that much," he said, obviously considering the thought, "you should."

I answered him with the seriousness he deserved. "I already figured that. I'm shooting straight for the heart," I told him somberly, and with that, I went into my room to play guitar.

COLDER

I have heard the story of the garden—
The serpent came and took it all away
I am always sorry in the morning
But right now? Let me slide in—let me stay

"I Fall"—Life Underwater

The audition-rehearsal went well—better than expected, in fact, because we'd left it with three brand-new songs and the beginnings of two more.

I liked Stephie and Jeremy. Stephie, who was a little taller than me and had this lovely angular look, was smart and tough and carried a very artistic picture she'd taken of her boyfriend; she'd designed his Mohawk, and she'd done a nice job. She'd done her own hair, too. It shaded from blond at the top to red to black; it looked like a match tip, and the ends curled under her ears.

Jeremy was the same height as Dee Dee and maybe a little darker, but that's where the similarities ended. He was shaped like a large bear, albeit a large, bass-playing, monster rhythm bear, and he kept his hair clipped as closely to the skin as possible and said he only took his army flak jacket off to sleep—or when his mother wrestled it off him to wash it—whatever came first.

Most importantly, though, we had fun, we had chemistry, and we knew we could make music. We planned to get together again in another few days and start planning some schedules.

I pulled my guitar out of the case, played a few licks, then put it back. I was restless and edgy. A lot had changed between the day before and now. I moved a few things into my new space, tried my guitar out in different areas.

I didn't know what was worse, trying not to remember Samantha at all, which was hard, because she'd given me my first few guitar lessons back when I'd just started playing, and now, boy did I play the shit out of it, or the image from the morning I couldn't get out of my head. Trace and Van. Did she like it? Did she really like him? Why him, if he was going to be so smug about it? Did it matter? Did she care?

Maybe, just maybe, it was me. Maybe it all meant nothing. Maybe I should just go ahead and do my own thing, before someone did their own thing to me. I was so tired of being cute...

I called the club and got one of the owners on the phone. "Hey, Mickey, it's Nina. Who's got the back room tonight?" Hell, if someone else was DJing, I'd go in and back the bar. At least I'd make some money, and in between I could check out the new disc spinner, dance, see if they were any good.

"It's Darrel, but I think he's gonna blow it soon," Mickey told me. "He's been doin' whatever at the booth again." Silence.

"You guys set up the rear lounge yet?" They'd recently bought the adjacent building and were setting it up with both a booth and a stage—capacity 500.

"We're wired for sound, why?" Mickey asked me.

"Let me run a session in the back room?" I asked. "Test the wiring, bin placements, all that sort of thing. That way you don't have to bring me in for a day session."

I could hear the wheels in his head churn. If he let me in tonight and it went badly, he'd gotten the room tested for free. If it went well, more people could fit in the club. The bar staff might be a little shorthanded, but there'd be more money all around—no one would complain too terribly.

"If you get people, you can stay back there. If no one walks in, just give me a rundown on any bugs you find—if any—and you wanna bar back tonight?"

"Yeah, sure. I'll be there in twenty minutes."

I hung up and got dressed fit to kill. I grabbed a stack of my favorite tunes and quickly stopped by the bathroom—had to check my hair.

Cap was right, I thought as I made sure everything was how I wanted it to be. I'd had no problem with Candace. Thinking of her made me smile. She was sharp, sexy, direct. She knew what she wanted—and wasn't afraid of it. I could deal with that. Hell, I should probably learn from that.

Everyone was doing whatever they wanted but me. I was stupid enough to think that caring meant anything, when pretty obviously the only thing that had any meaning was the fuck. No wonder everyone treated me like such a baby—I *was* one.

Not tonight—not anymore.

My hair was perfect, and I looked pretty damn good, if I did say so myself. Okay, I thought as I contemplated myself in the mirror. I had a room to check, and if it was up to me—and it was—I was gonna have that room full and rockin' way before it was time to close. Fuck bar backing tonight. And maybe, just maybe, if the music was good—and it would be—and the mood was right—it definitely should be—I'd invite someone up to the booth to party with me.

Fuck Trace, fuck Van, fuck Cap and Jackie. Fuck everyone who kept treating me like I was some precocious little idiot. Fuck 'em all.

SAVE A PRAYER

Now I'm pretty—do you like me?
Now I'm smarter—do you like me?
Now I'm angry—do you want me?
Do you want to lead me on?

"Lead Me On"—Life Underwater

"Oh, God, Nina, what do you want?" she groaned as we pressed into each other, kissing desperately as we lay entwined together on her bed—shirts off, pants and shoes gone somewhere with the shirts. Don't even ask about the socks; I still don't know.

I slid my tongue deep between her lips and was met by hers. "You know what I want." I broke off and caught a breath before I trailed a line from her collarbone to her jaw. "I want you." I gently bit her throat, then scraped it with my teeth before sucking on the skin. "I want you…I want all of you."

I kissed her lips again, and the sensual fullness of her response, the sincerity of it made me feel faint with rising desire.

"This," she whispered and thrust her body up to mine as she kissed my throat, "this is all I have to give, Nina, please…" Her fingernails ran sharp across my shoulders, and somehow she flipped me onto my back. She ground herself into me and my body responded, my hands on her hips and aching need returning her pressure. Her eyes drove, begging, pleading for understanding, into mine. "This is all I have," she whispered. Her mouth was soft and achingly sweet on mine.

I splayed my hands and ran my fingers down her back, sensuously massaging along the way as I wrapped one of my legs over her hip. One of her hands ran down lightly along the curve of my breast, down my ribs, and past my stomach to my waist, then grabbed my hip, bringing our bodies harder together. The other repeatedly ran across my face and through my hair until, finally, I lifted my chin and broke that soul-searing kiss.

She raised her head and leaned up for a moment on an elbow, and I stared straight into her beautiful gray eyes. "Okay, Trace, you win," I told her huskily. "We'll just give each other what we can."

"You don't know how much I...I want you," she said softly, tracing my face with her fingertips. Slowly, softly, she leaned in to kiss me again, and I closed my eyes to the feel of her lips pressing blatantly carnal kisses down my chest and stomach toward my...

No, this wasn't a dream, this wasn't even a stroke-fantasy, although it seems like it might have been a good one. This was really, truly happening.

By late August, Candace had returned to Merry Olde England, and after a good-bye that was harder than I really let myself feel, I'd thrown myself into my work and my music: the band was going great guns, and although we'd been through two drummers already and were searching for a third—I swear, I'll just never know what it is with drummers—we'd started to write a couple of songs and were really getting to know each other, bond, and have fun.

"All right, I've got to split in a few, I've got dinner plans," I announced to Jeremy and Stephie as the last notes of our latest tune died down in the air around us.

Crunch sounded through the room as Jeremy unplugged his bass, along with the soft thud of Stephie putting the microphone back on its stand.

I shut down my amp and unplugged my guitar, carefully setting it in a stand, then began to disassemble my wires and pedal effects. I shoved the pedals into my bag and stood to coil my patch cord.

Jeremy came over, bass slung in its bag over his back. "Gonna ravish some poor innocent?" he asked me with a sly grin.

"Yeah, right," Stephie came over and interjected, punching my arm lightly, "like Nina ever has to work for it."

"Hey, hey, hey!" I faced them both, placing the now-coiled cord in with my effects. "I take offense to that!" I joked, and picked up my guitar to zip it in the gig bag. "I work my ass off in here!" and gave a little wiggle to emphasize my point.

"Yeah, like that's not part of the attraction," Jeremy answered, staring pointedly.

All right, maybe I shouldn't have done that. "Cut it out, man."

"You're such a jerk sometimes," Stephie reprimanded, and smacked the back of his head.

"Ow! Hey! Ya didn't have to go and do that!" he protested, rubbing his scalp vigorously.

"And you know, it's not like any of them are innocent anyway," Stephie informed him, pointing to the small window in the studio door.

He and I both peeked out and saw some people out there, trying to see in.

"That's the next band, hoping we're done," I hazarded, shrugging my shoulders.

"Yeah, that's the next band," Jeremy agreed.

Stephie rolled her eyes at our collective denseness, and I grinned and shook my head in response, then returned to my equipment.

I slung my bags with their effects, cables, and guitar strap over one shoulder, hoisted my guitar over the other, and we all reached for the door.

"Right," Stephie finally said sarcastically, "that's why they don't have any instruments." She opened the door and made a sweeping gesture out into the hall.

Once out of the studio, it was pretty obvious that Stephie had a point. It was three, no, four girls, um, young women, and she was right—not an instrument in sight.

"Oh, hey, you girls a singing group?" Jeremy stopped to ask one of them amiably, flexing his shoulders.

Stephie and I shared a look and kept walking toward the store at the end of the hallway where the exit was, nodding polite hellos as we passed.

"Yeah, we're working on a single," one of the girls answered, laughing, and another giggled with her. Stephie and I slipped through the exit and down the stairs that led to the store front.

"Think he forgot to tie a shoelace or something?" Stephie asked in the companionable silence as we descended.

I snorted a laugh. "No, but how much do you want to bet he ends up catching one?" I countered as I stepped carefully down—I didn't want to trip and hurt my guitar. "Those lines of his are pretty awful," I commented as I waited for her.

Stephie rolled her eyes again. "God, he can be such a jerk!"

I smiled but said nothing as we walked through the repair shop and picked our way through the various disconnected and disassembled instruments that littered the area. What was there to say? That pretty much described everyone, anyway.

A bell tinkled as we entered the store and headed to the register.

"Hi, Stephie, hi, Nina," said the long-haired young man behind the counter. He gave us each a big smile, but his eyes rested on Stephie.

"Hi, John." I smiled back, watching his eyes on Stephie, and dug into my pocket for my money.

"Hi." Stephie flushed and made a big production out of digging into her bag for her wallet. I grinned at her but quickly hid it. I knew she liked him, and I was pretty sure he liked her, too.

John waited patiently as I found my money and put it on the counter.

"Stephie, we want the same time next week?" I asked as she found her wallet.

"Yeah, let's do that. Hey, do you have the jerk's money?" she asked with a smile.

"I don't have jerk money," I smiled back, almost laughing.

The bell tinkled again as Jeremy stumbled into the store. "Can you believe it?" he asked loudly. "They're," and he pointed with his thumb over his shoulder, "doing a single for DJ Nina to play on Dominion nights. That's just unfucking believable."

It was my turn to blush. "Got your share?" I asked him and looked down at the money under my hands.

Since I'd done the sound check in the new back room at the club, well, believe me when I tell you I blew it out; it was now mine. So, Darrel and I both worked DJing Saturday nights; he was in the old room, and I had the new one. And, yeah, Saturday was Dominion night in my room—that was what everyone who attended called it, anyway, in tribute to that night with Candace. In honor of that, I occasionally entertained company in the booth. Everything has a consequence, right?

"Oh, yeah, here you go," Jeremy answered quickly, handing his money over to John. "Are we booked for next week?"

"We're done, we're good," Stephie answered him quickly and rushed out of the store and into the street.

"Oh yeah, yeah, we're all set." I smiled. "See you next week, John." I readjusted the strap of my guitar and stepped to the door.

"Cool beans, dude," John answered. "Tell Stephie I said bye," he called to my back, the jerk, um, Jeremy, behind me.

"Yup," he answered, and we were out the door and on the sidewalk, the still-warm air smacking our skin in the early twilight. Stephie waited for us, smoking a cigarette and enjoying the weather.

"That was a pretty good rehearsal, guys. What did you think?" I asked, looking at each of them and lighting a cigarette of my own.

Stephie blew a few smoke rings just to prove she could, then grinned back at me. "We're doing fine, we're getting stuff down!"

Jeremy shrugged a shoulder under his gig bag. "We're really starting to groove. If we could just find a drummer..." He trailed off, frowning.

Stephie and I shook our heads in chagrined agreement. Where the hell were we going to find one, anyway? Ah, well. I had the next few days to ponder that and discuss it with the two of them as ideas came and went. For now, though, I had plans, and none of them included a drummer.

Despite the fact that Candace had left a few weeks ago, I still rarely spent time at the apartment. I just couldn't deal with anybody except for my brother and the band, especially after the last time I'd spoken with Trace. And I either made sure I was home at a time when everyone was out, or staying somewhere else—either visiting my family or jamming all night at Stephie's with Jeremy: composing, rehearsing, and making ourselves sick on ice cream. Yeah, we were musicians that didn't do drugs; sue me.

Maybe it was because of my absence that Cap decided we needed a "roommate party." He'd very assiduously combed through all of our schedules and picked the one night everyone happened to be off, then asked us all to meet him at Dock Street, another popular bar on Bay Street. The invite was an open one. Bring anyone—siblings, friends, significant others, and outside of rehearsal, well, that was all I had to do that night. I'd already invited my brother Nicky—I mean Nico. He would meet me there later.

I was suddenly inspired. "Hey, do you guys want to come with me? I mean, to Dock Street?" I asked Stephie and Jeremy. "It's my roommates and their friends, and you guys haven't met my brother yet—he'll be there. What do you say? Wanna go?" I asked in a rush. "I mean, if you guys don't have stuff to do," I added awkwardly. This would be the first time we had all hung out together—outside of rehearsal, I mean.

"Sounds good to me." Jeremy smiled. "You up for it, Stephie?"

Stephie pursed her lips and considered. "Trace gonna be there?" she asked me in an undertone.

As Stephie and I had become better friends, we discussed a lot of things, and of course, we discussed the weird mess that was our lives. I had confided in her about the strange relationship that Trace and I had and that I was trying to avoid, and yeah, Trace *would* be there, and I hadn't really seen her in a while.

"Yeah," I answered. "I'm a little nervous about that."

Stephie nodded. "I'm there, then. You need backup." She grinned at me.

"Thanks." I grinned back in relief.

"Hey, no worries, that's what friends do, right?" She punched my shoulder lightly.

"Yeah, we're your backup," Jeremy confirmed, and punched the other arm, quite a bit harder than Stephie had.

"Ow," I groaned, rubbing the spot out. That really had hurt. "Jerk!" I scowled at him. "I'm a girl, not your bass." Then I elbowed him in the ribs, 'cause that was all I could reach; he was darn tall, after all.

"I am so sorry." He shook his head in self-recrimination. "I'm really sorry, I didn't mean—hey!"

Stephie had whapped the back of his head again. "From now on, you're the Jerkster, Jerkster," she told him, then whapped him again for good measure.

Jeremy, um, I mean, the Jerkster, kept rubbing his head. "Fine, fine, just stop hitting me," he agreed, scowling as he tried to heal himself with his fingertips. "We should make you the drummer, you like to hit so much."

She and I both laughed, and we walked to Dock Street.

Cap had managed to get three tables pulled together, and we all sat around laughing, eating, and drinking, and for the first time in ages, I was having fun with my roommates. Jackie was being hysterically funny, and even Trace, who'd shown up with Van, was being nice for once.

I sat with Nico, Stephie, and the newly christened Jerkster, kidding around, sort of having our own party within the party until the larger conversation caught up with us.

"That's it for me, I've had it for the night," Nico announced, pushing away from the table and rubbing his stomach.

I dug into my pockets and pulled out my keys. "Here you go, Nico," I tossed them at him, "you know where my room is." He was staying at my place tonight since we were drinking and I didn't want him to drive. Since I lived only two blocks away, this was not a problem.

"Yeah, I didn't wear my drinking clothes," he joked with me, referring to those parties all that time ago and the guy who always wore a plastic garbage bag just in case he puked.

I laughed with him.

Somebody said something, I don't remember what, and I quipped back to the table at large.

"Shut up, Nina!" Trace called jokingly down the table.

"Why don't you make me?" I joked back and returned to my conversation. Come on, now, I had every right to say stuff, too.

In what seemed like half a second, Trace came over and yanked my chair out. Momentarily off balance, I raised my arms trying to get my bearings, and, in a flash, Trace slipped around, threw a leg over mine, and stood before me, straddling my legs.

I looked up into her eyes, unreadable in the dim light, and kept my face expressionless.

"I think you should shut up," she warned me, her voice a deadly quiet. The bar had gone silent around us, and I could feel everyone's eyes on us in the ringing emptiness.

"Yeah?" I asked insolently, tilting my head in challenge. "I think you should make me." There was no way I was going to let Trace intimidate me, especially not in front of my brother or my band.

We watched each other a moment, no quarter on either side, then suddenly her hands were on my shoulders, her lips were on mine, and her tongue slid deeply into my mouth; and while my brain was stunned, I gave back as good as I got. This was war.

We battled in that sensuous way for however long until we mutually declared temporary detente. Trace lifted her head from mine, her hands still on my shoulders.

"Got anything else to say?" she asked, a triumphant laugh in her voice.

"Yeah, actually." I curled my lip at her. "That the best you got?"

Good. Now she was shocked, and I grabbed her hips, bringing her down firmly onto my lap. Don't ever dismiss the notion of Dutch courage, because that must have been what was fueling me now. Well, that and the fact that I absolutely refused to lose face.

Releasing one side, I touched her face and gently brought it to mine. I looked into her eyes and whispered, "I don't think you can handle me," then kissed her softly, my lips and tongue an easy glide against hers. Her fingers slipped from my shoulders to run through my hair as she responded to me, her stomach pressing into my ribs.

"Hey, get a room!" someone called out, probably Cap, I thought, and various other catcalls followed. Again Trace lifted her mouth from mine, and she carefully stood up directly in front of me, sliding her body not half an inch from my nose. It would only have taken the slightest movement for me to catch her between my teeth.

"Do you wanna take this outside?" she asked me, her voice all throaty challenge.

Her smile was ironic, but the silent gray of her eyes had deepened, and they searched mine with an intensity that I knew was no joke. But still…that smile…and the message everyone got…I knew how to play this.

"Nico, take my guitar home?" I asked him, and didn't even glance his way when he agreed.

When I stood I deliberately gripped her hips for leverage and let my breasts skim lightly against her on the way up. The sharp hiss of her breath as I did it made me smile. Finally, we were eye to eye, and I dropped my hands.

"Fine, then."

She neatly stepped out from our almost-embrace and made way for me, and I strode to the door, stopping only when I got there. I faced her, mutely waiting. This was the last chance to back out and down, and the perfect opportunity for either of us to crush the other in front of everyone. Forget points; we're talking burning scorecards here.

Everyone in that room must have known this could go only one of two ways: we could either punch the fuck out of each other or fuck.

If the room had been quiet before, it was now graveyard silent. It seemed like every eye was upon us as Trace sauntered over, all liquid curves and predatory grace. I held out a hand for the last few steps, and when she grasped it, she reached up with her free one and drew me in for a bloody, searing kiss.

This time, the room erupted with cheers, and when we broke off that kiss, I glanced around to see everyone on their feet, even Nico, Stephie, and Jerkster. Nico's expression was inscrutable, Stephie gave me a small grin, and Jerkster, well, he held his beer up in a congratulatory toast.

The sharp sound of glass being struck rang out across the crowd, and we all saw Cap putting down the cutlery he had just used to ring his glass with.

"Nina, Trace," he began, his tone somber, but his eyes twinkling, "go. Go and either discover that it's destiny or..." and he paused dramatically, then grinned at the rest of the room before focusing on us again, "get it over with, so the rest of us can get some peace!"

Everyone laughed, and somewhere, almost under the table, I heard Van's muffled, "Hear, hear!"

Trace rolled her eyes and turned away, ready to leave, but I couldn't just let it go yet. "Fuck you!" I mouthed to him with a slight grin, then followed Trace to the door.

"Ah, ah!" I heard Cap call out to our backs as we made our way outside. "That's not who you're fucking!"

Not even half a step past the door, Trace pounced. It was all tongues and hands, aching, grinding need and nipples hard enough to hurt—and that was the way back home. My next conscious moment, I found myself in Trace's bed, and as her lips and tongue tortured me on their way to the waistband of my button-fly jeans, I groaned when she reached the top one.

"God, I want you, Nina," she stopped a moment to tell me, and her hand splayed out against my belly. She ripped the first button open with her teeth. "I want you so fucking bad," she whispered into that first opening. Then one by one, she released the rest of the brass buttons— her lips, teeth, and tongue sending waves of sensation that crashed through me.

When Trace opened the last button and discovered that I wore no underwear, she planted heated kisses at the V where the fly ended. I squirmed lightly under her, and as she reached to jerk the jeans off, I sat up and blindly reached for her face, pulling her up for another deep kiss. We lay back down together, and while her hands continued to push my jeans off, my hands reached for her waist to help her remove hers.

Between the pushing and the pulling we somehow finally managed to get everything removed, and as I lay between her legs, I gently stroked the high sharp planes of her cheeks, the luxurious length of her neck, and the sharp cut of her shoulders. She was so achingly beautiful, I wanted to cry from the pain of it, because I was touching her skin and I wanted to touch her heart.

Some of this must have translated through from my fingertips to her, because that's when she asked me what I wanted, and as I closed my eyes and enjoyed the trail of fire that Trace blazed down me, an image of sunset over the desert formed behind my eyes.

Her lips came softly to the top junction between my leg, and my desire and I exhaled a long, low breath as she pressed her lips first to one side, then the other.

My whole body ached with a deep, wrenching need, and I wanted this—I wanted Trace, and here she was and I was, together, in this intimate space, and I certainly thought that I was ready when she pressed her lips against that desperate ache. I groaned and arched my back a bit as her tongue slipped between my folds and teased my clit lightly.

With a slight tilt of her jaw, Trace stroked me with her lower lip from right below my opening to the base of my clit, and she pulled her head back a moment before bringing it back down and sucking my clit between her lips, hard.

That felt really nice, truly, but somehow not as intense as the anticipation had been. Maybe it was positional, so I sat up on my elbows and flexed my legs, raising my knees. That did help somewhat, and Trace wrapped her arms around my thighs, using her hands to spread me as her hair draped over my legs. I had a flash of memory—of the last time I'd been in that room, of the last time I'd seen her over the edge of that bed.

Van. Fucking Van. Mother. Fucking. Van. I shoved that thought down as hard as I could.

Oh, but this wasn't working, and as much as I knew that I should just relax and enjoy this, and I really, really wanted, no, I *needed* to get off, I was slipping out of that desire-induced haze and feeling less and less physically, and more and more acutely conscious of the blue sheets curled under me and how quiet the room was, of the light coming through the window to tell me the sun was coming up, and of the fact that I was naked with a beautiful woman's head between my thighs, lips riding my pussy, and I was feeling absolutely nothing, not physically, not emotionally—just a dull gray weight that seemed to spread through my chest. I knew two things: I was the desert, and the desert was cold.

Finally, I reached down and gently lifted Trace's face away from me. "Trace..." I spoke into the silence that filled the early morning air.

Her gray eyes filled with concern as they met mine. "Are you okay? Something wrong? I really want to..." She trailed off as I shook my head negatively.

Yeah, something was wrong, probably with me and my retarded body, I thought wryly to myself, but I was careful to keep both my expression and my voice gentle, because her expression was so vulnerable, so childlike. I didn't want to hurt her. "No, I'm fine." I smiled. "Just, come here," I invited her, indicating that she lie either on top of or next to me.

Trace slid up my body and settled next to me, one leg still between mine. I put my arms around her and cradled her head to my shoulder, then leaned back against the pillows. We snuggled for a moment, and I kissed her forehead. All I could think of was Van fucking her.

She raised her eyes to mine a moment, then shifted her hips so that she lay between my legs again. Trace wrapped her arms around my ribs and kissed my chest, over my heart. "I really want to make you come," she murmured, pressing her lips against me again.

I ran my fingers through her hair and lovingly stroked her shoulder. "It's okay, don't worry about it."

She slid a hand down and cupped my pussy. "Well, what if we..." she asked me with a sexy grin as she began to press her palm against me.

I put my hand over hers to still it. "It's not, it's just..." I pulled her in for a kiss, hoping to distract her or something, I'm not sure what. We broke for a moment.

"I think I drank too much," I lied. "Just stay with me."

I thought of all the girls I'd had and the way they made me feel. I'd really, really want to, then whammo! Nothing. But I always made sure they came. Maybe, just maybe, the difference here was that Trace was drunk. I'd wanted this so much, but I'd wanted it clear and memorable,

not accompanied by a headache and a hangover. But right now, it wasn't
Trace's fault, no matter what. For the record, I have to say that from the
moment Trace had grabbed my chair, I was stone-cold sober.

"C'mere." I smiled at her and pulled her up over me so that her
legs tangled with mine. "Now let's," I licked her neck and flipped her
over, "just not worry about this…" And I lightly nipped and licked a
path down her chest as our hips ground against each other.

Frankly, Trace was way too drunk, and while it became an
incredibly sensual make-out session (and I think I still have scars from
it on my back—somewhere), eventually, every caress became slower,
and her eyes stayed shut a bit longer. Finally, she snuggled under me
and fell asleep, but not before turning one last time. She nuzzled the
space between my breasts.

"You've got perfect breasts," she breathed with sleepy warmth
against my nipple before she pulled it lightly between her lips, teasing
the peak with her tongue.

"Thank you," I whispered, and kissed her ear. "Shush now…
sleep," I said, stroking her shoulders and carefully removing myself
from her kiss. Her lips were soft on my breast once more, then, with a
little sigh, she rolled over, tucking her body into mine.

We lay like that for a while and I listened to her breathe, the
cadence soft and easy as it always was when she slept in my arms.
I slowed my own breath and tried to sleep, but I was now overtired,
overwired, and overwrought.

Finally, when I knew that Trace was fully asleep, I left my arm
under her neck as I rolled onto my back, tucking her against my side so
she wouldn't get cold.

This wasn't the first time I'd wanted, really wanted, sex, but
somewhere, somehow, I'd lost the desire. It was frustrating, touching
and not being able to be touched, and although I usually was able to
avoid the awkwardness, there were times, like tonight, where if Trace
had been more sober, it would have just gotten stressful. I mean,
what person, except for the occasional callous asshole, isn't going to
have their feelings hurt if the person who just made them come can't
reciprocate? I know it would bother me if I was on the other end. But I
couldn't fake it, either, so I just avoided it altogether when I could and
made it up to myself later.

But it didn't make sense. I mean it couldn't be biological, because,
hell, on occasions, things did work—okay, not as well as they worked

by myself, but still, both those things proved that it had to be something other than physical. Not that technique doesn't count, of course, but still...

Candace was gone, and even though we'd promised to keep in touch, we weren't anything more than friends. Trace was right here, and even though it could have been so much more, it was never going to be. Dammit. Had we both been sober this could have potentially been something amazingly beautiful. And no matter who it was with, if I wasn't doing it for myself, I wasn't getting off. Not that I didn't enjoy and get really turned on, because I did, but it was like no matter what anyone did, they just couldn't touch me.

And if it wasn't them—and I didn't think it was—then it was definitely me. And if it wasn't biological, then maybe it was something else. Maybe Trace couldn't deal with being gay—maybe she needed to get drunk and play all these games just to get to a place where she didn't feel so afraid. Oh, hell, maybe I just had to get my head together; maybe I was just coming (no pun intended) from a different place. If it hadn't been for the band, I wouldn't have done anything even remotely beneficial for myself for the last several weeks. I'd been drinking too much, I'd been fucking around too much, and nothing felt good. I was disgusted with myself. Okay, then. I had made a decision.

I sighed and quietly slipped my arm out from under Trace and got out of bed, careful to tuck the blankets around her. She might be disappointed, but she wouldn't be terribly surprised if I wasn't there when she woke. Plenty of times I'd left her place early to go for a run before she opened her eyes. Usually, she'd meet me later upstairs and we'd eat together. But not this morning, I thought with slight regret as I dressed in the early morning light.

Maybe it was all in my head, and maybe it was my environment. Maybe there was nothing wrong at all, and this was just not the right place for me. Well, it wouldn't be the first time, I thought wryly.

I watched Trace sleep for a long moment, her lips a perfect bruise in her pale face, soft and peaceful in the morning sun.

Moving carefully so as not to disturb her, I leaned over and kissed them. Trace stirred. "Love you, Nina," she mumbled sleepily and kissed me in return, then settled back into sleep.

Stunned, I merely stood and stared a moment. "Love you too, Trace," I finally whispered back and noticed that my voice sounded thick and harsh. Dammit. I was crying. About Trace. Again. I let the tears fall as I padded to the door, and as I stood in the frame, I looked back at her sleeping form.

"Bye," I whispered in that same choked voice, and I walked out, quietly closing the door behind me and careful not to make any noise as I exited her apartment.

I had come to two conclusions: I had to leave. I just really couldn't take it anymore—not Trace, not Jackie, not even Cap, even though he was well meaning when he wasn't horny. I had to get away from all of these places and these people and find out who I was, because I didn't like the person I was being.

And the other thing? I wasn't going to even so much as kiss another human being unless the words right before it were "I love you."

That was it. No heavy making out, no crazy lines and wild sex with what amounted to friendly strangers. Dates. I was going on dates like a normal person, and if I liked them, there'd be another, and if there wasn't, well, hopefully I would have spent time with someone interesting. I'd know the right person when I met them, I figured as I walked through the corridor.

Instead of climbing the stairs to my apartment, I let my feet lead me down. I meant it. I was going to Jerry's Pancake Place to pick up the newspaper and check out the adverts for, well, if not an apartment, then at least a room.

I fumbled in a pocket and found my cigarettes, then lit one as I went through the door, closing it behind me. *What if there isn't anyone for you*, my brain asked me; *what if you end up alone?*

I pondered that possibility as I trudged down the block I usually ran down. The answer was simple. There was a difference between lonely and alone, and if I never met "my match," well, I liked my own company well enough. And with all the music and art I had to constantly work on, I'd never have time to be lonely.

Okay, my brain countered, *what about sex? What about it?* I asked back. I mean, it's not as if I enjoyed it too much. Okay, I loved the thrill of the chase and enjoyed nothing better than reveling in the ability to create all those delicious gasps and moans, feeling when a woman was so ready to—okay. Stop there. Yes, I enjoyed that when it was happening, but still, it left me empty. Besides, I told my brain as we entered Jerry's Pancake Place, it's not as if I didn't still have my favorite sexual partner—and I had never let myself down.

No, we, meaning my brain and I, were going to get out of there, focus on art and music and the things that were important. It would be fuckin' nice if I took some time somewhere and went to my favorite comic book store, Universe, and picked up the *Love and Rockets* that I had fallen so far behind in. It was time to get some clarity. Fuck it. I was hungry, and after paying for the paper, I sat down and ordered breakfast—cream of wheat with a soft-boiled egg on the side.

If I was never going to feel something, that special pull, then I wasn't going to settle for something else, either, I thought as I spread the classifieds before me. I wasn't going to waste my life pining for things that wouldn't happen, and I was going to take some responsibility for who I wanted to be—someone honest and real. If I wasn't going to settle for less in myself, I wouldn't settle for less in someone else, either.

I circled a couple of likely candidates for a place as my food arrived, and as I ate in silence, I studied the want ads, too. Oh, hell, maybe I'd just change everything while I was at it. Why not, right?

I found a few things that seemed likely. As soon as I was done with eating, I would go to my apartment, shower, dress, and wake Nico. Maybe he'd look at a few of these places with me, I thought; in fact, maybe we could do that, then visit our parents and baby sister for a little while. Heck, now that we were finally all talking to one another again, it might even be nice.

I smiled as I got myself together and went to the counter to pay. I counted my change and, paper clutched under my arm, took a moment to just feel the air around me when I stepped back outside. Yep, I agreed as I smiled back to the brightly shining sun, today's a brand-new day.

JUST ADD WATER

Somebody tell me where to find the things I had before
I never asked for nothing much but now I'm needing more
Than a slap on the back or a kick in the teeth
and a look that says that I should go
Now I'm dressing in black and I'm dragging my feet
and I feel like I've got nothing to show

"Just Add Water"—Life Underwater

Nico did come along with me to check out a couple of places, though he didn't say much. He would look around and nod judiciously. I agreed.

Nothing knocked me out either until I finally found it—a huge one-room studio not too far from High Rock Park, a nature preserve right in the middle of Staten Island. It wasn't right off the park, but only a few blocks away—perfect for my morning runs—while the yard in the back had plenty of room to work out in—it was time to revisit my martial arts training. Heck, the room was large, especially compared to the closet I'd lived in.

In short it was perfect, and except for the excited sparkle in his eyes, Nico and I managed to contain our excitement while I worked out the rent details with the landlord, Mr. Rabbitz—the place would cost less than the space with my roommates.

I handed over the money and got my keys.

"Where to now?" Nico asked as we got into the van.

I had lots to do and lots to think about, but first— "Let's make a quick stop at the hardware store?"

"Done, chief." Nico smiled at me. "Dude, you've got some beautiful space in there. What are you going to do with all that room? And did you check out that incredible light?"

"Oh, yeah! I think I'm gonna…" and we discussed the possibilities on the way to the store.

"This is for you," I told him as we settled back into the van, "'cause if my mama is your mama, then *mi casa es su casa*." I handed him a copy of my new key on a red carabiner key chain.

Nico's eyes went wide with surprise, then he grinned. "I'm so glad your mama is my mama. Sperm to worm?"

"You know it. Womb to tomb, bro, womb to tomb."

I celebrated my twenty-first birthday by taking a single trip with Nico's van to get all of my stuff—clothing, books, and instruments— and another trip to Jerry's Pancake Place for fuel and to beg for a bunch of old milk crates. Sunlight streamed in on two sides of my room most of the day, and, using crates for book shelves, I had two completely separate areas—one for my bed, the first one I'd ever bought. It might have been cheap, but it was new, clean, and mine, all mine.

I kept my guitar in a stand right next to it, while a trunk at the foot of it held my notebooks, my letters, everything important to me, such as postcards from Samantha before we'd lost touch, my yearbooks, things like that.

The rest of the area, separated by a bookcase I'd created out of the milk crates, housed my equipment and my art supplies, while a nice-sized closet contained all of my clothes.

Mr. Rabbitz, an older bachelor, shared the house with his nephew. At one point, the house had been a funeral parlor, so it had two kitchens, living rooms, libraries, one on top of the other, with a small barn in the back that had been converted into a garage with a loft on top. While both my "room" (which was on the second floor and directly above the library) and the loft were big enough to have the entire band over with equipment for practice, the loft over the barn was almost four times the size and would make a great complete living space. It needed fixing up, but as soon as I had the cash, I was going to inquire about maybe renting that part and doing the repairs. Hey, I'm a lesbian—I know how to use a hammer!

But since Christmas had come and gone a bare month before, my cash supply was a little lower than I normally liked. I'd started working a new job right before the holidays, because I really needed to just get away from Staten Island and the whole gang. Yeah, I maintained my DJing status most Friday and Saturday nights at the Red Spot, but I was getting sick of the whole scene and trying to slow it down. However, the more coldly polite I got, the more persistent everyone became.

I got offers to do private parties, including a few great gigs at NYU's legendary Fiji House, with their very well-deserved and many-times-over earned reputation as the all-time best-time party house around—when a Fiji party gets louder than it ought, the mayor knocks on the door in his bathrobe.

Stephie and Jerkster came with me to one of them so we could throw in a little "unplugged" performance—test the water, so to speak. After, we decided to grab a bite and walk around the Village, to enjoy the twenty-four-hour surround-sound scene.

Buddies that they were, they figured it was time I saw a gay bar that wasn't the depressing dive on Staten Island. Oh, hell, maybe what I needed now was to be more heavily involved in gay culture or—more specifically—lesbian culture.

The more I thought about it, the more sense it made. Maybe part of the problem was that I was inundated with straight messages, on every level. Besides, part of my new rule was "Don't mess with straight chicks." Yeah, they seemed to like me, but they were nuts (um, Trace, remember?).

Anyhow, I'd walked into the bar with the band, had a cranberry and orange drink (I'd already had some alcohol—I didn't want to get wasted, at all), and looked around. Crowded—and way after midnight, too. One bartender in the front. One bar and bartender in the back. One bouncer by the door. No waitress—anywhere. They needed help, in my humble opinion. Hmm…

The bouncer was a big, and I mean big, woman. She was at least 5' intimidating 10". The arms crossed against her chest, spiky haircut, and the set, straight line of her mouth didn't do anything to add warmth to her, and the scowl she wore as I approached wasn't encouraging, but hey, what the hell, right?

"Hi there, I'm Nina," I said, and held out my hand with a smile, "and you are?"

Her scowl deepened and her arms flexed before she uncrossed them to shake my hand. "Jen," she growled at me finally. "Whattayawant?"

"Nice to meet you, Jen." I smiled even wider as I shook her hand. Okay, this wasn't someone who believed in social niceties. I took a breath. Straight to the point, then.

"You guys are really busy tonight," I observed, and Jen glanced around the bar before nodding in agreement. "Looks like you can use some help."

Jen squinted at me, a survey that went from my hair to my boots and back again. "Yeah, and...?" she asked helpfully, and crossed her arms over her chest again.

"I can help," I stated simply and shrugged nonchalantly. All right, I'd put it out there; guess I'd see, right?

The worst that could happen was nothing, and since nothing happens without anyone's help anyway, I'd wouldn't lose anything—unless that deepening groove between Jen's brows meant she was getting ready to toss me through the window. I'd deal with that too, if it came to it, but she'd have to catch me first—and I hadn't been caught yet.

Still, I watched her face as I waited for an answer. Man, if those eyebrows came any closer, they were gonna stay that way forever, I thought as I calmly met and withstood Jen's glare.

Finally, she nodded. "You," she pointed at me, "wait here." She craned her head around to shout over the people sitting at the bar. "Hey! Dee! C'mere a sec!" Jen crossed her arms still again and favored me with her grim expression. "Let's see what the manager says."

Stephie and Jerkster had stepped away from the bar, and I mouthed "dunno" and shrugged at them while we waited in silence. When Jen narrowed her beady focus on Jerkster, I could swear I heard him yipe.

"I'm, uh, gonna find a bathroom, uh, yeah, gotta go," he muttered behind me, then slipped and squeezed away through the press.

"Chicken!" Stephie hissed at his retreating form. I glanced over at Stephie, and we grinned at each other for a moment before Stephie looked suddenly stricken.

"Ah shit!" she exclaimed in an undertone, peering after the trail Jerkster had left behind.

"What?" I asked in a stage whisper. The Lady Grim was still staring at us, after all.

Stephie leaned over to whisper in my ear. "He's got the bottle!"

"Shit!" I exclaimed in a low tone. Shit was right. Drinks were a little pricey there, so we'd snuck in a bottle of plum wine (what can I say, it's a guilty pleasure of mine—and it was a gift from the head of Fiji House), and after buying a beer apiece and drinking it, we'd take turns going into the bathroom and filling the beer bottles with wine—well, at least before I'd switched to "just juice."

I'd never done anything like that before, but Stephie and Jerkster had, and it seemed like a good idea at the time. Okay, I'd let Stephie drink my beer and gone straight for the wine; I'm just not a beer fan, well, except for the occasional Guinness. Besides, I wasn't worried about germs—alcohol killed them.

But still, there were two things wrong with this scenario. First, if we got caught, we were out of there. Second, since Jerkster had the bottle, it could end up empty, he would end up stupid, and we would end up caught. This would end any chance I had of ever coming here again, forget about getting a job. Oh, and a drunk Jerkster was very difficult to guide; he was heavy!

"Go get him!" I hissed, hoping that Granite Sides wouldn't hear us over the din. Judging from what I could see of her personality, I figured she'd think we were just two stupid kids having an argument.

"I'm on it!" Stephie agreed, and off she elbowed through the crowd.

Jen's eyebrows touched as she watched me, and I answered her gaze nonchalantly, standing as comfortably as I could.

For a moment, I felt like I was back in high school with all those nuns and tried to mentally picture Jen in a habit. I shook my head. Nope, didn't work for me; those muscles would never fit through the sleeves. And she didn't scare me—not the way the nuns did, anyway. They'd had a direct connection to God; all Jen had was that scowl. And her size. And those arms. Okay, so she was scary. Never mind.

Finally through the madding crowd eased a figure I thought at first I recognized; then, two seconds later, I did.

"*Liebchen!*" exclaimed Dee Dee, waving her ever-present bar rag before tucking it into her waistband so she could scoop me up into an embrace and kiss each side of my face. "Where have you been?"

I returned Dee Dee's greeting with a hug and a quick kiss of my own, very glad to see her. She'd left the Red Spot a while before I did, which was part of what made the job not so fun anymore; she was not only cool, but also the only other female who'd worked there who wasn't a waitress.

I attempted to explain over her repeated exclamations.

"Ah, Dee, this girl," and Jen said it with such disdain I wondered for a second what I'd done to piss her off, "here wants to know if—" Jen continued officiously, but Dee Dee waved her off, put an arm around my shoulders, and faced her.

"No, no, Jen, this gorgeous creature is none other than Nina the DJ. *Und* she can have whatever she likes. What would you like, Nina?" Dee Dee asked. "I am not just *bierwert*—barkeeper—here, I am the manager!" She beamed at me, her eyes sparkling. I guess it had been longer than I thought since we'd spoken, because her accent hit my ears freshly and made me smile. She'd been like that at the Red Spot—the happier she was, the stronger her accent. Cool.

"Hey, that's great! That's truly terrific!" I congratulated because I truly meant it. I took a breath. Might as well just get to it.

"I was really wondering if—" I began, but Ham Hands interrupted me.

"The kid wants a job, Dee Dee," she told her in a loud, bored voice. She focused her attention narrowly on me and said, "Hey, are you even old enough to be here? Let me see your ID."

I reached for my jacket pocket, but Dee Dee placed a restraining hand on mine. I had only recently reached legal majority, but no one at the Red Spot, or any other place I hung out or worked, had cared—or even noticed.

"Now, Jen, that's not necessary," Dee Dee scolded. "I haf told you, this is DJ Nina. We worked together. But I'm sorry, Nina," she said with true regret, "we don't have a cabaret license, *und* so a DJ is not possible at this time." She put a warm hand on my shoulder, and her voice went from regret to concern.

"But are you okay? Do you need any help, can I gif you some money or anything?" she asked me, reaching into her back pocket and pulling out quite a cash stash.

"No, no, I'm fine. I don't need any money," I said, embarrassed, waving her hands away, "but it looks like you could use a waitress. What do you say?"

Dee Dee grinned at me. "You were always a smart girl, Nina. Smart and proud. With that face, you'll make great tips!" she enthused, and pinched my cheek. "Done, then! *Und* when it's quiet, you'll work with me on the bar—I'll teach you everything I know!" she announced, and promptly hugged me again.

"Oh, Nina, we'll have such fun working together, I know it!" she said, and impetuously crushed me to her. I murmured some sort of agreement; I don't know what because I couldn't breathe. Finally she released me and cast her eyes on Jen while I surreptitiously restarted my deflated lungs and fixed my hair. As far as I could tell, they were still functional.

"You'll get the paperwork, Jen," she asked her, "and introduce Nina around? Nina," she said, "come tomorrow afternoon at four, and we'll start from there, okay?" She stroked my shoulder and I nodded in agreement.

"That's great, thanks," I answered, and could feel my smile stretch so wide my face hurt. Cool. A steady job that got me off Staten Island and away from everyone I didn't want to deal with anymore. DJing was great, but I didn't want to rely on it as my only source of income, and, as much fun as it could be, I was starting to get frustrated, too. I wanted to focus on *my* music, not someone else's.

"No, no, no thanks for me, *liebchen*. You'll be doing me a favor," she smiled, "*und* now I've got to get back to all those thirsty women!" She pinched my cheek. "Tomorrow, *liebchen*. For now, I leave you in Jen's capable hands, no?" she asked, looking at Jen.

"Of course," Jen answered stonily.

As soon as Dee Dee left, Jen rolled her eyes and shook her head as if she'd just been asked to scrub a prison bathroom with her toothbrush, again. "C'mon, kid," she said in that same you're-buggin'-me tone, "let me take you 'round." She gestured and I followed.

She was able to walk me through the bar rather quickly, since her size made a nice-sized path. "And don't think your friends can drink for free," she warned me as we passed Jerkster and Stephie, who waved. I smiled back and gave them the thumbs-up from behind the Iron Giant's back.

"Oh, uh, yeah, of course not," I answered as her glare fell on me again. Apparently I hadn't answered quickly enough. Mollified, she continued the tour, including the basement, where all the kegs for the bar taps were. It was a crawl space accessible from outside the building, and while I had to walk bent over, Jen was bent almost double.

I tried very hard not to laugh—I didn't want to have to deal with that glare again—and I was pretty certain I'd see it again soon. I have to admit, I wasn't wrong.

After the tour, Jen asked me to show up the next afternoon at two so we could do all the paperwork, and with no "good-bye," not even a "see ya," she steadfastly ignored me the rest of the night. I made sure to find and thank Dee Dee before we left, though, and also made sure to get phone numbers: the bar, her home, and her cell. Hey, you never know when something might happen, right? I just wanted to be prepared.

Jerkster fell asleep as Stephie and I made plans on the ferry ride back to the rock we called home.

"Oh, hey, want to come back to my place or we going to yours?" she asked. "We still going over that stuff?"

She was referring to our upcoming gig. Our upcoming first gig as a full band—ever. But man! It had been hard to book even a crappy night with a crappier time slot. It took two weeks of phone calls just to find out there was a twelve-week wait for an available slot, then another two weeks of trying to get in touch with an actual person in charge to get scheduled into the twelve-week wait. The good, no, the best thing about it? We were in. But that was also the scary part, too, so we needed to use our time wisely. We'd planned to just hang out tonight, then go back to one of our places and work out the rest of our set and rehearsal schedule, and the three of us were supposed to be there—the drummer we were working with had already promised to work with whatever schedule we came up with.

But even if Jerkster was there physically—and that looked doubtful, given that we couldn't budge him—he was too drunk to be any good. Still, we had work to do. Stephie and I could figure it out. We usually handled all the scheduling anyway.

"Uh, your place, it's closer," I decided.

"Cool, then. I've got Fudgesicles."

"Awesome," I smiled, "and I know an all-night pizza joint—my treat."

We walked off the boat together, leaving Jerkster to sleep it off. He'd show up at Stephie's house later—that's where he always went.

After a meal of pizza and frozen chocolate-flavored chemicals, Stephie and I mapped out all the details for our next few rehearsals, the songs for the show, and how we'd meet up to get there. This was CBGB, which was a big deal for us. The fact that the place was so famous made it intimidating, but the fact that we were the last act on a Sunday let us know our place in the pecking order—nowhere.

FAITH

I never thought it'd be so hard now just to crawl
But it's the thing that keeps me from the fire
And I can't stop now because I know how far I'll fall
I'm hand-over-hand on a thin red wire

"Sensation"—Life Underwater

In between rehearsals and sleep, I worked. And worked. When Dee Dee wasn't there, Jen constantly picked on me.

"Hey, kid, go across the street to the White Horse Tavern and get ice—here's your bucket," and she'd hand me a five-gallon bucket and smirk. Or "Hey, bar's backed up—grab two cases of beer from storage," referring to the crawl space under the bar.

What she didn't know was that when I used to bar back for extra money at the Red Spot, I'd handled ten-gallon buckets, and the boys and I would race to unpack the beer, carrying four cases at a time. So it was my time to smirk to myself when I saw her or Grace, the other bartender, sweating and straining while they carried two. Hell, compared to my labor at the Red Spot, this was a vacation. Well, except for Jen. What a bitch. And what was with the "kid" thing, anyway?

"Kid, there's a couple waiting in the corner," she'd order. Like, duh, I was already getting their drinks. Or, "Hey, kid, grab a broom, will ya?" Uh, just finished with that.

It was constant, and if it wasn't about work, it was about something else. "Kid like you should be going crazy—playing the field like tomorrow won't ever come," she told me seriously one day when she caught me pocketing a phone number with a tip without a second glance.

"Not my thing." I smiled over my shoulder as I walked my tray to the bar.

I worked the rest of the night, like I did the others—fetching drinks, cleaning, making chitchat and correct change. When we'd closed and the lights had come on for the cleanup, Jen approached me again.

"Is it 'cuz you're small town, or is it 'cuz you're a virgin?" Jen asked me as I sat at the now-emptied and shiny clean bar, sipping a Coke and waiting for Grace to come up front with tonight's pay. The few patrons that remained—all half dozen or so—were well-known regulars either waiting to meet someone, hooking up with someone from the staff, or just keeping us company, I guess. I suspected one or two of them had romantic inclinations toward Grace.

"What?" I asked casually, not rising to Jen's bait. I figured that as long as I kept perfectly calm and didn't react to anything Jen said, maybe she'd eventually back off. So far my strategy hadn't really worked, but it was better than losing my temper.

I beat the shit out of the trees in the yard when I got home.

But still…she was the boss when Dee Dee wasn't around—and that was a lot, because it seems that managing a bar has a lot more to do with schedules and paperwork than it does with bartending.

"Your attitude," Jen answered, skipping snideness for directness this time. "Are you just really that provincial?"

I sipped my soda quietly as I considered how to answer, then put the glass down carefully. "What are you talking about? What attitude? And secondly, how do you know I'm not racking 'em up on the side?" I stared into those dark eyes.

Jen's lip curled into a sneer. "Kid, I had to rip them off of you tonight, and you didn't even respond. And it's not the first time that happened, either. You get numbers shoved at you left and right, and you don't even glance at them. You just smile thanks and stick 'em in your pocket. What's wrong with you?" She finally got to her burning question. "Are you deformed or something?"

Well, it wasn't snide, but it was still rude. I raised an unamused eyebrow.

Jen did have a point. Women stuck money in my bra, their numbers written on the bills. When I brought them their drinks, they'd ask if I could give them a cherry, then tied cherry stems into knots with their tongues and smiled sweetly as they handed them to me. They brought me cappuccinos and pizza; one even made me a sweater, and another gave me a leather jacket I still have. One called me edible, and another asked what afternoon she could pencil me in for a session of cunning linguistics—and yes, I know what that means.

The night before, some guy (an occasional guy came in. They were either gay or vouched for by the women they were with) offered to pay me if I would take his young friend to a prepaid hotel room and help her celebrate her twenty-first birthday—by "making her a woman." These women were pretty, smart, charming. They were sexy, bold, creative. Some of them were aggressive, and some of them were shy, and through it all, I smiled, I thanked them for the cappuccino, I listened politely—and I said no. Every time.

For those that got a little too aggressive for my taste, there was Jen. And in all honesty, it didn't matter how crowded the place got—and sometimes there was barely breathing room. All I had to do was turn my head and lift my chin, and in seconds, I'd receive an apology—or there'd be room for one more on the dance floor.

Earlier this particular evening a group of women were celebrating something, I dunno what—could've been a softball game, could have been a corporate merger, the clientele was so diverse—and I'd had to take two trays of drinks to the table they'd found in the corner. While I was holding the trays, about four of them tried to strip me—and I mean strip me.

I didn't know what to do, and when I looked around for Jen to call her, I just made eye contact and she was there in less than half a second flat. Good thing, too, because my shirt was already open to the waist, and the first button of my jeans had gotten undone.

"I mean, nothing fazes you. You know, one day when you're older, you're gonna look back at this time and wish you'd done something with it." Jen nodded at me solemnly. "They're not always gonna throw it at you like that."

I toyed with the edge of my glass. It's not like she was saying anything I hadn't thought before; I just didn't believe that shit anymore. Besides, how did you explain to someone that you were already, in your heart of hearts, sick to death of the whole, empty, ugly thing?

None of it meant anything. At the Red Spot, the women had

wanted me because I was the DJ—no other reason. After the incident with Candace and some others, they'd wanted me because they "knew" I'd make them come. Hell, women and girls, even straight ones, would accost me in the club and try to kiss me. I knew which were straight, though. The gay girls would try to kiss me wherever; the straight ones tried to steal my kisses in the bathroom.

Me, well, I was no innocent. Sometimes I'd taken someone who kissed me into the booth to make out and dance with them there, sometimes two. More than several nights I'd left the booth and prowled the crowd, so restless, so high on that feeling that rides right under the skin through the blood, that unquenchable thirst, that I took the maximum the booth could hold—three—back with me.

I hadn't cared who they were or who they were with—it didn't matter. For as long as I wanted, they were mine. Any of them. All I'd had to do was walk up, smile, and nod toward the booth. They knew what to do, they always did.

Usually a party in the booth had meant just that, a party. We'd make out, we'd dance, and the girls drank for free. It was sensual more than sexual, and I'd sent more than one back to her boyfriend or girlfriend (but usually a boyfriend—the girlfriend usually came in too) more than ready for whatever they were going to do next.

Unless we were dancing or kissing, though, I let no one touch me. I fucked some of them, and on at least two occasions I'd fucked one while making out with another. No one ever, ever, got invited back a second time. My nights had gotten more and more crowded; the dancers themselves took on a new edge. I no longer wore black most of the time—I wore it all the time, and I'd earned it.

Jen's voice broke in over my thoughts. "Really, Nina. One day, you're going to be old and alone and not as pretty, I mean, as young as you are now. You should just get out there and enjoy it, you know? Rack up the points while you can."

Ah, points. There it was again, the concept that got me into so much trouble in the first place. I smiled at Jen, trying not to chuckle. She was being sincere, and I didn't want to hurt her feelings. Besides, this was the first time she'd ever spoken to me without her customary growl or glare, and I didn't want to spoil the moment.

But it was fucking ironic. I mean, everyone put so much pressure on getting laid. Why? There had to be something more to being "young, dumb, and full of cum," as Cap described everyone under thirty. Wasn't there? Something more, I mean.

And I was surprised, too. I mean, okay, I knew straight guys had to deal with that sort of pressure from their peers all the time; I could see that with Nico and the other guys I knew. But I was shocked to experience the same sort of pressure from women, I mean, from gay women. Wasn't that the sort of thing every woman pretty much complained about? How all anyone wanted to do was to fuck 'em? Part of the negative aspect of patriarchal culture or some such stuff? So why repeat the pattern? And why, why of all people, pick on me?

Besides, what the hell did Jen know about me anyway? She had no idea of who I was or what I'd done. I mean, for fuck's sake, one night while I was DJing, during the beginning of a really hot tune, I'd descended from the skybox to hunt—that was what it was, essentially. In seconds, I found the right girl. This night had brought me a blonde with an attitude I liked, and as I stepped up to her, a familiar voice spoke over my shoulder.

"Trace always said you were really cute," said Van. What a fuck. But interesting, though, I noted, because he and Trace weren't together; but he was with the girl I wanted.

The last time I'd seen him had been a few weeks before—after Candace and before my first anonymous guest.

In my mind's eye, I could still see the quirk of his lips. "Don't talk to me," I told Van and laughed lightly, never taking my eyes from his dance partner, who smiled back a bit nervously. "Go wait by the booth."

I've no idea what had possessed me to order him like that, but whatever the reason, I wasn't terribly surprised when he did it. I'd tracked him until he settled by the door, then returned my attention to the blonde before me. She wasn't a girl, exactly, and she was a bit more than a young woman. Whatever she was, she was definitely beautiful, with lanky legs, and, as I said before, I liked the way she tossed her head. It was that simple.

"I'm Nina," I smiled and introduced myself, although I knew it wasn't necessary. "Join me for a drink." It wasn't a question; we both knew the answer.

"Simone," she answered with a coy look and licked her lips. "I'd love to."

Yes, this was going to be a great night, I'd thought as I took her hand and led her back to the skybox. I didn't even look at Van, and they both followed me in.

"Lock it," I ordered casually over my shoulder as I strolled to the request window and signaled for Andra. I glanced down at my meters as I passed; I was good for time.

"What would you like to drink?" I asked Simone cordially.

"Corona. Corona with—"

"—with lime," I finished for her with another smile, and the one she reciprocated with packed some serious sensuality.

Van piped in. "Hey, I want—"

I held up a hand to forestall him; I didn't want to hear his voice if I could help it.

"Tequila. Beer back, right?" I asked, finally looking at him and arching my brow.

Van seemed impressed that I knew that as I returned to the window.

Andra had arrived and I told her what we needed. "Oh, and the usual for me." I grinned at her. She smiled and nodded, then eased back through the crowd.

"Make yourselves comfortable," I invited both of them. "I've got to set a few times."

At my tables, I checked my mix, my mike, and my headphones. As I slipped them over my head, I asked Simone, "Any special requests?"

She and Van had made themselves at home along the back bench, but at that, she stood up. "Only if you'll dance with me," she replied, her voice throaty and low.

"Of course." I laughed lightly, because that was the point, because it was part of the plan, and she was eager to play my game. "What will it be?"

She told me, and I programmed my next set. By the time I was done, the drinks had arrived and I tossed mine down—a shot of scotch followed by a shot of blackberry brandy. If I was going to poison my liver, I didn't want all the extra calories that a mixed drink would provide. In fact, it was a good thing I didn't like beer—turns out that just one serving has a full pound of them.

Everything and everyone set, I'd danced with Simone, and Van danced behind her. She was a good dancer, and when the timing was right, I kissed her, a thorough, sensual kiss that made promises I just might keep—tonight. Simone's hands clutched at my waist as mine tickled, traveled, and teased up her spine. With my tongue I drew delicate lines into the hollow of her throat that I knew, from the deep sound that rumbled beneath and through my lips, she enjoyed.

When Van reached forward, I slapped his hand away.

"Don't touch me," I told him with a deadly smile over Simone's shoulder. "You don't talk to me, and you don't touch me."

"Sorry," he'd muttered and looked away, over at the dancing crowd.

"Now…where were we?" I asked Simone as her hips swayed dangerously close to mine, but I held them tightly, less than an inch away from me, building, playing, delaying the inevitable. "Oh, I remember." I smiled. "Right about here," and I returned my lips to her neck.

By design rather than by accident we'd ended up with Van on the back bench and Simone between us. Van spread his legs, and Simone nestled between his thighs, her ass grinding against his denim-covered cock as we continued to dance, a dance that was more dry fuck than music. When Van groaned, I had to really force myself not to think about the last time I'd seen him.

I'd nibbled on her lip and let my fingertips trail along her thighs until I reached her cunt. What a nice surprise, I thought as she tossed her head and leaned back against Van, clutching his thighs. No underwear and shaved. She spread her legs for me, and I slid my fingers between her warm, wet lips, enjoying her silkiness. She groaned, and I licked the column of her neck.

"God…" Van muttered, his hips grinding behind her.

"If you're not quiet, I'll stop," I warned him as I gently played in Simone's waiting cunt, teasing the emptiness that waited for me to fill it, "and if I hear you come, I swear to heaven, I'll slap you."

I meant it, every word of it, but far from upsetting him, my words had seemed to excite him more, and he visibly shuddered. Good. If I had to watch, then he had to witness.

"Shh, Van," Simone warned, and she swayed a bit against the constant play of my fingers, her knees giving momentarily before she righted herself.

"Good," I'd smiled sweetly, "we have an understanding." I took a moment's pity on him. "Here," I told him, grabbing one of his hands that had clutched the bench, "hold this." I took his hand and put it on Simone's skirt, lifting it to her waist. He got the idea and did the same with his other free hand. She was naked from the waist down, and I was right—she was shaved, except for a small tuft at the top.

Simone caught my eye and I watched her, still teasing, until we both looked down to see what my fingers had found—a small barbell above the base of her clit. I couldn't let that go.

"What do we have here," I commented as I knelt between her legs. Her shorn pussy looked vulnerable, even more so with the metal running through it. I glanced up to see Van's fingers had gone almost white with the strength of his hold and control.

I flicked the barbell with my tongue and Simone moaned heartily, tossing her head back onto Van's shoulder. He leaned back for better balance and pulled her with him. His hard cock now pressed up between her ass cheeks.

I trailed my tongue along her length a few times, from her opening to her clit. She tasted like pineapple, I thought, as I slid my tongue inside her. Her hips jumped, and I could swear I could hear her mutter "Oh yeah," as she fucked my face.

I gently pressed against Van's balls, rubbing lightly with my thumb along the denim as it got damp from Simone's pussy. Then I placed the very edges of two fingers against her opening, slick with invitation, and played my tongue rapidly against her clit.

Two things went through my head, not necessarily at the same time: I could have done anything I wanted, anything, to Van. He had given me complete control, and I liked that a lot, too much. The other was God, but she was ready, more than ready, and as I teased a third finger there, I stood and replaced my tongue with my thumb.

Van had burrowed his face into her neck, and with the same hand that had gently stroked his balls, I took his cheek in my palm and pushed his head firmly back against the wall as I leaned in to replace him. Pressing my thumb firmly on Simone's beautifully hard clit, I slid my fingers ever so slightly inside her. Her cunt was hot.

Simone rubbed her cheek against my neck, then blindly lifted her lips to mine. I kissed her fully, deeply, and let her savor the taste of her wanting cunt in my mouth.

Raising my lips to her ear, I raked it lightly with my teeth. "Are you ready?" I whispered.

"God…yes," she groaned, her hips moving in synch with my thumb.

"Are you sure?" I teased mildly, but sincerely. She could have backed out if she'd wanted, but I was pretty sure she wouldn't.

"Yes," she hissed at me, breathless, and I slowly thrust all three fingers into her waiting hole, then just as slowly eased out again, letting her pussy adjust, feeling the length of it.

"Oh…" she sighed as I pushed slowly within her, a smooth back and forth. Two fingers would have been okay, but three meant she was tight around me—and I wanted her to really enjoy this, and I wanted Van to know just how much. I could feel him grit his teeth under my hand, and his body gave a slight jerk, which shoved her pussy firmly on my fingers.

I finally released Van's head and buried my fingers in her hair, drawing her face again to mine to kiss her once more before I fucked her earnestly, her cunt sucking on my fingers as I moved inside her, her hips adding to the motion. She tucked her face into my neck again, and I held her firmly as her pussy drew me into her again and again.

Finally, she tensed and bit my shoulder as she came, a soft sound issuing from her throat. I let her relax against me as I carefully withdrew, then stroked her head where she rested it on my shoulder.

"I've got you, you're okay," I whispered into her ear, and she sighed.

I finally looked at Van. His head lay against the wall, his eyes closed. His face seemed soft and vulnerable, and I noticed a dark stain on his lips. I realized he must have bitten them until they'd bled to keep quiet.

Fuck the points. I'd sunk his battleship and burned his board.

"Good boy." I smiled at him, but I didn't mean it. Why did he do that? Why give anyone so much power over you? Nothing could possibly be worth that, could it? And I'd enjoyed it, all of it, not only my own violence, but most especially Van's complete submission, which frankly left me pretty disgusted with myself. I'd felt like the biggest piece of shit.

"I'm not worried about points," I told Jen, because I meant it. I'd done enough of that, had enough of that. It was probably up there on the list of stupidest things I've done. Jen's eyebrows fused—dammit—as she focused on me. "I'm not worried about being alone either." I smiled at her, picked up my drink, and stood.

"There's someone for me, or there's not. Either way," I saluted her with my glass, "I like my own company." I finished my drink with a little flourish and put the glass back down on the bar. Jen got up too, and we walked over to the locked door where a woman knocked. Probably here to meet someone, I thought, or a very last-minute drink.

"Besides, between work and the band, I've got a lot on my plate," I added. "I don't have time to get involved in that romantic crap."

"Kid, you're wrong," Jen stated flatly as she put her hand on the lock. "All that one-person shit is just that—shit. You're gonna waste your looks, you're gonna waste your energy, and you're gonna waste time—time that could be spent having fun—and then, you'll get screwed over. Ya gotta make hay while the sun shines and all that," she warned.

"C'mon, Jen," I smiled as her hand twisted on the key, "you've gotta have a little faith."

I stepped in front of her before she opened the door. That was our custom. I'd greet and speak, and if I needed backup, Jen was a breath behind me. The door swung open, and I began to say the usual.

"Sorry, we're closed," I recited, not really looking at the woman who stood before me.

"Nina? Nina Boyd?" she asked, and now I looked—closely.

"Fran? Francesca DiTomassa?" I asked as I recognized an old friend from high school. The honey blond curls spilling over her coat past her shoulders and almond-shaped brown eyes were enough to tell me, but if they weren't, there was her picture-perfect smile, just as I remembered it. "Oh my God!" And ignoring the glare I was sure was aimed at my back, I let her in.

"God, Fran, it's been ages!" I exclaimed as we embraced.

"Nina, I knew it! I just knew it!"

She leaned back to scrutinize me and cupped my face in her hands, shaking her head. "I can't believe I'm really looking at you." Fran's warm brown eyes twinkled. "I knew in my heart it wasn't true!" She gave my cheek a solid smooch for good measure, and I heartily hugged her back.

"What wasn't true?" I asked, puzzled. That was a pretty strange way to say hello, wasn't it?

She shook her head, unable to answer while she played with my hair and patted my shoulder as if checking to make sure I was solid.

"Friend of yours?" Jen asked dryly as she locked the door behind us.

"Oh yeah," I enthused. "Hey, Jen, this is Francesca...Fran," I introduced, then corrected at the raised eyebrow she gave me. "Fran? Jen."

They shook hands as they repeated the polite social formulas.

"Like a drink?" I asked, walking behind the bar. I ignored the glare coming from Jen. I was allowed buy-backs and hadn't used a single one since I'd started working there. The one whatever it was Fran wanted certainly wasn't going to hurt anyone.

"Sure," she agreed, settling into a stool in front of me, "that's what I was stopping in for. Guinness, if you've got it."

Jen checked the door again and came over to the bar, grabbing a seat close to Fran.

"Guinness from the gun," I agreed, and got a mug. "Want one?" I asked Jen as she settled in.

"Yeah, why not?" she answered with a tired smile. Huh. She could smile. Well and good, then. I grabbed two frosted mugs from the stainless-steel freezer, then opened the tap. As the beer flowed, I watched to make sure it came out right, because there's nothing better than a good head—if you're into that sort of thing.

"Here," I presented the beer with a napkin to each of them, "enjoy." Fran smiled at me and hefted the frosted glass, and Jen wrapped her hands around hers. Satisfied that they were well served, I drew myself one, too. What the hell. It was only one beer, and it was Guinness, after all.

"To your health," Fran toasted and smiled, then took a hearty swig.

"Yeah, your health," Jen agreed with a twist to her lips that I assumed was a grin.

"Thanks," I returned, with a sip of my own. Grace came ambling out of the back room as I put my mug down. She had three nicely thick envelopes—seemed like we'd had a good night. The tips bulging in my back pocket agreed.

Mutely, I held up a mug and offered her a beer, and she grinned and nodded. She sat on the other side of Jen, and as she passed us our envelopes, I handed her the beer. I didn't even look in mine, just tucked it into my waistband.

Now that everyone was settled and watered, so to speak, I figured I could have a conversation with my old friend.

"I just can't believe it, this is totally fucking unreal," Fran said, leaning her head against her hand to stare at me.

For whatever reason, I was starting to get a little anxious.

To avoid more of that uncertain feeling, I lifted my glass and took a hearty swallow. Eesh. I'd forgotten how bitter it was.

Fran took a sip and put her mug down, then reached across the bar for my hand. I would have moved it away, but her expression, a combination of wonder and sorrow, stopped me as she traced her fingertips over my knuckles and veins with a touch so light, I would hardly have known she was there if I hadn't been looking. I definitely felt the tear that hit my skin, though.

"Fran...what's the matter?"

It's funny, isn't it, how sometimes between people the years and the distance don't matter; once you reconnect, it's as if you'd never parted? That's how I felt seeing her, well, after the initial shock had worn off. I was back to swimming pools and driving lessons, pre-meet pasta dinners and post-race bullshit, shared lockers, shared clothes, shared friends. Samantha. That made me stop cold—maybe something had happened to her, maybe something terrible.

I rubbed Fran's hand.

"Kitt, what's wrong?" I asked gently, using her old nickname. "Can I do something?"

Fran exhaled and squeezed my hand, lifting her filled eyes to mine.

"You're not going to believe this." She tried to smile and gave a little laugh through her tears.

I needed to get around to the other side of the bar; I had to sit next to her. I glanced over at Grace and Jen.

Grace gave Fran a sympathetic glance, then reached over the bar and grabbed a tissue, placing it next to our conjoined hands before she excused herself.

Fran took the tissue, and although she remained silent, she buried her face in her hand, and her shoulders shook as she began to cry in earnest.

I stole a glance at Jen, who looked back at me with alarm in her eyes, and I mutely asked her with a lift of my chin if I could have a private moment.

Jen instantly understood and nodded in agreement as she hastily got up. I guess she'd felt awkward about just leaving someone to sit at the bar and cry.

I bent my head closer to Fran's. "Hey, give me a sec, okay?" I said softly. "I'm just coming around."

She squeezed my hand, then let go. "'S all right, I'm okay," she sniffed, and grinned at me.

"Okay," I agreed with a small smile of my own to make her feel better, but I moved quickly so she wouldn't feel alone.

Once there, I took one of her hands, and as she swiveled to face me, I gently cupped her shoulder.

"What's the matter, Fran?" I repeated, searching her overfull, shiny eyes. "What's wrong?"

She increased the pressure on my hand and tentatively reached for my face. I let her fingers touch me, and she lightly rubbed her thumb along my cheek.

"You're supposed to be dead," she whispered, an awestruck look on her face.

Did she just say what I thought she'd said? I sat up straight and gave her shoulder another reassuring rub. I could feel my eyebrows doing a great imitation of Jen's. "Did you say...?" I trailed off as she nodded.

I leaned back in my seat, shocked. "What...how?"

Fran took my hand back in both of hers and leaned in so closely that I could count the tears in her lashes.

"I called you, Nina, I swear I called you," she said, her eyes wide as they stared into mine, "and your father, he—"

"No, no, it's okay." I held a hand up. I knew exactly what she was going to say.

Shock and anger warred in me; I suddenly knew what it was like to burn with cold fury. But none of this was her fault, so I forced those feelings down and away and propelled myself back to the present. My chest hurt seeing how much pain Fran carried in her eyes, and it was horrible to know that she'd felt it because of me.

"I'm so sorry..." I apologized, and put my arms around her. "I'm just so sorry." I pressed my cheek against her head as her hands wrapped around my ribs.

"Looks like a good time for a drink," Jen said. I jumped a bit, and Fran and I looked up to see her standing behind the bar. As we let each other go, I quirked Jen a quick grin.

Jen flashed the tiniest of smiles back to me, such a brief little thing I almost missed it—but I didn't. She was okay, after all.

"'Nother Guinness for you?" Jen asked Fran, her hands already pulling the mug out from the freezer.

"You know, I need a shot," she said thoughtfully. "Walker Black, straight up."

Great idea. A shot sounded just about right to me. Maybe even two.

"Righto," Jen agreed as she pulled the bottle, "and you?" she asked me, and I grinned as I watched her visibly refrain from adding "kid."

"Same," I answered Jen, "with a blackberry brandy chaser."

Jen squinted at me as she poured my shots. "Oh, yeah, I forgot you do that."

"Want to try it?" I asked Jen.

"Hell, why not, right?" She surprised me by smiling as she pulled another pair of shot glasses.

"You know, me too," Fran chimed in.

Finally all the shots were on the bar, and I took mine in hand.

Fran eyed hers a moment, then sighed. "Okay," she drawled, and picked hers up. "I'm as ready as I'm gonna be." She smiled and I brought my own glass up, ready to swallow.

"Wait!" she exclaimed, "we have to have a toast. We can't just discover you're alive and not celebrate!"

I smiled. "I knew I was alive," I told her, "but I'm happy enough to celebrate seeing you again. What do you say we toast to that?" I again held my little shot to the ready.

"Or how about to absent friends reunited?" Her smile practically gleamed, showing off her perfect white teeth.

Jen walked up behind me and clapped me—hard—on the shoulder. "Howzabout...to faith?" she suggested, more than a touch of irony in her voice, at least to my ears. "Nina knows all about that one, don'cha, kid?"

Fran didn't catch the sarcasm. "Hey, yeah!" she enthused. "All things in their own time, all things for their own reasons, and," her face grew serious and her eyes overbright, "we'll stay in touch from now on?" She grinned at me crookedly.

Touched, because the girl whose nickname was Kitt had been kind but stoic and because the woman before me was willing to let me see she had feelings, I gently clinked my glass against hers.

"Yes," I told her and took a sip, "I absolutely promise."

"Me too," Fran agreed, and drank some of her own. "Oh," she smacked her lips, "that's really sweet—what a great contrast."

"Yeah," I began, "that's why—"

"It's time to go," Jen informed us both, a hand clapped on either of our shoulders. I looked around. Oh, yeah. The bar was empty. She was right. I just had to—

"I'll take care of those," Jen said, taking the now-empty shot glasses from our hands. "I'll lock up." She herded us forward with her frame and a light wave of her arms.

"Yeah, I'm sorry," Fran apologized as she walked. "I didn't realize—"

"No need to apologize," Jen said breezily, "just have a nice night. You can wait here in the vestibule. Nina'll be with you shortly," she informed us both, then gazed at me for the last part with an intent that I understood instantly.

"Yep, I'll be done in a sec." I smiled at Fran, but inwardly, I sighed. I should have known that Jen would make sure that it was time to pay the piper.

"What do I owe for the drinks?" I asked her as she closed the door behind Fran. I walked over to the first window to pull the internal gates, first one, then the other until the lock rings met.

"Naw, nothing kid," she answered as she reached over my head and popped in the first of four padlocks we had to take care of, "not a thing."

Surprised, I arched a brow at her. "Thanks," I said quietly as we worked our way to the next window.

"Don't mention it," she said as she stood back to admire our handiwork. Two more to go. When they were done I went behind the bar and made sure everything that needed to be off was, checked the dishwasher once more, and made one last inspection of all the garbage pails to ensure that they were not only empty, but ready to go for the next round. Finally, everything was away, locked down, and we were just about good to go. I grabbed my bag (black, messenger style—of course) and my coat out from behind the little cubby behind the bar where I'd stashed them when I arrived.

"Ready for the outside gate?" Jen asked as we stood by the door, the place now lit only by the low security lights that never went out.

"Sure 'nuff," I answered. I slid on my coat and pulled my scarf out of the sleeve where I'd tucked it for safety, and as I wound it around my neck, Jen unlocked the door for the last time this night. Fran had waited in the vestibule and stepped over as we walked out.

"Hey!" She smiled. "You done?"

"Just about." I grinned back at her, then faced the vestibule again. While Jen reached into her coat pocket for the last of the padlocks, I jumped and reached for the final gate that would seal and lock the bar completely.

I grabbed an edge and let gravity and my body drag it down to just above my head. From there I muscled it to the ground—Jen couldn't bend because of a back injury—then held it in place by sheer will as Jen snapped the remaining locks in.

Once I heard the pop that meant we were really and truly done, I straightened out and dusted my hands. "Another one down," I commented to Jen as she bent back from the waist to stretch her spine. "See you in the afternoon?" I asked and, tired, smiled. It was almost five in the morning, after all, and we'd both be back by four thirty that afternoon.

"Yeah, definitely," Jen agreed with an equally tired grin.

Hey, wait, were we having a friendly moment? Did anyone have a camera to capture this for the permanent record? Wow, maybe we'd even have friendly conversations and, who knew, maybe go crazy and maybe—gasp! get along! I was pleasantly surprised.

"Hey, have a good one, 'kay?" I waved to her in friendly parting, intending to get to Fran.

"Yeah, you too," Jen agreed with a little wave of her own. "Oh, by the way, Nina?" she called to my back. "You know, there's a word for people like you."

Well, as pleasant as our earlier interchange had been, I guess I couldn't have expected it to continue, could I? Ahh….whatever, dammit. I thought we'd made some headway. Frustration rose through my head to meet the ache that had started behind my eyes, but I let none of that show. Instead, I merely arched an eyebrow at her in question.

"Yes?" I drawled out, letting the sound flow low, rich, and syrupy. Not for nothing was I a singer, after all, and this was one of those times I remembered it (the rest are subconscious). I pursed my lips as I watched her, waiting for whatever was coming next.

For once, Jen seemed to lose all of her cocksureness and even some of her constant anger as she mulled over her answer. She clapped me on the shoulder. "I'll tell ya when I think of it, kid," she said, patting my shoulder awkwardly. "See ya later."

Um, okay, that was strange, but it was better than what I'd been expecting—something along the line of "dumb" or another related word. Relieved, I tucked this thought into the back of my head: whatever she'd been going to say, she'd obviously changed her mind.

"Yeah, when the sun's out," I agreed, and waved good-bye for the final time this night.

Fran had retired a few feet away under the lamp post on the corner, and I hurried over, happy to be done and happier still to have run into Fran. Okay, technically, she'd run into me, but the end result was the same, right? Now that I'd seen her, I didn't want to say good-bye just yet, didn't want to just say "nice seeing you" and exchange numbers and lose 'em in the wash. I didn't know what I wanted, I didn't know what I needed. All I knew was that I didn't want to see her go.

"You up for a bite? My treat," I offered as I reached out to tuck her arm in mine, where I briskly rubbed her sleeve. Besides being the polite thing, it was cold out here, and she'd been waiting for me outside, even if part of that time had been in the vestibule. We started walking north on Seventh Avenue. Not that we knew where just yet, but I did know several places in that direction that would still be open and served decent food.

Fran shone her brilliant smile back at me. "Don't you have to catch a boat or something?" she asked, lightly tweaking my forearm as we walked.

"Nah, there's always another one. Besides, *carpe noctem*, right?" I watched her profile as we walked. The sky had developed that heavy hush of expectation, and the skyline had turned gray and red with clouds.

I couldn't believe that running into Fran like this had me feeling as happy as a puppy who'd just been given a treat, and even with the somewhat strange twist our conversation had taken earlier, it was somehow still almost all I could do to keep from skipping. How weird was that? But judging from the way her eyes shone and from the wattage in that grin, she felt the same way.

"Seize the night—what, is that like your motto or something? Are you going to melt in the sun?" she joked.

"Hey, it's just because I work nights." I laughed. "It's the only time I've got."

"Oh, so that's it," Fran said. She dropped her arm from mine and stopped to look at me directly. "I thought maybe, you know, the black clothes, pale face, disappearing for a couple of years and then reappearing as this gorgeous—"

I stopped her right there. "Okay, okay, enough," I shushed, and placed two gentle fingers on her lips. My breath puffed out in the chill air, and her eyes locked into mine.

That's funny, I thought. The last time we'd seen each other, she'd been taller than me. Not by much though, true, but now, I was taller. Okay, so it wasn't a huge height difference, but still…

The caramel of her eyes seemed to warm, glowing under the streetlight with a honey-clear intensity, and I enjoyed the fact that she was examining me with the same emotion in her eyes.

I brought my hands down to rest by my sides as the air seemed to mass and warm around us, and the tiny smile I could feel playing around the edge of my lips was mirrored by the one that bordered the corner of hers.

"You don't know how good it is to see you," Fran said softly, "or how unbelievable." She shook her head lightly as if to wave away the disbelief.

The air thickened around us, and the night took on a red glow, the one that always means…

"Snow," I said quietly as I carefully wiped a few flakes from her hair. Still she stared at me with that look of wonder.

"Huh?" she asked softly, breath misting in front of what could only be described as perfectly kissable lips.

I sighed softly with a feeling I recognized as regret. Of course, it figured that I had made that vow of celibacy, including the whole I-love-you-thing, before even kissing someone, because I'd always had a crush on her anyway. We'd even kinda sorta quasi-dated in high school, although we'd called it "wanna hang out" with a lot of unresolved tension. But still I'd made that promise, because otherwise I would have already—

Well, if you ask her, Fran will plead the fifth—she *is* a lawyer, after all—(and she always smiles when she does). I don't know exactly who started it, but I can say for certain that her ever-perfect smile, matching teeth, and gorgeous lips were just a hint of the promise that her kiss held—soft, warm, and full of sweet affection. I have to admit there was something infinitely soothing in the press of her lips on mine, and just as my hands began to come up of their own accord to bring her even closer, I realized two things: I wasn't supposed to do that, and Fran and Samantha had actually, officially, dated in high school.

The realization was like coming to after being doused with cold water, and perhaps she had thought along the same lines, because we broke apart mutually.

I stared at her—dazed, shocked, a little embarrassed. "I...um, I'm..." I tried, lamely. I settled for one of my crooked grins.

This time Fran placed shushing fingers against my lips. "I always wanted to do that." She smiled impishly at me.

I could feel my eyes widen in surprise as I thought about her words. It took me absolutely no time at all to process them and realize, yeah, me too.

"You know what?" I grinned back at her.

"What?" she asked, as the snow lay like crystals in her hair.

"Me, too."

Fran tossed her head back and laughed, a light, pure sound in a world rapidly turning white, and I joined her.

"So," I asked as I took off my scarf, "did it fulfill your expectations?" I gave it a good shake and brought it over her head and around her shoulders.

"What're you doing?" she asked as I brushed her hair lightly with my fingertips under the cloth.

"Keeping you warm. It's snowing," I explained, then tucked the ends into the *V* of her peacoat, taking a moment to button an anchor-engraved button.

"There. So..." I paused and stepped back to admire my handiwork.

"So...what?" Her gaze was frankly evaluating.

"Did it fulfill your expectations?" Uh-oh, I thought as I watched her face; I was going to stop being quite so cavalier with my questions. That smile became slightly shy, and unless it was a shadow from the scarf, a faint blush rose in her cheeks.

"Well, let's just say," she began, as she watched the flakes hit the sidewalk, "that I'm glad it happened." She glanced up at me as those last few words emerged, and there was only one way to describe the look in her eyes: smokin'.

"C'mon," she said, brushing the flakes from my head and breaking us from the strange envelope we seemed to be caught up in, "let's get going."

I ran a quick hand through my hair—hey, snow or no, it's got to look good—and allowed her to take my arm.

"What's your plan?" I asked as we waited at an intersection for the light to change.

"Well," Fran paused a moment for breath, "we grab a cab back to my place. I'll make something quick, you take a nap, and I'll send you back to the island later today in a car, whattaya say?" she concluded as we reached the next corner.

I considered. "How about," I counteroffered, "we walk and try to catch a cab on the way." I glanced at the obviously taxi-empty streets. Don't ask why, but it's the unwritten Manhattan rule: when the first drop of moisture hits the ground, all forms of public transportation—especially taxicabs—disappear. Come to think of it, that rule applies to the rest of the city, too. Damn.

"Okay…and?" she prompted.

"We pick something up on the way."

"Okay—"

"And I'll leave after that," I concluded.

Fran stopped suddenly and whirled to face me.

"Nina, no way."

I let my expression ask why.

"It's late, it's snowing like hell, and you've got to be exhausted."

I opened my mouth to protest—I didn't want to impose on her hospitality—and I certainly didn't want to give her the wrong idea after that kiss. Not that I didn't, I mean, not that there wasn't—ah, never mind. I didn't know what was in her head, and I didn't want to find out that Fran was like everyone else—all about the fuck. It was a kiss, just a kiss, and as nice and as warm and as sweet as it was (okay, and sensual too, she absolutely knew how to kiss well), it wasn't "I love you." I might have made a misstep, but I wasn't going to make another, I hoped.

I began to explain about not imposing or some such, but Fran waved my words away, sending eddies of snow clouds around her.

"I haven't seen you in four years, thought you were dead, and now that I know you're alive and well, how do you think I'd feel if I let you leave to freeze to death or get into some sort of accident during a blizzard?" she cajoled with a smile.

I laughed and looked up, blinking away the flakes that fell into my eyes. She was right, though, and if it wasn't exactly a blizzard yet, it was snowing hard enough to be its younger sibling.

I let my breath out in a huff. "Fair enough," I gave in with a smile of my own, "you win."

Fran slipped her arm into mine. "Well, of course I do." She laughed as she rubbed my forearm briskly.

We found a bodega (that's Spanish for "deli") somewhere on Avenue A and bought the same stuff everyone buys when it snows: milk, bread, and eggs. I don't know why. I mean, what's everyone doing, making French toast? I took the bag in one hand and her hand in the other.

We didn't really speak as we walked; we just kicked up the snow and pointed out different items that looked surreal and magical in the falling white.

As we approached her block, I grew uneasy. I mean, I knew this block, I knew the building we were approaching. Nah, couldn't be, I thought. What are the odds, right? But that funky sense persisted, and judging from how cool it suddenly got, I think the blood had drained out of my face and was rapidly descending into my feet.

We stopped by the steps that led to her apartment, and I let go of her hand so she could dig for her keys.

"Hey, Fran?" I asked as the snow blew around us. It was really starting to come down.

"Yeah?" she responded distractedly. "I can't believe I can't find them!" she complained, mostly to herself, her focus on searching her pockets.

"You wouldn't, um, happen to have had a neighbor named Candace, would you?" I asked as casually as I could.

"Ah, got you!" she exclaimed triumphantly, holding her keys out so I could see them. "I'm sorry—what did you say?"

I put the bag down to give my hands a break and tried my best to nonchalantly shove them into my coat pockets. "I was just, uh…you have a neighbor named Candace?"

Fran whirled so quickly to face me I only had a moment to see the shock in her eyes before it changed to alarm as she lost her footing in the fresh snow.

Her arms flew up, the keys went wide, and I rushed forward to catch her before gravity did. It got us both, and she landed on top of me with a solid, breathless "whump" as her body pushed my ribs one way and the slippery sidewalk another.

I lay there a moment and took a deep breath, then wiggled my fingers and toes. Everything was operational; therefore, I was fine. I blinked the snow out of my eyes and opened them to first find her curls sliding over my cheeks, and as I gazed past her chin, I found her lips, grinning widely. I smiled back ruefully. So much for my rescue attempt.

"Thank you," she said.

"You're welcome."

We studied each other as the snow continued to fall, thick and heavy, and Fran wiped some off my face, her thumb lingering against my chin.

"Are you okay?" I asked finally. She'd fallen, after all, and even if we seemed to be sitting rather comfortably, it was still possible that she could have injured something.

"Oh, yeah, I'm fine. In fact I—oh shit!" she exclaimed, and sat up with a panicked expression, looking about her wildly. The movement put her solidly and squarely on my groin, sending a bolt from my buddy to my brain, which made me jump in return. I swallowed the sensation and sat up on my elbows.

"Problem?" I asked mildly, arching a brow.

"My keys! I dropped my keys!"

"I'll help you find them. I think I know where they fell," I offered. I did have an idea, really. I'd seen them fly, and if I wasn't mistaken, they were probably behind the bushes that lined the front of the building.

"Sure, thanks," Fran agreed. All of a sudden, she seemed to realize exactly the way we were sitting.

She looked down to see just how we were joined and bit her lip. "Uh, sorry," she said finally, giving me a sheepish look. "Are you okay?"

I let it go for a heartbeat, then gave her back a slow grin. "Never better," I drawled. "Do you think you'll need a hand getting up?"

"Oh. Ah, no, I'm fine." She scrambled a moment in the snow before she stood, but, finally, she regained her feet.

"Let me help you," she offered when she was steady, and extended a hand.

As soon as I was on my feet, I brushed the snow off. But, man, was it cold to do barehanded!

"Let's find your keys," I suggested, and we moved in the direction I indicated. We searched through the dried brush together—Fran got the front, I got the back.

"So…did you say Candace?" she asked casually as we searched.

I was so sure I'd seen her keys fly over to this exact spot—between the dead brush and the wall where the snow didn't reach, but neither did the light. I felt my way along carefully—I didn't want to cut myself on a stray piece of glass or get bitten by whatever passed for local fauna and die of rabies. Yuck.

"Yeah," I answered Fran, who hovered somewhere behind me, "is she a neighbor of yours?"

Just scant inches beyond my fingertips some streetlight broke through the bracken, and I thought I saw a gleam. That had to be it!

"British?"

"Huh?" I asked back, not certain of what she'd said as I inspected what I'd found. A pull tab from a can—damn. I discarded it and followed that gleam before me. That just had to be it.

"Was she a Brit, you know, from the UK?" she repeated and clarified.

Almost, almost, just another…there. I snagged the loop with my fingertip, hauled back, and was rewarded with a jingle that could mean only one thing.

"Got 'em!" I announced triumphantly, and passed the keys behind me to her. Still bent double, I tried to carefully back out; I didn't want to rip my coat or my face on a branch.

"Yeah, she's English," I said as I crawled. "I take it you know her?" I was almost out, just a little farther now and…

"Know her?" Fran echoed. "She sublet my apartment this summer. She's Sam's girlfriend."

Holy shit! Shocked, alarmed, and otherwise totally taken aback, I stood straight up, slammed my head into the brick window ledge above me, and went straight back down. I saw stars, I saw God, I think I spoke a foreign language as adrenaline beat up through me and the pain in my head floored me.

"Ow," I muttered, scowling and rubbing my head. That fucking hurt.

"Are you all right? Are you okay?" Fran scrambled through the branches to ask.

I leaned my back against the building and rubbed my head some more. "I'm fine, I'll live," I told her, still scowling.

"Are you sure you didn't hurt anything?" she asked again, and reached down to help me up.

"My ego," I answered with a self-deprecating smile as I took her hand. "I think I broke it." This time I stood and managed not to injure myself.

"Looks fine from here, Raze," she smiled at me broadly, using my old nickname from swim team—Razor. "And besides," she continued, "you're safe with me."

"I think I knew that." I smiled back genuinely and brushed myself off as best I could as I squeezed out of the space between the steps and the damn dead twig collection. I stopped a moment to pick up the snow-covered bag and cautiously walked up the steps.

The snow had picked up volume and momentum, coming down hard and fast enough to have already covered the area we'd fallen onto in a fresh coating of white and fill up Fran's original footsteps.

Fran unlocked the door, and as it swung open into that very familiar corridor, my brain cleared enough to ask, "Did you say Candace was Samantha's girlfriend?" My mouth was dry as those words came out.

"Well, you know," she explained as she went to her mailbox, "it's one of those on-again, off-again sort of things. How do you know Candace?" she asked, giving me a quick and curious look, before she went back to sorting through her envelopes.

My guts froze. I was going to hell, I knew it. I was absolutely, positively going to hell, because I had committed the worst sin I could possibly think of—I'd slept with my best friend's girlfriend. Dammit, dammit, double damn. It didn't matter that we hadn't seen each other in years, didn't matter that I hadn't known because Candace had told me her ex was named Annie—and definitely an ex.

The facts remained the facts—did I sleep with her? Okay, all right, we didn't sleep. So did I have sex with her? Forget all those who-touches-who equivocations, because I knew how she liked her nipples sucked and how she loved me in leather. I had not only a mental picture, but a visceral one of the taste, the touch, the scent, and the gorgeous fit of her pussy and how she loved it best when I fucked her slowly and very deeply until I wanted and she needed to come, so I'd bury myself inside her tightening cunt until she was screaming my name and her pussy flooding my hand, and we'd relax a few moments while her cunt pulsed slowly around my buried fingers—Candace called them thank-you kisses—until I gently withdrew. And we'd start again.

How did I know Candace? Cunt thump surrender, to borrow a phrase; that's how I knew her.

"Oh, uh, we hung out over the summer a bit," I answered instead. It's not that I wanted to lie; it's just that, well, I'd really liked Candace, and it's just not my thing to kiss and tell—ever.

"The only place Candace really mentioned going to was Staten Island," Fran said conversationally as we walked down the hall toward her apartment. Snow dripped in gray and muddy bunches off the bag and my coat. "She said she wanted to know about Samantha's hometown."

I swallowed nervously as she keyed the lock. God, I knew that door and how strong it was—I'd fucked Candace mercilessly against it.

"That's cool," I answered noncommittally.

Fran swung the door open and flicked the light switch. "Yeah, I guess," she responded with a shrug. "The only thing," she said as she reached down to unlace her boots, "is that she met someone," she placed the first boot on a nearby mat and reached for the next, "and I know she and Sam have an arrangement, their understanding, but," and she got the other one off, "it made me a bit uncomfortable, you know?"

"Hmph," I responded blankly. This had the potential to get Mama-don't-know-ya ugly, and I didn't have the first clue as to what to do about it.

"Boots here, give me your coat," Fran indicated with a sweep of her arms.

Wordlessly, I took off my coat and handed it to her, then began to carefully slide off one boot.

"Yeah," she continued as I eased my foot out, "she said it was the DJ at the Red Spot—you go there?" She moved into the kitchen with our coats.

"I used to work there," I called back as I eased off the other boot.

"Oh, hey, then you must know who it is," Fran called back from the kitchen. "Is she as hot and wild as Candace said? You know, her hair up in a sort of half Mohawk and with what Candace called her Elvis smile?"

My hair was no longer sopping wet, and though I hadn't worn it like that in a while, I maintained the cut, and there was still some gel left in my hair from earlier. Even though it had been some time, I'd done it so often for so long that I set it with one hand as I walked to the kitchen and carried the shopping bag in the other. I could feel that wave settle perfectly into place.

It was time to settle this. Elvis smile—I never knew Candace had thought that, but I was pretty sure I knew which smile she meant. That was pretty cool.

I got to the kitchen and leaned in to put the bag on the counter, then put my hands on either side of the archway that led to the kitchen, watching as Fran hung up our coats. Then I cocked my head and my hips and set that half-pursed smile I knew Candace meant on my lips. "You mean…like this?" I asked. Funny how all it takes is the slightest changes in the angle of the head and the way the lips are held to be "on."

When she finally saw me, she was obviously surprised.

Well, we were a long way away from our high-school-uniform days, after all. But I had to let her know who I was, who I'd been, and who I'd become so she could make her own decision as to whether or not she wanted to continue our rediscovered and renewed friendship. If she did? Great—that would make me pretty darn happy. And if not, well, I'd lived without her for four years. She might end up wishing I was still only a pleasant if sad memory.

I tracked her as she came closer and watched her eyes go from serious surprise to smoky contemplation as they traveled from my head to feet and back again.

Slinging a thumb through a belt loop, I leaned arrogantly. The look in her eyes told me that she—at least a part of her—liked what she saw. It also told me…well, I didn't want to think about it. As stupid as it sounds, it would've really bothered me to think of Fran as "easy." But still, that look she threw? Smokin'.

With a last lingering glance, she took the milk and eggs out of the bag on the counter and put them in the refrigerator; those were lucky eggs—none of them broke. Fran pulled out a coffee pot and walked over to the sink.

"Don't pretend you don't know where the bathroom is," she said finally, a sly smile edging the corner of her mouth. "Go take a shower—there's fresh towels—and I'll toss some sweats in before you're done."

I dropped back half a step and glanced at her sharply. I'd intended to dry off as best I could, then change into the clothes I'd packed; they'd be drier than what I had on. She finished setting up the coffee pot, then peeped over at me.

"It's not as if I've never seen you naked before, you know," she reminded me with a wry grin.

True, it wasn't. We *had* been on swim team together in high school, and if we did see each other nude on our way back, forth, or in the shower, well, it was a locker room, after all, and no big deal anyway.

"I wasn't going to mention that." I grinned at her. "I was going to ask, what color?"

"What color what?"

"What color sweats?"

I gave her my jauntiest smile, and she returned a look that almost scorched me from head to toe then back again, complete with a slow, sexy smile.

"For you?" She licked her teeth, those perfect, perfect teeth. "Black, of course."

There was nothing else to say except, "Perfect. Thank you." We smiled at each other, then I gave a little wave and sauntered to the promised shower. Fran was right, of course; I did know the way.

I ran the water a little warmer than usual—a trick I'd learned from Cap. All cold water does is drive your blood farther inside and spikes it harder through the part of your anatomy that you're trying to cool off. But…and this is important: a warm one dilates your blood vessels, which spreads your blood out a bit. Yeah, you're still hard, and you might still be aching, but at least it's not like a bolt through the groin. Okay, it's still rough, but it's handle-able—sort of.

Showered, warmed, and dressed in the promised black sweats (and after Fran had done the same), we sat there together and caught up on everything we could. I told her about school—I wasn't going this semester; DJing—I was taking a break; work—keeping me crazy; and the band—which was my obsession, while Fran told me all about being in Columbia Law School—she had a scholarship; her summer internship in Los Angeles—in the legal department of a movie studio; and her plans after graduation—get sunny and warm or find people that were.

By unspoken mutual agreement, neither of us mentioned Samantha or Candace, until later.

DRIVEN

I'm not always right, I may not be the one
But one step closer to paradise
Is one step closer to paradise
I'll bring you one step closer to paradise

"Dani's Tears"—Life Underwater

Eventually, after about half a dozen cups of coffee, followed by hot chocolate, the demolition of a few boxes of microwave pizza, and a pint of ice cream, we noticed the sky outside the window had lightened to a murky gray. I stood from my seat to stretch, then walked over to the window to peer out, pressing my fingertips to the frosted glass.

"Holy shit!" I exclaimed. Holy shit was right. In the time since we'd gotten there, the snow had apparently come down even harder and faster than before—and it showed no sign of stopping. A thick white blanket covered the ground everywhere, and even the few cars parked on the street had been transformed into soft and rounded sculptures; there was no trace of color left.

"Holy shit!" Fran whispered from behind me as she came closer to see for herself. Her hand came up and gently held my shoulder as we contemplated a blurred and rounded world. The scant distance between us gradually shortened until that same hand that had been on my shoulder came to rest lightly across my waist, while my arm draped softly behind her neck.

She sighed quietly, staring out into the stillness, and for just a moment, one of us—and again, I don't know who—pulled a little closer, and I let myself enjoy the warm, solid sense of her next to me. It was just nice, you know?

"Bed," she announced suddenly, breaking our reverie.

"Huh?" I asked, momentarily nonplussed. I mean, I liked Fran and all, but I wasn't, I didn't, well, I couldn't—you know.

"Bed," repeated Fran succinctly, dropping her arm from my waist. "We've gone from 'it's really, really late' to 'it's really way too early' again, and I know I, for one, could use it."

She was—again—right, and I was tired, too. But I certainly didn't want her to think on the one hand that I was there just to get into bed with her or, conversely—no, no conversely. I didn't want her to think that I was even remotely thinking about the possibility of us having sex.

"Great idea," I agreed, following her out of the kitchen. "Just show me where to grab a blanket." I indicated I'd sleep on the sofa.

Fran narrowed her eyes and gave me a strange look. "Nina, it's not like I don't know you slept here before—without me."

Memories of exactly how I didn't sleep in her bed flooded across my mind's eye, and my skin grew so warm between the comment and the mental images that I could feel my ears burn red, and I was glad my hair was down so she couldn't see them.

"Yeah, well…" I tried. "I didn't want you to think I just—"

"Want to fuck me?" she asked, an amused smile playing about her lips.

Geez. What a loaded statement. I think if anyone but Fran had made it, I'd have had a snappy comeback; at least, I like to think so. I mean, sure, yeah, she was attractive, even better looking than she'd been in high school, with that sharp jaw angle and a new humorous sparkle in her eyes. There was also that kiss to contend with, too. Fuck it.

I couldn't figure out if she was trying to read my mind (and if my discomfort was that obvious) or if she was trying to proposition me. I also had nothing to say in response that wouldn't get me into trouble, one way or another. Boy, did it figure that she was going to law school.

I mean, if I said yes, was I agreeing that yes, that's what I'd want, that's what I'd wanted, or thanks for offering, yes? And if I said no, did it mean I wasn't thinking she might be concerned about that (which was a lie), that I didn't want to (sort of a lie—I didn't want to "fuck" her like that), or thanks for asking, but no? Not to mention I might inadvertently insult her. You know, imply that I found her undesirable or whatever, and not only was that certainly untrue, that would also hurt her feelings—I know it would have hurt mine. I wasn't going to do that to her.

But...I could handle this. I was Nina, after all, and I wasn't going to let a nice kiss and a pretty face rattle my cage, right? Right. I took a breath, let it out slowly, and smiled. "Does that mean you don't have an extra blanket?"

Fran's eyes widened, and I could see that she appreciated my nonresponse. "You're still a wisenheimer, huh?" She grinned at me. "C'mon, this way." She laughed and led me down the hallway to her room. I waited in the doorway to this bedroom I'd already visited several times in the past while she opened up her closet. After disappearing into it for a moment, she emerged with the disputed blanket, placed the folded brown square in my hands, then touched my arm.

"I don't bite, you know," she told me softly.

I smiled and took a step back. "How do you know I don't?" I searched her face for her answer. It was true—I was behaving—but I wasn't sure how far I could push that, given the circumstances. I mean, an old friend who happened to be beautiful, and I suspected more than willing, and not only that, but also in a place I already had some very intense sensual history. And...I wanted her.

Besides, my own promises to myself aside, I sensed danger here, that this would get me even more deeply involved in something I really didn't want. I had this instant understanding: sleeping with Fran would mean committing myself to her. And while I knew that even after all this time, we probably still had tons in common, would get along tolerably well, and could probably be quite happy together, it wasn't that amazing bolt from the blue that I was waiting to feel.

But even if it was, well, I had nothing to offer anyway. I mean, she was in law school, for chrissake, hooked up with an internship that would probably become her career, while I had not only just stopped going to school, I was working nonstandard jobs with nonstandard hours and spent every spare minute obsessed by music and art. The only thing I had to offer besides my dreams and my loyalty was the one thing that everybody wanted anyway—my participation in their orgasm. As far as I was concerned? That wasn't enough.

No, tempting as she was, if I slept with her and didn't make some sort of promises to her, I'd hurt her; and if I made those promises, I'd let myself down—because, well, just because.

Still…holding the blanket in one hand, I put my arms around her. She seemed surprised, but only for a moment, and as she pressed my body to her, I allowed myself to remember that she had been a good friend to me back then. Hell, she'd even let me borrow her car for my driver's license exam. She'd been solid then, and she was solid now. A few years might have passed, but the innate person—girl to woman—was the same. I don't know how I knew that, but I did. Bottom line? Fran was a nice girl—I wasn't. While I might have previously been in the habit of following a lead, I'd never been in the habit of breaking hearts—and I wasn't going to start now.

"I can't believe I'm holding you," she said, her voice a whisper against my throat. "I'd always thought we'd get a chance…I called you, I swear I did. Nina…" Her words seemed to catch in her throat. "I spoke with your father." Her voice rose slightly in pitch. "And he told me…he told me you had died, and then, he asked," she swallowed, "he asked that I please respect the family's privacy by not calling or sending anything."

I didn't know what to say. The anger that I'd thought long gone at my father threatened to roar through me, but he wasn't in the room. Fran was, though—real, solid, crying in my arms, and that was more important than anything else. I did the only thing I could think of—I dropped the blanket so I could hold her tighter and rocked her against me.

"It's my fault, you know," she said. "I told Samantha, I told her not to call, and she did anyway. She didn't believe me, she couldn't believe me."

"Shh…it's okay…it's okay," I soothed gently. I raised her tear-stained face to mine. "I'm so sorry," I told her and kissed her forehead, "I'm so sorry you had to go through that." I meant it, too, really meant it.

I quickly realized that even though my dad had lied, the pain she had felt had been very real, and I had better get my head out of my ass pretty darn soon and be a lot more sensitive. This was definitely, no, *Fran* was definitely not all about the fuck.

"Stay with me," she asked. "I don't want to let you go. I'm afraid you'll disappear." She placed a gentle kiss against my collarbone.

God. If I got into that bed with her...I didn't want to *fuck* her, but I did want to soothe her, to comfort her, to let her know I cared, that her pain touched me, deeply, and that I found her beautiful. But if I did that—if that happened—well, I just didn't know what else to do.

"Sleep, I promise, just sleep," Fran said, looking up at me again. I laughed lightly under my breath. Either we were on the same page, she was reading my mind, or I had been that readable. Since I prided myself on being rather inscrutable, maybe it was the first option.

"Ah, Fran," I sighed. "I can't promise that."

"Really?" she drawled, her eyes still managing to convey a layer of sensuality even through her tears and something else too—something like genuine affection. "And why's that? You don't like my bed? Too firm? Too soft?"

I shook my head no at each of those options and smiled. "No, no, nothing like that." I let my hands slide down her arms.

"Well, what then?" she asked, an amused if slightly exasperated expression crossing her cheeks.

It was time to come clean and just tell her. I mean, any more of this, and Fran might begin to think it was her personally, and I didn't want that.

"Uh, well..." I stalled, playing for time. It was amazing how quickly my cheeks and ears could burn. One second, normal skin, normal temperature, and the next, I was an overheated Christmas tree. I think she may have noticed.

"I'veneversleptinthatbed," I told her in a rush.

Fran shook her head in disagreement. "Nina, I know you were here before—with Candace. She told me all about you, well, except for your name, or I might have known it was you. It's totally okay, you know?" She gave me a bemused smile.

"No," I said, and took a deep breath. "I've never *slept* in that bed." I widened my eyes a bit, hoping she'd understand.

"Oh." Suddenly, she got it. "Oh! Okay, so you don't know if it's comfortable or not." She laughed and threw her arms around me, and after my eyebrows simmered down a bit, I laughed too.

I bent and picked up the blanket and what was left of my dignity. "So…where's the couch?"

"What, you've never been in the living room?" she teased.

"Nope, not once. I've never even been here while it was this light out."

Fran laughed again and rolled her eyes at me. "What are we gonna do with you?" She grabbed my hand. "This way."

I followed her down the hallway. It was true—kitchen, bed, bath? Been there. Living room? I knew where it was because I'd passed its entrance on the way in, but I'd never been through that portal, and frankly, the only light Candace ever had on was the light by the bed.

Fran didn't need to flip the light switch because, as bad as the weather was, it was still daylight. Murky, gloomy, snowy daylight, but still, somewhere above those clouds, the sun was shining and we were getting what was left.

"Here you go." She indicated with a sweep of an arm to indicate her sofa—and damn if it wasn't the required East Village futon with a very cool Chinese symbol printed on its fabric: the "double happiness" one, if I had it right.

After taking the blanket from her hands, I bent to pull the futon out into its sleeping position.

"Hey, let me help you with that."

"Sure," I agreed, and it was done in seconds.

She straightened, and we faced each other awkwardly.

"Sleep well," Fran told me softly, and bit her lip.

I half smiled back at her, fiddling with the blanket in my hands, running over a seam with my fingers. "Yeah, you too." We stared at each other, the silence growing even more awkward.

Finally, she gave me a little wave and began to ease away, but I couldn't, I just couldn't, after that whole emotional scene not five minutes ago, just let her go like that. Yeah, yeah, I know, I know, I was tuff and I was cool, but I couldn't be cold—not to anyone really, and especially not to Fran, not after what we'd just shared, never mind the fact that we'd been friends and teammates in the past.

I made a quick decision. "Hey, Fran?" I called to her retreating back. "Stay out here with me?"

"Yeah?" she asked, sounding uncertain and shy.

"Yeah," I affirmed with a smile and tossed the blanket on the sleeping platform. I sat on the edge and patted the spot next to me. "C'mon over."

Fran gave me one of those amazing smiles, and I swear I could feel my heart lift up with it. I'd missed her. It might have been my father's fault for telling everyone that stupid lie, but it was also mine for hiding and not trying to find her—or anyone else. The blame for that lay with me and me alone.

"I get the outside," I told her with a grin.

"*No problemo*," she agreed, climbing over to the wall side.

We got under the blanket, and I shifted to face her so I could say good night, only to find her already watching me.

"I've missed you," she said softly, tears threatening to fall from the corner of her eye. She patted my shoulder awkwardly.

I couldn't believe I was lying next to her, Fran, the ultimate scholar-athlete—and so fucking pretty—she'd been my friend, and I'd let time and distance come between us. I shouldn't have allowed that to happen—I'd been wrong, very wrong.

I reached out and gently stroked her errant locks back over her forehead. "I missed you, too," I told her sincerely. "I'm so sorry."

Her hand came off my shoulder, and her fingers carefully circled my wrist. She kissed my palm and the touch was so sweet, I couldn't help myself—I wrapped my arms around her and rubbed my cheek lightly against hers.

"It's my fault, you know," she whispered into my ear, "all of it."

"What's your fault, huh?" I asked gently. "You didn't do anything wrong."

Fran shifted against me. "It's my fault about Samantha that she changed her name and stayed in England."

"Now how could that be possible?" I asked. "I'm sure Sammy Blade's a big girl now, making big-girl decisions."

"You don't understand," she said, and pulled slightly away, "I'm the one who told Sammy—"

"That doesn't make anything your fault," I interrupted quietly and kissed her forehead.

"But it does," she insisted. "She wanted to hear it for herself when, before, she was just going to come back and surprise you. Instead, she made that call and," she sighed, "she never came home."

I simply held her and listened as she nestled back into me.

"When we finally spoke?" she continued, "she asked me not to call her Samantha, Sam, or Sammy—because the two people she missed most had called her that. She said she'd be called Ann or Annie from then on."

Fran's tears soaked my shirt and traveled down my neck. All I could do was hold her and do my best to soothe her as I absorbed her words and took careful note. Candace hadn't lied; her sometime-girlfriend's name *was* Annie. That made me feel better, because I really would have hated to think that Candace had lied to me. I also knew who both people were that Samantha, Ann, had referred to. One was me, and the other was her father, a fireman who had been killed "in the line of duty" as they say, during her junior year of high school.

"I think…I think she'd have found you that summer, if she'd been left alone, surprised you like she'd wanted," Fran said. "She'd have found you. She wouldn't have fallen apart the way she did."

She buried her face into my shoulder and shook. "And now you're here…and I still can't believe it."

Her tears tore through me, breaking me, pushing me against a wall I didn't want to hide behind anymore.

"Fran," I sighed and gathered her into my arms. I kissed the top of her head as she sobbed into my collarbone, then kissed her brow. "I'm right here," I assured her, and brushed the hair out of her eyes, then kissed them too. I was frantic with her pain, the need to erase it. She shifted against me again, sliding her legs against mine, and I was half on top of her when she raised tentative hands to my face. Her fingertips stroked my cheeks as I balanced myself on my forearms and gazed into her tear-starred eyes, eyes that wouldn't let me go.

"You're not going away?"

Oh, she was breaking my heart, breaking my mind, and I'd never before felt my whole body ache with the need to prove my words.

"I'm not going away. I promise." Every other thought, every promise I'd made to myself, flew out of my head in the face of that need. I brought my lips to hers.

Her kiss sent a line of fiery ice straight to my belly, and when her tongue played softly against my lips I could only invite her in: her mouth was everything I'd discovered before and more. It spoke to me, spoke to me of loss and longing, and when I lightly bit her lower lip I tasted something different—not the usual desire and need, though that was there too. I tasted her pain, I tasted her tears, and I felt driven to soothe her, to prove my intent beyond the force of words. Actions, not words, were what counted. I had to get under her skin and erase that hurt—hurt that I'd caused—forever.

Fran surged against me, her hips pressing against mine, and the cold fire in my belly lurched, then spread to my thighs. I leaned over her just the slightest bit and took hold of the edge of her sweatshirt, letting the back of my fingers trail against her warm skin as I lifted it off her.

Fran lay for a moment with her arms above her head, and her eyes were like molten gold. I trailed the back of my hand between her graceful breasts, down her taut stomach.

"You're very beautiful," I told her, because it was undeniably, incredibly true.

She smiled at me as I leaned over again to lay a kiss between my spread fingers over her navel.

I reached up again to kiss her, and as her lips pressed, gently insistent against mine, she rose up to sit with me. I couldn't stop running my fingers through her hair and over the high planes of her cheeks, simply in awe of her.

Her fingertips sketched my face, then my neck, and her lips followed—short, sharp little nibbles followed by languorous strokes along my throat. Her hands trailed down to my waist where they grabbed a gentle hold of the sweatshirt she had lent me earlier. "May I?" she asked, her thumbs sliding softly along my skin.

While I shuddered lightly in response to her touch, my heart warmed. No one had ever asked me before.

"Yes," I told her simply, and in less than a second, it was done. I shivered in the sudden cold, and Fran wrapped herself around me.

"Come here," she murmured into my ear before she nibbled along my earlobe, "let me keep you warm." The kisses she gave me were tender as she laid them along my shoulder and throat. The sudden heat and press of her breasts against mine sent a thrill of electric shock right through me, and the feel of the beat of her heart against mine made me want to weep. How could I have let her go? I could have called, I could have asked her parents; there was any one of a dozen different things I could have done, and didn't.

"God, I've missed you," I gasped, and pulled her even closer, kissing her softly, deeply, my hands first lightly tracing, then molding against her. Arms. Ribs. A shoulder blade as defined as an angel's wing. Fran.

I wanted, I needed to show her in a definite way that I had admired and loved her as a girl, that I was so sorry, sorry for the passage of time, for the loss and the pain. I needed her to know how I wouldn't let that happen again, and as I planted soft kisses on her neck, down the hollow of her throat, and right over her heart, I slid my fingertips beneath her waistband and looked up into her eyes to see if this was okay, if it was what she wanted. That was all that mattered.

"Let me help you," she offered. She sat up slightly, placed her hands on mine, and together we peeled her pants off. I crawled up the bed and lay down next to her, and she twisted on her side to face me. We simply stared at each other.

She drew her fingertips from my cheek down my neck, to my chest. Her fingers whispered on the curve of my breast, and when she reached my waist, her eyes traveled back to mine. "May I?" they asked, and I smiled my answer. "Yes."

I let her slide them off me, and she kissed my navel, then my thighs as she bared them. I sat up on my heels and shivered in the morning cold, and she flowed up the bed, bringing the blanket with her and throwing it around us both like a cape. Her skin was soft against me as she placed one hand on my face and the other on my waist.

The kiss we shared now had a new taste—it still held hints of loss, and it spoke of desire; I didn't recognize the other part, but it was something I instantly craved. She trailed her thumb along the edge of my jaw until it came to my chin again, resting and rubbing lightly in the curve beneath my lip. I had never been so aware of that spot before as her lips kneaded a path to that sensitive place between jawline and neck.

"Let me love you," Fran asked, her voice a low stirring in my ear.

My heart hammered in triple time: with an emotion I couldn't name, with pure arousal, and with confusion as she pulled back a moment to look at me. What did she mean? Was this just another way of saying "fuck"? But nothing about her spoke to anything I'd ever known. Bemused, I smiled and shrugged—I didn't know what to say.

Fran's eyes went wide for a moment, then she gave me such a beautiful smile my chest tightened with the joy of it. She took both my hands in hers. "I'm not going to hurt you," she promised as she kissed each hand in turn, then held them both against her heart. She rose slowly on her knees and leaned into me, touching my face as I pressed my hands against her chest where I could feel the flutter of her breath and the solid thump under her ribs.

She kissed my cheeks and my eyes; she stroked my hair and ran gentle hands down my arms and up again before she embraced me and laid me down beneath her.

At that very moment, I grew afraid, desperately afraid—I don't know why. I knew I could stop this, this whatever was going to happen, knew I could change this, flip it; all it would take was a toss of the head and a sharp twist and I could ensure that this would be just like any other time, any other person, and I could walk away without having lost a thing.

But I couldn't. Fran's touch was so tender, she'd been through so much, and I could absolutely feel that she loved me. We'd been friends before, and I knew that no matter what happened, we'd be friends after. That, I could trust. She didn't want points, she didn't want bragging rights, and she didn't want a fuck. All she'd asked was if she could love me. And I owed her something, didn't I?

I twined my arms around her neck and buried my face in it. Her hands trailed along my spine, then held my head very gently to her shoulder. I pressed my cheek into her collarbone and laid soft kisses into her throat before she raised my face to her lips again.

"I won't do anything you don't want me to," she whispered. Her chest pressed against mine again, and I wanted so much to simply just believe as her heart pounded against me. I reached for her face and kissed her desperately, then ran my hands through her hair and across the span of her shoulders, down the narrow valley of her back, and spread my hands across the tight width of her hips as she etched patterns down my ribs.

She slid down my body, licking and nipping along the way while her fingers alternately splayed, then gripped my skin.

"I need to feel you," she murmured into my navel while her fingertips rolled my nipple. She fit her shoulders between my thighs and bit the tendon next to my aching cunt, then placed her hands on either side. Fran raised her eyes to mine.

"I need to drink you in," she told me, and dipped her head to my need, kissing my cunt the way she kissed my mouth.

I sighed with the sensation, and when her tongue slid between the lips of my pussy, she did it with such perfect precision I involuntarily arched my back and cried out. Fran's tongue drew soft circles around my clit, and I was floating again, my world coming to pieces as she moved my pussy with her lips. I didn't know what to do with my hands, and as if sensing my confusion, she reached up and laced her fingers with mine. I held on to the only anchor I had as she brought me higher and higher. When she began to use the flat of her tongue to stroke me, creating a constant pressure on my clit, my body swam along the crest, riding the top, riding her tongue. Until it reached the edge of entrance.

Suddenly the wave I'd been riding gave way and crushed me under it. Van's smirk and Trace's eyes, the feel of her hands pushing against me in the skybox, the sudden hard cool of the floor smacking my head when my mother tried to beat the gay out of me, Cap's enthusiastic "there's the money shot," and the sound of every woman I'd ever fucked, all combined with the guilty knowledge of Fran's tears, were pulling me, shoving me into a tightening spiral, and I was going to drown.

I sat up almost involuntarily. "Fran—don't—" I gasped, fighting to breathe.

She'd stopped before I'd even really asked. Wordlessly, she shifted until she was next to me, and while I didn't resist when she wrapped her arms around me, I couldn't look at her. I felt about twenty shades of stupid. Maybe Jen was right; maybe I was just a kid.

Fran wrapped her legs around my waist so that one supported my back and pulled me closer. I leaned my head against her cheek, and she played with my hair, brushing it off my neck and shoulder.

"Nina," she said gently, "I would never do anything you didn't want to do. I don't want to take anything you don't want to give."

I smiled despite myself, because deep inside, I knew that. "I know that, Fran," I replied just as softly, "it's that…I'm not the person you think I am."

Fran shifted until she kneeled next to me, and I instantly missed her warmth as I gazed out the window. It was so gray out, I couldn't tell if it was still snowing or not.

"Look at me," she requested gently.

I glanced over and met her eyes, then dropped mine. I couldn't. I was such a jerk.

"Nina, please," she said again, and laid tender fingers on my face, "look at me."

It was her touch, matching her tone as it did, that convinced me, and I finally turned my face to hers, afraid of what I'd find. I stared at her wordlessly and discovered nothing but kindness shining out at me.

"I know you," she told me, stroking my face, and her perfect smile beaming at me. "I *know* you."

I shifted restlessly and tossed my head in negation. "No, you don't," I told her sadly, staring at her. My hands wanted to touch her, but I stopped myself and put them in my lap. "And I don't think you'd like me."

Fran closed the space between us and cupped my face in her hands. "You're wrong." She smiled at me again, a soft lift of her lips. "I *do* know you." She stroked my cheek, then placed the flat of her palm against my chest. "I know this—I've seen it."

I was touched, but I shook my head again. "No, Fran, really. I've changed—a lot. I'm not who you think I am."

I met her eyes once more, and she gazed at me with such warmth I wanted to cry. I wanted her to understand: the girl she'd known *was* dead, had been dead for a long time. I didn't know who I was, but I wasn't her—not anymore, anyway.

Fran sighed, cupped my face with one hand again, and drew soft lines along my shoulder with the other. I leaned into her touch. "Don't you think I'd know you'd be different? And," she kissed my lips softly, "think, Nina. Would you have walked me home, lent me your scarf, God," she laughed lightly, "saved me from breaking my ass in the snow?"

Fran had my attention, and this time, I didn't look away. Could she be right? Was a part of me, any part of me, still the person we both remembered? I shifted self-consciously.

"I've done some pretty callous things."

"Who hasn't?" she asked me simply.

"But they haven't done the things I've done," I responded. "They haven't—"

Fran hushed me and gripped my shoulder. "Nina, you could have lied to me about Candace from the start," she said, staring at me intently, willing me to understand. "You didn't have to say anything—she won't tell Samantha more than she told me. Well," she smiled wryly, "maybe a little more, but not much. There's a very good chance that no one would have known anything." She cupped my chin with her free hand and again ran her thumb into the hollow she was fond of. "Don't you see?"

"But, Fran." I shook my head in confusion. I mean, I thought my reasons for telling her were pretty self-evident. "Why would I lie? I mean, you had to know. This is your home, for chrissake." I could feel the heat rise up in my face as I said it, but I said it. I mean, how could I *not* tell her? And even if it hadn't been her home, it was someone she knew, people she knew. She had a right to know who she was dealing with so she could make informed choices, right? Well, I thought so, anyway.

"You're proving my point for me." She smiled and pressed her fingertips lightly against my sternum again. "This is the same. All the rest? It's just the outside. You know," she laughed lightly, "you were always so tough. Even as a freshman you had this fierce nobility."

I took her hand in mine. "Fierce, huh?" I chuckled. "In that uniform?"

Fran tossed her head back to laugh again that pure bell note, her hair flying about her like a golden mane. "Are you kidding?" she asked. "You actually made postman blue look hot!"

I laughed with her—those uniforms were terrible. "I thought you and Sammy Blade had, you know, a thing?"

Fran shook her head and told me with a wry smile, "We did—until you."

"What?" I asked, shaking my head a little with confusion.

Fran placed a warm hand on my shoulder. "Nina, we used to fight over you. First I'd said it was because of detentions, but that wasn't exactly true." She grinned at me, charmingly half embarrassed. "And then you joined the swim team, and it became who was going to give you a ride if you needed one, whose car you'd borrow, all sorts of things. You know, I'm amazed we didn't try to kill each other, but it was a relatively unspoken rivalry." She laughed, and that sound took me back to a place, a place where we'd all been together, back racing competitively in school.

We'd called her Kitt back then because under the cool, collected, and ever-poised exterior, Fran was fire, a jungle cat in school colors, so fucking hot and so fucking fierce she never left the pool without placing first. Hence "Kitt," because she'd been a tiger in the water ever since she was a cub.

Samantha had just come out of a first-place win in the pool, and I hurried carefully over. "Hey, nice dice, Blade!" I gave her a hug.

"Thanks, thanks," she said, returning the pressure before we awkwardly let each other go.

"Oh hey, refreshing electrolyte drink?" I asked her and waved in the general direction of the large orange monstrosity that held water and what we generally referred to as powdered urine, colored for misdirection.

"Definitely. Required. Now," she answered with a smile as we tried not to slip on the tiles over to the cooler.

I grabbed us each a cup, then handed one over.

"Nice. Very nice race," Kitt said to Samantha over my shoulder.

"Thanks," Samantha answered shortly, then downed the cherry-flavored drink. I glanced over to see a bored expression on her face. Not a good sign.

"Well, we've had the slice, we've had the dice. You guys will have to show us all how it's done in the third heat—after the next event, to give us a break." Kitt's eyes traveled to the other side of the pool, where the overstocked opponents sat. Samantha looked with her.

"It's a little rest, better than none," she commented flatly.

The silence dragged out.

"Hey, Sam, where's your towel?" Kitt asked into the silence.

She shrugged in response. "Probably in the locker room," she said blandly. "Don't worry about me." This time, Sam stared at her and I watched as Kitt's face worked.

She opened her mouth as if she'd wanted to speak but had thought better of it, then took her towel off her shoulders and tossed it at me.

"Share it," she said curtly, "I'm up for the medley now." She stalked off to the starting blocks.

Well, that was certainly bizarre, I thought. Maybe it was me, and I walked in a circle of chaos, bringing those around me into confusion and personality morphs. That sounded about right. Or maybe everyone was PMSing. That was more likely. Whatever.

"And you?" Fran continued, bringing me back to the present. "You were so immune to either of us."

I was more than taken aback—I was shocked, although maybe I shouldn't have been. I mean, I'd had the same crush on her that the rest of the student body'd had. Well, maybe a little more, in reality, since we did hang out, and I knew that Samantha and I had had—well, we never got that far.

Something, I don't know what, shifted within me, broke, re-formed, changed. I owed Fran—for her time, for her feelings, for what she had felt then, and for what I was putting her through now. An amazing new thought ran through my head—maybe I owed myself, too.

I gave her a soft smile as I touched her face, framing her cheeks with my fingers. "I'm sorry," I told her, and I meant it—I was sorry for everything —"I didn't know." That would be the last time either one of us mentioned Samantha or anything about her for some time.

She seized my hand and kissed it. "I don't...I mean...it doesn't matter if we make love or not." She kissed my hand again, then folded my fingers over and held my hand to her heart. "I don't care what you've done and I don't care where you've been," she declared. "I just love...that, that you're really here."

How could I not respond to that? Here she was, so loving, so kind, and, a part of my mind said, so aroused and cheated; how could I deny that? My former roommates? Honestly, they sucked. The women I'd fucked? Didn't care about me, well, except maybe for Candace. I think she might have tried. The women at the bar? Just wanted to score. Besides, it's not like I hadn't seen what happened to anyone I'd observed—lovers came and went. Declarations of romantic love would spread like confetti one night, only to be followed by heartbroken sobs the next. I didn't want that.

And as far as Samantha went, well, she wasn't here; she was a stranger, lived across the pond, had never come home. And given that Candace was her girlfriend or ex or whatever it was, that meant that she had more than likely known how to get in touch with me for several months—and hadn't bothered. She wasn't interested and didn't care.

No. I deserved something more than that, didn't I? Fran had made no demands, had pushed no agenda, was still giving me every opportunity to handle this any way I wanted. I made a decision: what I needed, what I wanted, was her.

If I was going to do this, it would have to be now or forever hold my peace about it because I didn't know if I could do this tomorrow— and I saw that this, this whatever could grow between us, had the potential to be beautiful. I wanted something beautiful, I wanted someone beautiful, in the exact way that she was—inside as well as out. Maybe that was something I could be too, someday.

I kissed her cheek softly and took both her hands in mine.

"Francesca Kitt DiTomassa," I whispered in her ear, "it matters to me." I kissed the corner of her eye where another tear threatened to fall.

"I...I want to make love with you," I said quietly. Her breath caught, and she absolutely stilled. Her eyes searched mine, and I answered honestly. "I want you to love me."

She smiled at me with such fierce joy, then looked at my lips with such a sensual twist to her own that the first part made me feel like I had stepped into the sun, and the second simply thrilled through me.

I was scared, so scared I could feel myself shake as she laid me down with contained strength and kissed me again. This time fire lanced through me in tightening strings that ran to my wrists as my tongue slipped between her teeth and savored the taste of my cunt on her tongue. Her skin was velvety warm as her legs molded to mine.

My fear ebbed when she ran her fingers down my ribs, and I gasped when she grasped my nipple, teasing one, then the other, to hardened, sensitive peaks.

But it was when her teeth closed on the tendon of my neck as her belly pushed into mine that the fire that had shot through me before came racing back like high tide, taking me with it, settling in my cunt.

I seized Fran and kissed her fiercely, trying to show her with my tongue how she made me feel, and when finally, finally, I felt the solid heat of her pussy on mine, I let her slide between my legs.

"Thank you," she sighed into my ear before she arched her back away from me, which brought even more pressure to bear on my tightening clit. She began a slow and steady glide against me, and as I scratched my fingertips along the lines of her back, I snaked the other hand between us so I could spread our joined lips.

"God..." she groaned as our clits met, and I agreed. Fran slid against me with a purpose now, and my hips moved to the same rhythm. Every kiss of her cunt took away another part of the world; each time her clit licked mine my skin grew hotter, until I couldn't take it anymore, and my hands, which had been alternately stroking her shoulders and grasping her breasts, teasing her nipples, tasting them, flew to her beautifully toned ass that flexed against me. I pulled her as hard into me as I could. I so desperately needed to hold her, to be completely with her, to get even closer under her skin that I wrapped my body around her, my knees pressing behind her shoulders, and my hands guiding her ass firmly on my cunt.

Fran instinctively spread her legs a bit and gasped at the increased pussy contact. I felt desperate as those slick, wet lips hugged my clit and hers ground into me.

The first time it happened I wasn't sure. The slip of her cunt on mine felt so amazing that even though I felt something different, the sensation was so brief and this all felt just so good, I didn't care. When it happened again seconds later, I definitely noticed, and so did she.

"Oh," she groaned, a low and throaty sound, and she buried her face into my neck.

I opened eyes I hadn't realized I'd closed. It felt exactly like, well, I couldn't tell you then, but I can certainly tell you now: the tip of a thumb when it moves just inside you.

Fran's luscious cunt now thrust more than slid, and I was so amazed by this new sensation that was in me, even the slightest bit, that I literally stilled.

"Hey," she asked softly as her pussy eased against mine, "are you okay?" She lifted herself up and looked at me.

I gazed back into her tawny eyes and stroked her magnificent shoulders. Even had we not been on swim team together, even had I not known anything else about her, I would've been able to tell she had at least been a swimmer by those shoulders. I traced the muscles with my fingertips, then returned to her face and neck, pushing away the unruly locks that fell across her cheeks.

Her face flushed, skin sweat-shiny, and hair loose, she awed me. I had never seen anyone more beautiful than she was at that moment, a lioness above me, and the expression on her face threatened to bring me to tears.

I relaxed my legs, content to twine them around hers, and she relaxed as well, settling her legs under mine, propping herself on her forearms. Her cunt still pressed against mine, for which I was grateful— I didn't want this to end. Her fingers were warm on my cheeks, and she rubbed her thumb across my chin while she waited for my answer.

"I'm okay." I smiled and got a sudden attack of the shys. "It's just…I mean, I…" I took a breath and tried again. "It's just…I mean, I never—"

Fran cut me off with a kiss that shot straight to my clit and wrapped me in her arms. She was a phenomenal kisser, and as I flicked my tongue against hers, I pushed my hips into hers.

She tore her mouth from mine and scraped her teeth against my neck. "I know, Nina," she whispered hotly into my ear, then kissed my throat. "I know."

She ran strong fingers up my leg and slipped her arm under my neck, and just as neatly, she shifted over until she was lying next to me, almost on top of me. I didn't wait for her to lean in to kiss me—I wrapped my arms around her shoulders. I'd found her full breast and stroked along its curve before catching her nipple, tweaking it. Her kiss set my skin dancing while her fingers nimbly played with my short pussy hairs.

"Mmm..." she murmured, "you know, I've kept the habit myself."

I chuckled despite the rising heat—I knew she meant the swim-team trim. Hey, it's a habit you don't break. Why? Someone's got to buy all those trimmers, right?

I replaced my fingertips with my lips and sucked in the honey-sweet taste of her skin. Her nipple felt gratifyingly hard under my tongue, and I let my free hand glide down her taut stomach muscles to find out if what she had said was true. I had thought so—it had felt that way when her pussy was against mine—but I wasn't sure. When my fingers found her, I knew.

"I see," I whispered back. She groaned when I cupped her cunt in the palm of my hand, my fingertips alternately squeezing and massaging her full lips, swollen with such need that they'd parted, her clit so hard I could feel it throb against my palm. I wanted so much to be in her that my fingers twitched and my clit jumped with hers. It jumped even more when she slipped two fingers around it and slid them slowly up and down my pussy.

"You're so soft," Fran said. She explored my cunt and stroked back up. "And you're so...hard..." she added, squeezing my clit between her fingers.

I couldn't take it anymore. I had to touch her. My pussy hurt knowing she was ready for me, slick and open and hard. I took her clit between my thumb and forefinger and began to gently jerk her off while I let my middle and ring fingers play right around the hot wet entrance to her cunt. Oh yes. That. Felt. Good.

"God, what are you doing to me?" Fran groaned, her hips surging in time with my strokes and pressing against my clit even harder, which made me groan in response.

"I'm jerking you off," I told her honestly when I could think for a moment. She tossed her head and exposed her neck. It was a target I had to take, and I dragged my lower lip along its length before I bit down lightly. "You are so hard...and so wet," I added, teasing my fingers against her opening.

Fran rolled over me slightly, and the hand that had been under my neck cupped my head. My lips met her halfway, and she pumped my clit harder, faster, her hips timed to her thrust, my body meeting hers.

I hadn't slipped my fingers completely inside her yet, but I was dying to, and though I was surprised when she anticipated me and placed a fingertip by my opening, I was ready.

"God...yes," I told her when I opened my eyes to see her watching me.

"Are you sure?" she asked, searching my face. "Really sure?"

I switched the angle of my hand and brought my thumb against her clit, the very tips of my fingers almost, but not quite inside of her. She was so wet I wanted to come right then.

"I want to feel you come inside of me," I told her. I wasn't afraid anymore. I needed her to feel everything I was feeling—all those wordless emotions that were all about her, everything I'd ever thought or felt and how much, just how so much I cared. And I did. The combination of her tears and tenderness, my memory and my crush made me love her. *She* made me love her.

"Fran...I need to be inside you...please..." She shifted her leg in response, opening herself up to me in such a trusting gesture it nearly undid me.

Her pussy was such welcome relief to my fingers—hot, tight, and soft. God, she was soft and slick, and I moved slowly within her, the feel of her loving cunt driving me insane with the twin drives of lust and humility. This was Fran, and Fran loved me. I knew it, I could feel it. Her body told me.

"You feel so good," I choked out, overcome by the amazing sensations she was stroking out of my clit and the way her pussy hugged me as I moved within her, each stroke an embrace.

I thrust my hips against her, bellies meeting, and still, she wouldn't enter me; she maintained her fingertips at my entrance. I pushed against her, trying to embrace her in return.

"I don't want to hurt you," she gasped into my ear.

I loved that—that she was thinking of me even as her cunt began to pull on me, urging me farther within.

I thrust deep inside of her and wrapped my leg over her hip. "You won't," I told her. "I want you to *know* how alive I am."

"Oh, yeah…" she groaned as I ground my thumb against her clit and pressed my fingers up inside her. Her fingertips moved against me, almost inside of me, making me frantic with need, my cunt aching to hold her.

"You're so open," she murmured, voice catching as she moved her fingers ever so slowly into that ache, "you are so beautiful, Nina, so damned beautiful."

She paused for one heart-stopping moment, raising her head and shoulders, and stared at me, eyes shining bright and wordless.

Lowering her lips closer to mine, she whispered, "I love you. I've always loved you."

I smiled gently up at her. "I know, Fran. I know." I kissed that perfect mouth again, and as she slipped her tongue between my lips, with careful tenderness, Fran slid her fingers inside of me, filling me.

It hurt—a sweet, aching pierce that went through my cunt to my chest—and I gasped into her lips as her tongue tangled with mine. My back arched to make room for her inside me.

She watched me closely, her eyes full of love and concern. "Did I hurt you?" she asked, stilling her fingers within me.

I breathed around this, this new thing, around the feel of her, the knowledge of her body in mine, the absoluteness of it.

"It hurts," I conceded, my voice sounding soft and small to my ears, "but…don't stop…it feels good, too."

She slid deeper within me, and I could feel every single little bit of her moving in there. I stared with wonder as the pain receded and the pleasure that had been at the back of it came roaring to the front. I had stopped moving within her, and I kissed her hungrily as I resumed. God, she felt good—inside her pussy, inside of me.

I moved on nothing but pure instinct as I dug the fingers of my free hand into her back and hers pulled at my shoulder, rolling me even closer to her. Sweat-slick, her belly rode against mine, and she buried her head into my neck. There was nothing but the sound of our breath, hard and harsh, and the feel of skin to skin until I heard it—soft and wet, like the most tender of kisses.

Fran's cunt tightened around me, and I could feel my own bear down on the incredible feeling of her inside me.

"Kiss me?" she asked hoarsely, and I glanced at the amazing

flush of her skin and the golden flash of her eyes before I did. Her body jumped as we thrust in and against each other, the agonizing cunt tension riding, tightening, pulling like a thread of light.

Fran broke and took me with her as I felt the unmistakable lock of her cunt.

"God yes," I ground out, "please come."

Her forearm pressed over mine with such force it was almost painful. I didn't care; it didn't matter at all because there was nothing but this—this unrelenting, beautiful tension, this barely chained divinity. I prayed to it.

"Come deep inside of me."

She moaned at those words, a low and desperately sensual sound as she tensed against me. "God…Nina," she cried, her free hand digging into my back, "I love you," and she thrust so deeply within me it I felt it in my heart. "Come with me," she choked out, then kissed me—hard. "Come with me."

My body exploded at her request. "I am," I gasped out, amazed with the realization that *this* was *it*, and it was too much, just too much—the feel of her on me, in me, the pounding wave that ground me down before it. I pressed my head against her chest and the sound that her heart beat back at me, and I cried out as the storm rode past.

"Hey, easy, easy now. It's okay," she murmured into my hair. "I've got you." Her pussy softened around me, and as reluctant as I was to leave that warmth, I withdrew gently, knowing that pressure would soon become uncomfortable for her. I laid my hand on her chest next to my face. And cried.

Fran slid gently out of me, leaving me empty. She crushed me to her.

"It's okay, it's okay," she soothed, kissing my head in between her words, her hands strong on my back. "Oh, Nina…"

She covered me with her body, soothing me with tender kisses and words that I gratefully drank in. Finally, I blinked up at her to find her gazing at me with the same brightness in her eyes and gently cradled her face with my fingertips. Brushing a tear from her cheek, I let my thumb remain there, just enjoying the feel of her.

"Are you all right? Did it…did I hurt you?" she asked with the same concern she'd shown me this entire time.

"I'm fine," I smiled at her, "never better." And honestly, for the first time in a long time, it was true.

"I'm glad," Fran grinned back at me, "that was—"

She stopped abruptly, staring at the hand she'd been about to stroke my forehead with. She sat up and flipped it over to examine it. I sat up with her and leaned over to see for myself.

"What's the matter?" I asked as I stroked her long curls from her cheek back over her shoulder. The face she gave me was stricken—then she showed me her hand. It seemed fine until I took it into my own and examined it. The back was flecked with dark red—the same red that outlined her nail beds had settled into the knuckle creases of her fingers. Paint. Okay, so?

"I don't understand."

Fran closed her eyes a moment, then opened them. She showed me the other side of her hand.

"Oh…" I gasped softly, understanding what I saw, what it meant. It was as if she had dipped only the front of her fingers in a red so brilliant it seemed almost unreal, while the center of her palm gleamed wetly, a darker color, from where it had pooled. Blood. My blood.

Fran closed her hand and pulled it away from me. "Nina…" she began and stopped, staring at me with golden eyes gone dark. "Nina… why…I mean, just—oh!" She pulled me into her arms and began to truly weep, tucking her head into my shoulder.

I wrapped myself around her as her shoulders heaved, rocking her, hopefully calming her.

"Shh…shh…" I murmured, planting kisses into her hair. I took her hand, the one she had curled to her chest, and laced my fingers through it. I made her open it up and pressed my palm against hers. It seemed appropriate—this, my hand, had been the one inside of her. Essence to essence. It seemed right to bring them together.

"Fran," I sighed. I kissed our joined hands, kissed her knuckles, her fingertips. I spread her fingers open and exposed her still-damp palm. I touched my fingertips to it and on impulse, painted a dot on my chest with it. I did the same to her.

Finally, she spoke. "Why, Nina, why did you—"

She shrugged helplessly when I put my fingers to her lips.

"Don't you see?" I asked, smiling at her gently. I could feel that smile widen as I remembered the sound that I'd heard, the sound of soft kisses. I knew what it was—it was the sound of us, the sound of making love, and despite the cool morning air, the realization warmed me throughout.

Fran shook her head, not yet knowing what I saw or heard.

The warmth of my heart grew through me, filling me, overflowing until it floated above my skin, and I had to share that feeling, that knowledge, with her. I shifted so that her back leaned against my chest, and I still rocked her lightly as I told her what it meant.

"No matter what happens," I whispered, "this is yours." I kissed her head, then moved her hair so I could kiss her neck and shoulder. "If I died tomorrow…"

She shivered violently at those words, then twisted around to kiss me fiercely. "Don't say that! You're not allowed to say that," she pleaded as she bowled me over with her strength and her fear and her love.

Her kiss was fueled by adrenaline, and I let her surge against me, reassure herself again that I was solid as her lips crushed mine.

"Whatever happens, Fran," I explained softly as we broke apart and she gazed at me, "this…" and I took her hand and closed her fingers over her palm, "this will always be yours." I rolled her gently over to prove it.

I woke up on an unfamiliar world, a different, softer world—one that held the unbelievable sight of Francesca Kitt DiTomassa wrapped protectively around me, her golden mane spread across my throat, her hand cupping my breast and its thumb occasionally tracing its curve, and a splendidly shaped leg draped over mine. I lay there, absorbing the experience, then lifted my head to look out the window. It was still gray out, and from what I could see, the world outside had become soft and white.

CHEMISTRY

Love and laughter—
it's what we're all after
Skin to skin—it's all chemistry

"Chemistry"—Life Underwater

You would think that being involved with Fran would force me to think about Samantha, and it did, sometimes: the realness of her was an occasional haze on my skin, and I rounded corners and expected to see her or looked up and expected to catch her eyes. Those times I was haunted at work, at home, even when I was with Fran.

On a few occasions we'd be in the middle of making out and I'd think "she and Samantha did this," or we'd make love and I'd think of the two of them together, which kinda flipped me out. I didn't know who I was more jealous of, and the thought of them together made me so fuckin' hot I twitched. I didn't think it made me a bad person. I chalked it up to being young, dumb, and full of, um, hormones, honestly.

After those first few days, when we were snowed in together, she must have thought about some of the same things, because the very next time I'd gone to her apartment, she'd changed the cover on the futon, rearranged her bedroom, and managed to mention that she'd bought a new mattress. I took the hint and broke it in with her. Yes, it was quite comfortable.

Life consisted of work, rehearsals, and Fran, who was amazingly supportive of my music. She'd never really heard it. I mean, I took my guitar over and played a bit, practicing lines over and over, writing lyrics and rehearsing melodies, but she'd never heard the band.

Something in me had changed—and not just the fact that my pseudo-virginity was now a myth. I got a brand-new pair of buzzers and retrimmed my hair, dyed it black, and with Stephie's help placed a bloodred inch-wide stripe down the back center. Oh, the smell of Manic Panic hair dye in the morning—crayons and Play-Doh—who could ask for anything more?

Strangely, though, my pants felt different. Nothing sat right over my hips or thighs; everything just twisted and made me uncomfortable, and I abandoned anything but button flies and army pants. I also started to wear underwear because I was just too damn sensitive, but I wore only thongs. Besides, Fran liked them.

Things had changed a bit at work, too. Jen stopped calling me "kid" as much, and while women still came on to me with alarming frequency, I didn't need her help quite as much. In fact, I'd been semi-promoted. I now backed Jen up at the door and occasionally filled in for her, while Dee Dee was showing me how the books worked. In fact, I'd been coming in some afternoons when we were closed so I could review the bar order and receive deliveries with Dee Dee.

"A head for business, that's what you've got, Nina," she'd tell me when I asked her questions. All that math with Atilla the Nun hadn't been in vain.

The night was quiet. I'd had a rehearsal earlier with the band, and Jerkster had decided to come hang out for while, which was fine by me.

Jen had called to say she was coming in late so I was "doing the door" until she arrived, but since only three people were in the bar, Dee Dee sat with me, reviewing the bar order and asking my opinions and reasons about why we should order what.

The bar phone rang and Dee Dee answered it.

"For you," she told me after asking whoever it was to hold on a moment. She handed me the receiver. "It's Fran."

"'Lo, Kitt," I said, with the lowest, sexiest tone I could muster. It was funny; no one used her nickname anymore but me, and it was very special between us. I could tell she enjoyed hearing it—her smile would brighten and her eyes would sparkle more.

"Hey, baby," she answered. I could hear the smile in her voice. "You working tonight? Rehearsing?"

Honestly, no matter what my confusions were, I loved her with everything I had, and make no mistake, that's never gone away.

"It's gonna be quiet tonight," I told her.

"Well, I'm free," she said, "and…I'd love to see you." She drew the last few words out with a little roll that made me smile at the image it conjured in my head. I wanted to see her, too.

"I'd love that too, but I have to go back to the Rock at some point. I have a rehearsal tomorrow."

"Lucky for us both then that I'm free until the day after. Stay over tonight, and I'll go back with you tomorrow."

"You're gonna come by here, then?" I asked, pleasantly surprised.

She had hung out there while I was working, but not very often. She *did* have classes to attend. I also suspected that the attention I got on some of the more crowded nights bothered her. So even though we'd never formally defined what we were or called each other "girlfriend" or anything like that (and I really *hate* the term "lover"— it sounds so, so, just, I don't know—I just don't like it as an overall blanket term) I made sure she *knew* whose bed I was going to be in— hers, without a doubt.

"Yeah, absolutely. I, uh…" and she hesitated, something she rarely did. "I really want to see you."

"And I'd like to be with you," I returned. "I miss you." I meant it. I hadn't seen her in a few days, and although we'd spoken during that time, it wasn't the same thing at all.

"Yeah?" she asked, her voice softer, uncertain.

"Absolutely," I affirmed.

"Great!" she answered cheerfully. "I'll see you in a little while. Ciao!"

"Ciao, Francesca," I said, and clicked off. I returned my attention to the bar, only to find Dee Dee smiling at me.

"What?" I asked, grinning. I couldn't help that.

"*Sie hat dich gern.*" Dee Dee smiled at me.

I gave her a puzzled look, not understanding what she'd said. I hadn't gotten really past the basic greetings yet—but I was trying.

"She really likes you," she translated, her eyes sparkling.

"Well," I glanced down at the books before us on the bar because Dee Dee's regard made me feel a little shy, "I certainly hope so."

"Love is a very strange thing, Nina," Dee Dee said solemnly, "and it makes us strange even to ourselves." She paused, then grabbed a few glasses from under the bar. She poured cream into one, juice into another, vodka into the third, and plain old soda into the last one.

"Which ones would you absolutely not mix together?" she asked expectantly.

"Cream and juice."

"And why is that?" she prompted.

"It'll curdle the cream, of course," I explained, puzzled. I knew she knew this; she was a chemistry major.

Dee Dee promptly mixed some of the juice with some of the cream in a separate glass. "And you are right, of course," she said as we watched it transform into cheese. She held up the glass to show me the results, then deftly flicked it away under the sink. "But," and she held up her index finger to make her point, "watch this." She strained some vodka through ice and carefully mixed it with the cream and the juice. Even though I was watching, I can't tell you exactly how she did it—but a few good shakes later, she poured a thick and creamy mixture that looked exactly like a pale orange shake.

"Try it," she urged, so I did. Jerkster came bopping over from the corner where he'd been sitting, and I offered him a sip, too. It was very nice, actually—smooth and cool, velvety and light, with a summery orange taste. It tasted just like a...

"A Creamsicle!" Jerkster announced, and I agreed. That's exactly what it tasted like, a grown-up Creamsicle with just the lightest of kicks.

"How did you do that?" I asked Dee Dee, smiling. "That was some trick!"

"Ah, nothing," she said, waving away the compliment. "You like?" she asked Jerkster, raising her eyebrows at him.

He peeped over the straw he joyfully sucked on. "Uh-huh," he said from around the plastic. The cup started to make that burbling sound as he got to the bottom, and he bopped happily off back to the jukebox.

Dee Dee observed him for a few more moments, then returned her attention to me. "It's...it's a lot like love, Nina," she said, pointing to the two empty glasses. "In the first example, we have two items—mutually exclusive, so different, and when they mix? One tries to become the other or the other tries to absorb the first to such a degree that they create something useless—and both are ruined. But, in our second example?" She paused and smiled. "There's something else—a catalyst that shares elements of both, yet it is separate, different. When it is used in the proper way, all these pieces give up a part of themselves, yet here they are, uniquely themselves, and together, something uniquely different—each a contributing element."

I got it, I really did. "It's a bit like being in a band." I nodded. "Everyone does their thing, but together..." We both looked over to the jukebox where Jerkster was dancing, badly. "You know what I mean." I grinned at her.

"I know what *you* mean," Dee Dee smiled back, "but do you know what *I* mean?"

I reflected. I thought I did, but maybe I'd missed something. I scratched my chin. "You know, Dee Dee, I'm not sure," I admitted, paying her the serious attention her tone deserved.

Dee Dee pinched my cheek. "You should never, ever, give anything to the point you are lost. Your life will become dreck, useless, and you," she pinched me again, "have too much to offer to waste it."

Her regard was so genuine it embarrassed me, and because I'd freshly cut my hair I knew she could see my ears burn as I dropped my eyes to the bar.

"So," I said as she let go, "does that mean I should be more like vodka than cheese?" I gave her my biggest grin and jumped away from the towel that flew at me.

"Wisenheimer!" She laughed. "Nothing cheesy about you!"

"You missed!" I laughed back.

She fixed me with her bright green eyes. "I miss on purpose," she grinned, "or you'll spend another hour on your hair."

I clutched my chest like I'd been mortally wounded. "Oh! You're killing me!" I mock-complained, then straightened up and put my hands on my hips. "Hey, I *like* my hair!" I told her, half joking but serious.

Dee Dee smiled at me again. "I like your hair, too," she nodded in agreement, "but it's your face that makes you money."

"And all this time, I thought it was my sparkling wit and conversational skills," I countered.

"*Ja*, there's that too," Dee Dee said as she wiped the bar, "but you must know by now how stunning you are, no?"

"Uh, no?" I answered as I walked back to the bar. I sat on a stool and pulled the books she'd left on the counter back to me. "People always say it, but it's, like, just bullshit, you know?" I started to review the numbers. "It's just what people say because they want to fu—um, have sex," I corrected myself, "right?"

"There's always that," Dee Dee said, and straightened from her task, "but someone's done you a great disservice." She waved her rag at me.

"What do you mean?" I asked, confused. I mean, yeah, sure, people said I was cute or whatever all the time, while the ones that said I was beautiful were the ones actively trying to get me into bed.

To tell the truth, sometimes it seemed like everyone was always trying to touch me; I was starting to find ways of walking around them without any contact—I couldn't bear it anymore. I was even occasionally uncomfortable with Fran and just didn't want to be held. But I figured people did that because they were, you know, rude, grabby, and horny— there was nothing real behind it except their physical need.

And as far as those who said I was cute (and I could swear the breath of cold air that whispered beside me for a moment was the touch of Trace's gray eyes), went, well, I'd never heard cute equated with stunning before—unless it was a cartoon and someone was dropping a brick on someone's head—now *that's* stunning. I said as much to Dee Dee, well, except for the part about touch avoidance, and she frowned at me.

"No, Nina, you're wrong, quite wrong," she told me, her voice husky and low with her soberness. "People don't do that to everyone— they do it to *you* because they want to be near someone with your kind of—ah!" she grumped, obviously frustrated, groping for the right word. "Light, Nina. They want to be near your light."

Now I was really confused—what the hell did that mean? "What?"

Dee Dee poured herself a soda and mixed some cranberry and orange juice for me. "Here," she said, sliding the glass to me, "listen."

"Thanks. *Salud!*" I smiled as I lifted it and took a sip.

"*Prost!*" Dee Dee returned. She put the glass down with a bit of force. "Let me see your eyes," she asked abruptly.

I looked straight into hers, letting her search for whatever it was she wanted. I loved Dee Dee's eyes—the startlingly amber-to-green combination that tonight shone a mellow grass color. Finally she nodded.

"Your heart is always in your eyes, Nina, and that's what they want, the part they want to touch," she told me, "the part you never share."

I had no idea what she meant—she'd lost me somewhere between heart and touch.

"Even I feel that, but I don't want to *fuck* you." She grinned and pinched my chin this time.

"Okay," I said slowly, "I'll keep that in mind." Yeah. Now I was *really* confused.

Dee Dee shook her head and chuckled as I got out of my seat.

"I'm going to go check the lines," I told her, meaning the vast cylinders in the basement that hooked up to the tap lines in the bar. "We're getting something weird from the soda gun."

"Okay, go check," she agreed, outright laughing now. "Too much for you, huh?"

I grinned back as I felt a slow burn rise up my neck. "Something like that," I agreed good-naturedly, still not knowing what I was really agreeing to. She'd given me a lot to think about, but no matter what anyone said about my heart, I knew Dee Dee had a good one. I was glad she was my friend.

A kink in the soda line was forcing it to send out a less-than-ideal mixture of syrup and carbonated water. I spent a good ten minutes wrestling with the valve seal so I could unhook it, straighten it out, then hook it up again. It was a good thing I knew my way around a wrench, I thought as I wiped my hands on a nearby rag.

I locked the storm gates behind me and walked back into the bar proper. Fran had arrived, which made me smile, but what I saw through the windows erased that.

One of our regulars, Yvonne, had probably had a little too much to drink. She wouldn't be the first, or the last, to do that, but I'd be damned and double damned if she thought she could cause a problem in the place I worked—especially not with Fran.

I didn't know what it was about, and I didn't care. Yvonne's arms were flailing, and she spoke vehemently to Fran, who had taken a step back and squared herself off in a defensive position.

In two steps, I was there and stepped between them, facing Yvonne. "Hey hey, cool it…what's the matter?" I asked her. She glared at me, put a hand on her hip, and shook her head, gazing silently at the floor.

I checked on Fran. "You all right?"

"Yeah," she nodded, "it's all—" Her eyes widened and she pointed behind me. "Look out!" I twisted my head to see what she meant, and as I did, a thousand points of light exploded in my head.

I rocked on my heels a bit as the explosion faded. Fuckin' stupid. I'd let myself get coldcocked by a fuckin' amateur.

Deliberately squaring my shoulders and hips, I smiled and faced Yvonne, who took a step back, breathing hard.

Warm moisture fell in a tickling run from my nose and lip, a sensation I knew too well. I wiped my fingers across my face, looked at the blood that covered them, and considered Yvonne coolly. "First one's free," I told her, then sucked the blood off my fingers. I never took my eyes off her, but I glimpsed Jen coming up the walkway as I waited to see what would happen next.

Yvonne seemed shocked, and her eyes flickered with something that might have been remorse, but I knew, in the same way I knew I wouldn't want to be in her position, that pride was about to overtake common sense. Her face hardened. "This one will be worth the price, then," she snarled and swung.

Too easy, way too easy. Her swing was wide, and I caught it with a simple forearm block, while my palm went straight to her shoulder. I could have easily gone for her chin, but it wasn't necessary—that was overkill, while a chest shot would have just pushed her farther into the bar. Besides, I already knew I'd win in a fight if it came to that—and I wasn't going to let it come to that. The move I chose used her own motion to spin her around and helped me propel her, one arm locked behind her back, to the door.

"*Aprèz vous!*" Jen said sweetly as she held the door wide open. She gave a slight bow as I shoved Yvonne through it, then she tossed the door shut. I knew Yvonne was not one of her favorite people to begin with, and she'd been longing for a reason to ban her from the bar. This must have been a pretty sweet moment for her.

My blood sang in my ears even as it dripped down my face. Jen grinned at me. "Nice one, buddy!" she said as she clapped my shoulder.

"Thanks," I said shortly through the pounding in my head.

Fran rushed over, and Dee Dee tossed her a clean bar rag that I was pretty sure had been soaked in ice water. I shivered violently when it touched my face as Jen and Fran forced me to sit on the nearest bar stool.

Jerkster came over and started singing, and I burst out laughing when Dee Dee joined him on the chorus of "Berserker."

"Hold still!" Fran admonished, because I'd made a bit of a mess when I'd laughed—my nose was still bleeding.

"Hey, glad you're on our side, kid," Jen said, still smiling. She patted me on the shoulder again, and this time the "kid" thing didn't bother me. She was all right, you know?

"Ow…" I complained when Fran moved the towel. It was a mess. Dee Dee took it and replaced it with another.

"Are you guys trying to tell me something?" I asked, my voice muffled through the cold, wet towel.

"*Ja*, Nina." Dee Dee smiled. "That was—"

"Totally cool!" Jerkster jumped around, "you were soooo cold, dude. You were laughing!" His eyes were wide, and his arms windmilled as he mimed what he'd seen with such enthusiasm that I was afraid someone else was going to get whapped in the face.

"I laughed? No way!" I said, looking at Fran and Dee Dee to either confirm or deny. I didn't remember that at all.

"Stop wiggling!" Fran exhorted as Dee Dee deftly exchanged the less-bloody-than-before rag for another one—this one full of ice. Ugh. I gently pushed Fran's hands away.

"I'm fine—look—it's stopped." I indicated the towel that was now only faintly spotted with pink.

"C'mon…for me?" Fran wheedled.

I sighed and rolled my eyes. "Fine," I capitulated, but only because you never deny a lady a direct request.

Fran gave me a self-satisfied smile and patted my shoulder. Great. Awesome. Now I was a good dog.

Jerkster kept rehearsing that block and punch (well, technically it was a palm-strike, not a punch) with Jen, while Dee Dee stepped to the other end of the bar. She came right back with two shot glasses.

"Here," she said, sliding them over, "this is good for you."

I eyed the little glass warily. Whatever was in one of them looked a lot like bloody mud with a bit of grass sprinkled on top—and I was pretty sure I'd already had my daily limit of that taste. The other looked like clear glue with little things suspended in it. I glanced up at Dee Dee, who had fixed me with that firm look of hers.

"I make special for you," she warned me.

Dammit. Another direct request. "Okay, all right, I'll drink it," I groused. I handed Fran the rag and returned my attention to Dee Dee, only to find her eyes still frying me. Damn, I thought, she would have been ideal as one of the nuns I'd known back in high school. I picked up her concoction.

"You have to swallow it all in one go, or it's no good," she advised.

Yeah, that just figured for me. I took a deep breath; I had the feeling I was going to need it. I brought the rim to my lips, and in the split second that the gloop was in the air before it hit the back of my throat and swallowed, I knew this was a bad idea.

Oh My *God*! Nose? What nose? I couldn't feel my fucking nose because my throat closed, my ears burned, and my eyes were on fire. Who the hell cared about anything else? And then there was the hot eel sliding down my chest. Jumping out of my seat, I did an impromptu little dance—it might have looked like I was praying for rain or suffering from chicken pox in my crotch.

"Christ, what the hell is that, Dee Dee?" I gasped, choking. "Is that horseradish and cough syrup?"

"Jagermeister," Dee Dee nodded, "and whiskey and Tabasco with some little, little herbs for flavor." She made a sprinkling motion with her fingers, rubbing them back and forth.

"Flavor? Flavor?" I coughed again and hoped desperately that I wouldn't spit out a lung or a kidney. "You should serve that with a fire extinguisher!"

Dee Dee laughed long and loud. "After that shot you took? Nina, you shouldn't taste anything—but you do, because you are berserker."

She laughed again while Fran seized the opportunity to put the ice back on my face. "C'mon, baby, your face is gonna bruise, and you have a show coming up," she reminded me. She was right, and she knew I knew she was right, so I let her freeze my skin.

"I am *not* berserk," I said to Dee Dee with as much dignity as I could muster from under the towel and Fran's firm hold.

"Hey, it's a compliment," Jen walked over and told me, Jerkster following her.

"Yeah, a compliment," Jerkster seconded. "'Cuz, like, the berserkers were, like, these German-Scandi-cold-weather dudes who went totally nuts when they were in a fight. They were, like, the ultimate warriors, and you could tell who they were because they would laugh the whole time, and then, after that, they were okay again."

We all looked at him in amazement. I'd never heard so much information about *anything* come from Jerkster at one time.

"What?" he asked, looking around at us. "I used to be into heavy metal. There's at least one song on every album all about it."

That was it, that was the living end, and I started laughing so hard my nose started bleeding again.

"Well, that's about right, anyway," Dee Dee said, as impressed as the rest of us. "Now drink this, too," she requested, pushing the other shot glass to me.

"Does this one also require any special equipment or precautions?" I hadn't totally recovered from the last one and wanted to keep the few taste buds I had left.

"Funny, funny," Dee Dee mocked lightly. "No, that one was for your blood, strong for strong. This one is for you—for your spirit, that it stays fiery but sweet."

That was about as much reassurance as I was going to get, so I went for it. This time, instead of downing it, I sipped and was rewarded with a pleasant tingle.

"Cinnamon?" I asked as I put it down.

"Cinnamon schnapps," Dee Dee corrected, "with gold flakes. The best for the best."

"I like it," I commented as I took a final sip. No, really. I liked it a lot.

"You would." Dee Dee smiled at me. She collected the glasses from the bar and put them in the sink, then gave the bar a good wipe-down. I watched her for a bit—Dee Dee and her endless supply of spotlessly white bar rags.

I sat there with the towel on my face while Fran stroked my hair. "You okay?" I asked her again. "What happened?"

Fran sighed. "Nothing. She was just a little drunk and a little disappointed, I think," she answered. "And it looks like you've cemented her disappointment."

I put the rag down to gaze at her directly. "Did I, now?" I asked dryly.

Twining my arms around her waist, I gazed into her almond eyes, then down at those lips that curved into the slightest of smiles.

"Can I kiss you hello?" I asked her, the heat of her body wrapping around me like a fog.

"Please do," she pressed against me, "my hero."

"Whatever it takes." I was instantly rewarded with the feel of that incredible mouth against mine, followed moments later by the warmth within it.

"Careful, careful," Fran cautioned, pulling away. "Your lip is cut, too."

I ran my tongue carefully around. She was right—I could taste the blood. "I don't feel a thing," I told her, and pulled her closer.

"Good, because your lips are way too far away from mine," she purred, then proved it. Her fingertips dug strong lines along my neck and shoulders as mine outlined her shoulder blades. I would have loved to have done the natural thing and reached for her amazing ass, but I wouldn't do that in a public place—that wasn't something I felt a need to share with the world.

"Harumph." Dee Dee coughed none-too-subtly behind us. Yeah. I was supposed to be working, not making out. "So I was saying…I think I should send you home tonight."

I whirled to face her. "No, Dee Dee, I'm fine, there's no need—"

Dee Dee held a hand up. "No, you should get some rest, and besides, it's quiet tonight. Francesca, you'll take good care of her, no?" She looked at her directly.

"Absolutely," she smiled, "she's in good hands." She took mine in hers to prove it.

"I thought so," Dee Dee nodded, "so here," she gave me my bag from behind the counter, "and here," she pushed some money at me, "so you can get a car home—you shouldn't be riding around on trains and ferries."

I stared at the money, then tried to give it back. "Dee Dee, I usually walk to the boat. Besides, I've got money."

"You got hurt at work, no?" she asked rhetorically. "So work pays to send you home. Now go," she shooed me away, "and let Francesca nurse you!"

I watched as her lips quirked just the slightest bit at her last words. Uh-huh. There was a faint whiff of something in the air, and it wasn't cinnamon schnapps.

But you know what? I didn't want to argue. "All right then, thank you," I told her. "'Night, Jerkster!" I called as Fran dragged me to the door.

"Hey yeah, see you tomorrow!" He looked up from his intense study of the jukebox and waved.

Jen was already outside in the street hailing us a cab.

"Thanks, thanks a lot." I grinned at her when a yellow car stopped.

"Yeah, you're welcome, kid," she said, "get some rest. And you," she nodded to Francesca, "don't let her fall asleep too early—she might have a concussion."

"No worries," Fran answered as I opened the door to the car. "I'll take good care of her." She got into the car and slid along the seat.

I gave Jen a sharp glance. She was being way too nice, and her lips had the same slight quirk Dee Dee's had. Uh-huh. Weird.

I got in the car and stuck my head out the window. "I'll see you tomorrow?" I asked, giving her the this-is-way-too-weird eyebrow raise.

"When the sun's up, kid," she promised with a smile, "when the sun's up."

"Cool," I answered, and waved good-bye. I settled into my seat, and after we told the driver where we were going, off we lurched into traffic.

"Come, put your head down," Fran smilingly invited, patting her lap, and I complied.

"You know," she commented thoughtfully, "that's the second time you've shed blood for me."

I shrugged in response as I settled against her. What could I say?

She threw her peacoat over me. "Got to keep you warm."

I brought her face to mine. "You do that well enough." I grinned and kissed her softly. "And I promise, the third time will be interesting."

"As long as it doesn't involve your head," and she kissed my forehead, "or this beautiful face," and she kissed my cheeks, "or these lips," and this kiss was delicate and tender and worked its way into something much more intense. I was so deeply into the consummate sensuality that was her kiss that when her hand slid down my stomach and into my waistband, I thought nothing of it—until the car stopped short.

"Kitt, baby, what are you doing?" I whispered to her as her fingers tickled even lower and the car moved on.

Her fingers stroked lightly against my pussy, teasing me, caressing me with promise. "I'm not supposed to let you fall asleep, so," she explained as her fingers slipped between my lips, "I'm taking care of you."

I felt the moan that was trying to make its way out and reached up for her head to bring her lips to mine. "You are evil," I whispered before I let that moan out into her mouth.

Her tongue mimicked her fingers as she slowly stroked the length of my swollen cunt. "God, you are so fuckin' hard," she breathed into my mouth.

"Francesca…" I murmured in half-hearted protest, "we're in a cab."

"Then you're going to have to lie still and be quiet," she answered as she rapidly fingered my clit. Damn, but she felt good. Fine. I'd be quiet. It wasn't going to be easy.

Her hand stilled on my pussy as she shifted positions. "Did you know," she whispered throatily, "that I can place one, two, three fingertips," and she paused as she did it, "along your clit when you're this hard?"

Between the words and the actions she had me ready to explode in my pants, and when I felt her hand move again, the sensation was so fuckin' intense as it bolted through me that I stretched my head back against her.

"God, baby, what are you doing to me?" I groaned. Fuck the driver—if he didn't know what had been going on before, I was pretty sure he did now, and I didn't fuckin' care.

She nibbled along the line of my neck, and I rolled against the added sensation before she answered. "I'm jerking you off." She smiled into my eyes, then kissed me again. When the steady pull on my clit became that cunt throb that lets you know the edge is getting close, all I could think of was her pussy descending on mine, swallowing my clit. I wanted to do that so badly, I thrust my cunt against her hands as she pumped me good and fast.

"Yeah, baby, just like that," I groaned out. "God, I want to be inside you."

I heard her breath catch. "You're making me so fucking wet, God," she growled. "Whatever you want, do that when we get back."

She was jerking me off so good, nice and hard and tight around my clit, and that combined with the thought of her wet pussy waiting for me—I couldn't even answer her as I thrust hard and came into her hand, my face pressed into her chest and my fingers rapidly playing her hard nipple.

I kissed her chest and climbed my way up her neck to her lips, straddling her thigh. "We're not done yet," I told her, and slid my tongue between her welcoming lips. I tongued her mouth exactly the way I planned to taste her pussy as soon as we got to her place, but I was going to have her right then and there because her kiss told me how bad she needed it.

I undid the top button of her jeans and slid my hand down, knowing I'd find her wet and waiting. I wasn't disappointed. Her cunt was an ever-thrilling combination of hard clit and soft open pussy, and I tickled through her slick lips for a second before I found her clit with my thumb and thrust two fingers into her hungry cunt.

She gasped and bit my shoulder. "Shh," I cautioned with a little smile of my own, "you're gonna have to be quiet."

"I didn't know," she licked my throat, "you were such a bitch." She bit my neck—God, I loved that.

"Right now?" I said as I pressed against her solid clit and did her pussy hard. "I'm your fuckin' hero."

She sucked on my skin in response and spread her legs a bit on the bench. I pressed up, deeper inside her, and her hand came down on mine. That move got me, got me so good it made me want to come again, and I made no protest when her other hand moved into my pants again, then moved around to my ass. When her fingers quietly made their way to my cunt, sliding between the folds and tweaking my clit, my hips jerked in response, and she had me where she wanted me.

"Oh, yeah, baby," she hissed as her thumb slid inside me.

"Kitt, are you insane?" I gasped with the rare sensation—rare because I seldom had her inside me. It really wasn't my thing. Besides, at the moment, my mind was still aware that we had company, even though my hands and cunt weren't caring.

"It's been three days," she answered, leaning her head back against the rear dash, "three whole fucking days."

The reality of her words swelled in me as I leaned down to kiss that irresistible mouth that sighed as we made up for lost time.

Come to think of it? I don't remember paying for that cab ride. I still don't know how I feel about that.

ENJOY THE SILENCE

Woke up in the morning underneath the sunlight glare
You know I'd never ask you but I wonder if you care
It's so hard to believe—and easy to deceive
Do you want me for me?

"Me for Me"—Life Underwater

Fran lay next to me on the bed, drawing lazy circles on my chest with her fingertips as I held her close and kissed her head.

"I asked Dee Dee if you could leave early," she confessed quietly as we enjoyed our closeness.

"Really? When? Why?"

"Yes, really, when you were in the basement playing with the taps, and because I needed to spend some time with you," she answered in the order that I'd asked.

The gig was in a few days, and after that, I was taking some time off from work—I'd planned to spend that time with her. If she'd really needed something, I'd have absolutely made sure I was free and there for her. Something must be wrong then, right?

"Kitt, love, is everything okay? I mean, why—"

"Shh…" she said and slid her body over mine, then kissed me sensually. She touched my face, running her thumb into that spot on my chin she loved so much as my hands skimmed along the smooth muscles of her back, then caressed the span of her shoulders.

"I have to go away…" she sighed and murmured into my throat. I lightly traced her arms as she snuggled on my shoulder. "I'm leaving Friday afternoon."

"That's tomorrow," I realized aloud. "So soon? Do you have to go for a long time?" I didn't ask her when or where. She had never pressed me for anything, and I wouldn't do it to her.

She propped her head on her hand. "Long enough that I won't be in town for your gig," she answered, "and I really wanted to go."

I leaned up to kiss her head and she sat up with me. "I'll miss you," I said as I reached to play with her hair as it lay across her shoulder. I caressed her neck as I pushed the long strands back. I would, too.

I might not have been ready to set up householding with anyone yet—and I absolutely hated that oft-rumored lesbian tradition, you know the one, how everyone moves in together on the second date? But I loved her and wouldn't dream of doing anything that would harm her or us.

Yeah, I might still flirt a bit, but that went with the job territory. I might not have liked to deal with it, but it wasn't just my sparkling wit and conversation that made me money; it was my face, too—and I was the lead guitarist in a band. However, in light of the intensity of what Fran and I shared, I doubted I would ever sleep with anyone else. In fact, I never even thought about it.

"I'll miss you every day until you come back," I told her and kissed her cheek, then put my arms around her and she nestled into them.

"Will you, really?" she asked, whispering into my breast in a small voice, and I pressed my lips to her head again.

"Of course I will, Kitt. You're my golden lion," I assured her in between kisses. "You're the pride of my heart."

At those words, she gazed up at me with such a vulnerable expression that the emotions that rose in me threatened to make me cry and forced me to wrap myself around her, holding her close, protecting her innocence.

"I didn't know that," she said simply and kissed my collarbone.

I rocked her closer, loving her, her body curled within my embrace. "That's a mistake on my part, then," I murmured, "because you should know."

We sat that way for a while, skin to skin, while her breath dusted over my breasts where she laid her head above them.

"I got you something," she said finally into our quiet, lifting her head and tossing it to shake her hair free.

"Yeah?" I asked lightly, loosening my hold. "For me?"

"Yeah," she answered, a smile in her voice and on her lips as she wiggled in my arms. She tweaked my chin. "For you."

She straightened and jumped up, onto the floor, then grinned. "What are you wearing for your show?"

"I haven't thought about it, really. Why?" I especially wasn't thinking about it now and figured I'd wear some variation of what I usually wore, maybe pay a little more attention to—what else—my hair.

"C'mon, get up," she exhorted, clapping her hands together briskly, "show me what you've got."

I raised my eyebrows. "What, you haven't seen enough already?" I asked, but I complied, stretching my arms above my head and enjoying the appreciation in her eyes.

"Shame to have to cover that."

"Really?" I asked cheekily, then caressed her waist and leaned in to kiss her neck. "I think you cover me quite well."

"Mmm," she responded as my lips caressed the column of her neck, "I agree...but I meant with clothes." She touched my arm and I raised my eyes to hers.

"Does that mean you have something in mind?"

Her eyes widened. "What makes you say that?"

"Because you're always taking my clothes off. Well, that and," I paused a moment for effect, "the fact that you never bring anything up without a reason."

"I do that?" she asked, laughing.

"Yeah, sometimes."

"Well, you happen to be right." She smiled. "I do have something in mind."

"It wouldn't have anything to do with my present, now would it?" I grinned slyly.

"It might, it might," she affirmed, nodding. Walking over to her closet, she pulled out her bag, then opened it to remove a plastic shopping bag that had been folded over.

She came back to me, took my hands, and held them gently between us. "Close your eyes."

"Closed," I told her as I did so.

Her hands left mine cold as she rummaged through her bag. Then I felt her warmth near again.

"Okay, lift," she ordered, patting my right leg.

I did, and she slid something part of the way up. I could feel it puddle around my foot—a texture, a scent I recognized, that made my nostrils flare.

"Other one," she asked, and I helped. When both legs were on, she slid them up me and rested her hands on my waist.

"You did not," I said, stunned by what I felt as I ran my hands down my thighs.

"Did not what?" she asked innocently. "Oh, you can open your eyes now, by the way."

I did. And couldn't breathe a moment as I looked down, confirming what my senses had told me. "Holy shit!" I exclaimed softly when my breath returned.

Soft black leather pants with a light sheen—and a lace-up front. They fit me exactly like what they were—a second skin. "Man oh man!" I said as I adjusted the laces. "And," I took a step and grabbed my boots, slipping them on, "straight cut! I love straight-cut pants!" I exclaimed as I examined the fit and the perfect drape over my boots. I did and do love a straight cut—makes my legs look even longer. Hey, just because I don't think I'm good-looking doesn't mean I'm not aware that I've got nice legs.

I looked up to see her watching me with the strangest expression.

"I don't know how I'm going to keep you…" she said softly as she approached. "Christ, Nina, you *look* like a Razor."

"Thank you, thankyouthankyou!" I enthused, grabbing her in my arms and whirling her around until we were at the foot of the bed where we fell onto it.

"You look *so* fuckin' hot!" she told me as she twined her arms around my neck.

"You shouldn't have, you know," I said as I brought my lips to hers.

"What, and miss this? Not on your life." She cupped my face the way she always did, running her thumb over my chin. Her eyes glowed at me, that melted caramel color that I could drown in. "This way, I'll be with you during your show," she said softly, "before you go off and become the star you're gonna be."

"Baby, that's not—" I began, but stopped as her eyes filled with tears. "Oh, baby, no, don't cry," I said, kissing her eyes, kissing the tears. I scooped her up in my arms.

"I'm not going anywhere," I promised. "I'm gonna be wondering when you're getting back so I can pick you up at the airport, and I'm going to take a few days off so we can go and do something."

She laughed softly through her tears. "Baby, don't write checks your reality can't cash," she said quietly, and kissed my chin.

"What do you mean?" I asked, confused. "This *is* my reality, I'm not going anywhere." In many ways, I thought that was true. I didn't have that piece of paper so many of my peers had that proved I knew how to at least read, didn't have a "real" job; I didn't have much except for the untouchables—the love I felt for her and the music in my body.

She smiled at me and wiped her eyes. "Nina, you're too big for this place, and everybody knows it, everybody knows it but you," she said, and kissed me again.

I kicked my boots off and Fran wrapped her legs around mine. We simply rested there together, my head under her chin as I lay on top of her.

I don't know how long we'd been there like that when the phone rang. Since it did that so rarely, I answered it.

"'Lo."

"Hullo!" cheered out at me. "Francesca?"

"It's for you," I told her. She took it from me, and I carefully moved so I wouldn't crush her. I lay at her side and got comfortable.

"This is Fran." From the way her voice bounced back from the phone, I could tell this would be one of those calls where everyone could hear everything. I put a pillow over my head in an attempt to muffle the sound.

"Hullo, Francesca!" the phone sang. I knew that voice, knew that cheery accent.

"Good morning, Candace," Fran answered formally. Her body stiffened as she sat up. I pulled the pillow from my head and read the rigid lines of her back. I pushed the pillow behind me and sat up too, wrapping my legs around her and pulling her into me, making a cage of my body for her to sink into, to take warmth from. I pulled the blanket up and tucked it around her waist and mine, then leaned back, Fran in my arms. She twisted onto her side and laid her head against my shoulder. I kissed her head.

I had no idea what the call was about, but I knew everything was about to change—it wasn't just the call, but her trip and my gig.

I suddenly got this sense that maybe, just maybe, this gig might be a bigger deal than I thought it would be, than any of us, meaning Jerkster and Stephie and I, thought it would be. Maybe not, though. Could be that sense was just because it was a first with a date, a time, and an exclamation point, and that alone made it important.

Still, and more important, we wouldn't be together for it, and I wanted to be as close to her for as long as possible before everything went wherever it was going to go.

She glanced up at me with a grateful smile, and I kissed her forehead. She sighed and snuggled back into me.

"To what do I owe this wake-up pleasure?" she asked with wry politeness.

I could hear Candace's little laugh that I remembered so well.

"You know," she began drolly, "if I didn't know better, I'd say that was my lovely lady Nina who answered your phone, Francesca," Candace teased, "but you know, I never could actually get her to stay."

Heat radiated from her body as she sat up, and when she glanced at me again before turning away, I could see (and I admit, this kinda thrilled me) the fire snap in her eyes.

"Perhaps because she wasn't yours to begin with?" she answered.

I gave her a hug and a kiss to remind her I was there, and she looked over her shoulder at me and threw me another brilliant smile, then settled more comfortably against me.

"Well, perhaps you're right," Candace laughed, "but then again, who could tame that? Hold on…are you saying that's her?"

Fran said nothing, she visibly stiffened and angled forward.

I straightened with a sigh. It seemed like the moment we'd been so carefully avoiding was upon us, like a bucket of water perched on a door frame. It hadn't fallen yet, but we were about to get soaked.

I reached over to the nightstand and grabbed my cigarettes.

"Oh, Annie, come here, this is just too rich," I could hear Candace call in the background. "Francesca has bagged my bird."

Fuck it. I lit her a butt too, as she raised eyes filled with anger and pain to me.

"It's okay," I whispered and tried to give her a smile. Hers was small and tight in return as she took the cigarette I gave her. We both knew I lied.

And then, I heard it, through the miles, through the static and that ridiculous tiny speaker. There was no mistaking that sound, the sound I thought I'd never hear again—

Samantha's laugh as she picked up the phone on her end.

"Hey, Fran," I heard her greet, still laughing, "Candace has convinced me to go back to the States for a visit, and since I have some things to take care of, it'll be New York specifically. Can I use the keys?"

She looked at me, trying to gauge my reaction, and I shook my head, not knowing what to say, because the moment I heard that voice, a tingle had spread through my skin until it felt like the top of my head, no, my whole body, was going to dissolve into an electric spark.

Fran took a slow, deep breath. "When were you thinking of coming?" she asked, exhaling softly.

I decided to stare at the wall. I didn't want to hear thisconversation, but I couldn't help it. I could at least pretend I wasn't paying attention.

"Why, Fran, is that a no?" Sam, I mean Annie, chuckled sarcastically.

"Of course not," she answered, obviously flustered. She jumped off the bed and began to pace. "It's just that I'm leaving for California in a few days and…"

My head snapped back around. "California?" I mouthed at her, shocked. I don't know why I was so surprised—I mean, that's where she'd done her internship, and where she wanted to go after she was done with her studies, and I knew that. But it was so far.

She nodded at me and continued her conversation. "…and I was just wondering if we'd get a chance to meet on your trip." Fran breathed hard, her entire body was flushed, and as she paced the floor again, she bit her lip nervously.

"Oh," Annie answered, "I thought perhaps you were trying to keep your new girl a secret."

Her lips tightened. "Annie, I just thought that—"

"I've an idea!" Annie interrupted. "Let's go to the Red Spot and see if we can find Candace's favorite attempt!"

"Ann, don't go there," she warned. "That's a hell of way to talk about an old friend—and someone you haven't even—"

Annie blithely ignored her and spoke over her.

"Sounds like she's enough to take us all on. Maybe it'll take all of us to keep her, what do you say?" She laughed.

"Watch your fucking mouth, Blade." She spoke sharply, fire cracking through her voice.

It hurt to hear those words come through the phone, to know that Candace had considered me more casual than I had thought. I'd considered us, at the very least, anyway, friends. But it hurt even more to know that after all these months, Samantha, I mean, Ann, Annie, whatever, had not only not tried to get in touch with me, but that I was probably the source of foreplay conversation between her and Candace.

The concept made me nauseous, crumbled something inside me. I looked up from my introspection to see Fran's eyes focused on me, fiercely concerned, hurt for me. She gestured to ask if I'd take the phone.

There was absolutely no fucking way, and I shook my head violently. "Candace knew how to get in touch with me. She could have called me months ago," I said in an angry stage whisper.

For fuck's sake, it wasn't as if I hadn't worked at the same place for months, and it wasn't as if Mickey and everyone at the Red Spot didn't get in touch with me from time to time. If someone had tried to find me there, Mickey would have passed the information on to me. I knew that for certain because he had. Fucked up, this was fucked up.

I jumped out of bed and stretched, then crushed the cigarette I hadn't been smoking in the ashtray.

"Blade? Blade? You haven't called me that since..." The phone went silent a moment, and as I focused on crushing the remaining embers, I glanced over at Fran long enough to see the spark flaring in her eyes.

"Since?" she prompted, her lips twisted in an angry curve.

"C'mon, *Kitt*," Annie drawled sarcastically, "don't fuck around. You know how I—"

"How you feel about her, *Sam*?" she interrupted. "Yeah, in fact, I do, every day. So watch your fucking mouth."

I couldn't listen to any more of this—not that voice, not that tone, and not Fran's responses. There was silence on the other end as I stalked to the closet, grabbed the closest T-shirt I could find, and yanked it over my head. I looked at it as I strode to the door. *Love and Rockets*, *Vida Loca*, or "crazy life" in English. How appropriate, I thought.

"Where you going?" Fran asked me in a worried undertone.

I gave her the best smile I could manage. "Just getting us some water." With the way my legs shook and threatened to buckle under me while waves rose in my gut and punched my throat, I figured I needed a bottle—and Fran looked like she could use some, too.

I opened the door just in time to hear Sam's voice cut across the planet. "You're fucking with me, aren't you?"

Fran closed her eyes and swallowed before she answered. "You know what? I wish I was."

I closed the door quietly behind me as I padded to the kitchen. Fuck. I'd forgotten my smokes. Back to the bedroom for me, then. I entered to see Fran had sat down again on the edge of the bed, smoking one of my cigarettes while she gripped the phone in her other hand.

"Hey, don't blame me, this isn't my fuckin' fault," she fumed into the mouthpiece. "Candace should have told you about Nina months ago," she said as I quickly grabbed my pack and left again.

I could barely hear the reply squawk to that—for which I was grateful. My heartbeat hadn't returned to normal yet.

I waved to catch her attention as I reached the door and blew her a kiss. This might not have been the world's happiest moment, but no matter who liked it or not, Francesca DiTomassa and Nina Boyd had something going. Besides, I loved her and didn't want her to think I'd forgotten.

She gave me a sweet and sad smile, then blew me a kiss in return. I spent a moment miming that it had landed on my cheek, caught it, and put it down my shirt, rubbing it over my heart. Fran grinned, and I sent her another one before I left.

Once in the kitchen, I forgot all about getting some water. I sat at the table and simply stared out the window where it overlooked the fire escape as I smoked. Finally, I muscled up the frame and sat on the ledge, just staring at the sky, watching my smoke float into it. The metal from the fire escape was a little too cold on my bare feet, so I tucked them up into the frame where I'd wedged myself—back against one side, feet on the other.

I thought of absolutely nothing, and I don't know how many cigarettes I smoked before Fran came into the room. She'd put on my shirt, the one I'd been going to wear to the show, over a pair of sleep shorts.

"Do you want to talk with her?"

I took a deep drag, then exhaled. "No," I said and shook my head, "I don't. She could have found me months ago." I took another deep drag and exhaled slowly before I faced her. "You didn't tell me you were going to California."

Fran eyed me, a bit warily I thought. She didn't have to worry—I wasn't going to bite.

"I was going to tell you, before the phone rang." She walked over and put a hand on my shoulder.

I blew the rest of the smoke out the window, then put my free arm around her waist, swinging my legs back in and onto the floor. Fran took the cigarette from my hand and took a drag while I put my other arm around her, burying my head against her ribs.

"Don't go," I asked quietly. "Stay with me or," and as it occurred to me, I thought it was a brilliant idea, "delay a few days and I'll go with you."

Fran gave a light laugh under her breath as she stroked through my hair and rubbed the back of my neck.

"I have to," she answered just as solemnly. "It's the only time I can, where I'm…it has to be now."

"Why?" I asked, kissing her nipple through the shirt. I accidentally tore the button when I reached for the curve of her breast. "Why now?"

Her fingertips strayed from my neck and began to dig into my shoulder as I breathed across her hardening nipple.

"Because…" she sighed as I teased that hardened end with my teeth. "There are some cycles you can't break…just like that…" She pressed my head against her while I massaged her beautifully firm ass with one hand. The other began making the journey where I knew it would please us both most.

When I reached the junction of her thigh and slipped beneath the leg of the shorts she was wearing, I smiled because they had been a gift from me.

"Don't…don't you want to talk about it?" Fran gasped as I pressed along the tendon, then ran my thumb along the groove.

I looked up at her finally, to see her undoubtedly trying to be rational, though her eyes were half hooded with desire. "No," I told her, my breath ragged with want, the need to touch her, "I just want you."

"She didn't know…Candace didn't tell her."

I heard her words, but they had no meaning, although some part of my brain realized that Candace had lied—to all of us; she'd known from the beginning exactly who I was. But right now, it didn't matter, it didn't matter at all. Fran, my glorious Kitt, was before me, and the scent of her desire was burning through my mind. All I wanted to do was make her call my name, her voice a trumpet to the sky when she did.

"I don't care," I told her as my fingers grazed her cleft. God, she was wet and she was mine. "Kiss me," I demanded, and she did, her mouth perfectly sensual, demanding, against mine.

I slid my fingers between her folds and glided along her ache, enjoying the moan that sang from her lips as I focused long strokes on her clit. My other hand had strayed from her delicious ass, and I pressed my fingers, gently insistent, into her waiting cunt.

Fran gasped and swayed, trapped between my arms and hands. I guided her to me, onto my lap.

"God, baby!" I choked out when her pussy encased my fingers and she threw her arms around me. She raised herself off me only to shift her hips a bit, because when she sat back down, she shoved me deep inside of her. Her face glowed and her eyes were both tender and fierce as she grabbed my shoulders.

"Kitt, baby, baby Kitt…you are so beautiful…just so fucking beautiful," I whispered into her ear because it was true, so true. I burned with the vision of her, lived and died with her breathless sighs, and I wanted more—more of her. I teased another finger by her cunt, feeling the other ones fly into her while my other hand lavished attention on her hard, hard clit.

"God yes, please…just…please…" she gasped as I began to slide that third finger inside her.

Ohgodohgodohgod I was going to die I was going to come—her pussy was so hot and tight, and she was so fucking amazing.

"Is this what you need, baby, is this what you want?" I breathed out as she pushed herself onto me again, and I was so deep inside her I could feel her womb, its hard prominence pressing against the back of my fingers. She rubbed her face against mine.

"Yes…" she hissed in that satisfied my-cunt-is-full voice as she rode me, her body a sensual wave, her pussy gliding off my fingers. "Just…God," she groaned aloud when I was sheathed in her again. I began to thrust into her—shorter thrusts, deeper thrusts, loving her, wanting her, needing her inside me, under my skin like bones, in my cunt like God.

"Just what, baby?" I asked as she buried her head in my shoulder.

"Don't stop," she groaned into my neck, "don't fucking stop."

Her words set me free and my body jolted with the feeling. I began to fuck her, really and truly fuck her with everything I had—my heart, my mind, I poured my soul out into her cunt through my fingers.

"I won't," I swore wildly as her pussy gripped me tighter. God, her clit was so hard and so big I wanted it in my mouth, between my lips, under my tongue.

"I won't stop because you're fuckin' mine," I told her, my words coming out in harsh breaths. They weren't the right words, but they were the only ones I had. I realized then and there that I'd never had the right ones, never would. How could I say thank you for bringing me back from the scary place I'd been? How could I tell her that her love for me made me safe, comfortable, easy in my skin, and capable of being more than I ever dreamed?

Yes, she was leaving, I was gigging, and there was that fucking phone call to deal with, and I knew, the way you know when you've just slammed your knee, that in half a second that it is really going to *hurt*, that everything was going to change—everything always does. But this? This was ours—our time, our moment, and we belonged to it, to each other. I gave myself to it, I gave myself to her.

"Mine," I growled, nipping lightly at her breast with my teeth. I'd already ripped the button off the shirt. "Mine…" I whispered again and pressed my lips to her chest, sucking on the skin as her heart beat madly against my mouth.

She crushed me to her, and I tasted blood as she swayed against me, her pussy so tight I was afraid I'd hurt her. I looked up, my chin pressed against her chest as I drank in the sight of her edges—the artful lines of her neck, her chin, the outline of my lion who cast golden eyes upon me, eyes full of love and passion, eyes that looked at me and showed me as beautiful.

"Yours," she gasped, and let go of me only to grab gentle hold of my face and kiss me desperately, as if she were dying and this was her last chance, her only chance, to let someone know she'd existed. "Yours…" she breathed again when she tore her mouth from mine, and she cradled my face in her hands, brushing her thumb over my chin, into the hollow below my lip. God, I was deep, so deep inside her pussy as those tight, slick walls held me, pulsed around me. Her eyes locked on mine, melting, incandescent, and I witnessed her transformation as she gave me everything she had, the rhythm of her heart beating in my hands.

The aftershocks raced through her, and she shuddered with them as I eased my fingers away, first from her now-too-sensitive clit, and then from the welcome warmth of her pussy as she hugged me and rested boneless, wordless, head tucked into my shoulder, cheek pressed against the beating vein in my neck.

I let the tears stream down my face, overwhelmed as I was by the intensity of everything, the magnitude of the gift that was my Kitt, Francesca, Fran, and I eased us from the ledge, sliding down the wall until I sat on the floor with my back against it, with her on top of me. I wrapped my arms around her, holding her, rocking her as she cried with me.

When through her tears she kissed me with hunger, pushing me back, forcing me down against the wall, I answered her need. When she reached for my pants I helped her open them.

Words were cheap. I used the language I knew best as we lay down.

LONDON CALLING

If you don't know what pain is—I can show you
That's the only way you let me know you
Think it over drink it through then feel it once again
Is this the only way that you can let me be your friend?
...
Take your mark, but think it over before you shoot me
through
This becomes the way that I will always think of you

"Carry The Stone"—Life Underwater

Fran left with the promise to call me after the gig and as soon as she knew when she'd be back. I didn't press her. Besides, since she was in California, I assumed her trip had something to do with her past internship and perhaps she didn't want to jinx it by discussing it.

Neither one of us brought up that phone call—at all.

In the few days left before the show, the band and I rehearsed, invited everyone we could think of—including my former roommates—and generally made the most out of our nerves. In reality, we'd be fine. The music was good, our rehearsals were tight, and we'd already done a few "unplugged" gigs, so this was just the same thing, only pre-announced and a little louder, right? Yeah, I didn't believe it, either.

Six hours to showtime and we had to be there in two. I showered, put on the pants, and decided to fuck the shirt—I'd wear a jacket instead. I spent way too much time, even by my standards, on my hair, and when I got my guitar and my stuff, it was time to load out into the van when Jerkster honked. By the time we got to CB's, we were all taking out our nerves in different ways, and me, well, I had nothing left in me emotionally but to focus on this—it was all I had.

So when Trace showed up and started coming on to me, I let her. It was odd—I think I felt bad for her. She needed something, something so much that she couldn't directly ask for it, couldn't reach out for it without hurting whoever she was reaching to. Besides, no matter what she said or did, I knew nothing would happen—I had no feelings for her other than that strange sadness, and I was way too into Fran to do anything that might damage what we had.

A moment of heart-throbbing fear grabbed me when we finally climbed the stage and I faced the audience after plugging in my guitar.

I swallowed, hard, Stephie and I shared a look, and I nodded to her—we were okay, we were going to be okay. Jerkster merely stared down at his bass, waiting for our cue.

The sound guy announced us over the PA, the drummer clicked in the time, and just like that, we were off and into it.

It was amazing, the way we worked together, the sound we created, the trip we brought the audience on with us—and they really were with us, every step of the way. As the set progressed we wore less and less—it's hot under those lights! The encore demanded still more, and we played the same set again.

By that point I'd lost the jacket and stripped down to my bra, Stephie had stripped down too, and Jerkster wore nothing but his kilt—and I mean nothing. I don't know if anyone picked up his underwear. We all had the same silky sheen of sweat.

The applause was very sweet when we were finally allowed to stop, and there was much back-slapping and congratulating as we disassembled our equipment and tromped off the stage.

When Ronnie the soundman asked as if we wanted another gig, I said "sure," then quietly packed my guitar and equipment on the side of the stage. It made me happy to see Nico when he came rushing over.

After he was done congratulating me and I recovered from the nausea his enthusiastic bouncing hug had created, I extracted his promise to watch my stuff when I excused myself to the bar for some water.

Trace came up to me out of nowhere, grabbed my head, and planted a solid smooch on my lips.

"That was great, baby, just great!" she breathed, and kissed me again. "Thanks, Trace, really. I'm just going to get some water. I'll be back by the stage in a minute, okay?" I asked with a tired grin.

She had grabbed my jacket from the stage and brought it with her. Putting it over my shoulders, she smiled and said, "You don't want to catch a chill." She must have had one of those rare moments of empathy, because she kissed my cheek again and walked away.

By the time the bartender finally brought me my water, my head was blank and muzzy, and I had this sense, the uncomfortable anxiety of expectation, like waiting for the mail. Probably a holdover from the pre-show nerves, I dismissively reflected.

I was annoyed when someone came and sat next to me, invaded my personal space, and I shifted in my seat to ignore their presence, to regain some sense of privacy.

I shrugged my shoulders into my jacket. Trace was right—I was starting to get a little cold.

A beer slid across the bar, and money hit the worn wood surface. Dee Dee would flip over that, I thought, as I rubbed a finger over a spot where the varnish had come off.

I caught the shine of silver as I sipped my water, and as my eyes insisted on focusing there, I realized it wasn't coins at all, it was jewelry, and I stared, stared because I recognized the piece, stared because I knew who it belonged to.

When I reached out to touch it, heat warmed my back.

"I don't like your girlfriend," said a voice I couldn't believe I was hearing. I closed my hand around that shiny little piece of silver, sat up straight, and carefully pushed my seat back.

"She's not my girlfriend," I answered with a steadiness I didn't feel. I put both hands against the edge of the bar to balance myself as I stood up.

Her hair was long and slightly wavy, darker than I'd remembered and parted down the center, and she wore a long black coat, but I would have recognized her and those diamond-bright eyes anywhere, no matter what she wore.

I folded her to me with an automatic response as immutable, unstoppable, and unquestionable as gravity. As I held my Samantha in my arms—and I couldn't help but think of her as mine—I could feel my heartbeat strengthen: a long, low, solid thump that rang right through me.

The phone call just scant days before, Candace, everything, everyone, disappeared in the complete surprise of her presence. "I can't believe you're here," I whispered into her ear and pulled her even closer. Samantha squeezed my shoulders, then buried her hands in my hair as she burrowed her warm cheek into my neck. I even forgot I was supposed to call her Ann.

"I can't believe you're here, either," she answered, her voice heavy and thick as it slid against my skin. Her breath caught and a tremor ran through her. Samantha was crying.

"Oh ye of little faith," I chided lightly and kissed the back of her head, "look harder next time."

Samantha chuckled through her tears and finally raised her eyes, those beautiful luminous eyes, to mine. I loosened my hold and rubbed my hands down the solid length of her arms.

"You're beautiful." Samantha smiled at me and held my hands. "You're right, and you're beautiful. What am I going to do about that?"

"Well..." I drawled, swinging our joined hands lightly, "I still have some work," I indicated the stage with a nod, "to do."

"Yes, of course," Samantha dropped my hand and backed up a step, "don't let me stop you. But after..." She trailed off, her eyes staring at me with something I'd never seen in anyone's before. I can only describe it as hunger.

"Yes?" I asked, uncertain before that gaze. She was here, and I was here, and this was just all so very strange. It felt good, but weird, too, because it felt so unreal. Were we really standing here, together, on the same planet, never mind the same continent? Maybe I'd passed out from stage fright and this was all some strange hallucination, and in reality Jerkster and Stephie were throwing water on me and trying to wake me.

Samantha reached to touch my face, but didn't. She dropped her hand like she'd been burned.

"I don't want to lose you again," she said softly as her hands clenched and unclenched at her sides, and I watched as her eyes grew overbright.

I didn't think about anything at all as I stepped back toward her and held out my hand, because if this was a dream, I was going with it.

"Come home with me," I told her simply.

Oh, it was agonizingly slow, the tentative reach of fingers, the wait for the custom fit of her hand in mine, and when it finally happened I could almost hear the tumblers of some giant lock click exactly into place.

"Really?"

Acting on impulse, which seemed to be all I'd been doing for the last few hours, I leaned over and quickly kissed her cheek.

"Truly," I answered her, and smiled. That smile grew until it threatened to take my ears with it. "Okay then," I said, maybe a little too brightly, "let's get this show on the road, shall we?" And without waiting for an answer, I half dragged Samantha behind me toward the table where everyone sat before the stage.

It might have only been twenty feet away, but it felt like twenty miles, and I was conscious with each step that the warm pressure in my hand was Samantha's fingers in mine, and while part of me was jumping up and down for joy singing, "Sammy, my Sammy! Yay!" the rest of me wondered what in the hell I'd just gotten myself into.

I mean, sure, yeah, we'd been great friends in high school, and I'd had feelings for her forever, but still—a lot of time had passed since we'd seen each other. And the feelings that I had for the girl I'd known, from the girl I'd been, well, here we were now, all this time later, young women, and, despite all that history, complete strangers, especially after what I'd overheard not too long ago.

Hey, she could be a homicidal maniac, and I'd just invited her home with me. Okay, not that I really believed that, but still, you could never tell, right? And whether I wanted to be conscious of it or not, I had to consider the strange arrangement that was our lives hanging in the background.

"Hey, guys!" I greeted the group at large as we neared.

Everyone looked up with friendly curiosity except for Nico. His eyes widened in shock, and he jumped out of his seat.

"Holy shit!" he exclaimed as his elbow jostled Jerkster's beer, spilling it—onto his prized kilt. Jerkster pushed back from the table and shook his head, dismayed.

"Holy shit is right." I grinned at Nico as everyone looked up.

"Everyone," I said to the table at large, "this is Samantha." They all nodded and said their various hellos.

"Samantha? This," and I waved to include the whole group, "this is everyone."

"Hi, everyone," she greeted the group, glancing from face to face until she reached my brother and smiled. "Hello, Nicky."

"Nico," he corrected tightly.

"That suits you," she smiled again, "Nico."

He didn't smile back.

"Damn, not another of Nina's girls?" Jerkster asked Nico in a loud undertone from his sodden perch.

"No. Definitely *not* that," Nico muttered back, and hearing that, I glanced over at him. To my surprise, Nico had crossed his arms across his chest, and his eyes had faded to stone gray as he stared at Samantha.

"Good," Jerkster muttered, "because I look like I peed myself." Someone threw him a bar rag and I chuckled a bit, full of high spirits.

"Get a move on there, dude," I teased unhelpfully, "we've still got work to do. Samantha," I said, "I leave you in," I looked around at the group, "interesting company." Good hands was certainly not the description, that was for sure.

Stephie, Jerkster, and I regrouped by the stage to ensure we hadn't forgotten anything. Ronnie came over to us as we started to arrange our shit so we could carry it out. He seemed so enthusiastic he was almost bouncing.

"Hey, guys!" he greeted. "You know, I just spoke with Graham, Graham Crack from the Microwaves. Their drummer, Paulie-Boy, was here tonight!"

We stared at each other in shock—the Microwaves? Dude, they were one of the coolest ska bands around. And if you don't know what ska is, you're really missing out.

There's a huge debate as to which came first, ska or reggae (and guess which side says which), but in a nutshell, ska is reggae sped up, with lots of horns and totally fun—whether or not the lyrics are political, satirical, or allegorical, and sometimes all three. The dance is called skanking, the Toasters are a hot group, and the people into it, who wear gray creepers, porkpie hats, and super-skinny ties, are called "Rude boys and Rude girls." That's the basics—oi!

I quickly hid my surprise, and so did Stephie and Jerkster—we were cool, after all.

"Anyhow, you mind if I spin off a copy of your tape tonight and give it to him? They're searching for a band to take on tour—you know, open for them."

Jerkster looked at Stephie, Stephie looked at me, and I looked back at them both like my mind had fallen to the ground. What? Yes? No? Really? No way! passed through all of our minds and faces as we searched one another for answers.

"Uh, yeah, hey, why not?" I answered Ronnie finally, swallowing through my dried throat. I kept peeking at the band to see what they had to add, but they just kept nodding at me like I had all the answers, so I continued. "Just, uh, we don't have an official drummer, as you can see." I pointed to the vacant spot our hired gun had abandoned. He was probably home sleeping already. "That's something—well, we've got to work on that."

Ronnie laughed. "That's an easy fix—Paulie-Boy loved you guys! So, I'll give the tape to Graham?"

"Yeah, sure," I said, nodding with a casualness I didn't feel.

"Yeah," Stephie finally chimed in—I glanced at her with barely veiled relief, "and uh, let us know what he says."

"Definitely," Ronnie agreed, and started digging into his pockets, pulling out little bits of paper. "Whose number do I have here?"

"Take Nina's," Stephie said, and Jerkster nodded behind her in agreement.

"Yeah, take Nina's," he echoed.

"She lives for that thing." She grinned at me, jostling my shoulder. I grinned back as I wrote the number down for Ronnie.

"Okay, great, I'll talk to you guys soon," Ronnie said, clapping his hands together as he walked back to his board. "This is gonna be so fuckin' cool…"

"Man oh man, the Microwaves—can you *believe* it?" Jerkster asked.

"Nah, it's all bullshit," Stephie answered, "this is fuckin' show business—everyone is bullshit."

I kinda sorta agreed, but still…this was New York, home of the "Hey, you never know."

"Nothing is nothing until it's something," I agreed with Stephie, "still…sometimes things happen, right?"

"Yeah, sometimes, things happen," Jerkster agreed.

"Uh-huh, and it's usually shit!" Stephie added, and we all laughed.

We grabbed our equipment and started hauling it out of there, taking it to the sidewalk so Jerkster could drive around with the van we'd rented and we could return it to our rock.

"Hey, seriously," I asked Stephie as I hefted an amp, "would you wanna go?" I walked to the sidewalk, Stephie carrying the bass drum behind me.

"What, you mean on tour with the Microwaves?" She put the drum down carefully between broken glass and gum on the cracked cement, then straightened. "Shit yeah! That's why Ronnie's got *your* number—I wouldn't believe it, and Jerkster still believes in the tooth fairy!"

"Hey!" I laughed. "I made some good money from the tooth fairy!"

"You know…" Stephie considered for a long second. "Me too." She grinned.

Stephie's words made me feel pretty darn good—as if there wasn't enough of that tonight. I was always a little bit aware that I was the newcomer to the Stephie-Jerkster friendship, even though we'd started the band together. Choosing me to take that call meant they trusted me, which was a good thing.

"But," I said as together we carried the drum hardware, "you'd go?" I asked again. Jerkster pulled around and hopped out, quickly opening a door and getting his muscle under that damn rack.

"Go where?" Jerkster asked as we slid our all-important shit into the cargo space.

"Tour," I answered succinctly, "open for the Microwaves."

Jerkster stopped what he was doing. "Oh my God, did they call? When? I need a new bass…"

I took pity on his enthusiastic panic, knowing how easy it was to rush over that ya-ya-ya-hoorah edge. I patted the arm of his army jacket.

"No, dude, they didn't call. But if they did, would you go?"

He stared at me for a moment, and his face seemed to glow.

"Nina…it would be my whole life," he said, his tone one of wonder and solemnity, something I'd never thought to hear from him. "You just tell me when and where, and I'll be there."

I nodded. I understood. I felt exactly the same way. Still do.

Stephie came round to stand by us. "Yeah." She looked at the ground and spit, then looked up again. "Me, too."

I studied them both, considering, nodding. "Me too," I agreed, "me too. I'll let you know as soon as I hear anything."

I don't remember how we got back to the rock we called home, barely remember the after-party our friends threw for us at the Red Spot—an after-hours event just for the band and what seemed to be over a hundred friends.

We laughed a lot, and there was lots of noise and what I thought was premature champagne, but it was great fun just the same—I think. Samantha's presence was like a constant heat at my back even though we weren't always next to each other; in fact, she seemed quite comfortable on her own—although every now and again we'd catch one another's eye and smile.

At one point Trace went to sit with her, and when I saw her a little while later, she looked extremely pissed. Poor Trace—I think maybe more than one person was immune to her charms.

I was tired and drunk off excitement and more than a little champagne, and I was relieved that Jerkster was taking everything to his place for the night—I'd go pick my stuff up in the morning—so all I had to do was carry my guitar (I never let that go) and call a cab. It picked me up in front of the Red Spot, and Samantha took the ride, sitting in the backseat with me.

I don't think we spoke at all. I leaned on my side and she on hers, and all we did was hold hands and stare at each other. I was so tired…

By the time we got to my place the night had chilled, threatening to become early morning frost, and the frigid air woke me up enough to feel how tired I was as the car pulled away and Samantha and I stood outside the door that would lead to my apartment, our breath steaming.

"Coming?" I asked her with a tired smile. I shifted my gig bag on my shoulder and held out my free hand.

"Where else would I go?" she asked me seriously, her eyes glittering in the streetlight as she took my hand.

I opened the door, then led her through the common-area kitchen in the back to my room, where I snapped one of the dimmer lights on. I can't deal with bright ones when I'm that tired—they hurt my eyes.

I spied small glowing embers on my bed. "Hey, scoot!" I chuckled as I put my guitar down in a safe spot nearby and reached with my other hand to pet a fuzzy head—one of Mr. Rabbitz's cats had gotten into my room. The fur ball scampered.

"Good-bye, Mr. Chubbles!" I called to the retreating waddle I recognized.

Samantha stood in the doorway, looking about. "Nice space," she commented, "it suits you." She indicated my art studio set up at the end of the room.

"Thanks." I smiled back in appreciation. Her eyes were the same blue I'd remembered, the same blue I'd dreamt about, and they held me in place as they came closer and closer.

When I barked my shin on the edge of my spare amp, I realized I'd been the one walking, which shocked me back to a reality where we stood face-to-face, alone together for the first time in years, maybe ever. She had the very lightest of lines around her eyes, and her face had grown thinner, perhaps a bit sharper, but the same soul sparked in those eyes and gave me that half-pursed smile I remembered so well.

"Let me have your coat," I asked her through dried lips, my voice sounding low and raspy to my ears. I shucked mine as she wordlessly removed hers, then handed it to me. It was a relief to move away from that intense connection. I walked to the closet to hang both up, and as I closed the door I felt her at my back, heat radiating like a rock left out in the sun to warm. Her arms closed around me, and I leaned back a moment to absorb her warmth before I faced her. I put my arms around her waist, and she buried her head in my neck.

"I thought…I thought you didn't want to see me," I told her quietly, my head pressed into her collarbone.

Samantha's hands tightened around me. "Not that, never that," she spoke hoarsely, her lips against my skin. "I died without you."

She sighed and shifted her grip, her hands strong and warm in mine. "I can't let you go," she said finally, quietly. "I never could. I can't go back to living without you." She took a deep breath and looked down at our hands a moment. Her eyes caught mine again, and she breathed out slowly. "I won't," she said vehemently.

I tried to remember to breathe as the sheer impossibility of everything rode down on me—the high of the gig, the perfect fit-feeling of Samantha, the dim ache in my gut over Fran. The right thing to do was to send Samantha back—back to London and Candace and her arrangements and her life, whatever it was she had created for herself, and for me to go back to the life I'd finally started living—my job and my band and, yes, my Fran, my Kitt.

I would, too, I absolutely would, but…not now, not this second. If Fran had brought me back to life, then just being with Samantha was that bolt from the blue that woke up something in me long sleeping. I was simply going to have to face it and, somehow, move on.

Oh hell, who was I kidding? "Me either," I admitted softly, "I can't do it either." I took my hands from hers, sat on the edge of the bed, and studied Samantha in that half-light.

"You're with Candace," I reminded her as she sat on the other side.

"No, I'm not, not since I spoke to Fran—it's way over," Samantha told me through tight lips. She wrapped her arms around me again, and I snuggled against her.

"I'm with Kitt—Fran," I corrected, and I admit I couldn't help smiling a bit thinking about it.

"I know," Samantha answered, her voice muffled in my shoulder. "I know she loves you."

"Sammy." I spoke quietly, and while I enjoyed the sound of her name in my mouth, she had to hear this. "I love her too."

Samantha's hands tightened on me convulsively. "I know," she answered, her voice an anguished whisper, "I just had to see you."

"I'm glad," I answered honestly, unthinkingly, and we held each other even tighter, still and silent in the dim light.

"I won't hurt her," I said finally into that heavy quiet. It was confusing because I ached with missing Fran, and at the same time the fit of Samantha's body to mine made me feel, well, whole, as if I'd been missing the last piece to my puzzle, and it didn't make any sense at all. But I knew that it didn't matter. I'd made a promise, even if I hadn't made it aloud. I'd made it, sealed it—in blood.

"I understand that," Samantha answered. "I don't want to—I won't either."

She kissed my neck and I shuddered slightly—not because of the sensuality of it, because it wasn't that, not really, but because this *could not* happen.

"I love her, too," she whispered.

I curved my head away from those baby-soft lips I'd dreamed

about, but pulled her closer to me anyway. My hands pressed against her shoulder blades and I rubbed small circles into her back as her fingertips drew stripes against my spine.

"Nina…" Samantha sighed, "what…what are we…"

"…going to do?" I finished for her.

God, nothing mattered. Time, distance, even the person whom I'd heard on the phone, what we'd done, become—it made no difference. We felt the same—to each other, about each other. What an impossible situation—because if Candace had been honest all those months ago, there's good money in betting that everything would have turned out differently. As much as I hate to admit it, I knew that, with a gut-twisting, bitter-tasting certainty. What made it bitter was that I would never, ever in any universe have wanted to miss the opportunity to love and to know Francesca—and I didn't want to give that up.

It wasn't fucking funny, though I laughed lightly, sadly, and rocked her the slightest bit in my arms before I let her go. "Nothing," I said finally, looking into her diamond eyes, "we're going to do nothing."

I shifted on the bed. "Come here," I patted the pillow next to me, "let's get some sleep. I'm too tired to deal with this right now."

She stretched her legs along the mattress and leaned on an elbow, a small smile playing about the corner of her mouth.

I kicked off my boots and lay on the bed over the blankets, and Samantha shifted.

"Are you sure this is okay?" she asked, uncertain. "I could—"

"What, sleep on the floor?" I asked with a smile. "I won't let you do that—that's not necessary. Besides…" I stretched my hands out over my head before tucking them under my head. Fuck it. I was too tired to even undress or change. I shifted and closed my eyes. "It's just sleep. We have the rest of our lives to work this out."

Samantha chuckled under her breath as she eased her length along the mattress. "Yeah, we do, don't we?"

"We do," I answered as firmly as I could. I lay there on my back with my eyes closed for a while, but as much as I tried, I couldn't ignore the burning presence next to me, inches away. I finally opened my eyes only to find Samantha staring at me.

Smiling, I turned on my side to face her. I stretched careful fingers to her face, gently drawing the curve of her cheek, and she returned the favor, sketching the line of my face with her thumb.

"Hey," she said softly, "do you remember that swim meet at Brooklyn College?"

"Of course I do. You kissed me."

Samantha laughed, a soft sound I almost couldn't hear. "Actually, I think you kissed me—that was the best kiss I ever had."

"Nah...can't be," I countered. It had been only one kiss—and one of those chastely romantic ones, to boot. Okay, so I'd never had one like that since, either, but still...

Her fingers stroked my cheek. "Yeah, it was," she affirmed. "You know, I'd been going to ask you out that night."

"I kinda figured that out later," I admitted. I ran my fingers down her neck and along her shoulder. "You should have, you know." I smiled at her.

"Nah, I couldn't," Sam smiled back, her hands trailing along my arm, "you had a very possessive girlfriend."

I laughed softly myself. "Kerry wasn't really my girlfriend. She was my friend and she was just—"

"Experimenting?" Samantha supplied, quirking her eyebrow at me.

"Something like that," I agreed. "It wasn't, it wasn't anything like..." Like you, I'd been about to say, but stopped myself—that was way too dangerous territory to step into.

Samantha chuckled. "Yeah, me and Fran, we were kinda like that, too."

How had we gotten closer? There had been at least a foot between us, and now I could see every detail of her lashes, the light freckles that sprinkled across her nose. I breathed in her air, and the hand that had been on her shoulder was now on her hip, while hers curved around to my lower back.

She moved it to my head again, gently stroking the long strands that fell over my cheek behind my ear. "I think you got further with her than I ever did." She sighed, and the sound was wistful.

We were face-to-face now, staring directly into each other's eyes, and the dark fullness of hers threatened to pull me in.

"Kerry or Fran?" I asked quietly. There was no mistaking the light press of her thigh against mine. We were simply falling into each other.

"Both," Samantha answered succinctly, her lips a whisper away from mine.

Oh. I hadn't known that, about her and Fran, I mean. I tucked that into the back of my mind to think about later.

"Oh," I whispered back. Wait a minute, did that mean…?

"You two never…?" I asked Samantha as I wrapped my arms around her and let her throw her leg over me when I tucked my head under hers.

"Didn't you and Fran ever talk about this?" she countered quietly.

I sighed. No. We never had. Maybe we should have. "No…" I answered, uncertain how to explain.

"You don't, um, talk much?" she inquired tentatively.

"You're not answering my question, Sammy." I grinned at her sleepily. I knew what she was asking, but that really wasn't any of her business.

"Not…not like you two," she said quietly, her eyes throwing obsidian sparks at me in the half-light of my room. She waited a beat. "You didn't answer my question."

Oh. Oh yeah. "We never talked about you," I admitted quietly. "After I found out about Candace, well, I figured, you know, you knew how to find me. And I've never wanted Fran to think…" I hesitated.

Jesus Christ. An icy chill bolted through my stomach. I disentangled myself from our embrace and sat up, running my hands through my hair. Shit. I had a bad feeling about this.

Samantha sat up with me. "Think what?" she asked with soft concern and laid a hand on my shoulder.

I took a deep breath and ordered my thoughts. "That I was with her because of you," I said breathlessly, shocked at the realization, shocked even more that I'd said it aloud in front of the one person I probably shouldn't have. Too late to take it back, though.

That's when the phone rang, the unexpected sound startling me so much that I jumped.

I reached behind me and grabbed it off my amplifier. "Nina," I answered.

"Hey, Nina!" Ronnie's voice, sounding way too wide awake, cut through the speaker. "You guys serious about touring?"

"Yeah, sure, we're interested." Even half asleep, I knew it wouldn't do us any good to appear overeager. "Who's sponsoring it?" Thank God my brain still worked without me. I didn't remember consciously thinking that.

"Uh, not sure," Ronnie answered, "let me get back to you on that."

"Cool, no problem."

"Cool. I'll call you back. Later!" and he clicked off.

I stared at the phone a moment, then put it back in its place so I could lie back down. "Sleep, Sammy," I told her as our bodies settled around one another, "I'm exhausted."

"Okay, love, okay." She kissed my forehead and lay back down, while I closed my eyes surrounded by the sense of home.

I was comfortably numb, dreaming about the gig, and I barely heard the insistent jangle of the phone break through the deep warmth of sleep. My arms felt like lead as I automatically reached to answer.

"Nina," I answered in a sleep-thick voice.

"Hey, baby, how was it?"

"Hey yourself!" I greeted, glad to hear her voice. I got out of bed and tiptoed out of the room, closing the door behind me. I didn't want to keep Samantha up, and I really wanted to talk with Fran—I'd missed her.

"So…how'd it go?" she asked, her voice warm across the wires. "You knock 'em dead?"

"I don't know about that but," I answered excitedly, "I just got called for a new gig. I'll tell you all about it when you get here. Oh, and hey—Samantha showed up after the gig. Crazy, right? She's sleeping. I miss you—when are you coming back?"

"I, uh, I don't know, but it seems like you're in good hands."

"Fran—what are you talking about?"

She didn't answer. "Where are you staying?" she asked instead.

"My place," I answered truthfully. Where was she going with this?

"You took her home with you," she commented mildly. "She probably landed today and you took her home with you."

Dammit. That's not what it was. "Fran…it wasn't…I mean, she showed up right after the gig at CB's. I couldn't just, you know? I mean, I wasn't—"

"Don't worry about it. It's okay."

I had to get her to understand that nothing had happened, nothing was going to happen—no matter what this thing was, it was her and I, wasn't it? "Fran, there's nothing going on, you and I—"

"You need to figure this one out—I can't help you," she interrupted again. She sounded remarkably even and calm, except for that little shake at the back of her voice. She wasn't doing this, she couldn't be doing this. I had to let her know something, anything, to make that sound in her words stop.

Every thought, every feeling I'd had about Samantha evaporated in the face of the pain I could hear in Fran's voice. I wasn't going to lose her. I knew, or at least I thought I knew, that the part of me that reacted to Samantha was just a hero-worshipping, infatuation-struck kid, but what I felt for Fran was the result of something different, something with a solid basis. And hey, if that sounds a little too much like the logic I used with myself the first night Fran and I made love, well, I was upset. "God, you *know* I love you…" I told her, desperate to get through to her.

"You've never said that before."

Ah, she was crying now, and I cursed myself miserably. She was right, I hadn't, because they were just words, and words could be so empty, so meaningless. But I had shown how I felt, hadn't I? Don't actions speak louder than words, and hadn't I spoken those words in so many different ways?

"Please believe me, Fran—I wouldn't—I didn't…I would never do anything to hurt you," I said finally.

"Ah, Nina, Razor Nina…I know where this is going to go—the two of you?" she asked through her tears. "Come on…you have to know what's going to happen." She took a shaky breath that cut right through me. "I'm glad we had our time. I'm glad I've helped you find each other again."

My heart pounded and I could hardly breathe. No. This was *not* going to happen. "Kitt, baby, please, come home, just please," I begged, "this will all be fine, I swear."

Too late, I remembered the adage the nuns had beaten into our heads—it wasn't enough to be good, you had to look good, too. I shouldn't have asked Samantha to come back with me. I hadn't been thinking about anything other than the gig, and I'd been so surprised. Maybe I could buy Samantha a plane ticket back to England or to wherever it was she wanted to go.

"I'm stuck here," she said, and for the first time, a slight bitterness crept into her voice, "and by the time I get there—Nina, it's already too late."

It was the finality in her voice that broke me. I started to cry. "It's not, it won't be, I swear, baby, it's not!" I sobbed. I'd fix this, we could fix this—whatever it took, and I meant it: anything, everything.

I could still hear her crying softly. "I'll call you when I get home. We'll talk then."

"Can't I pick you up from the airport?" I had to see her, to convince her.

"I need time—and you need to know once and for all," she told me firmly, evidently resolved despite her tears.

"Baby, you're wrong. I know everything I need to know," I insisted, "and I know who I'm with."

"The sad thing, Nina?" Fran said, "is that I know you mean that, that you'd give up your chance to finally find out what everyone else has known about the two of you forever—you match, Nina, you fit. God, the look on your face when she was on the phone! Your heart was never mine, Nina."

Maybe she was right, but I knew she couldn't be—my Fran, my Kitt, she was so deeply a part of me that it made words like "love" and "close" sound so trite when I tried to describe even to myself what we had. Didn't she know? I had given her everything, absolutely everything I had in me to give—what else was there? "I'd give you my blood, baby, I'd die for you—"

"I know what you've given me," she said quietly, "I'll always treasure that. But," and I heard her take a breath, "I'm not the one you'll live for."

This was ridiculous. This was insane, this was just plain-out wrong—there had to be a way through it. In person—if we were face-to-face. I knew if she saw me we would be okay. "Where are you in California? I'll come to you. I'll fly out as soon as I can get a flight," I swore, mentally reviewing airports and airlines. "Just tell me where you are."

She sighed, but didn't answer. "Where's Ann?" she asked instead.

"She's sleeping. I'm out in the hallway because I wanted to talk with you. Come on, Kitt baby, where are you? You back in LA?" I hazarded.

She exhaled slowly, and when she spoke, she didn't answer my question, and she no longer spoke with tears. Her voice was angry and resigned. "Trust me, Nina, she's not sleeping. In two seconds, she'll step out, put her arms around you, and these past months will be a beautiful memory. Then? She'll fuck you, then fuck you over."

She hung up on me.

Stunned, wounded beyond belief, I sat on the floor and dropped the phone, buried my face in my hands, and wept. When Samantha came out of the room, crouched down, and silently put her arms around me, I cried even harder.

"Okay, let it out, baby, it's okay," she crooned softly, "it'll work out." She kissed the top of my head.

"No, it won't," I told her, gasping, choking through the ragged tear that had split me wide open, "and it's my fault." But a part of my mind didn't agree at all. I'd given Fran everything I had and then some. And it hadn't mattered what I had felt for Samantha—I had honored what Fran and I shared, hadn't I?

"Francesca?" Samantha asked quietly.

"Yeah," I nodded, wiping my face, "yeah."

"She's mad…because I'm here?" Samantha asked slowly.

"She's upset because you're *here*," I corrected, indicating my place.

"But…nothing happened," Samantha said. "I mean—there wasn't…"

Something in me snapped. The memory of Trace rose in my mind and I remembered, I remembered everything she'd made me feel, everything I'd let her put me through—and I had let her do it. It left a bitter taste in my mouth, while a combined burst of anger and shame coiled through me. Fuck. It was icy.

I adored Fran, but I wouldn't do that to myself again, not for anyone, not ever again. Trace had made me feel like nothing; I wasn't going to let Fran do that to me. I wasn't ever going to be that weak again. I picked up my phone from the floor, dried my eyes, and wiggled out of Samantha's embrace. I can't really explain what had happened, but a different person stood than had sat there crying.

"Doesn't matter," I stated flatly. Suddenly, the ridiculousness of the situation hit me and I smiled, a twist to my face that hurt. "She dumped me," I laughed humorlessly, "she told me you'd fuck me over, and she dumped me."

Even in the gloomy darkness of the hallway, I could see Samantha's astonishment.

"You're kidding!"

"About which? The dumping me or the fucking me over?" I asked as I felt that painful grimace cross my face again.

Samantha waved her hands in the air. "Either…both—she broke up with you? On the phone? Just now?"

"Yup," I agreed, my voice sounding way too cheerful to my ears, so bright it literally hurt me to hear, "on the phone, just now."

This was crazy, this was insane. This was not how I'd ever imagined I'd end my first gig or—and okay, I admit, this had been a dream for a long time, too—see Samantha again. But honestly, I'd never imagined that Fran and I would end, either. I felt the shakes race up my body—you know, that internal shiver that won't let you go when you're just way too fuckin' tired? I was done, I'd had it.

"Bed," I said to Samantha and indicated my door with a nod, "I'm too tired for this." I dragged myself in and sat down on the side I'd slept on before the world had flipped upside down, then turned to see Samantha outlined in the doorway.

"Maybe…I should go," Samantha said. "I'll just call a cab."

Dammit. This wasn't Sam's fault. I was being rude and obnoxious, and that wasn't fair of me. Still clutching my phone, I walked back over to her. Her hands came up automatically to enfold me as I approached, and I put my arms around her shoulders.

"I'm sorry," I whispered. "I'm just really fucked up right now."

Her arms tightened around me, and I tucked my head into her neck.

"Don't worry about me," Samantha whispered back. "I just want you to be all right. I'll give her a call tomorrow, see if I can talk some sense into her."

That was *not* a good idea. If we couldn't straighten this out ourselves, then adding anyone else into the mix wouldn't help. Especially not Samantha.

I tossed my head. "No. She has no reason not to trust me, and if she finds she can't, well," I gave Samantha a tight little grin, "then we have nothing anyway."

"Don't you think that's a little harsh?" she asked, her voice low and concerned.

I dropped my arms from her shoulders and took her hand, leading her back to the promised land of sleep. "No, I don't," I answered, letting my breath out in a contained rush. "It's all about the bottom line."

I stopped by the foot of the bed and faced Samantha again. "Life's too short, Sammy, you taught me that, years ago. She loves me, or she doesn't. It's bone simple."

She searched my face, then finally nodded. "Yeah. I guess you're right," she said, looking at the ground, "but still—"

"I might feel differently in the morning," I allowed with a small smile. "Sleep now."

We gave each other a quick and fierce hug, and as I stepped back to my side of the bed, the phone went off. I answered it before the first note had completed itself as I sat back on the mattress, hoping it was Fran calling back.

"Hey," I said.

"Nina!" Ronnie's voice cheered out brightly. "Do you have a passport?"

Thrown for a moment because it wasn't the voice I was expecting, I had to think. "Uh, yeah. Yeah, I do. At least, I think so. Why?"

"You've got six days to get your band, your paperwork, and your gear in order. Rude Records and Skapunkt Records are jointly sponsoring the Microwaves tour—with special supporting guest, Adam's Rib."

"Are you serious?" I asked him, totally amazed.

Samantha stirred behind me, and I felt her sit by my back.

"Dead-on straight," he said, "bigger than a heart attack, but smaller than an atom bomb."

"Holy shit!" I responded, momentarily losing my cool. "Where we going?" I figured we'd be crossing the continent—East Coast to West Coast with a whole lot of "non-coast" in between.

"London, baby. You're starting in London—expect to be gone eight to ten weeks. Why do you think I asked about your passport?"

Holy Christ on a cracker. I fumbled behind the amp for the notebook and pen I kept there—for song-writing emergencies.

"We're there," I told him. "Who do I need to talk with, what do I need to know?"

I wrote down all the information he gave me, including Graham Crack's and Paulie-Boy's numbers. I promised to call him after I spoke with the band, then hung up.

I sat there, staring at the phone.

"Who was that?" Sam asked, gently stroking my hair away from my shoulder.

"That was Ronnie—the sound guy from CB's," I told her while I still stared at nothing. I grabbed a cigarette from next to the amp and lit it. I wasn't going to sleep after all.

"Oh," Samantha said. She waited a beat. "What did he want?"

I twisted around to face her, my mind, my hands numb. "To tell me about the Microwaves—we're going on tour."

FIRST AND LAST AND ALWAYS

Never thought I'd wonder if all that I feel is true
Right now? There's no difference between just me and you
I know you know me well
I know you lie like hell
Do you want me for me?

"Me For Me"—Life Underwater

Right after my call from Ronnie, I phoned Stephie, and I left it up to her to get in touch with the Jerkster. It was insane. We had to rehearse with Paulie-Boy, who would do two sets a night—ours and the Microwaves'. We got to meet all of them, including Graham, during rehearsals. Graham was from "Liver peeyool" as he said it; Paulie-Boy was from Boston. The rest of the band were from all over—the West Indies, London, the bassist was from South Dakota—how weird was that?

I liked everyone, but I found something about Graham intriguing. Not in an I-want-to-date-you way, but more in a there's-more-to-you-than-you-say-isn't-there way.

Anyhow, we somehow managed to get all of our papers and passports processed, and we all found the equipment we needed—especially those all-important current converters—just in time to get to the airport. Samantha had been the one to find the converters. "You'll need these, desperately," she'd said with a grin as she handed me five of them. She ended up being two hundred percent on the money.

Dee Dee threw me a surprise party two nights before we left. I had gone in on my next work night and told her directly—and requested the time off. I still needed a job when I got back, didn't I?

"Ah, Nina," she'd smiled and hugged me, "I always knew you were too big for this place." That had been almost exactly what Fran had said to me, and I froze just as I was returning Dee Dee's hug. She noticed.

"Nina, what's the matter?" Dee Dee asked as I stepped back. She reached to touch my face, but I pulled my head away, uncomfortable. I didn't want anyone to touch me.

"I'm sorry," she apologized.

"No...I am." I shook my head regretfully, ashamed of my behavior—I was being an ass to a friend. I was just completely out of sorts lately.

Dee Dee pursed her lips as she studied me. "Francesca?"

I glanced up into her eyes and nodded in mute acquiescence, trying to grin, but failing miserably.

At that moment, the door opened and Samantha walked in. When she saw me sitting with Dee Dee, she smiled and nodded, then found her own corner. This time, I smiled for real—I couldn't help that.

It was strange—she had a lot of errands to run during the day, which she vaguely told me about, just that they were work and family legal matters, and while she hadn't stayed over again (because we both agreed that the situation with Fran was bad enough, so she stayed at Fran's apartment like she'd originally planned), she made sure to see me every day—either after rehearsals, which were now in Manhattan in the Music Building on East Fifty-first on Tin Pan Alley, or she'd stop by the bar and say hello.

"Oh, I see why..." Dee Dee said, looking from me to her and back again.

"No, it's nothing like that," I told her, "in fact it's..."

I don't know why I did it, but I told her the whole damn thing.

By the time I got to the end, Dee Dee had tears in her eyes. I didn't understand—it seemed to me more like stupidity on my part than tragedy.

I should have never walked Fran home that night, I thought bitterly, but stopped myself right there, because I knew myself better than that. Given the opportunity, I wouldn't have missed the chance to love my lion.

Whatever had impelled Fran to her actions had come from somewhere, and I knew it wasn't me—not really, anyway. I truly felt bad for her, that something or someone had hurt her so badly that even though she said she knew me, she really didn't. I didn't realize I'd said the first part out loud.

"Nina, *liebe*, you don't really feel that way, do you?" Dee Dee asked me with warmth. This time when she touched my face, I let her.

"No, no, I don't," I told her sadly, "it's just...I'm so damned confused, I don't even know what to do."

Dee Dee sighed. "Have you considered staying, then?"

I had, I honestly had. But this tour was the opportunity of a lifetime; I mean, even *I* knew that this sort of thing might never come again. And I had to consider the band, too. I couldn't let them down now, could I? Hell, no.

"I thought about it," I admitted, staring down at the glossy shine of the bar, "but it's not just me involved." I looked up into Dee Dee's clear-sighted face. "It's Jer's and Stephie's dreams, too."

Dee Dee bit her lower lip and nodded. She took one of her ever-present bar rags out of her waistband and polished a microspot on the bar. I was starting to suspect that it was just something she did whenever she needed a moment to think. I started to grin, but quickly stopped; I didn't want her to think I was making fun of "her thing," if that's what it was.

"There are always other factors involved," she said finally, still scrubbing. She sighed and looked up at me. "It's very hard sometimes, Nina, to do what's right for you, for everyone, especially when your heart screams something different."

I nodded, unable to get words past the lump in my throat. Dee Dee had hit the spot, though, because in those rare moments in between rehearsals and work, I was tearing, breaking apart. I didn't want to go and I couldn't wait to leave.

Dee Dee patted my shoulder, and I could feel the warmth and support in her touch before she walked away, leaving me to my thoughts for a few minutes before I had to get back to work.

Samantha came over and stood next to my chair. "Hey there," she said softly, her mouth quirked into a little smile.

"Hey, yourself." I smiled at her through the weight in my chest. Fuck it. None of this was her fault anyway. I followed my inclinations and hugged her.

"How was rehearsal today?" she asked, hugging me in return. Her body next to me provided a sense of solidity I'd been needing.

"Fine, great, actually," I answered, speaking into her shoulder. "Paulie-Boy really knows his shit." And it was true. We were done with the songs themselves; we were now working out the set order and the stage show, such as it was. "How's all of your stuff going?"

"Fine, just fine," Samantha said. She held me tightly a moment, then let go, taking my hand instead.

"Nina...she's home," she said quietly, her eyes searching mine for a response.

Oh. Ouch. Fuck! I couldn't believe how much that hurt to know, that she was home and hadn't called me. I gasped and caught my breath, then twisted my head around and finally focused on the ceiling so that the stinging in my eyes wouldn't succumb to gravity and become tears. I'd already cried enough for one lifetime—maybe more. I wondered if anyone was counting—besides me, I mean. Hadn't I read somewhere that God counts women's tears? Maybe for tonight the universe could be satisfied with what it already had.

I wasn't ashamed of them anymore, well, at least not as much as I had been; I just had to work very publicly—and I didn't want to cry while in front of people, whether they were friends or strangers.

"When?" I finally got out, a part of me horrified to hear the wrench in my voice.

"Last night. Late last night," she amended, "too late to call."

That just pissed me off and don't ask why, but I laughed. I pulled my hand free of Samantha's. "Darlin'," I smiled, but there was absolutely no joy in it, "I'm up all night. That's the biggest bullshit I've ever heard."

Samantha had the good grace to look embarrassed and stared off at the floor before she looked at me again. "Come back there with me tonight. When she sees you, talks with you..." She trailed off as she read my face.

I shook my head. "No. She told me she'd call me when she was ready. I'm trying to respect that."

I looked around the bar. The evening had just begun, but it was already starting to get crowded. Soon, you'd have to yell to be heard across the background noise. Since Jen was working the door tonight, I'd be waitressing, and despite my personal problems, I had a job to do.

"I've got to get back to work, Sam, I'm sorry," I excused myself and stepped away, hardly able to see through the watery haze that held me.

"Nina, call her, just talk with her!" Samantha exhorted.

I took a step back. "I already have," I admitted, "and she wouldn't answer. Besides," I added, "I told her she was the pride of my heart—what else does she need to know?"

I walked away from Samantha's stunned expression, and this time, instead of hiding from the crowd, I hid within it.

I did send her flowers—Francesca, that is. I sent her tiger lilies and a card that said, "Please, love, call me." She didn't, and the continued silence hurt me so horribly I walked around feeling like I'd lost a body part somewhere in the vicinity of my chest.

I focused as much as I could on the things I had to do.

Two days later, the bar was set up for a private party that Dee Dee had asked the band to play at—and for the first time, there was a charge at the door. Graham and Paulie-Boy thought it would be a great way for us to test our act.

I wore the same clothes I'd worn for the last gig, and when we walked in, Stephie, Jerkster, Paulie-Boy, and me, I was thoroughly startled. Dee Dee waited by the door with Jen and started clapping as we came through it. The whole bar joined them.

"Nina, look!" Jerkster exclaimed and pointed.

Stephie and I both followed his finger, and I was so touched by what we saw it brought tears to my eyes.

"Congratulations, Adam's Rib," the banner said. "Next time, we'll toast you at the Grammys!"

I threw my arms around Dee Dee and kissed her cheek. "You're crazy," I told her with a huge smile, "and I absolutely love you for it!"

"How could I not, Nina, how could I not?" Dee Dee asked, then hugged me with such enthusiasm she lifted me off the floor and half spun me—right into Jen, who caught me up.

We stared at each other a moment, uncomfortable. I mean, we had that whole tough-dykes thing going—we didn't touch, you know? She'd slap my shoulder and I'd slap hers in return, buddies in arms; there's no touching with buddies (that kind of buddies, anyway). But what the fuck, right? I smiled and gave her a big hug, which took her half a second to return. She put me down and patted my shoulder roughly, her fingertips gripping slightly.

"You done good, kid, real good." She grinned.

"But there's more, Nina, look!" Dee Dee grabbed my shoulders and twirled me right around. Not only had she cleared a spot for the band to play, but she'd moved the back bar and transformed it into a DJ booth.

I stared at her, amazed. "But Dee Dee, what about the cabaret license?" I didn't want her to get fined just for throwing me a party.

Dee Dee grinned conspiratorially. "That's why tonight's a private party, *liebchen*," she said. "You can do whatever you want with a private club. Well, almost. So? What are you waiting for? Go—do your thing!"

I walked through the crowd, stunned. It had been a little while, but when I got back there, holy shit! Dee Dee must have called the Red Spot, because my crates with the discs I loved best were there.

I grinned to myself, because I knew exactly what to play, and my fingers rapidly found it.

I turned the system on, a "pop" running through the bins, making people jump as they craned around to see what was going on. Grabbing the headphones off the table, I slung them around my neck (they fit flawlessly), then set track one, backed up track two. This was oh so good to go, and I was feeling totally at home and perfectly fine—we were gonna have some fun tonight, for sure!

I set my fades, slid the 'phones over my ears, and clicked the mike.

"Dee Dee?" I called across the crowd, "this is for you—Kraftwerk: 'Trans-Europe Express'!"

Dee Dee covered her mouth with her hands, and I waved her over. "Come on, Dee Dee, dance with me?" I cajoled. She shook her head no, but her eyes were too sparkling for me to ignore. I had the next song cued to go, so what the hell, right?

I walked out from behind the setup and went straight to Dee Dee, gently took her hands away from her face, and dragged her out to the dance floor. "You can't turn the DJ down, Dee Dee, nobody does," I wheedled with a grin.

Dee Dee gave me a sideways glance. "Since it's a tradition..." She grinned finally.

"It certainly is."

Jen backed me up and agreed, and next thing you know, the place was jumping. I thanked Dee Dee for the dance with another hug, gave

Jen a quick hip bump, and went back to play with the tunes until it was time for us to perform. Graham walked in and smiled at us as we set up.

Samantha arrived halfway through the performance and gave me a thumbs-up, then found herself a corner to watch from. She made herself inconspicuous, but stayed near the front.

I smiled at her, then went back to the chorus I was playing. When I glanced up again, she was talking with Graham, who handed her something. Probably his number, I grinned to myself.

When I'd introduced them in the studio, Samantha had told me they'd met before—and that London was smaller than I thought, certainly smaller than New York. Graham had laughed and allowed that was true, but...I don't know exactly what it was I saw in Graham's eyes when he looked at her, but it was something, something I couldn't figure out. It didn't matter right now, anyway, because there was music to be played and performed, and I was part of it.

Toward the end of the night, we were just about to play our last song, when Jerkster nudged Stephie and pointed. Stephie glanced, then leaned over to me quickly. "Look out," she muttered to in my ear, then pointed as subtly as she could, "you're between the bitch and the barbed wire."

I peered over to where she'd indicated. Fran had come in, unnoticed in the crowd, and stood on the opposite end of the floor.

"C'mon, dude," I said just as quietly to her ear, "neither one of them is a bitch."

Stephie snorted. "Not from where I stand."

I shook my head. I'd told Stephie and Jerkster what had happened between Fran and me. It had been pretty obvious that I was miserable, and while I didn't appreciate the reference, I knew Stephie had my back, and I did appreciate that—and she was entitled to her opinion.

Fran raised her beer to me in salute with an ironic smile, while my hands froze on my guitar and my gut started to heave. I watched as Samantha strode over and jammed something into her hand as she spoke in her ear. Fran stared at it a moment, then gave it right back. If I hadn't been so stuck in my brain, I would have wondered what that was all about.

Suddenly, Paulie-Boy clicked his drumsticks behind me, which snapped me back. I was onstage, I had a job to do.

We rocketed into the song, and I let go and dove into the sound—

I jumped, I danced, Jerkster and I even did a little back-to-back shimmy, and by the way? You don't see anyone do those front to front because no one wants to get electrocuted. Touch another plugged-in instrument while you've got your hands on your strings, and you're toast. Literally. Complete with new hairdo, compliments of the local utility company.

Three encores later, we were beat, and Dee Dee came up to grab the microphone.

"And now…it's time for the raffle!"

"Raffle?" I mouthed at Stephie. She shrugged with a studied casualness, which I dismissed. The night had been full of many surprises. Probably Dee Dee had a great bottle of champagne or a basket or something along those lines.

"It's you," Jerkster said in an undertone as he unplugged and wrapped the patch cord from his bass next to me.

"What are you talking about?" I asked in the same undertone. I glanced back at Dee Dee, who held an ice bucket full of those little red tickets.

"Dude, look at me." He grinned. He had three rows of tickets strung around his neck—I'd thought he was wearing a scarf.

"You tried to buy me?" I asked him, incredulous.

"No, I tried to *win* you." He grinned again. "Hey, I was gonna share you with Steph," he added, and Stephie looked over and nodded, waving her wrist. She wore a couple of rows wrapped around it.

I shook my head at them. "I'm not kissing either one of you," I said, quirking my mouth to the side.

I walked up to Dee Dee where she played with the crowd, picking up tickets from the bucket and dropping them back in. "What are you doing?" I stage-whispered. "You can't raffle me!"

"Maybe this one?" Dee Dee asked the crowd, picking a ticket out. "Oh no, it's fallen!" she joked and dropped it back in.

"Hush, you don't know what you're talking about," she stage-whispered back out of the corner of her mouth. "It's the Return-to-New-York fund—they all want you to come back!"

This wasn't making any sense.

"What?"

"The money's for you!" she told me, her eyes and gestures still fixed on the audience. Paulie-Boy began a drum roll.

I looked over and rolled my eyes at him. Thanks, buddy, I thought, thanks a lot. I mouthed it to him and he smirked back at me.

"I don't want it—you keep it!" I told her.

"I'll hold it for you. Trust me, you'll need it!" she threw me a quick grin, then went back to the audience, who were stomping in time with Paulie-Boy. "It's showtime!"

Paulie-Boy really got into it and gave a drum roll so loud I wanted to rub my ears, making the silence that followed seem just as loud as we all waited to hear the results.

Everyone gathered as closely as they could to the makeshift stage, while Graham, Fran, and Samantha huddled together over the one ticket Samantha held.

Stephie and Jerkster unstrung their ticket garlands and went through them together as Dee Dee read out the numbers. I'd never noticed she had such a flair for the dramatic before, I thought as I waited with a dry mouth.

A muffled buzz went through the room as everyone checked their numbers, and Stephie and Jerkster were throwing the rejected ones at Paulie-Boy.

Finally, Samantha stood there with a strange look on her face, holding a little ticket in her hand.

Graham pushed her forward.

"Well, you won her fair and square," Fran said, and quickly took a drink of her beer.

I stepped down from the stage, took the little red stub from her hand, and handed it back to Dee Dee. "Well," I said as I stood before the three of them, "if this is the thing you guys have been playing hot potato with all night, then Graham won." I smiled at them, a stage smile.

I dramatically put my arm around his neck and got a very good look at his face as he bent me over backward. When his lips met mine, our kiss confirmed what my eyes had seen, and something I had suspected for a while—he was a she.

It was a very sweet and somewhat chaste kiss, and the room applauded when he stood me back up.

"Now you know." Graham smiled at me with a twinkle in his eyes.

"Now I know." I smiled back. "Does the band?"

Before we got onstage to play, I'd left the board programmed with a cycling set so Dee Dee could just flick a switch and have music for the rest of the night. She did as Graham pulled me into a hug. "The rest of the Microwaves do," he whispered, as we danced.

"I won't say anything," I promised as he took me through a quick two-step twirl.

"I wasn't worried about it." Graham grinned and put his mouth close to my ear. "What I *am* worried about," he said in a low voice, "is you."

"Me? Why are you worried about me?"

Graham gave me another little spin before answering.

"You're a great performer, Nina, a real natural. Paulie-Boy was right, we're gonna have a great tour," he began.

"So what are you worried about?" I questioned. I mean, if the music was good and the tour was on, then what was the problem?

"I'm betting…you've never been away for so long, have you?"

"No," I answered slowly, wondering what he was getting at.

"Things change—faster than you think." He tapped my nose lightly. "She's outside the bar—go talk with her." He spun me gently to face the door. "Go!"

I don't know why I did it, but I did, slipping through the dancers and other attendees. I stepped out through the door, walked past the vestibule, and saw her, standing a few feet away like she had that first night that felt as close as yesterday and as untouchable as tomorrow.

Tears shone in her eyes, and she merely watched me as I neared her under the streetlight, and I couldn't help myself—my hands reached out and gently cradled her face. I kissed that perfect mouth softly, my chest burning as I felt her respond.

"You're the only person I've ever made love with," I told her as I traced her cheeks lightly with my thumbs.

Fran blinked and looked down.

I put my arms around her. "Baby, please…don't do this to us," I asked into her ear. She wound her arms around my waist and buried her head into my shoulder, her cheek way too warm against my skin. I could feel her shoulders shake as she cried, could feel her tears slide down my chest.

"Nina, you hardly let me touch you," she said thickly, then grazed her lips against my collarbone as her hands dug into my shoulders.

I didn't know what to say to that, because it hurt, because it wasn't true, not really anyway, and her lips on my skin and her hands on my shoulders burned with memory, a fire that left me breathless, caught between hurting and wanting.

Finally, I found a way to speak through this paralyzing feeling, the cage that constricted my chest and throat, the words that had meaning for me, anyway. "You're the only one I've ever let touch me, love," I said, the words scratching their way out.

"No, baby, no," she corrected as she drew her lips along my neck. She kissed my jawline, then touched my face, her thumb drawing against my chin. "I'm your first."

She kissed me, deeply, desperately, those splendid lips against mine, maddening given her words, inflaming despite them.

"Tell me you don't love me," I broke off and said, breathing heavily. I leaned my head against hers. "Tell me you don't."

She kissed the spot right next to me ear. "I've always loved you," she whispered, and clutched me to her fiercely. "I love you right now, more than you can possibly know, and I will love you tomorrow."

"Then why...?" I asked helplessly as I held her to me just as tightly. The light breeze that blew over from the Hudson River felt cold on my face as I let the tears run freely down before I buried it in her mane. I breathed in her scent and felt her tremble against me, or maybe it was me trembling against her—I couldn't tell at all, it didn't matter.

"You're about to go see the world, baby," she said softly, "and it's a whole lot bigger than I am."

That didn't make any sense to me at all. "Kitt...do you want me to stay?" I asked quietly, prepared to do anything.

She laughed softly. "Yes...no...I wouldn't do that to you," she smiled at me, "and I wouldn't want you to do that to yourself."

Finally, I let her go and stood back a step. "What can I do?" I asked her. "Does it have to be like this?"

Fran smiled at me. "Come back. We'll see where things stand then."

I nodded and swallowed painfully. "You let me think this was about Samantha," I said, pain burning through me in strings that wiggled and twisted under my skin.

Fran nodded. "I know I did—and I'm sorry about that. I was... um...I overreacted," she explained, waving a hand in the air. "But...it's not going to change anything. The fact is," and she reached into her pocket, "you've been in love with her since we were kids—and it's not fair for you not to find out where that stands now."

She pulled her hand out of her pocket. "This…is for you," she told me, opening her hand to reveal an old-style silver chain with an ankh pendant—similar to the one I used to wear. There was something about the way it shone in the light that it made it look old, too.

She put it on me, fastening the clasp. She placed her hand over where it lay on my throat and gazed at me.

"Wear this," she asked, her eyes deep with meaning as they burned into mine. "Don't take it off—promise me that."

I didn't know why she asked, but the energy that emanated from her told me there were intentions behind this that were stronger than I knew.

I folded my hand over hers. "I promise. I won't take it off."

Prompted by instinct, I bent my head to hers, to kiss that mouth I could never resist.

"Oi there!" Graham's voice called out. "They want one more song before closing!"

The moment cracked in two.

"I'll be right there!" I called back as I faced her.

"Go, they're waiting for you." She smiled and waved me on.

I nervously swallowed and agreed. Graham was, in a strange way, about to be my new boss—and I didn't want to muff it up.

I started back to the door and had even taken a few steps when my brain snapped back to normal. Fuck it—he wasn't the boss yet.

I ran back, caught her up in my arms, and kissed her, one last beautiful kiss that would tell her more than my words would. "You'll always be my Kitt," I murmured into her ear, holding her close before I had to let go, "nothing will ever change that." I'd never spoken truer words in my life.

I let her go and didn't look back as I went to the door where Graham waited. He raised his eyebrows at me, but my expression told him nothing as our eyes met. He dropped his gaze and focused on the ground as I passed.

The place was crowded, and I bumped into Samantha as I moved through the human press to the stage. Caught short, I stopped to look at her, and her blue eyes, almost black in the light, widened as they rested on the ankh that hung around my neck.

Stretched between rage at the unfairness of everything and the absolute tearing that threatened to rip me down until I was nothing, when her eyes met mine again, I wrapped an arm around her waist, drawing her to me as she closed me against her chest, the thrum of the music I'd programmed bouncing through us.

"Do you want me to come home with you?" she asked, her voice low and throaty in my ear.

"Go to Fran—she's outside. She needs you," I whispered back as I let her go. I walked to the stage, feeling absolutely nothing.

I got home after six in the morning, the sunlight beaming. It was the last day, last chance before I left to straighten things out. I looked around my neatly packed stuff. That was good. I'd prepaid my rent, so that was taken care of. I walked out to the train station and hung out with Nico for a while. We stopped by my parents' for a few minutes because I wanted to see them before I left—well, that, and Nico insisted. It was a little less strained than usual—but not by much. I got an awkward hug from my mom and a vague "Be careful about the water" from my father. Nanny admired my ankh and didn't say much else.

My aunt, my mother's sister, embraced me warmly and told me to "show them what a Del Castillo's got," and I let my cousins, who shared my and Nanny's old bedroom, monopolize the rest of my time: little Elena and her doll collection and Victoria, who, even though she was too big for it, sat on my lap or rode piggyback while enthusiastically sharing her bug collection and took me through the little infirmary she'd created for Elena's dolls—they were really sweet kids.

I spent another hour at the comic book store with Nico before I went home. I knew at least he'd miss me, well him and Victoria, anyway.

A car would come to pick me up in the morning. I took a shower. With nothing left but to pick out my clothes for the next day and to sleep, I flipped on the lower light, lay down in my bed, and forced myself to think about absolutely nothing—the future was a complete unknown. I must have dozed off because the phone rang.

"Nina," I answered sleepily.

"I need to see you before you go," Samantha's voice said urgently in my ear.

I looked at the little travel clock by the side of the bed. "I'll never make it to you and get back here in time to get some sleep for tomorrow," I said, thinking for some reason that she was at the bar. Funny how it never occurred to me to say no.

"No need, I'm right on the corner."

I swung my legs off the bed, walked to the window, and there she was—same overcoat, hair gleaming under the streetlight. I didn't think about being naked until I felt a chill cross my skin.

I hung up the phone and grabbed my robe—a new one I'd bought for the trip. Belting it around me, I padded on bare feet out of my bedroom to the door. She was waiting when I got there.

Her face was pale, making her eyes stand out even more, dark burning holes that pulled me ever deeper into them. "I can't just let you go again," her voice was ragged, "I can't." She reached for me and I took her hands, pulling her inside.

"Fran—" I whispered to her as we walked backward toward my room.

"Has set you free," Samantha interrupted, and her voice burned with her intensity. She took a hand back and cupped my cheek, her eyes as intense as her words. "I know you love her, but I know, *I know,* you love me, too—you can't tell me you don't."

She was right. I couldn't. I tried, but I couldn't. God forgive me, but when I looked into her eyes to speak, to say something, anything, the words died in my throat.

I let myself experience what I really felt for her, all the things I'd closed myself off from, the things I'd told myself, convinced myself, would never be. The reality of Samantha's closeness flooded through me, the loss and the need, the stark fear of losing this moment, of losing her again, of never having this chance, despite the rawness that I felt to my bones over Fran, the desperate, desperate ache just to be next to my Samantha.

This was so much more than sexual, deeper, stronger somehow, leaping through my blood and setting icy fire to my belly.

I kissed her, I finally had her lips on mine, the memory and the promise merging into the beauty of the now, the real, creating an emotional landscape I could read without a single spoken world. I put my hands to her shoulders and slid her coat off her and onto the floor, and I felt her body shift as she kicked her boots off. Her hands were under my robe, caressing the skin of my back, graphing lines of heat that drew me even closer. I fumbled almost frantically for the belt at her waist and the button underneath. She gently grabbed my hand and guided it down her jeans.

"I have never been this wet before," she whispered into my ear, and I gasped softly because I swear it felt as if I'd touched myself; I could feel my cunt throb when my fingers encountered the thick and rich proof of her words. "Nina..." she groaned softly, warning me that she needed.

"Me either," I confided to her softly, because it was true. I never really had—before. I led her hand to me and she gave a sharp exhale as she softly felt what I'd said. Two sensations bolted through me—one a purely primal need to lay her down, and the other absolute relief and even joy that my body was finally doing the thing it was supposed to.

"You're wearing too much," I murmured, my lips on her neck. I bit lightly against the tendon, then scraped my lower lip against it as we both got rid of her pants. I ran my hands under her shirt and lightly over her breasts, feeling the hardness of her nipples as she pressed into me. I brought my hands to her neck and reversed their position, and in one sudden, savage motion, I ripped her shirt off.

She shuddered when the air hit her, and I sucked on the skin just under her throat while I undid the front closure to her bra and slid that, with the remains of the shirt, off her shoulders.

Her mouth was refreshingly cool, soothing my tongue, and she tasted like wine. Her hands slid my robe off my shoulders and tossed it behind her head, and the bed was behind her as she grabbed my hips and pulled me down on top of her, her thigh slipping between mine, pressed firmly against my cunt.

"Christ!" I gasped, because that truly felt great, and I had never, ever, wanted anyone the way I wanted Samantha. I looked at her face, into her eyes, eyes hooded with desire, and she gave me a slow smile. I returned the pressure she gave me and she rolled under me, slipping against me.

"I normally...don't enjoy this that much," she told me, breathing heavily as we slid against each other, "but you...are the exception."

I could feel the rising tide of sex control my face. "Same here," I smiled back at her, "same here."

I lowered my head to that mouth I wanted to drink from again and again, and I reached a hand around her hips, past her ass where her leg flexed into me and found what I wanted. My fingertips pressed very lightly against her opening.

When her hands, which had been guiding my hips, moved so that her hand dug against my ass and her fingers slid easily between my lips with the other, I leaned heavily into her, against her. I pressed my face to her neck, her head next to mine.

We rode through the moment, and as we did, I suddenly understood why we had always been told the body is a temple, because as we moved together, I felt like I was praying and Samantha's body was the altar through which I touched the face of God.

I don't know if she felt that or not, but I can say with certainty I was shocked when she surged up against me, rolling me onto my back, her leg still firmly between mine.

She leaned over me, then kissed me with fierce tenderness, the wine-taste of her mouth dizzying as her fingertips trailed along my chest.

"I need more of you," she said, her voice harsh and low with want, "please," she asked, and she slid her tongue deeply into my mouth and her fingers even farther inside of me.

"God…" she groaned, her lips against my neck, "you are so wet, love, so wet…" and she drew her tongue hotly against my ear.

I had frozen a moment when she slipped inside me—the unexpected intrusion, the suddenness of it, catching me short. But I could hear, I could *feel* that it meant a lot to her, and I forced myself to relax. It wouldn't hurt me, at worst, and as Cap had said once, I didn't have to worry about getting pregnant.

I let my breath out slowly.

"Are you okay?" Samantha asked me in the same low voice, her lips nipping lightly at my earlobe, her pussy an irresistible glide on my thigh.

I could have said no, but that wouldn't have really been true.

"Fine, you're doing fine." I forced myself to smile. This was okay, I was going to be okay. "I'm…I'm just not…not used to that." And it was true. Even though Fran and I had made love as often as we could, it was rare that she was inside me—it really just wasn't my thing.

Samantha raised her head from my neck and looked at me, her eyes ocean-at-night blue, for once the sorrow that always hovered in their depths gone. "I need you so much, Nina…you make me feel like I'm home." The chain and sword charm I had given her years ago stuck to the skin below her throat, glinting in the half-light of my room.

And that's why I let her continue—because everything in me

screamed that she was where she belonged: with me, in me. Fuck it. For once, I wanted this, I wanted to know, once and for all, what it was that everyone so enjoyed about this. I didn't want to just enjoy it in my head, I wanted to feel all of it. Samantha was the ocean I wanted to dive into. I grabbed her ass, pulling her tighter against my leg. "Come home, baby," I told her as she moved within me slowly, and she kissed my breasts and neck, "come home."

I tightened my cunt around her fingers, and she groaned again as I pushed my hips against her, driving her deeper into me and harder against my thigh.

"I love that," she rasped out, "the way you hold me in you." She pushed desperately against my leg, and her ass was so preciously tiny I felt like I could cup the whole thing in my hand. But what I wanted was more, more of Samantha, and I reached around her precious ass to spread her lips against me, so her exposed clit would ride the hard muscle of my thigh.

I slid my fingers along the length of her cunt and her hips moved, her cunt a thick, wet glide against my leg, amazingly hot, a sublime feel against my fingers as she began to thrust into me.

I had to be inside her, and I slowly moved against that delicious soft opening, carefully, slowly, moving my fingers against that tight, hot space.

"God..." she groaned and arched her back, trying to catch my fingers and drive me deeper inside her. But as soft and as wet as she was, her pussy was tight, and I didn't want to hurt her. Although I'd never felt anyone that wet before, I'd also never felt anyone that tight either, and if I hadn't known better, I would have thought, well, honestly? I would have thought she was a virgin.

"I don't want to hurt you..." I told her as her pussy pushed at me, urging me.

"You won't—I swear," she gasped, her breath ragged against my lips. "I need you, I want you, inside me."

I was full of misgivings. I was so scared I'd hurt her, but she'd made herself vulnerable by asking, and I couldn't deny her request.

Still, I was gentle as I pushed through and past the tightened muscle—God, her cunt was perfect, absolutely perfect, and before I was completely inside her she arched her back and slid fully onto me.

"Yeah..." she groaned, a sound so absolutely, primally sensual,

I stopped worrying because the blood rushed to my head as she sank against me.

The blood rushed right back to my cunt as she started to fuck me, deep, hard. I could feel the power in her arms, in her back, as she thrust, her hip driving her hand farther, adding to the almost-overwhelming intensity as she poured her life, she poured herself into me, completely. The fuck fit so precisely I felt it in my throat.

Her stomach was flat against mine, breasts rubbing, her free arm clutching at my shoulder, mine just below her ass, spreading her wider against the constant slip in and out of her pussy.

We kissed, openmouthed, hungry, my hands and cunt filled with her. I wanted even more—I wanted to be completely inside her, wear her under my skin. I pushed desperately into her, hoping she enjoyed this as much as I did, that her cunt was as completely full, as content as mine, because I loved the way she felt on me, in me, next to me.

I breathed in the air that she exhaled, the sweetest air I'd ever breathed, and I didn't know what I wanted more—her lips or her breath. Then and there I knew that I would never, ever, have enough of her.

"God, Samantha…" I breathed heavily. "Love you, I fucking love you." I was shocked to hear those words escape my throat; I hadn't even consciously thought them.

Samantha raised her eyes to mine, deep sapphire pools that pierced me, forcing me to realize how much I'd meant it.

"Come, love," she choked out, "come because I love you." Her lips scraped along my neck, her body waved against me, and I could feel the inevitable, the blind-rush end coming as her pussy bore down on me. Her fingers plunged so deep I felt my entire body tingle, as if I were electric, as if I was made of light.

"Look at me, baby," I asked her, wanting more than anything to know, to see, to feel and share everything, "let me see your eyes. I want you to see me."

She dragged her lower lip against my neck and my chin before she did, and her eyes glowed.

"Ah God, Nina…" she gasped as I dove into her cunt, wanting, willing her to come on me, in me, driven by the force she pounded into my cunt, into my heart.

"I love you," I exhaled, then caught my breath short as the light she'd sparked to brilliance within me overflowed and I was coming, coming in waves, over and over, a ferocious intensity I'd never felt in my life as my gaze stayed locked on hers, with everything I had, everything I was, pouring into her eyes.

"Coming," she whispered, a harsh breath over my lips, her eyes hooded as her pussy clutched and spasmed, her body shaking against mine, her skin soft, warm, and beautiful as it seeped into me. "I love you, I love you," she mouthed, over and over, her cunt, her hands, moving in with deep, hard thrusts, and I came again, watching her, feeling her.

I wanted to whoop with triumph. I got it, I mean, I really fucking got it. *This* was what it was about. This was better than *anything*, ever.

Samantha's eyes were still on me, and I took my hand off her ass and stroked the contours of her face, the face I'd dreamt about.

Her fingers still buried within me, Samantha propped herself on her elbow, her fingertips softly rubbing against my temple. "Are you comfortable?" she asked, her face inches from mine, soft and open, a tiny smile edging the corner of her mouth.

I arched my neck and kissed her, a gentle, reassuring kiss, and her tongue was once again soothing on mine, the taste of her mouth still addictive.

"I'm fine," I answered her, "you?"

She kissed the tip of my nose, then kissed my chin. "I'm perfect." She smiled at me. She wiggled a little, then settled her head on my chest, her lips brushing against the base of my throat.

I kissed her head and stroked her back. "Did you come good?" I asked, wanting to know, needing to know.

She nodded against my chest. "Uh-huh," she whispered. She shifted and raised her head. "You?" she asked, her face intense with concern.

I smiled at her. I'd never known her to be shy, I'd never known her to be insecure. I kissed her soundly in answer and was shocked to feel how freshly, how desperately I wanted her all over again as she stirred deep within me and I felt her answering need.

"Stay in me," she asked as I reluctantly slipped my fingers out of her.

"Just a moment, baby," I reassured her, and I shifted under her so that she lay next to me. I propped myself up on my arm and leaned over her, trailing my hand up her stomach, across her chest, and let her watch when I slipped that finger into my mouth, tasting her for the first time.

"You taste amazing," I whispered before my mouth closed on hers.

I couldn't let her wait, and I couldn't either. She was hot and wet and ready as my fingers flitted between her lips. Her clit was wonderfully hard, and I wanted to give it the attention it deserved.

Her free arm slipped under mine and she grabbed my shoulder, crushing me to her, her lips welcome on mine as her thumb circled my clit and her fingers withdrew a bit.

She felt so good, just so fucking incredible. "God, baby, you're fucking beautiful," I told her as I once again teased her opening with my fingertips, this time with my thumb pressing securely on her clit.

I kissed her, softly, deeply, timing my thrust to my tongue, and Samantha surged beneath me. "I came great," I whispered into her ear as she pressed her lips against my chest. "I've *never* come like that before."

Samantha groaned when I said that and thrust deeply into me, sending that amazing shock through me, short-circuiting my brain. "Me either," she answered, her body pushing against mine, "me either."

We were in it, deep in it, in each other, her head tucked into my shoulder and my face buried in her hair, that spiral light tightening when the thought blazed through my mind—I had to marry this girl before someone else did. That brought me up short. What? We barely knew each other—now, anyway. I mean, yeah, sure, this was the most intense experience physically or emotionally I'd ever had, but was that something to base an entire-life decision on? And I wasn't ready—I was leaving to go on tour, for chrissake, there was—

"Marry me?"

"What?"

Samantha shifted and leaned up on an elbow to face me, her eyes again glowing that deep, deep blue. "Marry me," she asked again, with that amazing smile, the one that had always reminded me of the sun coming out from behind clouds, "marry me when you get back from your tour."

How had she done that? Read my mind? Magic? Or something I really knew nothing about? It was something I would have to get used to, I thought, and surprised myself again.

I looked down our bodies, at the way we disappeared into each other, at how her leg wrapped over my hip and mine fit between hers.

"I think I already did," I smiled softly back at her, "a long time ago."

We didn't sleep at all. We spent the rest of the night mostly making love, although we took a few breaks—two for the bathroom and one for water. We talked—about the past, about the present, about how amazing this thing between us was. She wouldn't talk about work, though.

"I can't really tell you much about it right now," was all she said.

"Why, are you a government assassin or something?" I teased.

For the first time that night, the sorrow that had been banished from her eyes came back, and I was instantly sorry.

"Hey, I was only kidding," I said and laid a hand on her forearm.

"I know," she smiled back, the sorrow hidden again, but not fully, "and no, I'm not a government assassin."

She flipped her arm over to take my hand, and that's when I saw it—the horizontal slashes across her wrist, the burn scar that overlaid them. I wasn't conscious of reaching for the charm that hung from my neck, but as I rubbed it between my fingers, I could feel the similarity between what I felt and what I saw. Samantha watched me silently until I reached up to take the chain off my neck; I wanted to see if the charm matched the scar.

"Don't!" she warned, her hands immediately reaching for mine, her fingers checking the security of the clasp. That's when I saw the scar on the other arm, also on the soft inside skin, midway between elbow and wrist.

"Don't *ever* take that off," she told me with dead solemnity. I have no idea what my face must have said, but she took my hands in hers and tried to explain. "That…it was a gift, a gift given in love—it carries power."

I stared at her, shocked at her words. A part of me understood exactly what she meant, while another shied away. But the dominant part drew my hands to her arm, pulling it to me so I could take a look at the other scar.

It was burned into her skin like a brand, probably not as raised as it had been when it was first made, but still, it stood in relief to her skin, a shiny pale pink. I traced it with my fingertip, the exact size and shape of the charm she wore.

"When did you do this?" I asked, looking up into her eyes, eyes that had gone from deep blue to stormy gray.

"The day I spoke with Fran," she said slowly, watching for my reaction. "I had to sever a tie."

I didn't know what to think or make of that, but for some reason, all I could think of was Candace—she'd broken her tie with Candace.

It would be a long, long time before I learned exactly how right and wrong I was.

I carefully put her hand down on her knee and took up the other. As I tracked the angry red lines that ran across her wrist, I could viscerally feel the pain that had made her slash through her own skin, feel the dark joy she had taken at the first bright red drops that had fallen, and finally, the searing shock of a heated metal charm as it burned against the then newly healed skin.

I can't explain how much it hurt to see it, and Samantha gasped when my tears fell on her wrist, running down the channels the scars had left. She tried to pull her hand away, but I wouldn't let her. Instead I tenderly, carefully, kissed her scars.

"Why, baby?" I asked her, my words barely audible as they tore their way up through my throat. "Why would you do that?" But I knew, I knew, and my heart ached with the knowing as I looked up into her eyes, wanting to hear what she would say.

Samantha gently took her wrist away and pulled me into her arms, wrapping herself around me. "Shh…it's over and I'm okay," she murmured into my ear as she rocked me, "you're here, we're here, it's perfect." Once again, I was home and safe, safe in the circle of Samantha's arms, safe as I hadn't been in years; only this time, instead of her graduating in June, I was leaving in a few hours, and this time, I was the one who didn't know when I'd return—if ever. Hey, let's be super-practical: shit happens, and some of it's pretty fuckin' ugly bad.

I had things to tell her, things she had to know if she'd meant what she'd said earlier.

"Samantha," I stirred in her arms and faced her, "did you mean that?"

"What?" she asked, kissing my shoulder, "about wanting to get married?" She stroked my cheek. "I've never meant anything more," she assured me softly, her mouth a sensual curve.

I took a breath. "We need to talk," I told her quietly, "before we discuss that again."

Samantha reached around her neck and undid her chain, coiling it and the little sword in her hand. "This is the third time it's not been on my neck," she started, holding the ends out to put it on me. "The first was when I burned it into my arm." She stroked it as it lay on my chest, right over my heart, just below the ankh. She kissed it and the skin that lay beneath it.

"Now," she said, "I wear it always," and she took my hand and laid it on her arm, over the brand. "Wear this one until you bring it back to me—you carry a part of me." She smiled softly and ran her thumb against my cheek. "What you tell me won't change anything, I'm sure," she said. "I've been sure since the first day I saw you." She beamed at me with such gentle joy that I had to kiss the corner of her lips, then taste them.

Still, either way, I had to tell her.

"Sam," I spoke finally, "even if you're that sure," and I smiled as I took her hands, "there's stuff you need to know—things that must come from me so that nothing," I paused as I thought of how to explain, "nothing surprises you, or anyone outright lies to you or paints a distorted picture of the truth. No matter what the worst of it is, you heard it from me, and you heard it from me first."

In the past several years I'd learned one super gigunda lesson: people lied. They lied about themselves, they lied about you, they lied to themselves and to you, and when they had enough, they lied about the lies.

I had no idea how long Samantha was going to stay in New York, I had no idea where she'd go or what she'd do, but I figured that I'd probably met way too many people who'd be way too happy to put in a bad word for me. At least this way, no matter what anyone told her, she wouldn't have to ask herself, "Would/did Nina do/say that?" She'd know; I did, or I didn't. Anything that deviated from that? Wasn't true.

Samantha nodded. "Tell me then, baby, tell me what you think I need to know."

I did. Everything. From Trace to Fran and all the stuff in between. When I spoke about Candace (and I kept *that* brief), her arms stiffened around me.

"All Candace ever told me was that you were beautiful, you were sensually generous to a fault, and that you were a law unto yourself."

Huh? I thought. "I, uh, I don't understand," I said instead. Hey, I wasn't about to act dumb in front of my potential future, um, whatever, right?

"It means," Samantha explained, tightening her arms around me again and rocking me back against her, "that you, love," she kissed my neck, "wouldn't let her touch you."

Her lips trailed sensually up my neck, and her hands wreaked havoc on my body as she rolled the nipple of my breast with one, making me sigh, and slid the other down to my pussy. She began to stroke my clit—delicate, long strokes that made me roll my head back to search for her mouth while my cunt moved of its own volition into her hands.

"Yes," I hissed sharply as her fingers quested lower and she shifted her thumb to my clit. She slowly but firmly entered me.

"God, if I'd only known sooner…" she murmured into my ear.

All I could do was groan her name as she pistoned into my cunt, and I met her every stroke. She let go of my nipple and reached for my clit instead, milking it.

"I want to suck on that," she growled and shoved deep, deep inside me, sending shocks into my throat.

"I want to touch you," I groaned, desperately caught between the ever-growing, ever-better, satisfying cunt throb and the absolute hunger to bury myself into her, into her cunt any way I could.

"Soon, baby, I promise," she swore into my ear, "just…just come for me, now, like this, in my arms and wrapped around you." Her words were positively sweet and loving, and somehow they blended beautifully with the absolute gut-level way she pumped me, pushing me closer and closer to that point of light.

"Samantha?" I practically gulped for air as I asked her, almost at the edge of thought, wanting to take her with me and wanting even more to give her something that was unmistakably hers and hers alone. "Can I ask you something?"

"Anything, baby, anything," she assured me, her voice ragged.

I knew she was close too, almost as close as I was, and knowing how entirely turned on she was pushed me even closer. I trailed one hand up and over her shoulder to her neck, pulling her down to my mouth so I could feel her lips on mine. The other I trailed along the tensed muscles of her forearm. I circled her wrist lightly and felt the straining tendons, then let my fingers flow down her hand, feeling how wet I really was, the amazing vanishing point where she drove into me again and again.

I took a long breath—and went with it.

"Fuck me, baby. Please fuck me."

TRANS-EUROPE EXPRESS

All my life I waited for a time
For a dream to come that's locked inside my mind
And my days? I paint the ceiling blue
And I tell everyone that it's got nothing to do with you

"Paint the Ceiling Blue"—Life Underwater

We flew to Heathrow, and my first glimpse of London was from inside a train-tunnel in a car packed with people and equipment, followed by a dizzying unpacking session, loading everything into a car, dropping it off—somewhere—and then being driven to a hall. Stephie, Jerkster, and I were handed sandwiches and, of all things, cups of Tang—ugh!—told to hurry up and eat, our sound check was in ten minutes. It was a good thing we'd worked our set out before the flight—which I managed to sleep through until the last few minutes.

That was the relaxing start. After the show we unloaded from the stage and packed all our crap into a van—we had another show in less than twenty hours. Played still another in Leeds and a third in Liverpool. Slept on a train to Glasgow. We learned to like cucumbers and watercress. Okay, that's a lie. I liked them, Stephie barely tolerated them, and Jerkster would eat anything that didn't crawl fast.

We caught another train back to London, then Heathrow, then a flight to France. I didn't get to see the Eiffel Tower or the Louvre in person, dammit. A cold-water shower in a shared apartment in Paris—and I couldn't remember how to ask where the bathroom was! Boy, did that ever result in some mayhem, because I kept ending up in a washroom. Argh! Paulie-Boy took the time to explain to Jerkster what a bidet was.

From France, we took trains everywhere—and it was absolutely no fun waiting at a station madly paranoid about getting everyone and their gear on board. Train food was mostly these weird little sausages that tasted somewhat like hot dogs, with lots of coffee in the morning, more weird little sausages with wine at night. I'd never had so much coffee before, but it was either that or Tang orange-flavored crap. Why does everyone think Americans drink Tang? Everyone knows that you can use that stuff to scrub your bathroom with. And another thing—what's with the wax-style toilet paper? Sheesh!

There were broken strings in Belgium and the hunt for their replacements—I think in Antwerp. The little bit of French I knew did me absolutely no good there because they spoke Flemish—that wasn't even an option in any of the schools I went to! Ended up ordering strings from the States—Mandolin Brothers, to be precise.

Graham took us out to drink absinthe somewhere—I don't even know where anymore, if I even knew at the time. I kept dreaming about swords, vampires, and Tang. I think I was more afraid of the Tang. Then more traveling. We slept ten on the floor in Berlin where people said we were *absolut uber feist*, which I think meant we were cool, and learned that it was okay to call the booking agent (who occasionally forgot to pay us) *das Arschlock*, then showered in cold water again in Prague. It was back to Germany for one night (!) and we raced from there to Paris. There may have been breathtaking views into Spain, but I slept, one hand wrapped around my guitar, and I think both Stephie and I leaned against Jerkster—he made a good pillow.

I went crazy trying to find the right change per country and figuring out the different codes I needed to call. A few times I had to use either the bar phone or the hostel phone—and the fuckers almost always charged me double or triple whatever the rate was.

At least I could find a Coke anywhere we went—I count that as a good thing, really.

On the very few times I was able to get in touch with anyone, I managed to get through to Samantha's phone when she wasn't sleeping and I wasn't in the process of racing across the continent.

"How's it going, baby?" she asked me in that sexy undertone that made me sweat.

Christ—it had been over a month already. Speaking with her was worse than just missing her, because it made her seem closer than she really was.

"How bad is it?" she asked, teasing.

"Depends," I answered, "on whether I'm asleep or awake."

"Really?" she purred. "And why's that?"

"Because when I'm asleep, I'm either dead to the world or having nightmares—mostly about Tang," I joked, "but when I'm awake…that's different, because then I'm aware of how much I miss you. How about you?" I asked in return, pitching my voice lower. "How bad is it?"

"It's horrible," Samantha answered, all play and pretension gone from her voice, "it's been absolutely wretched."

"Wretched, huh?"

"Don't tease, Nina. I've lived in England for years—I've learned to say wretched." I could hear the smile in her voice.

"I wasn't teasing," I protested mildly. "I just like the way you say it. Besides," I added, "I don't want you to be wretched."

"There's a bright side," Samantha said cheerfully. "I'll be done in two weeks, and then I can come and meet you."

That sounded great! Two weeks? Awesome! Except…

"Sam, I don't even know where we'll be in two weeks," I reminded her. "This tour seems to be a seat-of-your-pants production."

"Well," she drawled, "I have a solution for that. Call my apartment and leave a voice mail when you know where you'll be. I'll pick up the message and come to you. Yes?"

"Yes!" I agreed immediately. "Brilliant! Two weeks, then?"

"Two weeks and I'll be wherever you are, and then," her voice dipped into a low-pitched roll, "I hope you have a few days off."

God…just the thought of being next to her was enough to make me want to jump out of my skin.

"Still there?" she asked.

Oh yeah. We were on the phone.

"It's going to be a long two weeks," I sighed.

"It's been a long month already," she returned.

Finally, I asked about Fran. As much as I both relished and in some ways feared this thing between Samantha and me, so full of beautiful, painful potential, I was still in many ways reeling from Fran—but I didn't want us to just drift apart, either.

"She's…she misses you, horribly," Sam admitted heavily.

"I, uh, I miss her too," I admitted.

"You would...you should," Samantha said, her words simultaneously sad as well as sympathetic, "you're blood-bound."

I considered her words. Sometimes, Sam said these things that sounded like I should really know what they meant, like I was remembering them or something, but they also confused me because I didn't—not really.

"Hey, you know, I tried absinthe—and now I'm sorry I did," I told her, filling in the quiet.

"Why's that?" Samantha asked. "Bad taste? Tired of seeing green fairies?"

I laughed at that idea. "You know, I don't remember. But no, it's the nightmares."

"Oh yeah? What kind of nightmares?" she asked, almost too casually. I answered anyway.

"Well, I don't know if they qualify as real nightmares," I cautioned. "It's mostly just these vague images, like, I don't know, these things are trying to catch me or something." I felt completely embarrassed telling her that, but truthfully, they were starting to get to me, just a little.

Samantha chuckled and the sound was reassuring through the miles. "Well, that sounds normal enough, love. I'm sure you guys are picking up more fans and more media attention. What's chasing you, baby, cameras or agents?" she asked, humor still in her voice.

"Um, honestly? They're these huge ten-foot shadow hounds."

"Shit!" Samantha swore and dropped the phone. "Ow!" I heard her exclaim in the background, along with the sound of plastic skittering on a hard surface until she picked it up again.

"Hey, still there?"

"Still here," I answered, bemused. "Did you hurt yourself?" I asked, thinking of the "ow" I'd heard.

"Yeah...no, I'm fine. I just jammed my finger in a drawer while I was looking for something," she answered, obviously annoyed with herself.

"Wish I could kiss it and make it better for you."

"Me too, but at least your wish already does."

"Does what?" I asked.

"Make it feel better."

Silence stretched out as we both really felt the miles between us.

"Take this number," Samantha said briskly, all business.

"All right, give me a moment to find a pen." I hunted around the front desk counter until I found one, then tested it on a scrap of paper to make sure it worked.

"Okay, shoot!"

She gave me the numbers and I repeated them as I wrote them down.

"What's this for?" I asked curiously. I recognized the country code for England.

"It's an emergency number," Samantha explained, "in case you can't get in touch with me—or I can't get to you."

"Okay…" I answered slowly, "whose number is it?"

I could hear Samantha inhale. "It's Candace's."

Oh. Wait. What?

"Samantha—no, absolutely not," I said flatly. "I'm not calling her."

I heard her let that breath out.

"It's only if there's a real problem. She will, absolutely, help," she said. "She *is* fond of you, you know." She let that sit there in the silence.

Yeah. I was aware of exactly why she was fond of me, too. In fact, I'd been fond of her as well. This sounded like the ideal recipe for a disaster. I promised myself that no matter what happened, that phone call wouldn't.

"Besides," Samantha added unhelpfully, "she might find you first."

I was starting to suspect that Samantha was taking some sort of subtle, okay, it wasn't so subtle, pleasure at my probably obvious discomfort.

Two weeks. Another two weeks, and I could breathe again.

I got in touch with my parents, who spent our precious minutes asking things like, "Are you eating? Are you watching your money?" and my dad chimed in with, "Hey, watch out for those fast European girls—they're not…well…just be careful."

I saved Coke cans with different labels and languages on them for Nanny—she liked that sort of thing—and sent them to her when I sent postcards. Victoria, I mean Tori (she'd hugged me tightly about the neck before I'd left and told me she wanted to be called Tori) I sent funny little toys that you could find in the middle of this very popular chocolate—Kinder Chocolate Eggs—we found everywhere we went (totally addictive! But banned in the US because apparently

Americans are too dumb not to eat the toy inside), while Elena I tried to find dolls for—those collectible ones that are dressed in whatever the national tradition is? Your mom or grandmother would remember them. Anyway, Nico I mailed these digest-sized comic books I'd picked up at different railway stations. They were, every single one of them, about World War II. The only exceptions were about World War I.

It made me wonder if Europe was like America in that way—you know, what they say about the Civil War—how way down South in the land of cotton, the Civil War is not forgotten? But I didn't really get time to ponder that too much; there was too much going on.

Nico sent me packages—books, clothes, whatever I asked for, complete with Oreos (couldn't find those anywhere—and I love those—Double Stuf, please) in care of the label, who'd send it on to me. I asked him for toilet paper in the next one.

As for the rest of the band, Stephie tried to call John every day and cried; they'd started dating about a month before we'd left—finally! The nerves made her throw up before every show, occasionally several times a day, and I felt pretty awful about that. Jerkster stopped using lines and finally got laid. It might not have been skill, though; it might have been the language barrier, because I think that happened while I was trying to track down strings in Belgium.

I lost weight. We all did, though I shared my Oreos with everyone as soon as I got them, but I gave most of them to Stephie. It seemed to be the only thing that didn't bother her stomach.

We washed stuff in sinks, sometimes ourselves, as best we could. I also discovered that when you wash leather pants in the sink, they feel like gooey mush when you put them on damp—and even worse when they get cold. The plus is that they molded to me perfectly.

Graham showed us the sights, such as they were—mostly bars and music shops and clubs, with some very cool shopping on the very few occasions we could get away. Of course, Stephie and I started adding to our now-collective wardrobe, and Jerkster bought a motorcycle helmet he insisted on playing in. Ah, so what, he liked it. Then he started buying bizarre stickers for it.

I did call Dee Dee at the bar, just to keep in touch, and besides, I wasn't counting on anything. Our contract wasn't forever, and I'd still need a job when I got home, you know? Just in case things happened and were, like Stephie said, shit.

I tried to call Fran—and got right through to her answering machine. I said hello and left it at that.

I started to lose track of days and started to keep a closer eye on the money. The promoter was "forgetting" to show up—again—which required many phone calls from me and from Graham to both labels and to a gentleman named Enzo at Rude specifically to straighten it all out.

More and more people attended every show, and we were starting to see more and more flashbulbs during and after. I didn't think about it much at the time—no one in Adam's Rib did, anyway; we were so caught up in the playing and the traveling. The fact is, we were getting more and more attention, and we were a band with no product to sell— no record, no T-shirts, nothing but a memorable show, just like a one-night stand.

We were so new to the business that it hadn't occurred to any of us that the combined facts of our schedule being a matter of public knowledge and our growing fan base meant that more and more of the attendees weren't coming just to see the Microwaves, but us as well—and even us instead.

A band that had been even a touch more seasoned than we were would have known that this meant negotiation, this meant a raise, that in fact, at five and a half, almost six weeks into the tour, we deserved a break. And Graham, even though he had his own stuff to look out for, looked out for us in this instance.

"We're going to Barcelona," he announced to us while we nodded along in the train. I glanced up from my book and raised an eyebrow at him. Yeah, duh. That's where we were going.

Graham cleared his throat in the resounding silence that met his grand announcement. "Then there's a show in Ibiza."

I didn't even look up from the book this time. So...what? We knew that too—and it would be a train and a boat, or a train and a plane. Probably train and boat, we figured, because it cost less.

"We'll be spending a few days there—just to relax, get drunk, get laid."

"Yeah heh!" Paulie-Boy screamed, fist stuck straight up in the air, the first to react. I looked up from my book again and glanced at Jerkster and Stephie. They stared back at me, just as confused as I was as the rest of the band jumped up and started dancing around the car.

Graham gave us each a sly smile and sat down on the arm of my chair. He casually slipped an arm around my shoulder. "You...don't know." He narrowed his eyes wickedly. "Ibiza is...*the* party capital of the world."

Jerkster, Stephie, and I looked at each other—we were from New York. 'Nuff said, as far as we were concerned.

Graham understood our silent exchange.

"It's not that sort of party," he explained, rubbing his hands together. "You will get to experience why," and he stood up again and did a little tango-style two-step, "the Latins are the better lovers and why," and he struck a very prim and proper pose, "we Europeans think you Yanks are so repressed."

Even Jerkster raised his eyebrows at him at that, and after looking at our faces, Graham cracked up hysterically.

"You'll see," he said as he walked away, back toward the dining car. "Lady of Spain, I adore you," he trilled, waving a hand behind him.

We eyed each other again.

Jerkster stretched out and went back to sleep.

It was midnight or thereabouts when we arrived in Barcelona, and since load-in for a gig usually started somewhere around seven in the a.m., it was right to bed, as soon as we could figure out where that was. This was the first time we weren't staying at the friend of a friend's cousin's wife's brother's dog's lover's ex-girlfriend's place. It was an honest-to-goodness hotel room—two rooms for the Microwaves (and they needed it) and one, count 'em, one for Adam's Rib.

I got to the room first, Stephie a step behind me. We'd left Jerkster back somewhere in the hall, playing with the ice machine.

Stephie stood next to me as I stared at the single beds from the middle of the room. We exchanged a look that said, "Where's Jerkster gonna sleep?"

"Not with me."

"Not with me, either."

Hey, it really is true what they say about band telepathy, though an observer would have seen only an exchange of arched brows and a couple of strange mouth movements. That's totally okay—Stephie and I knew what we meant.

He marched into the room singing something atonal, kilt swinging, and helmet full of ice under his arm.

"Hey." He stopped short as he saw us. He looked at the beds, then back to Stephie and me. "Who'm I staying with?" he asked, a wide smirk showing his teeth as he glanced from me to Stephie. "No, wait, don't tell me—you guys are gonna share!"

I put my guitar—which was still slung over my shoulder—down safely in a corner while Stephie and I exchanged another look.

She slapped his helmet off his hands and tossed it to me.

"Yo, wait!" Jerkster exclaimed. "Give it…" He lunged for me and I jumped out of the way. Since he'd had to bend when he reached, I did the logical thing—I dumped it on his head, then shook it to make sure all the water came out.

"Oh that sucks, that sucks!" he bellowed as the ice and the cold water flew over him.

"You're sleeping in the tub," I told him as he straightened, that smirk for each of us firmly in place. I tossed the helmet back to Stephie, and she held it dangling from the strap as she leaned her weight on the opposite leg.

"You're gonna need more ice," she told him, flicking her finger against the helmet.

"Don't do that!" Jerkster asked as he snatched the helmet from her. He inspected it. "Poor George, did she hurt you?" he asked the sticker as he smoothed it.

"George?"

"Yeah, for Georgie Porgie Pudding Pie," he said and showed us the sticker—a yellow square with a cartoon pig dressed in a blue sailor suit. "I'm getting more ice," he informed us.

"Okay," I drawled as he walked to the door. I picked a bed and threw my stuff on it while Stephie did the same on the other side of the room.

The next morning was as brutal as we'd predicted, and for the record? Neither Stephie nor I really let Jerkster sleep on the floor or in the tub—I called the front desk and asked if they could send us up a cot, a foldaway bed, or failing that, at least a half dozen pillows.

The fact is, we'd all bunked together on many occasions, but this was an opportunity to sleep on a for-real bed, not a sofa, a floor, or a seat that didn't recline enough while the ground whizzed by underneath and the overhead lights never really went out.

I'd already left messages for Samantha letting her know we'd be in Barcelona, and called from the front desk as soon as we'd walked in—after handing the clerk the equivalent of several dollars—to let her know there'd be some downtime in Ibiza before we went back to the mainland and on to Madrid.

I didn't know if I'd see her in Barcelona, Ibiza, or Madrid, but I was certain on one thing—I hoped it was sooner rather than later.

We took some time in the evening for general and maintenance grooming to make sure we'd hit the stage looking the way we wanted to.

I'd made a few small changes: I'd let the red streak fade, and the black, too; my hair was a bit closer to its actual color. I'd also started to let it grow on the sides by my ears so that it swept down into a curved point along the line of my cheek. Stephie thought it was cool—she said it matched my smile. Jerkster didn't notice, but I didn't expect him to. Graham thought it looked cool and apparently a little something else, too.

"Let me get a good look at you, love," he asked, catching my arm as we were about to troop to the immediate backstage. "Come on," he urged, pulling me to his dressing room, Well, at least he had a dressing room, I thought; we had an old storage closet. But fuck it, it worked, right?

"Let's see you, then," Graham said, narrowing his eyes and putting his chin in his hand. His index finger stroked his thin red-blond mustache. His delicate mouth scrunched up into an expression I'd learned was his "how do I change/work/fix/explain this?"

Not once did I ever, ever, think of Graham as a woman. He wasn't—not in his voice, not in his dress, not in any way, manner, or form. Graham flirted with *everyone* outrageously—male, female, gay, straight, whatever, and Jerkster had wondered if Graham was, "You know, gay?" but he never thought for a second that Graham was anything other, or different, than Graham—a guy with an almost too-pretty face.

"What's the matter," I asked him with a smile as I held my hands out from my sides, "something showing that shouldn't? Do I have a tag sticking out somewhere or a lump that shouldn't be?"

It was already pretty warm, and Spain was hotter than most places. I'd found an awesome pair of long cycling pants made of stretchy black material; they had a really neat two-layer checkerboard strip down the sides with a red stripe in the center, plus they were a lot cooler heat-wise to wear than leather or denim. Besides, the checkerboards were homage to the Microwaves—they were a ska band, after all.

Stephie and I'd discovered some really cool zip-top bra sort of things, and we picked up a bunch (we didn't know where in the world we'd be able to find those again, if ever—this is one of those secrets I'm not sharing); some totally formfitting, everything-holding tank tops; and some cycling jerseys—they were too cool! I stuck with basic black, although I had a few with some contrasting stripes—and my racing jerseys were wild! I wore one of those super-tanks tonight, because it had a similar checkerboard on the seams that matched the pants. I thought I looked pretty darn good.

"Put your hands on your hips?" Graham requested, so I did.

"Yeah, that's what I thought," he said.

"What?" I asked, puzzled.

"The way you stand—no, stay just as you are," he said as I started to shift, "just look in the mirror—here," he said, and stepped out from in front of it.

He stood behind me. "What do you see?" he asked softly.

I looked, I really looked. I saw me, booted legs planted wide, hip cocked to one side, cool new outfit, and the gleam of the two silver charms on my neck and throat.

"I look ready to play," I told him.

He put his hands on my hips. "Stand straight," he said, pushing my hips into position, "and keep looking." He took his hands off me.

It had been a long time since I'd really seen myself, seen anything but my hair or that my clothes were set right, that is, so I looked again.

Hair—cool! Shoulders—kinda wide. In addition to the width I'd gained over the years from swimming, I'd lost weight and developed that "T" shape that so many guitarists have. A large and well contained chest. Small hips, beat-up boots. My eyes were grayer than I'd remembered.

Graham stood behind me and placed his hands over my shoulders. He didn't touch them; he let his hands hover about an inch above them as he measured their width.

"You've got great shoulders…small back…small hips…" and he followed their outlines without touching me.

"Now look at that face—androgynous," he said, "very gamine."

I gazed at him directly. "Gamine?" I asked with an arched

brow, looking straight into his mischievous brown eyes. "What's that mean?"

"It means a young boy or girl—and you could be either." He gently faced my head to the mirror. "You should try drag."

"All life is drag," I shot back at him with a smile.

"Glad to see you're learning. Here…" He grabbed one of his jackets and threw it at me. "Put this on."

It was one of his black jackets—double-breasted, too, which I happen to prefer. I shrugged it on, and it fit. It did nice things for my shoulders. "Got a tie?" I asked him.

"What color do you want?" he asked, rummaging through his collection.

"Red. Bloodred, if you've got it," I decided. What the hell, right?

He tossed it over my shoulder and hovered over me as I knotted it.

"Hey, I do know how to do this, you know." I scowled playfully. "I've worn one or two before." Which was true, I had, because I could. Hey, I did work at a gay bar, after all.

"Really?" Graham drawled at me. "Well, knock me down and call me pretty. I had no idea."

I finished knotting the tie around my bare neck and rolled the sleeves for the jacket to my forearms.

"How do I look?" I asked him with my best half-smile.

"Halfway there." Graham nodded approvingly.

"Yeah, well, there's kinda no hiding these." I looked down at my chest.

"There's ways around that, you know," Graham said. "You can bind them, you can—"

I interrupted him. "Graham, it's way too hot to do anything like that and besides," I hesitated a moment before I continued, "I'm not sure it's something I want to do—just yet."

I glanced up over the mirror and at the clock.

"Holy shit! I've got to get to the stage!" I exclaimed, and almost ran to the door—it was two minutes to curtain.

Graham snickered. "Don't worry if you're a minute late—I know the main act. I'll take care of it for you."

I smiled back at him as I dashed out.

"Keep the tie!" he called to my back.

Fuck, I wasn't even thinking about that. I took it off my neck and put it around my waist as I hurried backstage and found Stephie and Jerkster, all ready to go. Paulie-Boy was already out there, settling into his seat.

"Where the fuck *were* you?" Stephie hissed, more out of concern than anger. She handed me my guitar.

"Graham wanted to talk to me," I answered as I slung my instrument. There, it hung flawlessly.

She did a double take and smiled. "Nice jacket."

"You're gonna sweat to death," Jerkster warned.

Personally? I agreed, but I couldn't take it off because I'd already strapped in and there were the opening clicks of Paulie-Boy's drum sticks. Time to hit the stage!

The show itself was a total blast—we'd written a few new songs during all those hours of traveling, and after we ran through them during sound check, they were pronounced good enough to perform— we debuted them that night. This effectively made our set about half an hour longer, which we all thought was really cool. I did take the jacket off about a third of the way through—it was way too hot for the way I played. I wondered how Graham managed it all the time.

After our set we left the stage and went into the hall behind it—the backstage area itself was crowded with the Microwaves horn players. Hey, it ain't ska if there ain't horns, ya know.

Graham came rushing over. "Hey, Nina, don't go off yet—I want to ask you something," he said, hustling me back over to the place I'd just left.

"Yeah, sure, Graham. What's up?" I asked, slinging my guitar behind me.

"I'd like you to come up and sing a few songs with us," he told me seriously.

What? Who, me?

"What about Stephie?" I asked, confused. "Shouldn't you ask her?" She did do most of the lead vocals, after all.

Graham's eyes twinkled at me. "No, love, it should be you—and Stephie agrees."

I was taken aback at that, but okay, then, I'd go for it. I was glad I'd held on to his jacket. Despite the heat from the stage, once you walk away from it, it's a pretty rapid cooldown. Besides, ska bands always wear suits so I fit in, although I still kept the sleeves rolled and the tie around my waist as opposed to my neck.

The Microwaves put on a great show, and as crowded as ours were becoming? Theirs were jammed to the rafters! This place was normally a nightclub with tables and chairs scattered around, but you wouldn't have known that—it was standing room only, though it looked more like leaning room, because there didn't appear to be any space anywhere. It is a very good thing people jumped up and down—it made room for others for about half a second.

I did three songs with them, and Graham kept me on for the encore—a down-and-dirty version of the ever-classic "Could You Be Loved" by Bob Marley.

You'd think that normally, between the lights and the crowd, anyone onstage could barely see people, never mind recognize an individual, and normally? You'd be right. You can't really see beyond the first few rows or feet from the stage unless the lighting levels out for a moment or you get a flare across an area.

But halfway through the encore, I saw her—that unmistakable flash of Blue—and I'd seen it plenty of times before in lower light than this. Her eyes locked onto mine, green glowing through the smoke and haze as she cut through the crowd the way I swam through water—smooth and fast.

From the corner of my eye, I could see Graham give me a sharp look, but we finished the song just fine, thankyouverymuch. However, by the time Graham got to the final introductions and the required "thanks and good night," I'd lost her when I smiled and waved at the crowd.

Lights came up, curtain came down, and I turned to Graham.

"Great show, Graham, that was a lot of fun. Thank you," I said as I hugged him.

"Wonderful job, Nina," Graham returned, slapping my back, "just perfect. Splendid, even."

I took a step back and beamed at him. Paulie-Boy stopped over. "Nice job, Nina." He grinned and gave me a high five. "Great show, Graham, really great show."

They smacked each other on the arm. Funny how it is that a band is like an athletic team—win or lose, the team supports each other. I like that. I grabbed my guitar from its leaning post on the wall and slipped it into its case.

"Well, Graham, I'd best—"

"Have a drink with me," Graham interrupted. "I'd like to speak with you." He smiled as he said it, but I heard something serious in his tone.

I thought about it. If I went back to my room, there'd be Stephie, probably crying about John—not that I blamed her, mind you; it was just sad to deal with—or sleeping. The other likely scenario was Jerkster either passed out or trying to rent porn. I hadn't heard anything from Samantha yet. I'd checked with the front desk so many times that the clerk announced "*no hay mensaje*"—there's no message—whenever he saw me.

Despite the intensity between us, Samantha and me, I mean, I was still more than occasionally confused by how I felt in general. I missed Fran, horribly. Without her, I felt somehow naked. Next to Samantha, I felt raw, as if the skin I lived through had been removed. I hadn't really given her an answer before I'd left—it was all too fast and too soon, you know?

And...I felt guilty. Fran had broken up with me, not the other way around, and that just fucking hurt, because I'd never considered what we'd had to be "borrowed time," as she'd put it the last time I saw her.

She'd repeatedly said that Samantha and I should absolutely be together, and now, after the fact, even though I mostly agreed, I still thought that we might have been completely happy and hated the fact that she'd possibly been right—again. It made me think she should have been named Cassandra—you know, the prophetess doomed by Apollo to speak words that no one believed until it was too late? She'd been unhappy in her life, mythic as it may have been. I didn't want to make Fran unhappy, I didn't want to hurt her.

Fuck it. I didn't want to spend all night thinking about it, and besides, Candace was lurking out there somewhere. Well, Samantha had warned that she'd probably find me first anyway.

A drink with Graham sounded like a good idea. Besides, we were taking a ferry over to Ibiza, and Paulie-Boy had warned us that it would be about a nine-hour float. I'd sleep on the boat.

"Sure, Graham," I smiled, "why not?"

"Great, then." He smiled back and clapped a hand on my shoulder as we walked to the stage exit.

"Find us a table, I've got some things," and he waved his hand to indicate the general area, "I've got to straighten out for tomorrow."

I understood. "Fine, then, I'll see you out there in a few," I agreed as I shifted my case. I walked out and through the hallway, away from the corridor that led back to the hotel proper and instead made a sharp right to a door that would lead back into the club itself.

Quite a few people still milled about talking, drinking, enjoying themselves. A few smiled at me as I walked past them, but no one bothered me. Cool music flowed through the room as I wandered about, looking for a table.

I found one finally, about two-thirds of the way from the stage, and quickly claimed it. No sooner had I sat down and settled my guitar next to me than a waiter appeared out of nowhere, handed me a menu, and asked me what I'd like.

Oh, how awesome—food. I loved when we played at places that served food. Even more important than getting paid sometimes, we got to eat.

I took a quick glance at the menu, but it required more thought. I asked the waiter for a few minutes, a glass of water, and a glass of sangria. Hey, I was in Spain. I wasn't going to skip the sangria.

"Can I join you?" Candace's green eyes shone at me through the haze.

I nodded and indicated a seat to her before addressing the waiter.

"I'm expecting another. Can I have two more glasses, and make that a pitcher instead of a single?"

He agreed, then walked away.

"Thank you." Candace smiled at me. "You're looking better than ever."

I reached over my gig bag and into the front pocket to retrieve my cigarettes and lighter. Taking one out for myself, I mutely asked her if she wanted one. She smiled her thanks again, and I slid my pack over to her, then lit her cigarette when she pulled one out.

I sat back and straightened up, still unsure what to say. I felt incredibly blank, caught between hot and cold, as I took a good long drag.

She wore her hair differently, long and loose with a bit of a wave, and she'd modified its color. There was a lot more red in it than last time. Her blue and black bodice-like top still fit her exactly the way it was meant to—like a second skin that held her breasts up to inspection. She was as beautiful as ever and I remembered—everything. And still I felt nothing, nothing at all. I had wanted her so much then, and now, well, she was as absolutely attractive as ever and I still loved that beautiful accent.

Could I have possibly loved her then, I asked myself? No, yes, maybe, but that wasn't the way it felt at the time. Had I liked her? Yes, I honestly had because she was so much more than incredibly attractive; she was bright, and funny. We'd had some very good conversations; we'd had really good sex.

Candace allowed the inspection, smoking wordlessly, a tiny grin, almost a smirk really, playing around the edges of her lips, lips that I knew tasted like cherries and something else, but always cherries, and technically skilled.

The waiter came back with three glasses and the pitcher of sangria—and I still hadn't picked anything to eat yet. I told him I would wait for Graham as he poured a glass for each of us, then left.

Candace leaned across the table and stared, hard, at the jewelry I wore, then sat back.

"So," she said softly, "no words for me now that you carry both of them with you?"

That bothered me. It bothered me that she knew what I was wearing, that she knew who they were from. No, I did have words, one specifically. "Why?" I asked her, leaning across the table. My glass remained untouched. "Why didn't you tell me? Why didn't you tell any of us?" I exhaled and waited for her answer.

"You've changed," she commented quietly.

I gave an ungracious laugh. "Who wouldn't?" I asked in return, not expecting an answer. Not that it was fair, the way I was behaving, not that it was her fault, not really. But everything was so twisted up for me, and somehow, in my head, Candace was at the bottom of it. That might not make sense, but it doesn't have to—most feelings don't. If they did, they'd be called logic, and probably? Life would still be as hard.

Candace sighed and stared down at the table, smoothing the cloth with her fingers.

"Look," she began, "I went to New York last summer for two reasons: one for work and the other specifically to find out if that cock-and-bull story Annie had been fed was true. I mean, it was a fine story to tell a young girl, and it would have worked, except it didn't really make sense, to me, anyway," she said in utter seriousness. "Believe me, I was surprised to find you as easily as I did."

I stared at her, hard. "Then why—"

"Please." She held up her hands to stop me. "Let me tell you the whole thing before you ask your questions. When I'm done, you can love, hate me, or," and she smiled a sad little smile at me, "you can invite me to your room."

I gave her a small smile of my own in return; we both knew that wasn't going to happen. But still, I had been "rather fond" of her, and we'd been pretty hot together. We'd had nice chemistry.

"I do want to hear what you have to say," I told her softly, because I wanted to understand.

She took a sip from her glass, then reached across the table to lay a hand on mine. "I was going to tell you, Nina. I was going to tell you that night at the Red Spot, until your friend barged in." She watched me expectantly.

"I remember the night," I said as neutrally as possible, "but then, why didn't you say anything later?" I took my hand back and hit a drag off my neglected cigarette.

"You were living your life, Nina, on your path. Do you really think you'd be here, now?" and she looked around us, waving a hand to take it all in.

Yeah, right. I wasn't buying it.

"That's bullshit, Candace," I countered. "Fran...Samantha—"

Candace nearly jumped across the table. This time she grabbed my wrist—not painfully, but firmly. She leaned in to me closely, her eyes barely five inches from mine.

"Died, Nina. Samantha *died* when she thought you were gone. Do you understand that? Have you seen the scars on her wrist? Felt them? There's a reason we call her Ann. There's a reason I didn't tell her what I was doing. Think, Nina," Candace shot vehemently, "would I risk her for *anyone*? What if you weren't who she would have wanted you to be? What if you weren't what she thought? Or what she needed? There'd be no one to save her this time."

I was shaken, shaken by the strength of her words and the memory of those scars under my fingertips. I'd known, but then again, I hadn't, not really, not so concretely. I narrowed my gaze at Candace, considering. There was more to what she was saying, because her words implied something deeper, and I spoke it as I thought it. "You love her—"

"That's neither here nor there." Candace waved impatiently. "I had to know if bringing you back into her life was worth the possible price that she, not you, would pay."

Now that? It really pissed me off.

"So…you had to, what, fuck with me a few times to see if I was worthy or not?" I pulled my wrist away from her, pushed my chair back, and stood up. "So worried about *her*, right? So worried, so concerned," I sneered, "that—what was it you said? Oh yeah, it was—"

I stopped myself. That was going too far. I wasn't going to do it, I refused to do that—I wasn't going to become an asshole like everyone else. But boy, did I want to. Tonight, I decided, discretion was the better part of valor. I was going to leave this alone before I said something I truly regretted.

I plucked my cigarettes from the table with one hand and grabbed my gig bag with the other, then slung my guitar over my shoulder.

"Drinks are on me, as always," I said coldly, politely.

"Nina—wait, that's not—" Candace began, but I ignored her.

"I hope you got the answer you were looking for. You certainly did your research thoroughly. Please tell the gentleman who shows up I had to leave." I gave her a little half bow and walked away. What the fuck, she probably knew him, too. Wonder if she'd slept with him too, I thought, but then, that wasn't worthy of me, and frankly? It wasn't any of my business, either. I didn't care.

I found the waiter on my way out and told him Candace was with the band so that she wouldn't have any hassle with a check. Hey, I wasn't a total asshole. When I went out into the main lobby, I didn't go to the elevator. Instead I went down to the other end of the corridor where rumor and the layout map said there was an outdoor pool. Both were right.

A row of chairs circled the pool, with two tables holding neatly folded towels at either end. I found myself a lounge chair and propped my guitar on one, pulled out my cigs and threw myself on another. I was angry, absolutely fuming, disgusted with myself. I'd almost reacted like my father, verbally vicious in anger. I was sorry I'd left before finding out what Graham had wanted to discuss, but I'd apologize when I saw him next. Right now, I really didn't trust myself, my feelings, or my words.

Dammit. I lit a cigarette and watched the smoke float up into a star-filled sky. I'd never seen such a clear sky in anything but winter; it was as clear as a windless January night, when it's so cold and crisp you can hear your breath crack—only here it was about eighty degrees out. I wished I'd brought the sangria with me, but then, no, I didn't. I wanted to be completely clearheaded. I chuckled at the smoke as it floated above me. Here I was, a thousand and more miles away from home, and I was angry with my father, of all people, angry because he had told that stupid, stupid lie, just to be vicious—angry because I wasn't any different.

I tipped my ashes into a nearby ashtray and looked out over the pool. Nice. It was a good sixty or so feet long, vaguely lozenge-shaped. Diving board at one end, and, according to the dark numbers set into the white tiles, it went from five feet to twelve. Most of the light came from the building behind me, the rest from the sky. I wondered if the water was warm and carefully kicked off my boots—a new pair I'd gotten in England. What the hell. I took my socks off, then walked over to the table and grabbed a towel. I sat down again, just staring at the water, and untied the red tie that was still around my waist.

Fuck it.

I slid my pants off and folded them neatly, took the jacket off, and peeled off my top, then put the jacket back on. I grabbed the towel and walked around the pool to the diving board, just looking at it, thinking of nothing except that it had been a long time since I'd been in the water. I hung the jacket on an entry stair railing next to the board, put the towel on the ground, and climbed up a couple of steps to the diving board. I walked to the end and hung my toes off the edge. A good racing start. I shrugged my shoulders a little, loosening them up, and hung them past my toes, letting my back stretch out.

Finally comfortable, I set myself into a starting crouch, my eyes focused on a patch of water that shone several feet in front of me, and sprang, through the air, into the water.

I'd forgotten that I normally would immerse myself before I dove in, and the water was an electric shock against my skin. It was warm, blood warm, and I let myself glide under for a while, using the lightest of kicks to propel me. Finally, it was time for air and I went up. Everywhere my skin broke the surface, I chilled as I pulled my way through the water to the other side. I could see just enough to make out the wall before me, and I pulled myself up in time into a flip turn, again enjoying the dark, silent world I glided in before it was time to breathe again.

This time when I came up, I flipped onto my back, put my hands behind my head, and just stared at the sky, kicking lightly every now and again to maintain my position.

I could understand Candace looking out for her Ann—that made sense to me. The rest didn't, though, not really.

I kept thinking about it. She'd said at the time that she and her girlfriend were "on-again/off-again," and Fran had said they'd had "an arrangement." So what did that mean? That they slept with other people? Or they got to test-drive the other's new model first?

I had to look deeper into this. I flipped over again and swam a few strokes, enjoying the feel of the water gliding over my back.

There was one thing, I mused, that was hard to fake with another woman in bed, and that was just how ready or not the body was. I felt a laugh rise in my throat and surfaced quickly so I wouldn't drown.

Pussy don't lie. Mouths do, hearts do, even the eyes, but the pussy wants what it wants and nothing else. Either you are that something, you get that something, or ain't nobody getting nothing, I thought.

What was it my first girlfriend had said? Oh yeah, solving the mysteries of the universe, especially the ones about sex. Maybe that's where all the solutions were, too. This time, I really did laugh.

God, I hadn't had any in weeks. I didn't even have time or the privacy to take care of myself, as if that would have helped. Pussy knows what it wants—and I knew exactly who mine wanted.

Shit, man, I had to get out of the pool; my brain was starting to get waterlogged. It was time to get out before, well, I don't know—maybe I'd stay there all night and float. No, not an option, not really, anyway, not with a trip and a show the next day.

I swam back to the diving board and the ladder next to it and did something I love to do when I climb out of a pool—just grab on to the bars and pull myself up, kick and jump over the wall. It's like flying for a moment. As I got to the top, ready for the kick, it hit me, hard. Samantha had tried to kill herself. For me. Over me.

Candace had asked if I'd seen those scars. Of course I had; they crisscrossed my mind when I closed my eyes. I and my fingers could still feel them—their sharpness, the angles, the ankh burned over them. Christ. Those angry lines on her wrist spelled my name.

I didn't complete the jump. I let go and sank down hard. I gulped before the water closed over my head and let my knees bend when my feet touched the bottom.

I exhaled and forced myself down until I was sitting and the world was black and warm, the only sound the water itself, heavy and moving me slightly as the filters worked. Even they were quiet.

I closed my eyes and the darkness was complete, not even the slightest bit of shine from above as I fought lightly against the pull of the filter to remain on the bottom and wondered. Wondered what it was like to be dead, dead and still. I'd almost died once; at least, I thought I had. That had been like swimming too, like dreaming.

What would have happened if I'd stayed in the dream? Did everything just go black? Did you know it? Would you care? Did a black wave crawl up on you, licking at your edges until it wiped you out and you exploded into space, or heaven, or something? Maybe you just lay there, forever, unknowing, unfeeling, the world going on and on and on like some giant fucking hungry machine, eating us up and spitting us out, and dead was dead like the meat on my plate or the dirt on the ground and everything still eating and feeding and dying forever and nothing ever came of nothing because it all became dirt until the universe itself blew apart into the great silence...

Better to end it now, right? End it because nothing, nothing would ever change; everything born to die and die again and again and again, the endless grind mowing it all down, the grass and the trees and the people I knew and everyone...dying as they breathed, dying as I looked at them, I was dying at that second and had been since the day I was born.

It was all one huge waste of time—because it would all be nothing but hydrogen and protons one day, a day we would never see because we'd have been so long gone that perhaps our atoms would have worn out, half-lifed into nothing.

If life was survival, then it made sense that the ruthless succeeded. If there was nothing but the ever-waiting darkness, then someone doing whatever they needed to do to ensure their continued survival was right—not necessarily ethical, but right according to the law of eat or be eaten.

You could take power—and even then, for what? Still the same black song waited to sing over you for the nanoseconds of cosmic time you bought.

End it now and stop fighting a useless, foregone, and lost battle. It would be easy. All I had to do was exhale and inhale, as simple as breathing, and then? I wouldn't anymore.

It was almost a song in my head, a clear whisper in my ear. *Do it*—didn't I want to know what it was all about, anyway? Samantha had tried—and would have succeeded had someone not saved her life, according to Candace. Was I any less than Samantha had been? We would all die anyway—did it matter? There was no such thing as eternal light. That was the eternal lie, because one day, even the stars would burn out; the light they shed was the evidence of their dying.

My eyes snapped open in the dark. I'd reached that point underwater where you think you've been breathing, but you're not, you're definitely not, and I was seeing my nightmares close around me—those giant shadow hounds that had started to haunt me. Only this time, instead of searching, they were circling.

Those words that had just passed through my brain didn't sound right. I mean, okay, they did in a very logical way, but the argument didn't sound like me, didn't feel like me. The half-life of protons was a theory, like every other theory out there.

I remembered a little factoid a physics professor had left on the bulletin board for anyone that was interested—a photocopy of a *New York Times* Science Section article. It wasn't just a theory, it had been proven.

"Photons, subatomic particles that are the 'building blocks' of light, travel at various speeds. Once they reach a critical number, they do the unthinkable: they gain mass." The article had gone on to say that not all of them did it, and no one knew why, but it was the ultimate marriage of the macro (space) and the micro (quantum). Energy to matter. Matter to energy. Neither can be created nor destroyed—but apparently they gave rise to one another.

Even in a vacuum full of nothing but waste and dust, even if the universe went cold and still, my photons would travel on until some of them gained enough speed to become something, or they would shine forever in the darkness.

Fuck the whole eternal-darkness thing. Of course everything "ate" everything, at least in my head—I was starving! Fuck, no, I didn't want to die, and twice fuck no in a pool. I'd been a fuckin' competitor, dammit; there was no way I was going to drown some like some negligent parent's accident.

My legs had started to cramp, and I straightened them with a vicious kick that sent me surging to the top. I gasped as I broke through and decided to swim to the shallow side and walk around instead of going back to the ladder. I'd been an idiot. You weren't supposed to swim alone anyway. I needed a good meal. Funny how weird your mind gets when your blood sugar is low.

I walked in water not quite shoulder-high when I got to the end, and I dipped my head quickly one last time, to sweep my hair back and off my face. Water streamed down my spine.

I stepped out of the pool and walked around the edge to the other end.

I hadn't noticed anyone else come out to the yard, but they waited at the other end, holding the towel out for me. I recognized Graham as I strode toward him, naked and wholly myself under the starlight.

"You're right," he said with a glance at my chest that had absolutely nothing lascivious in it, just a pure appreciation that I didn't mind. He firmly raised his eyes to the sky as he handed me the towel.

"Right about what?" I asked as I took it from him. I dried myself off quickly, then wrapped it around my waist and took the jacket he held in his other hand.

"Look, I'm a Brit. We don't have the obsession you Americans do with mammary glands, but it really *would* be a shame to cover a chest like that. You have to have those shoulders to carry it!" he chortled, not removing his gaze from heaven until I was covered.

His comment was respectful and I appreciated that.

"You can look now," I said dryly.

Still he stared up at the sky while I went back to my lounger and picked up my clothes. I put the tie around my bare neck where it flowed down my chest, nestling between my breasts, a bloodred stripe across my pale skin. I rebuttoned the jacket correctly, then slipped my boots on. The jacket hung about two, maybe three inches below whatever it needed to. Hey, I was dressed, at least. My ass was covered—it looked like I was wearing a suit dress or something like that, anyway. I put whatever was left into my gig bag, grabbed my butts, and hefted my guitar.

"Graham, I'm ready, it's totally okay," I assured him as I walked over.

Finally, he looked at me. "Holy Jesus Christ—stop!" he gasped.

"What?" I stopped, confused and vaguely alarmed. Was I about to step on a snake? Was there a spider hanging from an ear? I wasn't familiar with the local fauna, after all.

Graham walked up to me, stopping about five feet away.

"I have never, *ever*, seen that jacket look so good!" he said. I'd never seen Graham looked so amazed.

"Graham, you've been drinking, haven't you?" I asked him, taking a step forward.

"Hell no, girl!" he expounded as light flared from the doorway that led back to the hotel corridor. Guess someone else was coming out for a swim. "You look fucking hot, fucking sharp—"

"Like a Razor?" Candace's voice drawled out into the hot night air.

I snapped my head at the sound to see her backlit by the door. Her eyes flashed a moment in the light before it swung shut behind her.

"She told me you'd be out here," Graham said. Dammit. Was there *anything* Candace didn't know?

"I'm sorry I didn't wait for you, Graham," I apologized to him.

"It's all right—sometimes, things come up." He grinned. "Do you want me to get you out of this," and he jerked his chin over at Candace, who walked toward us, "or shall we try again tomorrow?"

Tempting as it was to take Graham up on his offer, the fact was that I might never get a chance to face Candace again—and there were things I still wanted to know.

"Good luck and good night, then. I'll see you in the morning?" Graham asked.

"Of course." I smiled back. "There's only one boat a day!"

"And don't you forget it!" Graham reminded me, shaking a finger at me with mock severity.

He nodded politely at Candace as he walked past her, and this time, I found another table instead of opting for a lounger.

A thought occurred to me. "Hey, Graham?" I called as he reached the door.

"Yes?"

"Could you ask someone to send some food out here? I'm starving."

"Consider it done, then," he said. "Can't have you wasting away."

Candace came over to the outdoor table I'd chosen as I once more put my guitar down. "Can we try this discussion again?" she asked me with a small smile, her eyes gleaming in the starlight as I straightened. She reached out and gently grabbed my tie. I let her.

"You're easy to fall in love with, Nina, but you're hard to love," Candace said quietly.

Whatever angry thing I was going to say in response died in my throat when I saw the sad twist to her lips and the tears in her eyes. "I'm sorry, Candace, but I don't know what you're talking about," I said. I gently took her hand from my tie and the skin that lay beneath it.

"Sit with me. Let's try this again. Do you want a cigarette?" I offered.

She sat, she took one of my cigarettes, and I lit it for her. Light flared again from the door, and we both looked when we heard a voice.

"*Están en esa mesa*." They're at that table, someone said, and over came two waiters carrying a small tray table and a cart.

"Coca-Cola, *señorita*?" one asked, pouring out a bottle for me as the other set the table down. Coke. Oh how awesome. And that tray, that smelled very much like…yes. Two cheeseburgers, with fries. *Oh, Graham,* I thought, *you're the best—fucking funny—but the best.*

"Eat with me," I offered, "heavy conversation after. I don't think well when I'm hungry."

"I suspect you probably think too well, either way."

What I recognized as mirth tugged at the corner of her mouth, and I arched an eyebrow at her and shrugged as I reached for my plate.

We ate in a companionable, civilized silence, quite a bit different from our last dinner together or our first.

"Do you remember Port Marseille?" Candace asked me with a small smile.

The waiters had turned on one of the torch lights that lined the edge of the courtyard so we were no longer in complete darkness. However, outside of that circle, you could see the star field again.

"It's not something I'll forget," I told her with a smile. "It *was* a beautiful summer night."

I have to admit that, at some point, I asked her if she'd felt the least bit bad about sleeping with someone her girlfriend had felt so strongly about, especially since she was "on a mission," I'd teased gently.

"Guilt is such a funny human construct," she answered seriously. "Should I feel guilty because a gorgeously dynamic young woman finds me attractive? Or because she responds to my interest?"

I thought about that. I guess, well, I wouldn't either, would I?

But Candace had more to say. "You carry a wall that says 'don't come near me,' and it's part of what makes you so damnably sexy. You're exceedingly generous with everything but yourself—you keep that for you—and for her."

Candace stood. "You mentioned before that I did my research thoroughly," she began.

I stood, too. "Look, I'm sorry I said that. It was completely uncalled for," I apologized and touched her arm.

"No, no, you were right. When I do something, I see it through." She smiled at me. "And honestly, Nina, you made it very enjoyable. I wanted to know what it was about you that could absolutely do that to someone, why she carried you in her heart like some carry those prayer beads."

"What did you find out?" I asked quietly.

She touched the charms that hung on my neck. "That you value life," she said as she touched the ankh, "that you value truth," she said and ran her fingers down the little blade under my throat. She looked into my eyes. "They're inseparable for you—and you are more than her match."

I was surprised when she lightly touched my cheek. "I was sending her to New York to find you—accidentally on purpose. I didn't tell her who you were because I didn't know if anyone could tame you." She moved her fingers from my face to my forehead, brushing my hair back. "I didn't know you were waiting for her."

I smiled at that because she was right—whether I knew it or not at the time, I *had* been waiting for my Samantha. "I was," I said. "I didn't know it, though."

Her hand moved from my hair to my shoulder. "I'm sorry…about what happened between you and Francesca," she said softly as she applied sympathetic pressure to the muscle under her fingertips.

"Are you?" I asked, stunned at the unexpected sting I felt in my eyes as my throat went tight.

"You've never really, ah, loved someone before, have you?" Candace asked delicately.

She could have been fishing, trying to find out how I'd felt about her maybe, or asking about how I might have felt about anyone, Trace included, since Candace had sort of met her that one night. But that's not what she was really asking. I knew what she really meant, so I looked Candace in the eyes and took that question right on the chin.

"No, I hadn't," I answered with simple strength. I would never be ashamed of loving my lion.

Candace dropped her eyes and took a breath before she spoke again. "A part of you will always be hers," and she touched the ankh on my neck, "just like a part of Samantha is Annie to me."

I shook my head, because at that moment, it felt like I had nothing. "That's just…that's just fucking great," I said finally. "What's mine, then?"

Candace grazed my chin with her fingertips. "Samantha. Samantha, whole and free. You knew her when she was happy, her potential spread out before her, part of her, before she…" Candace sighed, but wouldn't finish that thought. "I only ever got to see glimpses of that, and only on those rare occasions when she spoke about the past," she said instead, "when she spoke about you."

She leaned in and kissed my cheek. "I envy you, Nina," she said softly in my ear and put her arms around me.

I hugged her back, because I knew that despite what she said she did or didn't feel, what she didn't say was the important thing—the thing I'd known earlier. She loved Samantha, she loved her enough to see her happy, loved her enough to let her go, and like it or not, I was the one Samantha had gone to.

But still, there was one thing I had to know, after all that was said this evening. "Candace, everything between us…was it all just research?" I asked gently. I'd really liked her then, and honestly, I still did. I was sort of hoping that we could, I don't know, be friends, or something like that. I know that sounds weird, but that's how I felt—I don't know why. And I needed to know, needed to know if I'd really and truly been that wrong, that mistaken.

"No, of course not." Candace laughed and squeezed me. "I told you, you're very easy to fall in love with." She kissed my cheek, then pulled back to look at me as we let go of one another.

"Besides, as I told Annie," she tweaked my nose, "I've grown rather fond of you." Her teeth and eyes gleamed in the torchlight.

"I'd grown rather fond of you, too," I told her. I kissed her cheek. "Thanks for being honest, or something like it."

We really didn't have much left to say, so we walked back into the lobby together and said good night. Just before I was about to leave, a question occurred to me as I caught myself about to yawn.

"Hey, Candace?" I called to her back.

"Yes?"

"Why are you in Barcelona?" The real question was why didn't I ask that before, but I think I was so surprised to see her and so wired out from the show, my brain had fogged. Man, though, I needed to get some sleep if I was missing things like that.

"Two things, really," she said, her eyes glinting with humor.

I arched an eyebrow, waiting.

"I'm on holiday—and I love Spain," she said first.

"And...?" I prompted.

"I've been following your tour. I wanted to see you." She seemed pleased with herself.

Oh. Okay. I sensed something behind that, but I was too tired to really pursue it further at the moment. In truth, I would eventually find out much later.

"Will I see you again?" I asked, this time not able to swallow my yawn.

"Go get some sleep," Candace said kindly. "You'll see me again sooner than you think."

I grinned. Okay, I could buy that. This time, we said good night and I really went back to my room, where Stephie slept with a spoon in her hand and Jerkster slept in the chair, comic books scattered on the floor. *My* comic books, to be precise. Whatever. We could take care of that in the morning.

❖

Ibiza as a party town was like the Red Spot as a country. Everywhere, everything, was hot—the weather, the music, the people, the scenes—everything. It was whiplash city: you couldn't help but snap your head constantly at the parade of outrageously beautiful people and scenes.

We had rooms in a resort—an actual apartment with a little kitchen, two bedrooms, and a pullout couch. Jerkster wanted the sofa because he could watch TV all night. That was totally fine with me and Stephie, because each room also had its own bath—awesome! We had time to nap and bathe before hitting the stage. That...was heavenly.

I had enough time to go for dinner with Graham, and during our meal, Graham told me the tour would extend. After Madrid, we'd return to London after revisiting Paris, marking the end of our original contract, and we'd do a last London show before a week's break—the time necessary for us to get the new contracts reviewed and signed. He wanted to go back to Germany, head to Austria, jump to Italy, and then…Tokyo.

"They're gonna love what we're doing there," he enthused. "It's a huge market."

I considered. "Why not tell the whole band?" I asked him. "Why speak with me?"

Graham looked at me as if I'd dropped my clues somewhere. "Nina, you're the show. You write the music, you figure out the arrangements—including the harmonies. Nothing happens without you."

His perception of the whole thing shocked me—I didn't see it that way at all. We were a team, we all did our jobs. That's what it was all about, to me anyway.

"I'll talk with Stephie and Jerkster—let's all grab lunch together tomorrow, and you can explain it all then?"

Graham nodded thoughtfully. "Sure, we can do that. Noonish then, here?"

"Sure," I agreed, "that works."

We finished the rest of our meal chitchatting about the different places we'd played and comparing sound from one venue to another.

When I went back to our room preshow, I caught Stephie and Jerkster up on everything Graham had told me, and that we'd have lunch together the next day to figure it all out.

"Does he need to know tomorrow?" Stephie asked.

"I don't think so. We've got time to figure things out, why?" I asked her.

Stephie shrugged and shook her head. "No reason, just wondering."

"Hey, well, I'm signing the dotted line—I'm playing," Jerkster said enthusiastically.

I totally understood. I just figured we should know what we were getting ourselves into first and said so.

Jerkster nodded judiciously. "Yeah, you're right. I'll call my mom tomorrow. She does that law stuff, she can help us out."

"Hey, cool," I said, and dropped it from there—it was time to get going.

The show itself went great, and I did another set with the

Microwaves afterward as well. This time, Jerkster and Stephie stayed to watch, and it was so cool, because Graham had them come up to do the encore and it was, again, the ever-classic "Could You Be Loved." That's just such a rockin' tune…

When the show was over and we were all done hugging each other, I grabbed my guitar and walked backstage. I was still coming down from the very real stage high and rapidly falling into the sense of disappointment that had been building over the last two days. I'd heard nothing from Samantha—and I'd made sure to leave messages.

I walked back to our room. Everyone was going out, but for once, I didn't want to. I was going to watch some television, maybe rent a movie. I just wanted to be alone, you know? Besides, I hadn't had time to read lately; maybe I could read a few comics. Oh, hell, maybe there was an old *X-Men* or something somewhere I could pick through, take me to someplace different, and after, I'd work on some music. It was time to at least run through the basics, take my guitar apart, make sure everything was how it needed to be.

That was my plan, anyway, as I walked the corridor. As I approached our door, I noticed someone had left us flowers. "Nice," I thought as I slid my key card out of my back pocket. I opened the door and dropped my guitar off inside, then came back out for the blooms: irises and tiger lilies. They made me think of Samantha and Fran as I searched for a card, the irises for the amazing color of my Sammy's eyes and the tiger lilies for Fran's fieriness.

I found a vase under the sink in the kitchenette, and as I transferred them from the paper they'd been wrapped in, the card dropped out from the stems.

"Nina," it read, "this is a poor substitute for being there, I know. I will see you as soon as I can." It had a lovely single *S* beneath it.

I stared at it for a moment and drew the *S* with my finger. I flipped the card over, I don't know why. There was nothing, no actual information, time frame, phone number, anything. It was blank, as it should be.

Yep. Fine. I was staying in. Well, I might as well get my night started, right? I grabbed my guitar and sat down on the sofa to play.

I spent the next few days getting some sun at the beach with Stephie and Jerkster and enjoying the hottest nightclubs I had ever been to—before or since. There's no real way of describing it.

And then? We were back on the road. I took a single iris and a single tiger lily and pressed them in the back of a book so they could dry before we left, and made a bunch of phone calls to let everyone know where we would be. This time, I made sure to leave the label information on Fran's voice mail as well as Samantha's, just in case.

Everywhere we went as a band, we tried to take in some music— from the bars and the bands that played in them if we had free time, from the radio, from TV—and there was the whisper of a hot band called Loose Dogs and their lead singer/bassist, Ann R Key. Jerkster picked up their CD and we listened to it. The people were right—the music was hot, and Stephie and I could definitely hear what Jerkster loved about them. The bassist was phenomenal.

"I wonder why they didn't call themselves Cry Havoc, or something like that," I mused aloud. I looked up to find Stephie, who sat across from me, and Jerkster, who sat next to me, staring as if I'd dropped my mind off the train as we sped along the continent.

"You know, 'cry havoc and let loose the dogs of war'?" I asked as they kept staring. "No?" I shook my head lightly.

"No," Stephie shook her head, "that's why you write the lyrics, Nina," she said, smiling at me, "because you know shit like that."

Considering that the lyrics we had consisted of things like "we don't have cable anymore—someone threw the little box on the floor. The cat bit the wires and fried all night—Man it was terrible! But it gave light,"* I wasn't writing Shakespeare, so I laughed. "Whatever works," I answered, "whatever works."

Jerkster shifted in his seat and pulled the little boom box we carried around from under his seat. We kept it there so we could listen to our performances, review and dissect them, or, sometimes, just relax, listening to CDs we picked up wherever we went.

"Hey, let's listen to their album again?" he suggested hopefully, waving the jewel case in the air.

We all agreed, and Jerkster carefully balanced the player on top of the pile of stuff between our facing seats, then with a gentleness that would have surprised anyone who didn't know him, he put the disc in. I settled back and shut my eyes as he hit Play.

Their music did something for me, something very special, because it had the same sort of stirring beat that the Sisters of Mercy had, but added to it was a heavy sensuality coupled with a desolation

---

*"Cable No!"—Adam's Rib

that I responded to, in a very visceral way. I listened to the disc while we rode on yet another train, my eyes closed and feet stretched over our equipment. One particular track stood out for me.

As the lyrics and the music flooded through my brain, the unbidden image of my lion above me, before me, shifted, shimmered, became diamond-bright eyes and the sensuous curve of a deadly smile, deadly because it cut right through me. So real was the sense of imminent heat that I felt my body stretch and shift. Samantha. I missed her.

I sat up, banishing the too-real picture from my head, but it did nothing for the heavy throb in my chest. I caught my breath and let it out slowly, but the hammering didn't stop either. I ran my hands through my hair, tried to get my bearings, while Stephie and Jerkster stared at me with concerned puzzlement. Stephie clicked off the boom box.

"What's the name of that song?" I asked Jerkster.

He grabbed the jewel case he'd tucked next to him and inspected it.

"Um, track four, track four," he muttered as he searched. "Oh, track four!" he exclaimed triumphantly, "it's called 'The Kiss.' The bassist is singing lead on this one."

I bought my own copy.

BIZARRE LOVE TRIANGLE

*Now I'm standing here all by myself—I take the world from
my shoulder
Put my heart on the highest shelf and make my world a little
colder
Make my heart a little colder
Make my love a little colder*

"Colder"—Life Underwater

By the time we returned to London, Stephie was done, and it was
a very sad good-bye that led to panic—we had to rehearse the set with
me singing lead. This all went well until we arrived in Vienna where a
combination of alcohol, bad communication, and hysteria resulted in
Jerkster's wrist getting broken—he and the wrist got sent home.

I could have packed it in, too, but I wasn't ready to go back broken,
you know? Besides, my new contract was still good. Maybe I could do
something different, my own thing—something, anyway.

I lit out for Madrid and landed a job as a DJ at La Santa, a club
we'd played. What the hell, Spain had been the last place I'd said I'd
meet Samantha—not that I'd thought that would happen. I'd heard
nothing—absolutely nada.

No, I didn't call Candace. That would have been too weird.

Ah, fuck it. I lived in a little apartment on the roof of the building
and was supplied with the things that mattered: a studio in the club that
the owners, Carlos and Enrique, let me use to record in during the day,
a rooftop pool to ease tension and build my tan—the first one I'd had in
years—and time, free time to work on music, *my* music.

I celebrated my "new life" the way I did most major changes—I cut my hair. Short on the back and sides, with long spikes on top. I dyed the whole thing bright cherry red. What the hell, right?

I'd stopped looking, stopped caring, about anything, really. I'd given up trying to get in touch, too. No one called anyway, except for Graham and Enzo, the contact at Rude, and it wasn't as if I hadn't put the information out there. Even Dee Dee knew how to get in touch with me, and we spoke once every three weeks or so. She kept threatening to kidnap me back to New York, and I kept telling her she'd never want to leave Spain once she got there.

Once, just once, she asked me as carefully as she could if I had resolved anything with Samantha and Francesca.

I'd taken a very, very deep and slow breath before answering her as honestly as I could, as honestly as our friendship deserved, before I told her I'd completely lost contact with both of them—and this time, it wasn't my fault. I'd tried, I'd really and truly tried.

Dee Dee was quiet. I could just picture her nodding as she digested that information and thought of how to respond to it.

"Ah, Nina..." she sighed finally. "Maybe there are things you don't know about. I find it hard to believe that either one of them..."

We chatted a bit more and promised to touch base again soon.

It was okay, not hearing from either one of them, I mean. I was dealing, I guess, or something like it. I didn't understand at all, but I also tried hard not to think about it, because otherwise, it fucked me up and I couldn't focus, and I really needed to: I had a new contract and a new time frame in which to put a demo together and find the musicians to do it with.

Graham stopped by to visit, listened to some of what I'd composed, then boasted about the work I was doing back to the London office; they wanted me recorded and touring for the fall.

Enzo said they'd send me someone to work with, and by the terms of my contract, I'd have to. I hoped we got along, but really, whatever, because no one showed up for that either, so I enjoyed my life as best I could and wrote a lot of music.

Carlos and Enrique were generous enough to let me carve out an even larger sound studio from the DJ booth, and I spent hours every day writing, arranging, recording.

That's what I did when I wasn't out scouring for new sounds to add to my playlist or very occasionally socializing with the many beautiful young men and women the guys constantly introduced me to, but that was rare. It was a very focused, contained, and productive life.

I worked by myself during the siesta, the best time of day for it, since only Carlos and Enrique or any new trainees were in the building, so I was guaranteed the precious time I needed—I usually rewarded myself with a swim later on.

I had just recorded a tricky section for the second time and was listening to it back because I didn't like it, I wasn't happy. It needed, oh, I don't know, it needed *something,* and I was bouncing my head in time to the rhythm when, for whatever reason, I looked up across the board. Maybe it was the difference in air currents, or a different scent in the room. But whatever prompted the impulse didn't matter.

She was coming in from the corridor, and when she realized I'd seen her, she jammed her hands into her pockets. I put my guitar down safely, then cut the sound as she approached, a languid walk that spoke of determination despite uncertainty.

Her long curly blond hair was pulled into a loose ponytail at the nape of her neck, and she wore what most Spaniards on vacation did—a white linen shirt over white capris. Her skin was darker, her body thinner. Those shoulders, that jaw. I dropped the headphones and stepped away from my workstation.

"Kitt?" I whispered, unbelieving as I walked toward her. My hands started to tremble and the pulse beat in my neck. Even in the dim blue light of the club, she radiated gold. My lion. I stood not five feet away from her.

"Nina?" she asked softly, uncertain.

I nodded, dazed.

"You look…my God, you look amazing!" Her mouth, that flawless mouth, smiled tremulously at me, and she closed the distance between us. The tremble in my hands became a shakiness I couldn't control when she reached for my face. Her thumb brushed my lip, stroked my chin, then came to rest in that spot she had claimed as hers. I could barely breathe. My eyes stung and I reached for her blindly, pressing her to me, and her hands were on the bare skin of my back, holding me, caressing me.

I buried my face into her neck and kissed the warm pulse that leapt under my lips. "God, I missed you," I whispered, "I missed you so much."

"Nina, I'm sorry, I am so sorry," she told me in between the kisses she laid on my face. She held my face and kissed my eyes, and it took everything I had not to break into sobs. I stepped back and away from her brilliance before it blinded me, before it took away everything I had struggled so hard for, the things that were mine.

"What..." I swallowed and impatiently wiped my eyes. "What are you doing here?" I had to move, I had to get away from the warmth that radiated from her. I stepped back to my workstation and began to randomly organize things.

Fran sighed and lowered her head, accepting my distance. "Your mother...your mother told me where to find you." When she raised her head, I could see the glint of tears in her eyes.

I swallowed against the rising tide in my body. I wanted to hold her, I wanted to love her as I had, when she was mine and we both knew it.

"No. I mean," and I dashed the tears from my eyes again, struggling against everything, "why are you in Madrid?"

And then I heard it—the *a capella* (vocal only) version of "The Kiss" by Loose Dogs. I checked my board. Nothing was on. Was a radio playing in the outer bar? The sound was coming from out there, and no one was supposed to do anything to the sound system but me. I had to go investigate; the sound had a distinct quality I couldn't quite put my finger on.

"I heard you needed a bass player," Fran said with a tear-filled smile as I excused myself. Fran didn't play bass, I thought confusedly as the melody got louder. I was halfway across the floor when I realized the difference in the quality of the music: it was live.

This was beyond bizarre. Whoever the singer was, they were doing a dead on-spot imitation. Did one of the guys bring in a new waitress to train in the afternoon? I stopped and stood perfectly still, attempting to orient on the approaching source. My heart still raced from earlier, and when that person came around the wall, singing, walking straight to me, those diamond-bright eyes cutting through the dim light, I swear that beat stopped.

"You're fuckin' kidding me!" I spit out through clenched teeth when I started breathing again. I spun and stared at Fran, who came up to me, crying, smiling. I stiffened, my hands curled, and the tendons strained in my wrists.

I couldn't believe how angry I was. Maybe the last few years had been my fault, but this current disconnect hadn't been. I knew that. The only thing I felt was betrayed.

"Nina?" Fran sniffed, then recovered. "Meet Ann R Key, the bassist for Loose Dogs." She swept her arm in the direction of what was unmistakably, undeniably, Samantha, with a bass gig-bag slung over her shoulder.

Samantha smiled at me, a cocky little grin that was a quirk of her lips. It was only her eyes that looked sad, and for a moment, I wanted to touch that mouth, lighten those eyes, but I shook myself. No.

"Do you still need a bassist?" she asked softly.

I looked from one to the other. One of them showing up, maybe that I could understand, but both of them, showing up together, that was too weird, like they were ganging up on me or something, and I didn't like it at all.

Was this supposed to be some sort of fucking game? What the fuck were they doing? Whatever. I wasn't playing.

I shook my head and ran my hands through my short spiky hair. Then I took my guitar, and as quickly as I could without hurting it, I slammed it into its case and yanked at the handle.

"What the fuck do you think you guys are doing?" I asked, infuriated because I felt stupid for some reason, incredulous because I simply couldn't believe I was looking at either one of them.

"Six weeks. Six fucking weeks," was all I said as I walked past them to the wall that led to the corridor before I faced them.

The sense of betrayal persisted, I don't even know why, and all I could think was that I'd been so much better off, after all that silence, without them. I mean, one breaks up with me, the other promises, what, eternity? And breaks a date. What the fuck was that?

"How far do I have to go to get away from you?" I asked, not knowing which of them I spoke to.

Fran took a step toward me, but Samantha stopped her, grabbing her hand. Somehow, that little gesture, the implied intimacy of it, killed me. "God, just leave me the fuck alone, both of you," I snarled, and stalked out.

I assumed one of the owners had let them in, and even though he might not have understood the argument, since it was in English, I was pretty sure my tone was loud enough to be understood. The club was empty as I walked through it. Whichever guy it was had made himself scarce. I'd have words for one of them later, that was for sure.

I went to the back stairway that led to the roof, to my apartment, and when I got to the top and opened the door, the bright afternoon sun blinded me.

As I entered my apartment I glanced at the pool. A refreshing swim seemed like a good idea—time to float and think, think about nothing at all because I needed to cool off, literally and figuratively. Seeing Fran again had set my heart to racing, and the completely unexpected revelation about Samantha had just completely fucked me up. I realized I didn't fucking know her at all.

I settled my guitar in its usual spot and went to change into one of my swimsuits. I'd been there long enough to acquire a nice collection. I went with the turquoise string bikini I'd picked up when I first arrived; it looked great with my tan, or at least that's what Carlos said, and that tan needed some maintenance. I slapped some sunblock on. Even though I wanted to maintain the color, I was still naturally fair skinned, and the afternoon sun could be brutal. That was something I'd learned the day my face and shoulders matched my hair color.

I selected a towel and stepped into the kitchen, opening a cabinet for some olive oil. Pouring a tiny bit into my palm, I worked it into my hair—a neat little trick I'd learned from Enrique. He'd told me that it would prevent my hair from getting dried out as well as preserve the color for longer, and he was right.

Done with my sun preparations, I grabbed my sunglasses off the table, tucked them into the strap along my hip, and stepped out onto the roof. I tossed my towel down on one of the chaise lounges, walked to the board, and dove in.

The water was warm, heated by the sun all day, but it was still refreshing, I thought as I surfaced with a long stroke. Automatically, I began to swim the length, focusing on my arms, the position of my legs. I did about four laps before I decided to just float and let the sun warm me.

I swam to the cement and brick edge, then pulled myself out of the water. After dripping across the hot roof toward the closest floating raft, I returned with it, dropped it into the water, then carefully climbed on. A couple of strokes propelled me to the middle of the pool, where I pulled my sunglasses from my hip and slipped them on.

I lay there for a while, the soft slap of the water against the sides of the pool, the soft rock of the lounger and the warmth of the sun lulling me into a light doze.

"*Y qué?*" Enrique's voice cut across my peace. And what?

Lowering my sunglasses, I looked at him as he stood next to the pool, carrying two tall glasses and wearing the most popular form of male attire—a Lycra Band-Aid. This one matched my bikini—and Enrique looked good in turquoise. Frankly, Enrique looked good in everything. "And what what?" I asked archly.

He brought a lounger over, dropping it into the water. "Which one is the bass player?" he asked. He put the drinks down on the ledge and swung his legs over, dipping his feet in the pool.

"The one with the bass, of course," I answered, putting my sunglasses back on.

I heard him splash in, then lift himself onto the lounger, creating waves that lightly jostled me. "Here," he said, and bumped into me. I opened my eyes and took the glass he handed me.

"Thanks." I saluted as I sipped. Hmm. Rum and Coke, or *Cuba Libre*—Free Cuba, as they called it. You know, I'm pretty sure that I don't know anything that I probably should about Cuba, but I thought it was weird that they call the drink that in Spain; after all, they were once an empire.

Enrique settled back comfortably into his lounger. "Which one is the ex?" he asked, sipping nonchalantly.

I closed my eyes and leaned back, putting my glass into the holder in the lounger's arms. "The blonde," I answered shortly, "the devastatingly beautiful-didn't-believe-me-fuckin'-dumped-me blonde."

"Ah, a lover's quarrel?" he said lightly. "And it was over someone…another woman…" He let that hang in the air.

I considered how to answer. Since I hadn't given in to temptation, I hadn't sinned, right? And truth to tell, if Fran hadn't broken up with me, I know, for a solid fact, that I would never have let anything happen between Samantha and me, no matter what.

"There *was* no other woman, except in her mind," I answered finally. "Where's Carlos?" I asked, trying to change the subject. Usually we all ended up in the pool at the same time every afternoon.

"He's downstairs, putting in some new equipment. Enzo from Rude is setting up a new show."

I digested that news quietly. There had to be something else to it.

I knew Enzo and the label were waiting to see what I came up with. Graham had been really excited about the new material I'd developed, and in a very real way, I was "his discovery." Enzo had already more than hinted that he wanted me out on tour before long—to hit the back-to-school crowd, which didn't really make sense. Standard industry practice was not to release anything new between October fifteenth and January, going into February, really—the entire biz revolved around established acts at that time for the holiday rush.

Maybe he thought I didn't know that, and honestly, I hadn't before Graham explained it to me.

"And?" I asked.

"And what?" Enrique returned, lightly mocking my earlier answer.

"And what else did he want? I know Enzo. He doesn't call without at least several agendas, no?"

"No…and yes, you are right," he drawled, "he wants something else."

"Of course he does," I said, more to the sky than to Enrique. "Does he want a time line or a new demo?" For the last few weeks Enzo had been really been pressuring me to give him something, anything. I knew he wanted me to get back on the road. He was famous for saying "It's good enough for rock'n'roll," which meant slapping some shit together and putting it out there sometimes. But there were two things wrong with that, at least as far as I was concerned.

It had always been drilled into my head that trifles make perfection and perfection is no trifle. I wasn't going to just put some shit out there and attach my name to it—no fucking way. And I'd learned on tour that with no product, the show doesn't matter—you leave nothing memorable behind. Before I went out on the road again I was making sure that I had enough good music to perform and to sell.

"He wants you to work with Ann, thinks you'll be a good team." He resettled himself on his lounger as I sat up to stare at him and sipped on in silence. "Graham suggested it." He shrugged casually.

Fuck. What the fuck are you doing to me, Graham? I thought. At least he'd hooked me up with an excellent bassist, I grudgingly credited him.

"So, who was she?"

I sighed, resigned to playing the game. "Who was who?"

"The imaginary woman, of course?" he asked, eyes wide like an innocent. Which, from the lift in the corner of his mouth, I knew he wasn't.

I settled into the lounger, set my sunglasses back on my head, and picked up my drink. "The bassist," I said casually as I took a sip and closed my eyes.

"So the blonde is the one you were engaged to?"

"No," I answered shortly, "that was also the bassist."

I could feel his shock in the silence, then a sudden splash rocked my lounger. I opened my eyes to see Enrique in the water, shaking his head at me.

"*Muy chueca, chica*," he said. Very twisted, girl. I saluted him with a small smile.

"I know," I told him, that tight little smile on my face difficult to speak through, "believe me, I know."

"No, not just that," he said, wading toward me and pulling his lounger with him. "It's just that Enzo asked if we had an available apartment. And since the other one is being worked on and Graham said you girls knew each other, we thought, well—"

"They're staying with me," I said flatly. Great. Fucking great. Maybe I'd go back to New York early and find an apartment in Brooklyn—no, Queens. Everyone got lost in Queens.

My displeasure must have shown on my face, and Enrique misunderstood—he thought I was concerned about appearances, which, in conservative Madrid, many *Madrileños* are. But I wasn't a *Madrileña*; I was a New York City punk, and that shit never really mattered to me.

"Don't worry," he laughed, "we only dress Catholic."

"I thought gays weren't allowed to believe in God," I shot back at him, still not exactly thrilled with life at the moment, but willing to play with Enrique all the same.

"Someone better tell God that." He grinned maddeningly. "Besides," he added, "this is Spain—and you should have more than one lover. Damn, Nina, you should at least *have* a lover." He studied me for a moment. "Love is more flexible than you think," he said softly.

I really didn't want to get into that conversation with him. For the record, the word "lover" in Spanish—*amante*—sounds a heck of lot nicer than it does in English. It carries just so much more with it, which is why I didn't object to Enrique's use of it. I still don't like the word in English.

I hung my glasses from the center strap of my bikini top and decided to swim a few more laps to get my head clear of the adrenaline that was pumping my brain full of mush; and in the end, I must have done a few more than I thought, because Carlos and the girls came up the outside stairs and through the gate.

Carlos was funny. He had them walk outside instead of go through the club—I guess so that they knew the stairs were there or it was his way of introducing long-term guests to the place. The three of them waited: Samantha with her bass slung over her shoulder and holding her bag, Fran with her bags in front of her, and Carlos, a smug expression curving his too-pretty mouth.

I swam over to their end and climbed out, vaulting over the ledge the way I liked to. Besides, it showed off my arms, and for once in my life, I was aware that not only was I more than half naked, but that I looked good that way, and I knew that both of them would notice.

And notice they did. Fran's eyes cut across me before she focused on Carlos, while Samantha chewed the corner of her lip, then stared at the sky. Bad idea—it was way too bright out.

I ran my fingers through my hair, then pulled my sunglasses free from my top and slipped them on.

"How long will this unexpected...visit last?" I asked Carlos.

"Well, Nina," Fran broke in with a Spanish pronunciation that sounded slightly Italian, "we're both here at the label's request. The studio I worked for bought Rude, and I'm doing their contract fieldwork. Samantha's the musician they're lending you, and Enzo suggested four weeks to do the demo and review the contracts."

I stared at her in shock. "When did that happen?" I asked. This put a whole new twist on my life. It meant potential politics that I might have to steer far and clear from, if I had to work with both of them. It meant I might want to find a new label if my current contract was about to change. I was going to have to call Mrs. J—Jerkster's mom—sooner than I thought, then.

The sun beat on my head, and the slate tiles of the roof began to burn under my feet, which forced me to remember my manners. It really was hot out there, and Samantha and Francesca had just traveled quite a long way. That, and Carlos had made them take the outside stairs.

"You know what? Never mind, it's hot and I'm sorry. This way, ladies," I said politely and led them to my apartment—I guess *our* apartment, seeing as they would be staying more than a day or two.

"So," I said brightly as I opened the door and they followed me in, "this is it."

Samantha promptly selected the ideal corner for her bass guitar, and I gave them the nickel tour.

While they unpacked and settled in, each using one of the travel trunks that served as end tables, I decided I wasn't hanging around—I was going out before work tonight. I quickly showered to get rid of the chlorine and dressed. On the way out of my room, I grabbed some towels from the linen closet and made coffee.

Yeah, okay, I was pissed and confused and just generally off track, but still, they were staying in what was essentially my home, and I knew when I finally calmed down, I'd be happy to see them. In fact, part of me was; I just wasn't ready to deal with either one of them yet.

"Hey, go change, swim, relax," I said, and put the towels on the sofa. I'd already told them it was a pullout; they'd have to figure it out for themselves from there. "I started coffee," I told Fran with a weak grin. I'd learned to make it when we were, whatever we were, because she enjoyed it so much.

Samantha took a towel and nodded, silent, that heavy emotion she carried darkening her eyes.

Fran looked up from her bag. "Thanks, Nina," she said, her voice as gentle as always. "I know this must be quite a, a shock for you. Can we take you out to dinner and talk?"

I couldn't. I needed time to calm down, to wrap my head around their presence in my space—every aspect of it, including work. And I had questions, probably more than two. I shook my head and asked, "Um, let me rain check you on that, okay? I, uh, I've got a few things to take care of." Yeah, lame, maybe, but what was I supposed to say, um, you guys are really freaking me out? I don't think that would have gone over very well. No, that's a lie. It probably would have been completely fine, but I just wasn't up for it at the moment.

As I walked to the door, it occurred to me—by the time the night ended, I would forget what I was mad about, since I'd be tired because their combined presence was making my brain swim. And I was hyperaware of my skin—the water that had barely dried, the heat from outside, the slight hiss from the air-conditioning.

And in the end? I knew it wouldn't matter why I hadn't heard from either one of them for so long—because deep down at the heart of it, I missed them both too much to care.

I stopped with my hand on the knob. "Since you guys just got here, why I don't I take both of you out tomorrow, then. Let's say brunch, since I get out of work late?"

Samantha and Fran exchanged a surprised look, then Samantha gave me that smile that made me want to—well, it made me want, anyway.

"Sure, that sounds really good." She nodded lightly, and Fran smiled in agreement.

Okay, then. Cool.

"I'll see you in the morning, then." Okay, so I was fucked up, but at least I felt a little better as I walked down the steps and out into the parts of the city that would bring me a little distraction before I had to deal with the combined presence of my lion and the diamond edge of Sammy Blade.

❖

If I hadn't got so, so, I don't know, adrenalized is probably the best way to describe it, that I shook every time I saw either one of them, I'd say it all went very well. It hurt to see Fran, to be near her, to remember anything, everything, while Samantha left me raw, shaken, and confused—I didn't know anything at all about where we stood with each other, and the fact that they were together, in my face and in my space…

Once I got downstairs and into the "studio," things were fine. Working with Ann R Key was quite easy. I played her the pieces I'd written, and we would develop them, adding bass lines and occasional harmonies and trying to sketch out where percussion should go, while Fran worked in Carlos and Enrique's office during the day, reviewing the tons of paperwork the label sent her. Apparently, it sucks to be low man on the totem pole when you're working in the legal department.

The evenings weren't too hard because I worked, but on the nights and days I didn't, I started spending time with them, sometimes together, sometimes individually, depending on what was going on. I was the one with the scheduled time off, while Fran's job was really every day and sometimes late into the evening, and Samantha's revolved around me, with "other things" that she occasionally had to do. They weren't any of my business, so I didn't ask.

It started with them both coming to the club when I was spinning and grabbing a bite with me afterward. Then one night when I didn't have to spin, but Fran had to "review clauses," I took Samantha to one of my favorite places.

It was a hot-ticket restaurant where they served things like roast tuna with mango chutney in a white-on-white dining room. Mostly I tried not to spill anything while attempting to maintain a conversation, which is not something I usually had a problem with—I suspect it was either company- or subject-dependent.

"I met Trace…" Samantha said nonchalantly as she cut into whatever it was on her plate.

I almost choked and was afraid the chutney would come out my nose. Instead I hefted my glass of sangria and took a healthy swallow. Once I could see again, I said as calmly as I could, "Oh, that's, uh…you went to Staten Island, then?"

"Uh-huh." She nodded and sipped sedately. "She was…more than you said she was."

I stared at her, remembering quite well the "full confession" I had made to her before I'd left and sincerely hoping she didn't mean that I'd either omitted or changed the facts, such as I knew them, anyway. I put my fork down as safely as I could to prevent injury to myself or anything else in that white, white dining room.

"What do you mean?" I asked very carefully.

Samantha set her glass on the table and gazed at me, studying me seriously.

"Do the words…unholy, unclean, and undead mean anything to you?" She gave me a half-smile.

I thought about it. What was it Candace had said? "That one has fangs." Unholy, unclean, and undead. I grinned at Samantha.

"Uh, that sounds about right to me, yeah," I said. "I wish I'd thought of that."

Samantha laughed lightly. "Eeyeah…but you're okay, right?"

I didn't know what she meant by that at all. "Um, I'm fine," I told her, arching my brow, "although there might be a scar or two somewhere. Why?"

Samantha raised her glass and gestured. "Just making sure. People like that, they're...they're just vampires, you know?" She quirked her lips when she said it, and the half-smile reached everything but her eyes.

Now that bit, about the vampires? I did understand. The thought of Trace didn't hurt anymore, not the way it used to, but it still left me feeling, I dunno, dirty or something, and it still had this sense of "my fault" about it. Still, it was way over, and the best part of that was it was two oceans and more than two time zones away.

I don't really remember what I said, and the rest of the conversation returned to more mundane things, well, mundane for us anyway—like the studio and the work we were doing.

I asked Samantha when she'd switched from guitar to bass, about the band Loose Dogs and the work she did with them, and where she'd played. Samantha had never performed in the States; instead, she'd spent about half her professional life doing studio gigs, but she'd performed all over Europe, even in some of the places I'd gone with the Microwaves and Adam's Rib. We compared notes about venues and sound, bands we liked, and the things we totally hated—and we made lots of jokes about train food.

Samantha had "stuff to do" the next night, and Fran happened to be free, so I took her to a very traditional restaurant known for serving some of the finest Italian food in the city. It was great to hear Fran rattle off her order in Italian; she spoke it beautifully. My pronunciation wasn't bad, but really, I cheated, because I spoke Spanish anyway.

When I told her in Spanish that I admired her Italian, she blushed and looked at her plate a moment. I smiled but was a little embarrassed, too, because I hadn't meant to say that, and it crossed all the boundaries we'd been so very careful to maintain.

"Well, Nina, you've a beautiful accent yourself," she returned with one of her trademark smiles. I tried very hard not to stare at that gorgeous mouth and was grateful when the waiter came back with our food.

We joked and laughed with much of our old closeness as we ate, then spent the rest of the night hopping around from place to place, Spanish style. I really enjoyed seeing the delight on Fran's face as she observed the local social culture, the mix of people, the sense of friendly playfulness that seemed to be a part of the very sidewalks and buildings.

And we sort of fell into this habit, I guess, of Fran and me or Samantha and me going out and wandering around Madrid on nights when I was free. Or they went out and did stuff or came to hang out in the club, and we became, as weird as it sounds, friends, friends like we hadn't been in years.

I can't say there wasn't some tension, because in all honesty, either one of them near me made me vibrate like a live wire, and any time I was with both of them for more than a few seconds I had to keep myself at least three feet away from whoever was nearest because it felt like... Truth to tell, there really wasn't a single moment, not even in the studio, when I could forget what it was like to love Samantha, the primal intensity of her, or to be loved by Fran and her controlled fierceness.

Whenever I saw Carlos and I was with one or both of them, he'd give me an evil smirk and pretend all innocence if either one of them glanced over. I scowled at him a lot—then tried not to, because I didn't want my eyebrows to stay like that.

Enrique constantly asked me for updates. *"Y qué?"* almost every day, and he got some arched eyebrows and a lot of "And nothing, busybody," in response. He laughed at me every time.

Finally, everyone had two days off—it was a holiday—and in their respective travels around Madrid, Samantha and Fran had each happened upon a spot that everyone talked about as *the* place. I'd never been to it because it was famous for two things: the food and the very specific atmosphere. People went there for important dates: to propose to their intendeds, to celebrate twenty-five-year anniversaries, and to begin or consummate secret, undying trysts.

So, of course, that's where we went—and it was perfectly nice and perfectly weird, because it was a really romantic, candlelit spot where we had duck breast with something and way too much spiced red wine, and ordered some to take home. What the fuck, right?

After dinner, we took a walk in *El Parque de Retiro* or the Park of Retreat (and for the smallest bit of history, because, hey, it's Spain, not some mundane part of Staten Island's dump or something), which is what Felipe IV had built it for—retreat.

This park came alive at dusk and rocked through the night. Artists and vendors lined the walkways, selling everything from "authentic" bullfighting ad posters to castanets to a variety of foods. Scattered here and there were the occasional games of chance, such as darts and balloons, the shell game, cards. Gypsies offered to read your palm and your cards and solve your problems—all of them—for the right price. There were also street performers, individuals playing their guitars and singing their hearts out or groups doing complex flamenco patterns. This was Madrid at its most fun, and I was glad to be able to share it.

We passed the Crystal Palace and the San Jeronimo Church (which happens to be where the monarchs who'd financed Christopher Columbus got married)—imposing structures that looked a heck of a lot different in real life than they did in a small two-by-two picture in a textbook, and finally, we came to the lake path.

I was feeling pretty expansive and just generally good about everything, because we all felt just so very comfortable with each other that I could occasionally hold Samantha's hand or Fran's as we walked along.

I linked my arm through Samantha's on one side, then Fran's on the other. "So..." I started as we strolled along the edge of the lake, moving from patch of light to patch of light and watching as the rowboats slid by with their lantern-lit bows, "what are you guys really doing here? I mean, okay, we're all working for the label, in effect, but why both of you? Not that I mind, of course," I added, giving them each a smile.

We stopped walking.

Fran stuck a hand in her pocket and looked at the water. Samantha closed her eyes and took a deep breath.

"Well, Graham asked for Ann R Key specifically, and he told the new head that I know you both...so they thought it would be better all around if—"

"Um, would you believe me if I said we're courting you?" Samantha interrupted Fran, looking at me directly, her face inscrutable in the half-light.

What? Was she serious? I shrugged myself free of both of them and took a step forward so I could see them a bit better.

"You're not serious?" I asked.

"Yeah," she grinned crookedly, "pick one."

"Jesus, Sam..." Fran breathed out, giving her an annoyed look. She shook her head.

Jesus was right. And Mary, and Joseph, and anyone else you could name. What the hell was I supposed to do with that? How in the hell was I supposed to do that? It's not like I was trying to decide between two new pairs of boots. And besides, if I was? I usually got both anyway. Eesh.

"Well, what if I don't want to?" I asked. I mean, hey, ask an easy question, you get an easy answer, right?

They exchanged a glance, and Fran returned her gaze to the water.

"You could have us both," Samantha said softly, and shrugged.

Fran's eyes met mine. "If you wanted," she added quietly.

I picked a rock up off the ground and tried to skip it across the water. What the hell? Pick one, the other, or both? How was that supposed to work, anyway? One hop, two, three, and the rock sank in with a splunk. Besides, in a way, like Candace had said back in Ibiza, didn't I carry them with me all the time?

I touched the charms that hung from my neck and faced them again after I knew that rock was on its way down. "What do you mean?" I asked, looking from one still face to the other. "I already have you both."

Nobody said much of anything on the way back to the apartment, although there was this kinda loose agreement, or at least an understanding, that this was something we should probably discuss a bit more, and probably more than a bit.

My head was spinning with the weight of what Samantha and Fran had offered because it wasn't even remotely close to anything I had even—well, okay, that wasn't entirely true. There had been those few encounters, but…that was just sex, you know? I hadn't cared about those girls, or even myself if I was honest; it was still something I felt so disconnected from.

But Fran…if I really took time to let myself feel it, I adored. I couldn't get around it, past it, through it, or over it. The best I could do was ignore it, and I did that badly.

And Samantha? Samantha was under my skin in ways that I still can't describe, the beacon that called me like the sound the ferries made through the fog at night—constant, low, and wistfully mournful for a home that might never be reached again and remains forever missed.

I didn't know what to think as I sat between them on the sofa with a movie playing on the TV that none of us was really watching while we finished first one, then another, pitcher of the sangria we'd made from the wine we'd brought back from dinner—those bottles went pretty fast.

Somewhere in the back of my head, this one thought persisted. Maybe, just maybe, still, even now, this had nothing to do with me—it was between Francesca and Samantha, a dance of approach and avoidance that they couldn't resolve and in some ways used me to translate between them.

Ironically, that didn't bother me, at least, not in the way you might think, because in a very real way, I truly thought Sammy and Fran were good for each other. They'd been friends for such a long time, had remained close even with all the things they'd been through—and once they'd actively admitted to being attracted to one another. Maybe they still were and just couldn't deal with it, which is kinda silly, but, hey, people are, right?

That was all my brain could come up with, the wall I'd hit and couldn't get past right then—this was more about them than me.

I probably shouldn't have done it, but I did.

"This is not a choice," I warned Samantha as I faced to her. She stared at me a moment, her eyes almost translucent in the flickering light of the television. I took her hand from her lap, held it in mine, and softly pressed my lips to hers. The raw sensuality of her response made my breath catch into a knot in my throat where it flooded back down into my chest, making my heartbeat ragged, painful.

When I let her go, I kept her hand on my leg and went to Fran, who'd been studiously focused on the television. I cupped her face gently and turned her eyes to mine. "This is not a choice," I repeated, and her eyes widened when I leaned in to kiss her—those beautiful lips, that gorgeous mouth again on mine, and my heartbeat, still ragged from Samantha, sang at the reliving of memory.

When I finally let her go, I had Fran's hand in one of mine, Samantha's in the other.

"I don't think this is about me," I told Samantha and kissed her cheek. "I think this is about you and her," I said to Fran and kissed her briefly as well.

I let go of both their hands and stood up, then faced them both. They stared at me.

"You guys have to work this out." They glanced at each other, puzzled, before focusing back on me.

"Nina," Samantha asked quietly, "what do you mean?"

I smiled at her fondly. "I mean that...there's something between you, between the two of you," and I shared that smile with Fran, "that you have to figure out."

Fran shook her head lightly, like she didn't understand. That was okay.

"Well," I announced, because I'd probably done all the damage I could for one lifetime, "I'm going to bed. You guys…do what you need to do, I guess."

I leaned down and gave each of them another hug and kiss good night. "Let me know what you decide, okay?" I said as I went to my room and left them there staring at each other.

I flipped on the low light on my nightstand, got undressed, and slipped into my bed. I was tired, buzzed, and strangely happy—because I trusted Samantha and Francesca to work this out, and I loved them both so much, the thought of them together in any way had a beautiful feel.

I roused slightly as the bed shifted behind me and Fran wrapped herself around my back, her skin velvety against mine. I stretched a bit, enjoying the remembered warm fit of her against me, and twisted my head to enjoy the press of her lips against my throat as her hands molded the contours of my ribs, my waist, gripped and pulled gently on my hip.

"Missed you…so much," she murmured hotly against my jaw and touched my face in the way that was hers and hers alone.

I turned in her arms and cupped her face, then tangled my fingers in her hair as I brought my lips to hers. I lost myself in the welcome of her mouth, in the elegant play of her tongue against mine, and the strength of her hands as they retraced my body again and again.

I wasn't shocked, or even surprised, when the heat that I always knew as my Sam warmed my back again and her hands joined Fran's, cupping my breast, rolling the nipple between her slender fingers until it was hard, and I groaned with the sensation. I arched my back into Samantha, which forced my hips forward, my pussy against my beautiful lion, hers pushing back against me.

I let go of her hair and reached back and over my head for Samantha, bringing her face to mine, kissing her with the desperate hunger she raised in me, and Fran licked my throat, biting gently, then pulling on the tendon with her teeth. Her hand slipped down, scraping lightly between Samantha's fingers before it traveled farther, back to my hip, wrapping around me, grabbing my ass in such a way that she moved the aching lips of my cunt, and as I sucked on Samantha's tongue I tasted Fran.

Fire. I was molten fire, flowing between the diamond that was my Sammy Blade and the contained strength that was Fran. I loved her, I was in love with Samantha. I wanted them, needed them, both, here, now, and I slipped my hand away from my Blade's head and between us, behind me, gripping along the tightened muscles of her stomach until I found the treasure I'd been seeking, the fine, light hairs of her amazing cunt, the hard prominence that spoke of her desire, and I gratefully slipped my fingers between her wet lips, never more at home than when I was there, stroking the length of her, waiting to enter.

Samantha gasped and tore her mouth from mine. "I love you, Nina," she breathed into my ear.

Her head arced over me to meet Fran's, and she kissed her. It was heart-piercingly beautiful, the way their lips met and moved together— I was filled with an awestruck joy at their joined perfection. I had never felt so completely safe in my life.

My lion pressed harder against me, her hand gripping insistently as Samantha scratched lightly down between us until she cupped my pussy in her hand, squeezing, teasing, promising—everything. Her hips urged behind me.

Ah, but my beloved Samantha was gorgeously wet, and when Fran gently pushed me so that I was almost half on top of Samantha, my fingers found their mark and I slid into her cunt, tucking my thumb under my palm so I could play with her clit.

She bit my neck as Fran crawled down my body, nipping with her lips, light little licks with the tip of her tongue, memory and experience merging as she mapped me. She stopped and kissed Samantha's hand as it lay on me, then parted my lips with her tongue.

"Oh God, Kitt…" I gasped as she sucked me into her, and she caught my free hand, twining her fingers with mine as I curled the hand behind me deeper into Samantha, who shuddered behind me. She slipped an arm beneath my shoulders and around my chest, anchoring me to her. She laved my neck with open-mouth kisses, scraping her lips and tongue along the column of my neck.

"I adore you, I fucking adore you," she ground out between sensual attacks, and her cunt sucked my fingers, fitting on me as if I'd been made for her.

I cried out when her tongue entered me, and Samantha crushed me to her, trapping me, holding me still when I tried to arch my back.

"I got you…" she assured me, and her fingers slipped around my clit while Fran's mouth worked me relentlessly, driving me on and up. Her free hand wrapped loosely around the hand that drove into Samantha, moving with me, around me, a light tickle that urged me on, harder, faster.

Samantha shifted, her leg smoothing across mine, entangling it between hers, opening herself further to me, spreading me wider, and pushing my thigh against my hand, my thrust in her that much harder as I moved under Fran.

"Damn, I *love* you, Samantha," I whispered, craning desperately to kiss her as the two most beautiful women I would ever know or be this close to in this lifetime loved me and each other, pushing me to the edge, the power behind this, this thing between us, building, towering over me.

Her lips were instant relief to my thirsty soul. "I want you inside me," I told her. "I want you both inside me."

Fran heard me and raised her head. I caught my breath, gulping at the loss, and Samantha responded instantly, sliding into me so I wouldn't feel it for too long.

"*Te adoro*," she whispered, speaking the language of my childhood as she moved gently within me, and my cunt welcomed her home to me, "*te amo, te adoro.*"

Fran climbed up my body, straddling my leg, and her cunt was deliciously hot and wet, gliding along the hard muscle of my thigh.

Her irresistible mouth kissed me, and once again, for the last time, I enjoyed the taste of my cunt on her tongue.

"I love you, Francesca Kitt DiTomassa," I told her, melting into her golden eyes, "I will always love you."

I grasped her hip with my hand as she rode my thigh, her leg pressing between us, driving Samantha farther into me. Fran slipped her hand between us, cupping Samantha's hand under hers, and I could feel her fingertips waiting to enter me.

"Baby," she murmured, kissing me gently, "this is going to hurt. I want to do what you want, but I don't want to hurt you."

She was right, I knew she was right, because even Samantha inside me hurt a bit.

"You are really tight, love," she whispered, then caught her breath when I shifted my hip slightly, causing my fingers to reach deeper. Her hips jerked against me, and, honestly, I couldn't have cared less if my arm broke; I wanted this, wanted to be in her, wanted her to come.

Fran leaned across me and kissed Samantha deeply as she shuddered against me, and my hand traveled from the curve of Fran's hip to her ass, and I pressed my fingers along the length of her cunt. She groaned into Sam's mouth, her head under my neck, and I felt Samantha shiver as she tasted me for the first time on Fran's lips.

"Kitt, baby," I rasped out, losing my voice, my breath, my mind between them, "I don't care if it hurts, I want you."

She buried her head into my neck, between me and Samantha.

"Okay...okay..." she groaned as I pushed her over the edge, slipping my fingers inside her, letting her crush down upon me.

I felt Samantha ease out of me a bit and then...God. The world was going to fall apart and take me with it because it hurt, it fucking hurt, but it didn't matter because it was so fucking intense, so fucking good it spiked through me, and caught as I was between them, my body heaved anyway, light and pain and pleasure, and God, if it only happened once in this life, then it was enough to remember it always, the sweat-slick intensity as Fran's head pushed into my shoulder and her free hand pulled, Samantha's arm wrapped around me, fingers digging across my collarbone as I buried my face against her chest, her heart pounding into my ear, the straining, painful push of bone and muscle of my arm trapped to my side now so I could bury my fingers into Samantha's cunt, the bruising push of Fran's hip between my legs, driving, always driving their combined thrust while I loved her, deep and hard.

"God yesss..." Fran hissed against my throat as she shifted on me, her pussy pulling and gliding and loving me. When she bit at the bone in my shoulder, the sensation sent a chill through me, and I heard Samantha's breath catch as she surged against me.

My body relaxed, totally relaxed, and I felt their combined push become something deep and discrete—Fran steady and deep, my Sammy more of an urgent thrust in my cunt as she got ready to come. I could feel it—in her body, in mine.

I twisted my head and kissed the skin above her heart. "Come, love," I begged her, "come deep."

Her leg flexed over mine, pulled against me, and I could feel the tendons in my wrist strain between our bodies, the tension of her cunt an exquisite weight across my arm, the beloved absolute embrace of it almost blinding me as she took as much of me as she could within her and her painfully engorged clit pulsed under my thumb.

"Coming," she gritted out, a desperate sound that slipped between her teeth, and her body waved as she again crushed me to her, kissing me desperately as she rode the tension out of her and into me, forcing me to move against the twin pressures of them, creating a frantic need, a hunger that made my throat ache and made my hands move, almost frenzied as I plunged as far as I could in Fran.

"Stop…baby, stop," Samantha said, "too much," and she shifted slightly so I could ease my fingers from their home.

I won't lie, my hand hurt from that position, and I slowly flexed it, then wrapped my fingers lightly around Samantha's forearm, sliding down over her wrist, stopping only when my fingertips found Fran's hand crushed over hers.

Electric strings were racing out and under my skin, the arc starting from wherever I felt the raw intensity of my Samantha, the barely restrained fierceness of Fran, and the rush was coming up and over me as she let go of my shoulder. Her hand reached for my face, brushing over my cheeks with her fingertips, tracing my lips until her thumb rested below my lip. She raised her head and kissed me the way only she could.

"Yours," she whispered against my lips, and once again my beautiful Fran broke and took me with her, my body soaring, my heart torn between love and grief because I knew what she meant, what this was—this was good-bye—as her cunt held me as if she'd never let me go.

I moved the hand that had felt both of them within me to her back to feel the flex of the muscles there with the blade as sharp as an angel's wing, to trace the span of her shoulders one last time.

"My lion," I whispered back to her, "the pride of my heart." I kissed her with hopeless intensity and came, a sharp burst of pleasure and pain that pounded through me, tearing me, drenching me in love and sorrow.

Fran eased slowly out of me and the loss was painful, both physically and emotionally. She pressed her fingers against my neck as she rested the full weight of her body upon me and cried into my throat while Samantha murmured soothing little sounds into my ear and gentled my bruised and aching cunt.

I didn't need to see Fran's or Samantha's hands to know that I'd bled again. I'd felt the tear when they'd entered me, could smell the blood on Fran's hand.

When I moved my fingers to come out of her, she stopped me. "Please…stay," she cried softly, "just a little longer."

"Love you," I murmured and stayed, content to feel her for as long as possible before even this, too, had to end, and I rubbed her back as she lay on top of me.

Samantha shifted, sliding her arm out from under me, and lifted herself up on an elbow. She kissed me tenderly, kissed the tears that ran hot and free from my eyes, and when she finally left my cunt she placed her hand over mine where it rested in Fran.

I realized Samantha cried too, as she kissed her cheek. "I love you," she said softly to Fran, then Samantha kissed me again. "I adore you," she whispered into my ear, then settled herself over me.

It was some time later, but not too long, when we shifted and resettled into each other, and I let Francesca hold me as I'd never let her—my head on her shoulder, my leg over her hip and Samantha draped over my back, her arm reaching over me to hold my hand and Fran's, joined together, body and blood.

You'd think there would be, but there really wasn't any "morning-after awkwardness," and because it was a free day, we spent most of it quietly, together. We went out for breakfast, well, brunch really, and we went back to the park for a while. We walked over to El Prado and let ourselves get art stoned, lucky enough to be there during a huge Picasso retrospective—his sketches, his books, all on display.

Fran loved it, really and truly loved it, but I didn't get it at first, although I really enjoyed his sketches (I'm more of a Matisse fan, myself) until I saw *Guernica*. It floored, absolutely slammed me into shock (I can't even begin to describe it), and I was touched in ways I don't think I can explain when I saw that it brought Samantha to tears.

As we wandered through the galleries and I saw the work of Goya, I knew I would never, ever paint again. I could never hope to approach that level of brilliance; I mean, okay, the Saturn-eating-his-children thing was gross, but the way he painted light? I'd just have to try to do the same thing with my guitar and voice—I would never be able to do that with a brush.

Sometimes I held Samantha's hand, other times Fran's, they held each other, we walked arm in arm. It was just so very easy and very quiet, even when we discussed the paintings. We'd stand in front of them and whisper and point at different things. Honestly, we'd said everything we'd had to the night before.

During the siesta hours we went—where else?—back to the apartment and the pool.

There was only one awkward moment—when it was finally time to turn in for the night—and in the end, we all slept in my bed. It wasn't sexual, though. I suppose it could have gone that way if any one us had even slightly pushed for that, but this strangely sweet sort of shyness flowed between us.

There were whisper-kisses and ever-so-slightly suggestive caresses. We traded these gentle touches until we were all sleepily satisfied and wrapped sensually around each other like a pack of little fuzzy animals, curled together, warm and soft and safe.

The studio sessions? They were another story altogether.

Fran would work in Carlos and Enrique's office, reviewing the contracts that Enzo would send her while Samantha and I did our work: sculpting feeling into sound.

The music was really going great; it was just that these moments would occur between us, Samantha and me, I mean. We were a little shy with each other, a little extra-polite and oddly formal in a way I didn't understand, all things considered.

I'd catch myself staring at her, her lips, the exquisite line of her neck as she sang, the way her fingers ran up and down the fret board— long, lean, musician's hands, the veins standing out in sharp relief through her skin—like mine.

I'd catch her staring, too, her eyes sometimes glinting at me in the dim light that surrounded the workstation. When she leaned over me to check a pan level on the board for a new tune we were starting to lay tracks out for, her nearness made me catch my breath, and we stood there, frozen, afraid to move in any direction.

I shook my head and looked down at the board. "Set a midrange here, I think—you?"

Samantha hesitated a moment before answering. "Yeah," she croaked out, "mid, uh, midrange."

I reached across the board to set the dial just as Samantha did, and when our hands touched, I knew, whether or not she did, that the time for bullshit had come to an end. My nerves were frayed; I was jumpy and edgy and filled with this nervous energy that skittered through me that I couldn't control no matter how hard I tried.

I took her hand in mine and faced her. "I can't do this anymore," I told her. "I can't work with you."

Her hand was warm, electric in mine, and her eyes took on an edge in the work light that surrounded us.

She placed a gentle hand on my shoulder. "Do you not like the work we're doing?"

That was so far from possible that I just shook my head wordlessly. The developing material had the hallmarks of greatness, I could feel it.

I took a breath, then another. I had to say this, had to get it out there and in the open, because I couldn't take the shyness, the longing distance when every single time she was near me, and even when she wasn't, I could hardly breathe because all I could think, all I could feel was *her*—her presence, the taste of her breath on my lips, and the custom fit of her on my hands, the flash of her eyes when she came, and the exquisite softness of her skin as it melted into mine.

"Samantha," I said finally, looking into her eyes, eyes that made me want to jump in and swim through her, "it's not the music—it's us."

Samantha shifted her hand from my shoulder and stroked my face, lightly rubbing her thumb along the rise of my cheekbone. "Love, do you need time alone? Am I making you uncomfortable?" She gazed at me earnestly.

I let go of her hand and caught her face lightly between my fingertips. "You're making me crazy," I whispered, glancing at her lips before I pulled her to me.

God, I'd missed her, the taste of her mouth, of her breath as she breathed against me, her body molding to mine. When her lips parted it was as if my skin remembered everything we'd done, and blood pounded through my neck as images of all I wanted to do to her, with her, slammed through my mind.

"The feeling is quite mutual," she breathed into my ear as her fingers curled around the nape of my neck and dug lightly at the muscle. I licked the sharp ridge that defined the hollow of her throat, and my hands eased down her sides, memorizing again her shape.

Samantha's body eased before me until we were leaning against the board, and it was either her hip or my arm that brushed past the on switch for the DJ section of the board and set music flying through the room, a beautifully evocative trance piece by Bjork (she used to sing lead for the Sugarcubes—incredible stuff!). It couldn't have been a more ideal moment, except it got better.

Samantha tore her mouth from mine as my hips eased between her thighs. "Is this your choice, then?" she asked, holding my face in her hands, pinning me with her gaze, her eyes a deep midnight blue as they searched mine.

I searched myself, outside in, skin to soul, and back again. I kissed her, softly, thoroughly, then pulled away from her slightly. "Dance with me?" I asked, a quiet breath against her ear. I let my hands wrap around her waist and pulled her gently to me, away from the board.

She followed and we moved out onto the open floor. I touched my lips to the vein that jumped in her neck as we swayed together. It occurred to me that at some level, even though I had to leave New York to go on tour, I had run away from Samantha, not then, but after, after Ibiza, after I'd given up trying.

Her hands were warm, strong, loving, as they held me, and her cheek rubbed against mine. I was again struck with how absolutely safe I felt with her, how completely, utterly loved, without expectation, without reservation, and then it hit me—I hadn't welcomed Samantha home to me, she'd made me feel at home with her.

That scared the fucking shit out of me.

She'd asked me if this was my choice. Choice? What choice did I have, really?

"Samantha?" I asked lightly, afraid to break this beautiful spell.

"Hmm?" she responded, a soft burr as her lips brushed against my ear.

"Fuck the demo," I said, "take me home."

JÓGA

I know that you don't want us to fall apart
Don't be afraid—it's love we made
The truth? It's in your heart

"Face The Rain"—Life Underwater

I don't know why it took me so long to admit, to know, what I guess was so obvious to everyone, even me when I wasn't so busy trying to pretend it wasn't true.

But when we got upstairs, in my room, in my bed where we groaned and cried and whispered the most solemn and holy of promises to each other, and it seemed even the very walls glowed and echoed back at us, I knew where I belonged when Samantha welcomed me to her, wrapping herself around me when our bodies met, drawing me to her, in her, as we continued the dance we'd started earlier, part of the dance we'd started so long ago.

When her fingers scratched into my back—long, intense, sharp lines down my spine—I swore I heard music (don't laugh too hard, but it was Vivaldi's Suite in D Minor, specifically), and I closed my eyes as I bit down lightly on her collarbone, then laid my ear against the pulse that beat under her skin.

"Do you hear music?" she asked me, her voice low and halting as her cunt moved gracefully under mine.

"I do," I whispered into her neck and kissed just under her chin when she angled her head. "I can hear your heart beating." She opened her eyes, diamond bright for me.

Samantha massaged along my ass, then traveled up my back, tracing across my shoulders and up my neck. She cradled my face. "I'm so sorry I couldn't get here sooner," she said. "I missed you so much..." She slipped her fingers down to touch the sword that still hung from my neck, pressing it into my skin.

"Don't...ever...leave me again," she said, and I was startled to see tears in her eyes. I instantly wanted to make that hurt go away, so that she never cried for me, over me, again.

"No, baby," I promised, "I won't." I meant it. I kissed her eyes and tasted her tears and gently kissed those lips that were so soft I was afraid of bruising them. "I never," I kissed her chin, "want to be away from you." Taking one of her hands, I caressed her scars, her marks, with my fingertips. I kissed the hollow of her throat, and as her legs relaxed around me I slid down her body.

I let go of her wrist and rounded my hands over her flawless breasts, my lips tracing as much of her skin as I could, tasting the slight sweat that covered her, until I finally, finally, reached that place I'd wanted for so long. I reveled in the scent of her, of us, and as I dipped my head to kiss the short light hairs that covered her, Samantha laid her fingers on my head.

I glanced up across the tanned expanse of her stomach, past the sharp definition of ribs and past her breasts, to find her looking back at me, eyes dark, full of love and a hunger that matched my own. She lightly drew her fingers through my hair, then ran them down the side of my head until her thumb brushed against my cheek.

"Bring your hips up here." She smiled at me. "I want to taste you, too."

I was surprised, because as much as I wanted to taste her, I also wanted to know what it would be like feel those tender lips wrapped around my clit, that perfect kiss, her tongue jammed in my cunt.

But to share such marked intimacy? The thought made my gut tighten with need and the rest of me shy.

I rubbed my cheek against her palm and kissed it before I said anything.

"I, uh, I've never done that before," I admitted, watching my fingertips scratch lightly at the outer bounds of her pussy, run lightly in the groove that marked her thigh. "I mean..." I didn't really know what to say; I shrugged and finally looked up to see her smile had gentled.

"Me either," she said, "but I want to—with you."

Wow. That was just so, so...I didn't know what to say, really, because as appealing as the idea was, it scared me too. This was some whole new level of, well, of something, anyway. But...if I was going to try to make a life with her, and I knew, the way I knew that my heart was beating so loudly that I could hardly hear myself think, that was what I wanted—a whole life together—I was going to have to either get over it or let it go.

"Unless...you don't want to," she added, the slightest of tremors marring her words.

No...I wanted to, I definitely wanted to, but first I had to get rid of the shake I had heard in her voice, and I almost flew back up her body to reassure her, half on, half off her.

"God, no," I told her earnestly, staring into her midnight-ocean eyes to convince her. I combed her hair with my fingertips and carefully kissed her. "I'm just...you don't have to do that," I said, looking deeply into her eyes again.

"Nervous?" she asked, smiling her half-smile, that gentle, loving expression.

I had to kiss the corner of her mouth where her lips quirked.

"A little," I admitted.

"Then we'll go slow." Samantha sat up slightly to wrap her arms around me and nibbled on my lower lip, which sent shivers through me. I shuddered as I shifted carefully, sitting next to her.

"You're driving me crazy," she murmured into my throat as I greedily enjoyed the slivers of sensation she shot through me.

But it was time, more than time, to return the favor, and I stroked across her waist, her ribs, the defining lines of her as I gently pushed her back and forged a new trail down her body, headfirst.

I still lay to the side of her, and when I returned to the place I'd started from, I hesitated—this was a completely different angle and I was struck, struck hard, by how very vulnerable she was to me, in her need, in her love.

So soft, so open, so damned defenseless, and I wanted to cover her vulnerability, shield it from the world and keep it safe. I felt so humble in the presence of the trust she showed me, my heart caught up in my throat and lurched with it.

I outlined her edges again and rubbed my thumbs lightly against her tendons. "You are so damned beautiful," I whispered, "you're killing me."

She shifted under me as I finally lowered my head and kissed that open vulnerability with all the feelings that threatened to overflow through me because I was just so in love with her that my body felt heavy with it. I had never, ever, loved *anyone* the way I love my Samantha.

She inhaled sharply and let her breath out in a short gasp as my lips touched her, a cushioned descent between softness, to touch down on the warm slickness of her, and I scraped my lower lip against her clit, from base to head and back again, then kissed her as I would her mouth. Oh, sweet, she was so sweet.

"Please, baby," she said as she slipped an arm under my waist, "I need to taste you," and she literally shifted me over her. God, that she was strong enough to do that—it sent a shock through me, a combination of surprise and primal lust that made my kisses change from tender to the raw need to have her, and, careful not to rest the full weight of my body on her, I, thank God, finally, oh God, slipped my tongue inside her just as she settled me over her.

"God…" she huffed out, the word blowing hotly against my want before she wrapped her arms around my hips and pulled me to her.

Christ almighty, she spread my cunt with her tongue and sucked me in. She reduced me entirely to the primitive, the primordial, and our bodies pressed along their length as I wrapped my arms around her thighs and drove farther into her, the scent and taste, the feel of her absolutely gratifying as her lips moved me.

She reached up along my back and dug lines into my muscles, moving me, urging me on and shifting lines of place, of person, because I was so lost in her, lost in the feelings her tongue built in me, in the creation of the third, the "us," that I don't know when I noticed the pattern to the sparkling lines she drew on my spine.

She drew a single vertical line with her fingertip, then stopped, rubbing her palm across my back. A vertical line with a connected horizontal. A circle. An angled line connected to another. Three horizontals and a vertical, then she again rubbed her palm across my back. Writing. Samantha was writing on my skin what her tongue was spelling in my cunt, what hers said to my mouth as I loved her, too, and told her in the wame way, her clit, swollen and hard, between my lips and under my tongue. I reached for her arm, and she released my back to grasp my fingers, to entwine them with mine.

She squeezed my hand and let go, to grab my hips with gentle strength, then took her mouth away for one agonizing second. "Fingers, baby...please," she gasped before she plunged into me.

So incredible, so intense, I couldn't help but twist my head for a second as my lungs clutched for air before I buried my fingers and mouth in her.

I'd gone way past riding the wave. I was a drop merged in the ocean, we were the wave together as our rhythm synched and every thrust, every roll of our bodies as we slid against and within each other complemented, met, matched. We matched.

She'd been orphaned by cruel fate and me by cruel intention, but when we were together, none of that mattered—we just wore our scars differently.

As her legs tightened around and against me I could feel my own mounting tension, a tremble in my stomach as I tried not to crush her, and with my free hand I outlined "I love you" on her flexing thigh, like she had on my spine.

There it was, that power holding us fast in its grasp as we climbed and raced and built to that fine-line point that was the clit that pulsed and grew between my lips and under my tongue, the pussy that wrapped around my fingers with hungry love, and the lips and tongue and hands that held my cunt entrapped, enthralled, always needing and needing only her.

One more thrust, one more pull and another, and instead of falling apart I was falling together, the pieces of me I had thought dead or disappeared flying back to settle where they belonged, where I belonged, and I was so fully complete that when Samantha came in my mouth and tight on my hands I thought I might simply burst with the pure joy of it.

I kissed her pussy tenderly as I withdrew, pressing my lips to her with adoration, with reverence, for what she had offered, for what she had so willingly shared. I cupped her in my hand and rested my head on her thigh. She bit lightly against my muscle before I just as carefully shifted off her.

She sat up and I joined her. We wrapped ourselves around each other, a warm tangle of arms and legs as we leaned back against the wall and her lips searched for mine, then found them. I enjoyed the feel of our lips, the combined flavor that was uniquely us, and Samantha let me continue my languid exploration, joining me as we learned each other all over again. I put that charm, that tiny blade, around her neck again—I had promised I would when I got home.

I lay with my cheek drowsily pillowed on the yielding plain of Samantha's stomach, my fingers splayed along her ribs, the other resting on her thigh. The soft hairs of her pussy rubbed against my sternum as her legs warmed either side of me, and I curled between them.

When the lightest feather-touch of fingertips ran through my hair, I kept my eyes closed. I was so comfortable and warm I didn't stir when I felt the sheets that we'd kicked to the bottom of the bed slide up against me and fall softly around my shoulders.

I still didn't move when I felt them tuck around me a bit, because it was just so nice where I was, and I was so peacefully tired.

But when the feather-light touch returned briefly to my hair and was followed by a kiss on my forehead, I opened my eyes in the early sunset.

"Kitt?" I blinked and asked sleepily. I shifted my head slightly to see her, and she carefully sat on the edge of the bed.

"Shh," she soothed, "go back to sleep." She rubbed my arm lightly through the sheet, then stood.

"Okay…" I sleepily agreed and snuggled under the sheet. Samantha shifted beneath me, but didn't wake. The leg behind me pressed tighter along my back as her hand came to rest on mine.

"Nina, do you want me to put the lamp on?" she asked, standing in the doorway.

I opened my eyes again and shook my head. "No…but thanks." I gave her a small smile and closed my eyes.

❖

It was hard saying good-bye to Carlos and Enrique, and I not only promised to keep in touch, I promised to visit—and I would, too. If there was some way I could work it out, I'd go back to Spain; I loved it there. Hell, I wanted to live there.

In the end, we flew back to New York after stopping for two weeks in London to hand in the demo, argue out a recording and touring schedule, and work out new contracts since we'd now created a new musical unit that wasn't Adam's Rib and wasn't Loose Dogs, either, while Fran had gone two days ahead of us to get the paperwork started—and believe me, there was a lot of it.

Samantha had a lawyer—excuse me, a barrister—she worked with, and in fact, it was the same one Graham used, and offered to do introductions, but I'd already been working with Mrs. J (and Jer's last name was really and truly Jenns)—she knew my shit. Besides, I was already ignorant enough about our own legal system, never mind working with a foreign one, and frankly, she'd done great stuff for Adam's Rib, all things considered.

Maybe things might have been a little different had we actually spoken with her before we'd signed our first contract, but…you live and learn and sometimes you get a bloody nose, and if you're lucky, you live through it.

Samantha and I were pushing to get the recording done at a reasonable pace instead of the rush Enzo was asking for so we could spend some quality time together—and not just in the studio. We had stuff to work out for ourselves.

We had a solid plan with the timing we had in mind: we'd tour in the spring and into the summer instead, which would pack a bigger punch on our new release.

Yep, those were the plans Samantha and I had, well, that and we were really and truly going to do the crazy thing and get married. We discussed it on the flight back to Heathrow from Madrid. How had she put it? Oh yeah, over twenty thousand feet in the air, she asked, "Can we get married before you decide to join a new band and go tour Borneo, then give it all up to live with the aborigines in Australia?" She was nuts, but she was nuts about me, and that's kinda sorta what really mattered.

I laughed, though, and told her if I was going to give it all up it would be to bodysurf on the West Coast or, better yet, Hawaii. I'd start swimming and never stop until I was one with the great blue. She leaned over the seat, then wrapped her arms around me and laughed. "Only if you take me with you," she said, "only if you take me with you." I heartily agreed.

"Okay, we'll do that knot-tying thing," I said, "but there's a couple of conditions."

"Anything. Name it," Samantha swore, as she cupped my cheek and her eyes were that deep blue that made me want to do—everything.

"Full disclosure, Sam," I told her. I was dead serious, too. "I want to know where in the world you were for six weeks that I didn't hear from you and that you won't disappear on me like that again."

I was less than surprised to find that Candace worked for Rude—she was A&R, "Artists and Repertoire," which meant she scouted new talent and signed them. Oh, how it fucking figured, you know? It just fucking figured.

"Uh, I think tonight would be a good time to fill in the blanks," I told Samantha while we waited in Enzo's office.

She took my hand, kissed it, and swore she would. She was absolutely as good as her word. Samantha told me a whole lot of the things I didn't know (and a few I didn't want to, but that's another story—in fact, it's hers).

While in London, I finally got to officially meet her Uncle Cort, who really was as big as she'd described him to me when we were in high school. I loved him immediately, the big, almost burly, slightly gruff man who was probably one of the gentlest people I'd ever met.

He made me feel welcome, a part of the family that was he and Samantha.

Back in New York, I got in touch with Jerkster, I mean, Jer—I really couldn't call him Jerkster anymore since the accident—and Stephie right away. I really missed them! And tell you the truth, they were the people outside of Samantha and Fran I was closest to. That's the thing about being in a band—you really are a family, even if you don't play together anymore. It was hard to accept in many ways that Adam's Rib was over and gone; it had been such a nice dream! But that's life, and the most important thing was that we'd had a great time while it lasted.

Jer picked me up from my apartment; we were going to get Stephie and go back to his house. I wanted to meet his mom anyway—to thank her for everything she'd done for me and for us and offer her a retainer for all the stuff I was pretty sure she'd end up doing for me in the future. It ended up becoming a lot for a couple of years.

Jer really wouldn't be able to play again—not the way he had before, anyway. It could have been heartbreaking, but he was going back to school to study engineering—sound engineering. "Fuck the *sheiskopf* bus-driver thing," Jer said with a grin. "I'm going to be an uber sound guy."

I agreed with him. He would be great at that, and I knew right then and there who would do our sound on tour—and who'd run the studio I planned to open one day. Hey, it was okay to have a new dream, right?

The big shock was Stephie. I'd been smoking a cigarette while

Jer and I waited for her in his car, and when I saw her—I flung it away without even thinking about it—she was huge! She was due in about four months. Damn, that was why she'd cried almost every day—and explained a lot more than that, too. I wished I'd known, though. I don't know what Jer and I could have done differently, but maybe, something. I was glad I'd given her all those Oreos, at the very least.

Stephie was done with touring, though. But she mentioned that John was a drummer, and you could tell from the way the baby kicked anyway, sticking her little feet out of her mom's belly as if to say, "Here I am—let's kick it!"

"Yeah," Stephie said after she made us pet the belly and play tag with each foot, "not even breathing on her own yet and already a punk."

We laughed a lot about that, and in my head, Stephie worked in that studio I was going to have. I knew she still loved music, and she was super sharp—there had to be something we could do together. I'd find it, whatever it was.

I was definitely going to talk with Samantha about checking John out as a drummer. I mean, maybe he couldn't tour, what with a new baby and all that, but we were going to spend about six months in the studio—maybe he could do our recording sessions.

For the time being, though, I promised I'd bring baby April funky stuffed animals and write her silly baby songs.

"Why did you decide to name her April?" I asked.

"Um, uh, because that's when, she was, uh…" Stephie stumbled and blushed.

Jer and I looked at each other and burst out laughing. I high-fived Stephie.

"That's cool, that's way too cool." I smiled.

"Hey, good thing it wasn't in John's car," Jer laughed, "or her name would be Ford!"

When Stephie flushed beet red, we laughed so hard we started crying.

"Ah, shit, I think I peed myself," Jer said, and I fell off my chair and rolled on the floor.

"Stop, stop!" I kneeled up on the floor, held my ribs, and gasped between fits. "My stomach hurts!"

"When you're done laughing…" Stephie interjected, her lips twitching as she tried not to crack up.

It was a humbling moment when Stephie asked if Jer and I would be godparents—and he and I stared at each other.

Wow. That was, like, a big deal, like, a *huge* deal. I hesitated. I mean, maybe someone else would be more appropriate, at least more appropriate than me.

"Uh, what about, you know, your family?" I asked her.

"Yeah, your family?" Jer echoed. I smiled at him a moment because I knew for sure he wasn't nearly as out of it as he pretended.

Stephie frowned and stared at the ground, then spat eloquently. I admired the way she did that. If I did it? It would either land on my shoe or back on my shirt.

"Yeah, well…they're not thrilled that I'm throwing my life away on some waste-of-life, shithead musician." She looked back up at us and tried to smile, but the result was small, hard, and forced. I saw the tears in her eyes.

I hugged her carefully; I didn't want to crush April. The world could be a fucking lonely place, and I couldn't imagine how scary it had to be for Stephie while trying to bring this little innocent thing into it. I didn't know John well enough, hadn't really seen Stephie and him together enough, to know how solid things were between them, but even if it was sealed in stone, Stephie still needed her friends—and I was one of them.

"Hey, dude, I'm your backup," I said, and kissed her cheek.

Stephie hugged me back. "So yeah, then?" she asked, laughing through her tears.

"Ah shit, you guys are making me cry—it's a group hug now," Jer said, and put an arm around each of us.

"April's going to get the best guitar lessons," I promised Stephie. That kid wouldn't ever have to look too far to find a friend, not if I could help it, anyway.

We caught each other up on everything, and I told them about stuff between me and Samantha—and begged them to be in the wedding party. I told Jer to wear his kilt—with underwear, please.

And maybe, I thought as we hugged each other and played with the tiny feet that kept poking out to say hello, I had more than the beginnings of a studio here. Maybe one day, we'd be a label of our own. That dream was growing…

When I got to the bar, Dee Dee and Jen were happy to see me, although they expressed it differently. Dee Dee gave me rib-crushing hugs, laughed, cried, and kept playing with my hair—which was okay, because it was supposed to stick up all over the place anyway. Jen, on the other hand, gave me a quick, stiff hug and kept slapping my shoulder, and I was okay with that, too; it was part of who she was and I got that, really. I was happy to see them, too.

"When you settle in, maybe we'll talk about training you to manage the bar?" Dee Dee asked.

"I'll think about that." I grinned at her. What the hell, managing a business was managing a business, right? It would be an awesome learning experience, and I already knew Dee Dee was a great teacher. Besides, I had to earn a living somehow, right? At least until other things settled out—if they did.

Nothing was nothing until it was something, and in the music world, that meant signed pieces of paper and a check. I had to wait now and see if Enzo's people liked what Mrs. J thought was good for me, then review that and send it back, and so on and so forth until the thing was nailed to the ground.

It never hurt to hedge a bet, though.

Samantha had her own stuff to do, so I met Fran when she came back to New York. She teased—a lot—about the wedding while I reviewed the paperwork she'd brought with her, but we both knew she wouldn't miss it for the world. When the three of us got together for dinner the next night, she told me privately that the most beautiful things in the world she'd ever seen, she'd seen in Spain—and not in El Prado. I smiled at that; I knew what she meant.

Other people who needed to know were, of course, the various and sundry beings I was genetically related to. I took my mom out for lunch and told her this was it, I was getting married, and it was to Samantha. This was my life, to fuck up, fix up, and learn from any way I could, and yeah, I fell down, but yeah, I kept getting up—and if she didn't want to be there, I'd get over that, too.

I told her that she was my mom and I loved her, but this was my line and I wouldn't let her cross it, and we either could agree to disagree, or we could forget it. I'd still love her, I mean, of course, she's my mom, but I'd do it from a distance if I had to—she'd have to respect me.

My mom nodded at all of that and hugged me less stiffly than she had the last time. She then asked me to bring Samantha over next Sunday to the barbecue party they were throwing, so everyone could meet the person I wanted to bring into the family. I asked if we could invite Samantha's uncle, since he'd be flying in within the next two days. I think it made her nervous, but she agreed.

As nauseous as the thought made me—and I think I could have given Stephie a run for her money there for a few days—it wasn't nearly as horrible as I thought it would be, although for a moment when Cort shook my dad's hand his grin changed, became something slightly feral, and I couldn't see my dad's face, but he was subdued for the entire event, thankfully.

Cort fascinated Nico, I think he may have scared Nanny a bit, but he absolutely charmed my mother and my aunt Sophia with his knowledge of various cultures and legends. He told some of the best creepy stories around the fire pit in the yard after the sun went down while Victoria, uh, Tori sat in my lap and shivered at all the appropriate parts.

I didn't want any sort of pre-party thing, in fact it didn't even occur to me, but Dee Dee insisted and even called my mother (ugh!) to help arrange the whole thing.

No. Just, no. This was not—no! "Dee Dee...why?" I think I whined.

"She's your mother, *lieb*, she'll want to do this for you," Dee Dee told me when I buried my head in my arms to prevent myself from banging it repeatedly on the bar.

Dee Dee slapped my back with the towel before dropping it on my head, laughing the whole time. She was a great friend. Jen picked the towel up, looked me in the eye, and laughed harder as she dropped it back. She was a great friend, too.

Of course, it was part fun and part nightmare. The fun was, well, I'm not over it enough to think it's funny yet.

It's not so much that I thought the idea of a shower—party—whatever you want to call it is a bad thing, it's just that I didn't want to do the bachelor/bachelorette thing because I felt silly. And the shower thing, well, I knew it was going to get political—you know, family friends, work friends, work people you have to deal with.

Okay, the presents were cool, because, hey, who really thinks of buying towels or dishes, right? And you know, everyone needs a Crock-Pot and a steamer (okay, I've never used either one, and personally, I really liked the Gumby and Pokey cookie jar, and Samantha was into the silverware. Someone had to be, right?). Okay, I'm being an ass—it was all kinda cool, until Candace walked in with Enzo and handed Samantha the toaster.

She favored me with one of her brilliant smiles, kissed me, and told Samantha, "I wish you both a 'happy domesticity.'"

"If you let go of my intended, it will be." Samantha grinned back and put her arm around my waist.

I was grateful for her interference, because I admit, I stood there like a dummy—this wedding stuff was making my brain soft!

"Ah well, can't blame a girl for trying," Candace joked back, her green eyes glittering.

"But…it's the women who succeed," Dee Dee said, coming up behind her with a tray of drinks.

When Candace looked at her, I could almost feel the shock of electric connect between them. Cool, and…not, because I'd have to deal with both of them if they got together. Okay, I could live with that. In fact, I was totally fine for the rest of the party—until the strippers.

Yeah, strippers as in the plural, more than one (and one was far too many). They were Graham's idea. Wonderful. Great. Thanks again, Graham. In front of my mom and my little sister—just awesome.

I covered my eyes the third time my mom stuck a dollar bill in a dancer's g-string.

The night before the wedding I went back to my apartment and tried to settle myself into sleep, but it wasn't working. I tossed, I turned, and finally, I gave up.

I switched the lamp on and lay on my back, arms behind my head. I was going to get married the next day. How weird was that?

It was weirder when the phone rang. I jumped, because it had been so quiet it cut through the silence like lightning slashes through the sky in the heat of summer.

I got it on the second ring.

"Hello?" I answered.

"I need to see you," Samantha said urgently.

"We're not supposed to do that," I said with a smile I thought she could hear, "and you're too far away."

Her voice was soothing to my jangled nerves.

"Don't be so sure," she returned.

I snatched the blanket and wrapped it around my shoulders before

I swung my legs off the bed and walked to the window. I laughed when I saw her in the same overcoat I'd seen her in last time she'd stood there, her hair gleaming under the streetlight.

"Come on in," I said into the phone, and that smile in my voice must have been unmistakable, "you've got the keys."

She walked in seconds later, and I greeted her at the door with a very hungry kiss. "I couldn't sleep without you," I whispered in her ear before I scraped it with my teeth. I shoved her coat off and let it fall so my hands could roam her freely.

"What makes you think," she said against my throat as we half walked, half stumbled to bed, her hands firmly on my ass, "that you're going to sleep?"

We didn't make it to the bed.

❖

The wedding itself was a blast. I'd never had so much fun in my life—well, at least not with that many people at the same time. I can honestly say it was probably one of the *best* things I'd ever done.

I got teased a lot, but all things considered, I kinda expected it. The most important part was that I got to marry my best friend in front of my other friends and family, and I did it with my backup standing next to me: Nico and Stephie and Jer.

I was really nervous about that kiss part in front of the whole world, but it ended up being the easiest bit and something everyone at the wedding called for about every two minutes. I'm surprised more glasses weren't broken.

I smiled so much my face hurt.

It's been a few years now, and if you tell me what time it is, I'll break it down to years, months, weeks, days, and hours since that day. Samantha always laughs when I do that, but I've caught her doing it once or twice herself, and it always makes me smile, too.

I can tell you that it's been two albums and two tours and this will be our third album—the last we do for Rude Records, because after a long discussion, lots of paperwork, and a few of those horrible shot-things that Dee Dee says are good for you, we've opened our own studio. Now we're going to launch our own label.

Dee Dee and her brilliant business mind is going partners with us—Fran, Sammy, and I. Candace had given up the label for the camera and ad-campaign work. We'd contract her when we needed to.

Originally, Samantha's Uncle Cort had wanted to just give us the money for it, but I didn't want that. I didn't want anything I didn't earn, and I'm sorry to say that it was the biggest argument Samantha and I had: she said I was stubborn and I told her I was free.

We finally understood each other. She saw it as a gift and I saw it as something that could never be repaid. My concern was that the label would never feel like it was "ours," as in the team's; they might see it as belonging to Cort, that he'd funded it to Samantha, since he was her uncle, and not to all of us.

We worked it out. Fran's West Coast legal, Mrs. J is East Coast, Dee Dee's the head of general operations, and I'm creative development. Sammy will handle A&R and will fill in for studio sessions on bass (she doesn't like to tour as much as I do), and you know for sure who our engineer is—Mr. Jeremy J. "Bear" Jenns himself. Stephie has handled our schedule from flights to fittings to interviews for years; she'll be the general office manager, while her husband, John, is the studio drummer.

April is our resident cutie until she starts school. It'll be another year or so before she can start guitar lessons, but John's had her on drums for a few months now; the kid's got some chops for such a bitty thing! She's gonna be some talent some day, though, and that's not just a proud godmom talking. This kid has got *it*—in spades.

And yeah, Aunt Nina wrote some very silly songs for her, and I have to sing them to her whenever I see her, which is almost every day I'm in the studio. It's cool. It's fun to sing and do silly little dances about monkeys and chocolate soup.

We're signing Graham as a solo artist. Three guesses as to who our head of tour security is, and you're right if you say Jen.

You repay loyalty with loyalty. It's a solid start, and everyone has worked their asses off—and there's even more sweat ahead. All I know is, I'm not going to let them down: I still eat my Wheaties in the morning (but I still hate Tang).

I've learned that I won't say never. I keep myself open to all the possibilities, the good and the bad—I try to live them as they come. Fran's sunny and warm on the West Coast, and that's exactly what she said she wanted. Samantha and I stay at her place when we go out that way, and when she comes to New York, even though she finally bought her old apartment, she stays in ours—it works.

Don't misunderstand. Samantha and I don't share our relationship; it's her and me all the way; we belong together. We fit, lock and key, just like Fran said.

But when we see each other? Well, if we hold each other just a little too long or Samantha's hands linger a little lower than an observer thinks they should, well, honestly? I don't care—and neither does Samantha.

Now that I have a better understanding of the whole thing, I can honestly say that loving her was probably the sanest thing I've ever done—short of marrying Samantha, that is. I will never ever refer to Fran as my ex, because we still love each other even if it's different now. And we will, always.

You know, it's kinda nice to know that there's someone out there that loves us both, exactly the way we are, exactly the way I am. If someone asks me about her, I introduce her as my friend, my friend and Samantha's friend.

Here's a weird observation. At times with Samantha, if I really take the time to notice, I see bits and pieces of other people—Fran's gentle fierceness, Candace's abandon, Trace's sadness—that, and Trace's lips always reminded me of Samantha's—baby soft. I even see some of Dee Dee's good-natured dry humor and some of Jer's pretend dopiness, because who would have thought it; my so-serious Sammy is one hell of a prankster. I know it sounds odd, but it's what I see, sometimes.

There are things I see now about myself. I could have been a lot like Trace, more than a lot, honestly, and I'm very glad I'm not. I also know that whether I like it or not, I *am* a lot like my dad, both the good and the bad. I don't like accepting that, but I have to or I'll do and say things that aren't right. And you know what? I like being the good guy; I don't want to wear another hat.

Samantha says she never, ever, sees anyone else but me, and it makes me feel a little guilty sometimes, because while 99.9% of the time it's exactly the same for me, so help me, green eyes still slay me—I can't help it—but I would never betray Samantha's trust in me, I would never betray this very special "us" I love so much.

I know a whole heck of a lot more about what Samantha does when she's not with me, what her "real" work is. For the record, she's not a government assassin. And when I think about some of what she had to do during the weeks I didn't see her, my heart shakes with the knowledge of just how close I came to losing her. But…that's not my story to tell. It's hers, and maybe she'll share it someday.

That would be really cool—my beautiful Goth. She scowls when I say that and says, "I am *not* a 'Goth,'" and I laugh while I disagree.

My beautiful, beloved Samantha, with her scars and brands, her storm-tossed eyes that hold sorrow and clear only for me, in her black clothes and silver charms, and her deadly smile that only brightens to sunshine for the same reason her eyes do.

"Samantha, love?" I tell her. "You…are Gother than fuck." She shakes her head at me, but smiles anyway because she knows I love her.

This always ends with a laugh and a kiss or, better yet, just the kiss.

There's more to this story, of course; there always is because I'm not done growing, not done evolving yet. I don't think I'll ever stop, and I don't think any of us ever should, but that's just my opinion.

Some things you never get over—they leave a mark, a scar, a souvenir of some sort that becomes a part of who you'll be—forever. If you're lucky, if I'm lucky, we learn to live with it, to grow around it, maybe even make it a valuable part of our own foundations. I'm not saying I've done that yet; I'm just saying that maybe I'll get there, too, someday—when I grow up or something.

For at least a little while I've achieved my own sense of peace, of self, of balance, and if it's not ideal, well, what peace is?

Everything I've been through and felt and thought and become is with me now and forever in the studio. I briefly touch the charm around my neck that I never take off, and I inhale again. This is what I sing over the opening guitar riff I recorded earlier:

You and me together—we walk the longest mile
And falling down forever, we stumble, stand, and smile
Look at us—two crazy dreamers
We live on hope alone
But we are such as dreams are made of
Fire and wind and bone

Don't give up on your love

We've lived with misdirection—almost torn apart
But in the introspection, we got down to the heart
Look at us—we're still together
Though often thrown off stride
Take my hand, we'll make it happen yet—I swear
We'll let the passion ride

Don't give up on your love

I had a dream—you were with me—you were laughing, you
were singing
Out in the breeze, taking it easy...
Don't wake me 'cos you're happy
Don't wake me 'cos I'm happy
Please don't wake me 'cos we're happy, yeah
So happy together—don't give up
So happy together—don't give up
We're happy together, yeah
*Happy together**

*"Don't Give Up"—Life Underwater

About the Author

JD Glass lives in the city of her choice and birth, New York, with her beloved partner. When she's not writing, she's the lead singer (as well as alternately guitarist and bassist) in Life Underwater, which also keeps her pretty busy.

JD spent three years writing the semimonthly *Vintage News*, a journal about all sorts of neat collectible guitars, basses, and other fretted string instruments, and also wrote and illustrated *Water, Water Everywhere*, an illustrated text and guide about water in the human body, for the famous Children's Museum Water Exhibit. When not creating something (she swears she's way too busy to ever be bored), she sleeps. Right.

Works in progress include the forthcoming *Red Light* (June 2007), and *American Goth*, a novel related to but separate from the "Punk" stories.

Further information can be found at www.boldstrokesbooks.com, www.jdglassonline.com, and at the BSB Virtual Coffee House, http://lesfic.14.forumer.com, where you can check out "JD's Juke Joint and Den" for news, updates, and the occasional flash of wit.

The *Punk And Zen* soundtrack by Life Underwater is available later this year at www.lifeunderwateronline.com and www.mandoweb.com.

Books Available From Bold Strokes Books

Punk and Zen by JD Glass. Angst, sex, love, rock. Trace, Candace, Francesca...Samantha. Losing control—and finding the truth within. BSB Victory Editions. (1-933110-66-X)

Stellium in Scorpio by Andrews & Austin. The passionate reuniting of two powerful women on the glitzy Las Vegas Strip, where everything is an illusion and love is a gamble. (1-933110-65-1)

When Dreams Tremble by Radclyffe. Two women whose lives turned out far differently than they'd once imagined discover that sometimes the shape of the future can only be found in the past. (1-933110-64-3)

Fresh Tracks by Georgia Beers. Seven women, seven days. A lot can happen when old friends, lovers, and a new girl in town get together in the mountains. (1-933110-63-5)

The Empress and the Acolyte by Jane Fletcher. Jemeryl and Tevi fight to protect the very fabric of their world...time. Lyremouth Chronicles Book Three (1-933110-60-0)

First Instinct by JLee Meyer. When high-stakes security fraud leads to murder, one woman flees for her life while another risks her heart to protect her. (1-933110-59-7)

Erotic Interludes 4: Extreme Passions. Thirty of today's hottest erotica writers set the pages aflame with love, lust, and steamy liaisons. (1-933110-58-9)

Storms of Change by Radclyffe. In the continuing saga of the Provincetown Tales, duty and love are at odds as Reese and Tory face their greatest challenge. (1-933110-57-0)

Unexpected Ties by Gina L. Dartt. With death before dessert, Kate Shannon and Nikki Harris are swept up in another tale of danger and romance. (1-933110-56-2)

Sleep of Reason by Rose Beecham. Nothing is as it seems when Detective Jude Devine finds herself caught up in a small-town soap opera. And her rocky relationship with forensic pathologist Dr. Mercy Westmoreland just got a lot harder. (1-933110-53-8)

Passion's Bright Fury by Radclyffe. When a trauma surgeon and a filmmaker become reluctant allies on the battleground between life and death, passion strikes without warning. (1-933110-54-6)

Broken Wings by L-J Baker. When Rye Woods, a fairy, meets the beautiful dryad Flora Withe, her libido, as squashed and hidden as her wings, reawakens along with her heart. (1-933110-55-4)

Combust the Sun by Andrews & Austin. A Richfield and Rivers mystery set in L.A. Murder among the stars. (1-933110-52-X)

Of Drag Kings and the Wheel of Fate by Susan Smith. A blind date in a drag club leads to an unlikely romance. (1-933110-51-1)

Tristaine Rises by Cate Culpepper. Brenna, Jesstin, and the Amazons of Tristaine face their greatest challenge for survival. (1-933110-50-3)

Too Close to Touch by Georgia Beers. Kylie O'Brien believes in true love and is willing to wait for it. It doesn't matter one damn bit that Gretchen, her new and off-limits boss, has a voice as rich and smooth as melted chocolate. It absolutely doesn't... (1-933110-47-3)

100th Generation by Justine Saracen. Ancient curses, modern-day villains, and a most intriguing woman who keeps appearing when least expected lead archeologist Valerie Foret on the adventure of her life. (1-933110-48-1)

Battle for Tristaine by Cate Culpepper. While Brenna struggles to find her place in the clan and the love between her and Jess grows, Tristaine is threatened with destruction. Second in the Tristaine series. (1-933110-49-X)

The Traitor and the Chalice by Jane Fletcher. Without allies to help them, Tevi and Jemeryl will have to risk all in the race to uncover the traitor and retrieve the chalice. The Lyremouth Chronicles Book Two. (1-933110-43-0)

Promising Hearts by Radclyffe. Dr. Vance Phelps lost everything in the War Between the States and arrives in New Hope, Montana, with no hope of happiness and no desire for anything except forgetting—until she meets Mae, a frontier madam. (1-933110-44-9)

Carly's Sound by Ali Vali. Poppy Valente and Julia Johnson form a bond of friendship that lays the foundation for something more, until Poppy's past comes back to haunt her—literally. A poignant romance about love and renewal. (1-933110-45-7)

Unexpected Sparks by Gina L. Dartt. Falling in love is challenging enough without adding murder to the mix. Kate Shannon's growing feelings for much younger Nikki Harris are complicated enough without the mystery of a fatal fire that Kate can't ignore. (1-933110-46-5)

Whitewater Rendezvous by Kim Baldwin. Two women on a wilderness kayak adventure—Chaz Herrick, a laid-back outdoorswoman, and Megan Maxwell, a workaholic news executive—discover that true love may be nothing at all like they imagined. (1-933110-38-4)

Erotic Interludes 3: Lessons in Love ed. by Radclyffe and Stacia Seaman. Sign on for a class in love…the best lesbian erotica writers take us to "school." (1-9331100-39-2)

Punk Like Me by JD Glass. Twenty-one-year-old Nina writes lyrics and plays guitar in the rock band Adam's Rib, and she doesn't always play by the rules. And oh yeah—she has a way with the girls. (1-933110-40-6)

Coffee Sonata by Gun Brooke. Four women whose lives unexpectedly intersect in a small town by the sea share one thing in common—they all have secrets. (1-933110-41-4)

The Clinic: Tristaine Book One by Cate Culpepper. Brenna, a prison medic, finds herself deeply conflicted by her growing feelings for her patient, Jesstin, a wild and rebellious warrior reputed to be descended from ancient Amazons. (1-933110-42-2)

Forever Found by JLee Meyer. Can time, tragedy, and shattered trust destroy a love that seemed destined? When chance reunites two childhood friends separated by tragedy, the past resurfaces to determine the shape of their future. (1-933110-37-6)

Sword of the Guardian by Merry Shannon. Princess Shasta's bold new bodyguard has a secret that could change both of their lives. *He* is actually a *she*. A passionate romance filled with courtly intrigue, chivalry, and devotion. (1-933110-36-8)

Wild Abandon by Ronica Black. From their first tumultuous meeting, Dr. Chandler Brogan and Officer Sarah Monroe are drawn together by their common obsessions—sex, speed, and danger. (1-933110-35-X)

Turn Back Time by Radclyffe. Pearce Rifkin and Wynter Thompson have nothing in common but a shared passion for surgery. They clash at every opportunity, especially when matters of the heart are suddenly at stake. (1-933110-34-1)

Chance by Grace Lennox. At twenty-six, Chance Delaney decides her life isn't working so she swaps it for a different one. What follows is the sexy, funny, touching story of two women who, in finding themselves, also find one another. (1-933110-31-7)

The Exile and the Sorcerer by Jane Fletcher. First in the Lyremouth Chronicles. Tevi, wounded and adrift, arrives in the courtyard of a shy young sorcerer. Together they face monsters, magic, and the challenge of loving despite their differences. (1-933110-32-5)

A Matter of Trust by Radclyffe. JT Sloan is a cybersleuth who doesn't like attachments. Michael Lassiter is leaving her husband, and she needs Sloan's expertise to safeguard her company. It should just be business— but it turns into much more. (1-933110-33-3)

Sweet Creek by Lee Lynch. A celebration of the enduring nature of love, friendship, and community in the quirky, heart-warming lesbian community of Waterfall Falls. (1-933110-29-5)

The Devil Inside by Ali Vali. Derby Cain Casey, head of a New Orleans crime organization, runs the family business with guts and grit, and no one crosses her. No one, that is, until Emma Verde claims her heart and turns her world upside down. (1-933110-30-9)

Grave Silence by Rose Beecham. Detective Jude Devine's investigation of a series of ritual murders is complicated by her torrid affair with the golden girl of Southwestern forensic pathology, Dr. Mercy Westmoreland. (1-933110-25-2)

Honor Reclaimed by Radclyffe. In the aftermath of 9/11, Secret Service Agent Cameron Roberts and Blair Powell close ranks with a trusted few to find the would-be assassins who nearly claimed Blair's life. (1-933110-18-X)

Honor Bound by Radclyffe. Secret Service Agent Cameron Roberts and Blair Powell face political intrigue, a clandestine threat to Blair's safety, and the seemingly irreconcilable personal differences that force them ever farther apart. (1-933110-20-1)

Innocent Hearts by Radclyffe. In a wild and unforgiving land, two women learn about love, passion, and the wonders of the heart. (1-933110-21-X)

The Temple at Landfall by Jane Fletcher. An imprinter, one of Celaeno's most revered servants of the Goddess, is also a prisoner to the faith—until a Ranger frees her by claiming her heart. The Celaeno series. (1-933110-27-9)

Protector of the Realm: Supreme Constellations Book One by Gun Brooke. A space adventure filled with suspense and a daring intergalactic romance featuring Commodore Rae Jacelon and the stunning, but decidedly lethal, Kellen O'Dal. (1-933110-26-0)

Force of Nature by Kim Baldwin. From tornados to forest fires, the forces of nature conspire to bring Gable McCoy and Erin Richards close to danger, and closer to each other. (1-933110-23-6)

In Too Deep by Ronica Black. Undercover homicide cop Erin McKenzie tracks a femme fatale who just might be a real killer...with love and danger hot on her heels. (1-933110-17-1)

Stolen Moments: Erotic Interludes 2 by Stacia Seaman and Radclyffe, eds. Love on the run, in the office, in the shadows...Fast, furious, and almost too hot to handle. (1-933110-16-3)

Course of Action by Gun Brooke. Actress Carolyn Black desperately wants the starring role in an upcoming film produced by Annelie Peterson. Just how far will she go for the dream part of a lifetime? (1-933110-22-8)

Rangers at Roadsend by Jane Fletcher. Sergeant Chip Coppelli has learned to spot trouble coming, and that is exactly what she sees in her new recruit, Katryn Nagata. The Celaeno series. (1-933110-28-7)

Justice Served by Radclyffe. Lieutenant Rebecca Frye and her lover, Dr. Catherine Rawlings, embark on a deadly game of hide-and-seek with an underworld kingpin who traffics in human souls. (1-933110-15-5)

Distant Shores, Silent Thunder by Radclyffe. Dr. Tory King—along with the women who love her—is forced to examine the boundaries of love, friendship, and the ties that transcend time. (1-933110-08-2)

Hunter's Pursuit by Kim Baldwin. A raging blizzard, a mountain hideaway, and a killer-for-hire set a scene for disaster—or desire—when Katarzyna Demetrious rescues a beautiful stranger. (1-933110-09-0)

The Walls of Westernfort by Jane Fletcher. All Temple Guard Natasha Ionadis wants is to serve the Goddess—until she falls in love with one of the rebels she is sworn to destroy. The Celaeno series. (1-933110-24-4)

Change Of Pace: *Erotic Interludes* by Radclyffe. Twenty-five hot-wired encounters guaranteed to spark more than just your imagination. Erotica as you've always dreamed of it. (1-933110-07-4)

Honor Guards by Radclyffe. In a wild flight for their lives, the president's daughter and those who are sworn to protect her wage a desperate struggle for survival. (1-933110-01-5)

Fated Love by Radclyffe. Amidst the chaos and drama of a busy emergency room, two women must contend not only with the fragile nature of life, but also with the irresistible forces of fate. (1-933110-05-8)

Justice in the Shadows by Radclyffe. In a shadow world of secrets and lies, Detective Sergeant Rebecca Frye and her lover, Dr. Catherine Rawlings, join forces in the elusive search for justice. (1-933110-03-1)

shadowland by Radclyffe. In a world on the far edge of desire, two women are drawn together by power, passion, and dark pleasures. An erotic romance. (1-933110-11-2)

Love's Masquerade by Radclyffe. Plunged into the indistinguishable realms of fiction, fantasy, and hidden desires, Auden Frost is forced to question all she believes about the nature of love. (1-933110-14-7)

Love & Honor by Radclyffe. The president's daughter and her lover are faced with difficult choices as they battle a tangled web of Washington intrigue for...love and honor. (1-933110-10-4)

Beyond the Breakwater by Radclyffe. One Provincetown summer, three women learn the true meaning of love, friendship, and family. (1-933110-06-6)

Tomorrow's Promise by Radclyffe. One timeless summer, two very different women discover the power of passion to heal and the promise of hope that only love can bestow. (1-933110-12-0)

Love's Tender Warriors by Radclyffe. Two women who have accepted loneliness as a way of life learn that love is worth fighting for and a battle they cannot afford to lose. (1-933110-02-3)

Love's Melody Lost by Radclyffe. A secretive artist with a haunted past and a young woman escaping a life that has proved to be a lie find their destinies entwined. (1-933110-00-7)

Safe Harbor by Radclyffe. A mysterious newcomer, a reclusive doctor, and a troubled gay teenager learn about love, friendship, and trust during one tumultuous summer in Provincetown. (1-933110-13-9)

Above All, Honor by Radclyffe. Secret Service Agent Cameron Roberts fights her desire for the one woman she can't have—Blair Powell, the daughter of the president of the United States. (1-933110-04-X)